Wakefield Press

# THAT THING I DID

Allayne L. Webster is an internationally published Children's and Young Adult author. She also plays guitar/sings and sometimes she illustrates.

Allayne is the proud recipient of three arts grants and a South Australian Premier's Reading Challenge Ambassador. She has served on literary festival boards and her novels have been listed for various awards.

*Paper Planes* (Scholastic) was a 2016 CBCA Notable, shortlisted for the Adelaide Festival Awards, and has recently been included in the Australian Heritage Literary Project Untapped Collection. *A Cardboard Palace* (MidnightSun Publishing) was a 2018 CBCA Notable, published in Sweden. *Our Little Secret* (Scholastic) was listed for the Golden Inkys, and *The Centre of My Everything* (Penguin RandomHouse) was listed in the 2019 Davitt Awards and shortlisted in the 2020 Adelaide Festival Awards. *Sensitive* (UQP) is published in Russia and was shortlisted in the 2020 Australian Speech Pathology Awards.

*That Thing I Did* – YA (Wakefield Press) is Allayne's ninth publication. *Selfie* – YA (Text Publishing) will be out 2023.

# Praise for Allayne L. Webster

## Praise for *That Thing I Did*

'*That Thing I Did* is a rollicking, funny YA novel that bursts off the page with frenetic, youthful energy. Allayne Webster writes with wit and precision, delivering a zinging tale chock-full of non-stop humour and tonnes of heart. The twists and turns are so frequent, the pages practically turn themselves. This book is a wild ride from start to finish: it's witty, hilarious, hectic, manic and unabashedly irreverent!'
**– Holden Sheppard**

'*That Thing I Did* is a road-trip tale like no other. This raucous escapade through regional Australia has it all: from prison breaks to fancy dress party hijinks, from sugar hits to home truths.

Its unforgettable characters are joyous, outrageous, foolish and wise, all at once. There's Taylor, obituary-writer wannabe, recently friendship-dumped after committing a social faux pas; Chip, aspiring pornographer and Chuppa Chup addict who speaks to dead people; Chloe, a shoplifting heartbreaker; and Jackson, prison escapee who just wants to see his dying nan, the irresistible, potty-mouthed Daisy.

It is a hot mess of the best possible kind, and well worth the ride. If you do only one thing this year, read *That Thing I Did*. I loved this book.'
**– Erin Gough**

'A hilarious, punchy as hell road-trip story that's pretty much got it all.'
**– Robert Newton**

'*That Thing I Did* feels like a familiar road trip/buddy comedy/ coming of age/loss of innocence story, and yet it's fresh and edgy and like nothing I've ever read before. It's *Ferris Bueller's Day Off*, if it was directed by Kevin Smith!

Be grossed out, shocked, and snort your soft drink out your nose, while still getting the feels, on a rollicking, twisting and turning, road-trip adventure, sharing a hearse (yes, a hearse) with a truly unique and wonderful cast of (somewhat morally ambiguous) characters – both the living ones and the dead ones.

There is at least one laugh-out-loud moment on every single page and some major didn't-see-that-coming plot twists, which rival Hollywood's best filmmakers. But be warned: nothing is off limits and *That Thing I Did* is DEFINITELY not PG, unless by PG you mean Pure Gold (I'll never think of Winnie The Pooh the same way ever again)!

*That Thing I Did* is bawdy bonkers brilliance, and a book you'll never forget, for all the wickedly right reasons.'
**– Adam Cece**

'Fast-paced, funny and brilliantly written!'
**– Poppy Nwosu**

# Praise for Allayne L. Webster

## Praise for *Sensitive*

'*Sensitive* combines laugh-out-loud moments with the seriousness of being thirteen. I loved it.'
– Emily Gale, author *I am Out With Lanterns*

'Honest, funny-sad and real, *Sensitive* is an unforgettable story about living with chronic illness, and about being yourself when all you really want is to be somebody else.'
– Vikki Wakefield, author of *This is How We Change The Ending*

'Strong, funny SJ will win your heart, even as her situation breaks it.' – Bren McDibble, author of *How to Bee*

## Praise for *The Centre of My Everything*

'Both heartbreaking and heart-warming. Allayne Webster navigates the world of young adults living in a regional town with a deft hand and sharp eye. The characters are raw and beautifully realised and stay with you long after reading. I was hooked from the first page.'
– Sue Lawson, author of *Freedom Ride*

'A gut-punch of honesty with a sting in the tail.'
– Dianne Touchell, author of *A Small Madness*

'*The Centre of My Everything* will draw you in and warm your soul.'
– Nicole Hayes, author of *One True Thing*

## Praise for Allayne's other works

'Webster's characters, major and minor, are entirely believable.' – *Sunday Age*

'Webster offers insights into the futility of war.'
– *Australian*

'Lively, believable characters and positive role models for teenagers.'
– *Advertiser*

'The account of schoolyard bullying is particularly well done.'
– *Sydney Morning Herald*

'An incredible insight into the confused mind of someone who is little more than a child, and how adults can easily manipulate them but misunderstand and underestimate them.'
– *Courier Mail*.

'I was unexpectantly mesmerised.'
– *Read Plus*

'Shows you can grow and change, and winning isn't everything.'
– *Reading Time* magazine

'Webster uses language that will resonate with teenagers, yet she writes with skill and beauty. Funny, clever, honest.'
– *Good Reads* magazine

'Webster has woven a believable, credible tale that successfully draws its female readers into the character and captures the teenage voice.'
– *Magpies*

Also by Allayne L. Webster

Junior Fiction

*Barnesy*
*Sam's Surfboard Showdown*
(co-authored with Amanda Clarke)

Middle Grade

*A Cardboard Palace*
*Paper Planes*

Young Adult

*Our Little Secret*
*Stresshead*
*The Centre of My Everything*
*Sensitive*

# THAT
# THING I DID

ALLAYNE L. WEBSTER

**Wakefield**
**Press**

Wakefield Press
16 Rose Street
Mile End
South Australia 5031
www.wakefieldpress.com.au

First published 2022

ISBN 978 1 74305 863 3

Cover designed by Stacey Zass
Edited by Jo Case, Wakefield Press
Typeset by Michael Deves, Wakefield Press

NATIONAL
LIBRARY
OF AUSTRALIA

A catalogue record for this
book is available from the
National Library of Australia

CORIOLE
McLAREN VALE

Wakefield Press thanks
Coriole Vineyards for
continued support

*For my Sunshine Girl, Vikki.*
*Making you laugh is my favourite thing.*

# CHAPTER ONE

'I require a partner in porn.' My neighbour, Chip Carter.

Me: 'Come again?'

Him: 'Ha! Good one.'

This may take some explanation.

Rewind twenty minutes to me being dumped by my best friend, Cass:

'You're hard work, Taylor. You're not like the others.' She meant Lia, Jack and Riley. 'With them, it's easy. With you, there's always something.'

I fumbled the phone. 'So if we see each other, like, *out* ... do you promise to say hi?' I actually said this. Straight after, I wanted to jam my head in a garbage disposal unit.

Cass sighed. 'Now you're making me feel bad.'

'Is this about that thing I did?'

'No. This isn't one of your stupid fake death notices either. You don't get to write your ending.'

'Obituaries. They're called obituaries.' I wish I'd never let her read them.

'Look, I have to go. Mum's dished up pizza. Bye.'

And that was the end of twelve years of friendship. No parade or fireworks, no dancing chorus line or falling curtains. Dial tone.

Fast forward, and I'm sitting on my neighbour's porch being force-fed hot chips.

'Cass should feel bad,' Chip says, licking his salty fingers one by one. 'She's an insult to all things bovine.' He shoves a takeaway bag in my face and flips me the bird. 'For Cass, should you require clarification.'

I take a chip handful. 'Clarified.'

He pushes back his limp fringe revealing a moonscape; his skin is bumpy and pockmarked. 'I've seen her when she comes over. Her cheek does that weird twitching thing.' He shudders, shakes it off. 'Nope. You're worth way more than that, sister.'

It's pertinent to highlight something here: I'm a guy. I didn't make best friends with a girl to win any nice-guy awards. It's just how stuff went down. Let the record show: on the first day of primary school I peed my pants and Cass rescued me – a solid basis for any relationship when you think about it. But facts like, I'm not a *sister*, are irrelevant to Chip. Chip moved next door a few months ago and until now our conversations have occurred twice weekly over the garden fence, Ned Flanders Howdy-Doody style – except for today, when he witnessed me doing laps of my front lawn post-Cass-dumping fallout.

He shoves the greasy bag under my nose. 'Eat! Carbs fix everything, friend.'

We're scoffing Bill's Takeaway. Bill's is on the corner, less than a minute's walk from home. Chip made a phone order, and Noelene, the sixty-year-old on work experience, thought he was taking the piss. Their interaction reportedly went like this:

'Bill's Takeaway. What's your order?'

'Chips.'

'Size?'

'Three bucks' worth.'

'Name?'

'Chip.'

'Got your order, son. What's your name?'

'Chip.'

*'What's. Your. Name?'*

'Chip!'

Cue muffled arguing. 'Bill! Some kid's tuggin' my chain! If my case worker audits you about my performance, you'd better make up some bestselling fictional bullsh—'

Bill took charge of the call. 'Now listen up. If this is that little brat from Derwent Street, I swear I'll deep-fry your nutsa—'

'It's Chip.'

'Chip Carter?'

'One and the same.'

'Well, why didn't you say so? Here, I'll hand you back to Noelene.'

And thus, hot chips were ordered.

Now, I swallow a chip and ask Chip, 'Have you been perving on Cass?'

He makes a face as if I have worms.

'You eavesdrop?'

He shrugs. 'I have no life.'

I've never before considered whether Chip has a life. 'Chip, you know how we're neighbours—'

'Well spotted.'

'Why don't you go to my school?'

'I'm nineteen, dipshit.'

'Oh.'

'But you're a Middie, right?' He means Middleborough High, the place where hopeful teenage souls go to die. 'I've seen your uniform,' he says. 'Year Eleven?'

'So they tell me.' I extract a bruised chip. If I were penning my memoir, it would be excellent symbolism. I fling it into the rose bushes. 'You go to uni?'

'Nup.'

'TAFE?'

'Nup.'

'Work?'

He buzzers me. 'You're out.'

'What do you do all day?'

'Ah! The eternal question.' Chip takes a giant slurp of home-brand soft drink and pufferfish burps. 'Currently? I'm staring into a gaping crevasse filled with my self-doubts, fears and hang-ups. But let's call it a gap year.'

'And so vividly described.'

'I do a bit of Uber driving. I'm also housesitting for my life-giving alleged authority figures. They're in the UK.' Of the last part he doesn't seem sure. 'I'm your quintessential trust fund baby.'

'You're quintessentially on the dole, then?'

'Essentially, yeah.'

We stop talking and stare at his yellow lawn. A weedy garden bed swamps a cyclone fence, and beyond it, Adelaide's northern suburbs creak and moan, bend and waver. Somewhere, blocks away, a lawnmower roars to life, chokes and dies – a fitting soundtrack.

Chip reaches out to shake my hand. 'You know what, Taylor? Bye-bye, Cass. Sod off. Adios. Arrivederci. Quoting the musical genius of Bob Dylan: *It ain't me, babe.* Or more masterfully expressed by Lily Allen: *Fuck you.* I can quote you the entire country and western musical canon?'

'Nah, I'm good.'

'Well then! Congratulations! This is the start of something new.' He takes the sauce bottle that's wedged between his knees and squirts a bloodbath into the bag. 'What did your other friends say?' He doesn't bother to feign innocence. 'I told you I eavesdrop. Plus Facebook. You should check your settings. That retro pic your aunt posted of you in the bathtub when you were, like, eight? Those bubbles didn't cover *everything*.' He squishes potato and drops it on his tongue. 'Did Cass make a decree? *Year Eleven shalt not sprekin zee Deutsch with Taylor!*'

I shift my weight, a sharpness working its way from my stomach, lodging in my chest. Cass may have been my friend since I was knee-high to a Woolies checkout, but honestly, there are semi-automatic assault rifles less intimidating. (Rumour has it that Middleborough's principal, Mrs Fitzpatrick, has her on speed-dial for disciplinary advice.) When Cass is angry, she's angry, and you don't want to be on the receiving end.

I've always quietly wondered what it is she sees in me. Really, we're complete opposites. Cass is outgoing and mad popular, and I'm (if I'm honest) an introvert. Cass is ruthlessly practical and I have a tendency to dream/overthink things. Cass enjoys confrontation and I shy away from it. Cass thinks dance TikToks are this generation's cultural gift to humanity, and if I see another preppy tween hand-square-their-face-shake-their-booty I'll sign up for a lobotomy.

But they say opposites attract. I suppose I've made up for what Cass lacks and vice-versa. She is, all things aside, sharp-witted and she makes me laugh. And she has an infectious smile. Plus she has a complimentary story for every scenario, which I *do* admire. And you know when she gives you affection that it's genuine because it's hard-won. Till now, our strange little balance has worked, so I'm not sure where it started to go wrong. All I know is that it's going wrong a lot lately and it's not as simple as growing pains. More: growing *apart* pain.

Until now, I've taken the perks of being part of Middle-borough's inner sanctum for granted. That was a mistake. Excommunication will cost me dearly.

'Well?' Chip prompts.

'Cass would've taken a pre-poll to assess the electorate.'

'You're not going to ask your friends what they think?'

'No.'

'Wow. You really are a sap.'

'I thought you were on my side?'

He laughs. 'Did I say that?'

I stare again at his cyclone fence. It morphs into a post-apocalyptic, none-shall-pass, Gandalf-beating-his-staff, boundary-type thing – those who cross will disintegrate, those who stay will turn to stone.

'You need a distraction,' Chip decides. 'You shouldn't wallow.'

'Wallowing is expected. Some might say it's a healthy step in the grieving process.'

He strokes his chin. 'Look at it this way: you're on a road that's crumbling in your wake. Do you: (A) stand still and crap your dacks; (B) run like a motherfucker; (C) let the dark abyss swallow you up and—'

'What was (A) again?'

'The answer is: you get on your bike and you—'

'I have a bike?'

'—you pedal. You keep pedalling. It's all you can do.'

I chew a chip, then my lip, ruminating on this well-meaning, totally unoriginal idea. 'Where am I headed?'

He leans over to flick my temples. 'Use your imagination, dude! Read the signposts!'

I look *again* at the fence. 'They're in Scandinavian.' If I think this will save me, I'm wrong.

'That's quite fitting,' Chip muses.

'It is?'

'Yeah. Adult entertainment is *always* better when it's foreign.' He extracts a car key from his pocket, gets down on one knee and presents it to me. 'Taylor Kennedy, how do you feel about the pornography business?'

'The—?'

'I require a partner in porn.'

'Come again?'

'Ha! Good one,' he laughs.

And that's how I end up working with Chip Carter.

What comes next is in no way my fault.

# CHAPTER TWO

Chip Carter smokes Chupa Chups. (I'll wait here while you take that in.) First, he dispenses with the lolly part via a couple of gargantuan heart-failure dental crunches, then he gnaws the stick, flattening it out, making it ergonomically mouth-friendly. He brings it to his lips, draws back, holds, and after a heady moment, exhales. He flicks invisible ash into a SmokeMart ashtray nestled in his car's drink-holder and inhales again. Then he winds down the window to blow a lungful.

'Secondhand smoke kills.' He pulls up at the lights, flips the sun visor down, picks at a zit and flips the visor back.

I haven't asked where we're going. I'm along for the ride.

Chip leans across me to open the glovebox. It's a Chupa Chup treasure trove. With an overt eyebrow waggle, he asks, 'Tempted?'

'I'm trying to give up.'

He whacks it shut. 'I admire your strength. Unfortunately I'm saddled with an addictive personality. I figure I'll run with it.'

The lights turn green and we make a left, climbing the hill to Ingle Farm, a city shopping complex with a giant windmill but no farmland or animals in sight.

Curiosity gets the better of me. 'Chip, how exactly did you come to be in possession of this ... this ... vehicle?'

He lovingly strokes the dashboard. 'Long or short version?'

'Short.'

'It was a cold day in June ...'

'This sounds like the long versi—'

'It was a cold day in June when my uncle was arrested for public indecency. And before you judge,' he says, side-eyeing me, 'Uncle Roger anticipated a speedy trip through Macca's Drive-Thru. My grandmother's dressing gown should've been more than adequate.'

'You mean he was sans jocks?'

'*Cos I'm free! Free-balling!*' Chip sings. 'And he was headed home along Grand Junction Road.'

Grand Junction Road runs from one side of Adelaide to the other, from the beach to the hills. Affectionately dubbed The Mullet-Proof Fence, it protects eastern suburbs latte-sipping, bearded trendsetters from toothless rat's-tail bogans in the north. We live on the mullet side, the *wrong* side, next to Yatala Labour Prison. Our housing estate was once RM Williams' farmland but now there's a childcare centre, a nursing home, a suite of shops, and a bunch of God-fearing families living smack next door to rapists and murderers.

Town planning at its finest.

'Uncle Roger,' Chip continues, 'was chowing on his Bacon Double Cheeseburger Deluxe – which, might I add, he'd waited fifteen minutes for in a parking bay – the customer–retailer bond is well and truly broken, my friend ... and as he pulled out, this huge semi came out of nowhere and—'

'Woah. It hit him?'

'Nope. He dodged it and had an argument with a light pole instead. He managed to climb out, and being all concussed or disorientated or whatever, he peeled off the dressing gown and started wandering all over the road – *naked*. He was in the path of an oncoming hearse.'

'*This* hearse?'

He caresses the dashboard again. 'Yes. And the driver didn't see Uncle Roger until it was too late. Dude hit the picks and the onboard coffin slingshotted out the back: planed it about half a k, took out a sandwich board advertising *Deadset Awesome Getaways*. The coffin splintered and eighty-six-year-old Heathfield Smart, who apparently liked lawn bowls and the odd fling at the pokies, landed on his kisser.'

'Faaaaaark.'

He draws on his Chupa Chup, nodding. 'So the hearse driver, a subcontractor, is shaking like crazy, right? He gets on his knees in front of my uncle and begs him to get him out of trouble with his boss. The police show up, see them locked in this, er, *embrace*, and arrest them both for public indecency.'

'And the dead guy?'

'He wasn't a reliable witness.'

'No, I mean, what happened to him?'

'Oh. An ambulance picked him up. Turns out the hearse's gearbox shit itself. Hearses drive pretty slow most of the time.'

It's true, we haven't done over forty clicks.

'My uncle contacted the owner to apologise and rather than do the whole insurance thing, on a whim he offered to buy it. I have it for safekeeping while he's in Yatala.'

'Your uncle's in prison for public indecency?'

'Nah. For robbing a servo.'

We pull into Ingle Farm Shopping Centre. Chip does laps until he finds a double carpark space he can front-drive into, and I sweat over the fact I'm living next-door to a guy with criminal associates. And yes, I *do* see the irony in that statement given that I live next-door to a prison.

'Chip, you haven't told me what we're doing here.'

'Gotta see a man about the new iPhone. They've got the dopest camera function.'

He cuts the engine and gets out. I follow him. 'Is it hot?'

'The iPhone?' Cheesy grin. More eyebrow waggling. 'No, but what's in front of it will be.'

This provides me with little comfort. 'Chip, earlier you mentioned the adult entertainment business. I should raise a small but not unimportant detail. I'm seventeen.'

'So?'

'Adult entertainment shops have big painted signs screaming *R18+*.'

His brown eyes squint. 'You've never snuck a look at your parents' stash?'

It takes me less than half a second to realise that arguing would be futile. We keep walking. 'What's the plan?'

'Taylor, have you heard of creative licence?'

'Obviously.'

'Well, I'm exercising mine,' Chip declares. 'I don't need to have a firm plan and even if I do, I don't need to explain every aspect of it to you. It's perfectly acceptable to have a general idea of where I'm headed and let things evolve from there.'

'So what you're really saying is you have no idea what you're doing.'

'Untrue,' Chip asserts. 'I told you my business venture.

It's very straightforward. What more do you need to know?'

'The what, when, why and how?'

Chip waves a hand. 'Trivial details.'

I narrow my enquiry. 'Okay, specifically: the how?'

'Minor miniscule *microscopic* detail.'

'But Chip, earlier you said *porn*. As far as I'm aware that almost always involves nakedness and fornication and I'm just wondering how you plan to execute that.'

I'm kind of freaking out. I've never seen a real-life girl naked. Unless of course I count my mother, which I might add was completely unintentional and possibly the worst moment in the history of my life, and if the image wasn't burnt into my retinas and scarred into the very core of my being, I'd probably fail to mention it. I'll happily admit to screen-freezing *Game of Thrones* a few times (okay, every episode) plus I do tend to linger over the Big W lingerie catalogue (I'm a sucker for airbrushed perfection), but outside of that, I haven't so much as tweaked a nipple – other than my own. I've never kissed a girl. Never *been* kissed. And I'm not about to tell Chip because if he finds out I'm a seventeen-year-old virgin, he'll likely die of hilarity-induced asphyxiation right here in the carpark.

Instead I ask, 'Do you expect me to participate?'

He mutters something I can't make out.

'What was that?'

Louder this time. 'First things first. Hardware. Equipment. iPhone.'

I try not to look relieved.

Chip ditches his Chupa Chup and twists a flappy sandshoe on top of the stick, extinguishing nothing. 'Look, if you don't have the cojones for this project, it's cool, go home. Walk, my friend. I won't think any less of you. Well maybe I will, but I won't tell you about it.'

I consider my current friendship options. This is a nanosecond exercise.

'That's what I thought,' Chip says. 'Follow me.'

In the food court, Chip buys us each a Mega Slurp and picks a table. He keeps checking his phone – I note the screen is badly cracked – scrolling, screen-flipping, sneaking sideways glances at patrons between gurglish sips of blue what-the-eff-is-in-this frothy muck.

It's dead for a Thursday afternoon. There's mostly the after-school crowd plus a handful of shift workers stuffing their faces with a late lunch. A skeleton staff loiter at bain-maries tossing hours-old food, wiping down benches and trying to look like they're earning their keep.

Chip winces, rubbing his forehead. 'Brain freeze.'

I stir my drink and shuffle it from one hand to the other.

He kicks me under the table. 'Quit it. You're making us look conspicuous.'

'*I'm* making us look—?'

'Oh boy,' Chip whispers, his face turning pale. 'Here he is.' He stands up and thrusts out a hand with the vigour of an army lieutenant. 'Cam, my man! Glad you could make it!'

I turn in my seat and my line of vision collides with a well-worn jeans crotch, the contents of which can only be described as suspiciously sock-stuffed. I look up. Cam's freckled, pit-ridden face stares down at me, eyebrows weirdly arched like some evil comic book avenger. His mane of bright-red hair sticks up straight at twelve o'clock, ears at three and half-past nine.

'You right?' he sneers.

'Oh, um, yeah. Hi.' I put out my hand. He doesn't take it. 'Your name's Cam? Ha! That's funny.' Blank looks from both of them. Chip glares at me so hard my head might catch on fire. But my mouth is off its leash. 'It's just that we're seeing you about an iPhone with a fancy camera and your name's Cam, so that's kind of weird.'

One WTF look at Chip, then Cam asks, 'Why'd you bring this knobjockey?'

Chip gives a solemn headshake. 'His mother couldn't find the self-discipline to give up bouncy castles when he was in utero.' He pats my shoulder. 'Sit. Drink your high-fructose treat. Let the grown-ups talk.'

I slurp my Mega Slurp. Cam takes a seat. Only now do I notice his black backpack. After a covert sweep of the food court, he unzips it, parts the flaps and croons, 'Check it. It doesn't officially go on sale until tomorrow. My boss would lose his shit if he knew I was giving you a head start. Let alone that I was using my staff discount to take a cut. We have to sign a bunch of contracts to say we won't touch them until after twelve noon. What corporate wanky bullshit is that?'

I peer into the bag and spy a sealed iPhone box nestled in a bunched-up polo shirt with the business logo *Tony's Phonies*. I consider telling him it's the dumbest name in the history of store names and a miracle it scored an Australian Business Number, but think better of it.

'You haven't opened the box?' Chip queries.

Cam nods.

'How much?'

'Nine hundred and sixty,' Cam says.

'Fuck off.'

'Nine hundred and forty.'

'Double fuck off.'

Cam packs up his camera bag and salutes us. 'So long, losers.'

'Wait,' Chip says. 'Nine hundred. That's my final offer.'

It's been his only offer, but who's counting?

Cam eyes him. 'You good for it?'

Chip extracts a brown leather wallet and thumbs the contents. I spy a wad of pineapples and briefly wonder exactly how big Chip's quintessential-essential trust fund is.

Chip's eyes narrow. 'How do I know it works?'

Cam states the obvious. 'It's brand new.'

'What if it glitches? There's one in every batch.'

Cam blinks at him. 'You want a product warranty?'

'You *are* going to put it through the register,' Chip says. He turns to me. 'It's not like it's hot.'

'Well yes, but not till tomorrow.' Cam sighs, 'Can I email the receipt?'

Chip seems satisfied. He pulls a folded canvas bag from his pocket, unfurls it, takes the package and slips it in. 'Let's go,' he grunts at me.

I leave my Mega Slurp unslurped. 'Nice doing business, Cam,' I say, and this time I don't put out my hand.

Chip steers me through the food court, canvas bag slung over his shoulder. I look back to see Cam dart into Smiggle. If I were character-building in one of my fictional eulogies, it would make no sense (unless I described him as a complex contradiction), but given the fact he seems one-dimensional, I think not.

'How often do you deal with that guy?' I ask.

Chip shrugs. 'Now and then.'

'Is he a liability?'

'Say what?'

'Will he blab?'

'If anyone's going to get into trouble, Taylor, it's him, not us. You're overthinking it. Besides, he's plankton.'

'Huh?'

'Whales, sharks, fish, krill, plankton,' Chip says. 'End of the food chain.'

'Oh.' I want to know what plankton eat, but I also don't.

'You've obviously watched one too many crime shows. His goon squad aren't coming after us if that's what you're worried about. He's moved on to bigger adventures.' Chip shifts the weight of the backpack and rubs his hands together. 'Now the fun begins. Equipment? Check! Hired help?' He pats my shoulder. 'Check! Next, a venue.'

'A venue?'

'Yeah. You don't think we're operating from my garden shed, do you? I mean, that's cottage industry crap. We need a respectable shopfront to give us some credibility.'

I hadn't stopped to think about *where* we're doing it, I was still getting my head around the idea we *were* doing it.

'I want to make some classy advertisements,' Chip says. 'Maybe film us giving a mission statement. None of that doop-doop music overlay. You don't happen to play keyboard, do you?'

'I failed Year Four recorder.' Then it hits me. 'Wait. *What?* You never said anything about filming us!'

'Didn't I? Oh. Well yeah, we're obviously doing that too. We're the face of the business.' He rubs his forehead, thinking through options. 'I'm sure we can download some suitable melodies. Hey, didn't I see you post that you're interested in writing?'

He must've seen me sign up for a creative writing class. Dammit. I really should check my Facebook settings.

'What sort of writing are you into?' Chip asks.

'Oh you know, the usual stuff.' I'm not sure I'm ready to tell him about wanting to be an Obituaries Editor. He'll probably laugh and think it's stupid.

'Writing is writing,' Chip says. 'Can't be that hard. Most authors are nerdy dicks.' Then he rethinks it. 'Actually, there is this one Aussie writer who looks like Dave Grohl from the Foo Fighters. He's kind of cool. But I think he's the exception, not the rule. Anyway, what I'm saying is, I'm sure you'll manage it.'

I'm busy freaking out over authentic porno dialogue and copyright-free music search terms, when my phone buzzes. It's my mother. My brain synapses fire, frantically trying to disentangle the two.

'Yo Mum!'

'Found you!' Like she possesses GPS superpowers. 'I was worried.'

This is new. Mum doesn't worry. About anything. There are cucumbers that get more worked up.

'You left the front door open, the TV blaring, the remote in the fridge.'

The remote. *Shit*. I was mid choc-cake binge when Cass called. I think I left it on the top shelf next to the Vegemite. (Don't ask why my mother refrigerates Vegemite – she just does.)

'Where are you, TK?'

'Mum, I told you not to call me that. My gangster rap phase ended in primary school.'

'Fine. Where are you, *Tay-lor*?'

'Ingle Farm.'

'Keys didn't cross your mind? Security? Unintelligible hand-scrawled notes lying about one's whereabouts? We could have lost the family silver.'

'We don't own any silver.'

'We own that candelabra thingamee your dad stole from Aunt Henrietta's wedding.'

'True.'

'And Mrs Harvey was broken into last month, remember?'

Mrs Harvey lives across the street. She's one hundred and fifty, give or take a day, smells like decaying potpourri and farts without warning. She also steals stuff. A neighbour from four doors down has her on closed-circuit TV nicking a garden gnome. And a concrete bird bath. And a rope. Which makes me wonder if it was a gnome-asphyxiation shallow-water-drowning thing or if they weren't connected items. And how an elderly lady even transports a birdbath? Baffling.

'The burglars rifled through Mrs Harvey's underwear drawer,' Mum reminds me.

'I don't want to think about Mrs Harvey's underwear.'

At the mention of underwear, Chip cups his hands at chest level enquiring as to size. I mouth *gravity* and he's crushed.

Mum goes on, 'I'm pretty sure they used her underpants to parachute out of there.'

I laugh. 'Get to the point, Mum.'

'Remember when it happened to us?'

Our house was broken into five years ago. Dad came home, found the front door open and the place trashed. Whoever did it had been there a while: drawers upended, cupboards ransacked, belongings strewn everywhere. They took the TV, my Xbox collection, Mum's jewellery and handbags, even the microwave. They took things we didn't realise were missing until months later. But of all the stuff they stole, my diary was the most shitty bit. Obviously they didn't mean to take it. I can't imagine any burglar worth their salt heads into a house thinking *Top of the to-do list is get that kid's diary!* I'd kept it inside a lockable briefcase that had belonged to my grandfather. The thieves must've thought it was something valuable. And it was – *to me*. It contained a childhood's worth of scribbles: notes Cass and I had shared in class, drawings, photographs, Sport's Day ribbons, pressed daisies from my grandmother's garden, a recipe for the best toffee I'd ever tasted. A poem by 1800s poet Christina Rossetti, 'Remember', that's often read aloud at funerals. When I'd read it to Cass she'd screwed up her nose and told me it was morbid and I should stop dwelling on the bad stuff. But I liked it and kept it anyway. Long story short: getting broken into sucked dog's balls.

'You can't trust people, Taylor,' Mum prattles. 'You can't leave our house unsecured. This isn't the sixties. It isn't *Mad Men*.'

'Are we done?'

'No. Your father's thinking Mexican.'

'I don't care what we have for dinner.'

'Fine. Mexican it is. But he's secretly googling Salma Hayek again, I can tell.'

She's messing with something, making a clanking noise. I hear a beep and the clack of paper trays as the printer fires up. Mum's a self-employed tax agent. She works odd hours, harbours coffee-ringed mugs, and lives almost solely on a diet of ham sandwiches and takeaway.

'Are you *sure* you're okay, Taylor?'

'I'll tell you over tacos.' But I have no intention of doing that.

'Don't be long, okay?'

'Yep.' I hang up.

'Parentals?' Chip says.

'I should make a move. It's a school night.'

Chip pats my back. 'One more stop. We'll be quick, I promise.'

We make it back to the hearse. A group of kids about age ten have their noses pressed to the back window. One of them, the short one with what looks like Doritos cheese dust stuck to his lips, asks, 'Is someone dead in there?'

'Your mother,' Chip says.

Doritos-face's friend says, 'That's not funny. His mother has cancer.'

Chip gapes. 'I'm so sorry!'

'Nah, she has herpes!' And they fill their dacks laughing.

'Go on,' Chip says, recovering. 'Get out of here.'

The kids take off in the direction of Hungry Jacks. Chip opens the hearse and we get in.

'That must happen a lot,' I say, putting on my seatbelt. 'Questions about the hearse, I mean.'

'Questions come, questions go,' Chip says.

He starts the engine. We drive forward, give way to a moronic speeding P-plater and make a right out of the carpark.

'Anyway,' he says. 'What would those cheeky brats know? Hey, I told you I'm with Uber, right? People go ape for this ride. My rating is through the roof.'

We pull up at the lights.

I decide to press him on the grand plan. 'So this pornography thing. You're serious?'

He thumbs at the shops. 'You think I bought the iPhone to shoot Instagrammy sunset shit? Of course I'm serious.'

He looks genuinely peeved. 'No one gives me any credit, I swear.'

I feel kind of bad, so I try to sound more interested. 'Would you say it's a permanent career move?'

He gives me a considered look. 'Taylor, at school, you know how they ask you to fill out those career questionnaires?'

I nod. I filled one out last week. I wrote *Obituary Editor*. Cass scoffed and rolled her eyes. I noticed she hadn't written anything on hers. It'd always been a sticking point with us – I knew what I wanted, she didn't. But I didn't judge her for that – even when she seemed jealous. Most people my age don't know what they want for breakfast, let alone a career.

Chip says, 'And they're like: do you want to be a doctor, a lawyer, an engineer, a fashion designer? Hairdresser? Hypnotherapist? Hovercraft specialist? Hazmat suit maker? And you have to choose. Right then and there, you have to choose.'

'Yeah?'

'Well I want to be a pornographer. There was no box for that. *Where is the box for that?*'

'You could've pencilled it in.'

'For real, dude. It confused me. I thought, *How come I don't fit a box?* But during my gap year—'

'Extended gap year.'

'I thought about it long and hard—'

'There are numerous quips I could make here, but I'll restrain myself.'

' – and I thought, what do I truly love?'

'You and most of the population who won't admit to it,' I say.

'And the answer came to me like a thunderbolt. Since then, I've never known such calm. My heart and my mind are totally at ease.' Chip smiles serenely. 'Ask yourself, Taylor. What are you truly passionate about? What's the one thing you're absolutely sure you could spend the rest of your life doing?'

I thought it was honouring people by writing their life stories. Now, for some reason, I'm not so sure.

He dips his Chupa Chup stick at me. 'It's a good thing you have me to guide you.' He flicks the radio switch and Cannibal Corpse screams thrash metal. 'Strap yourself tight. We have one last stop before I drop you home.'

# CHAPTER THREE

I stumble through my front door, dazed and traumatised by the Adventures of Taylor and Chip – which I promise to revisit once I recover.

Mum is on the phone. 'You're calling from the Accident Investigation Claims Department?' She cradles the landline between her shoulder and ear while stirring taco mince on the stove. She gives me a wooden-spoon wave. 'Yeah, right, and I'm Ed Sheeran.' She hangs up. 'Why do scammers always call at dinnertime?'

Dad dons his well-rehearsed scammer persona. 'You have won the Lotto. We are needing your account details. Give us remote access and your passwords.' He gets up from his dining chair, goes over and grabs Mum by the hips, pressing himself against her, swinging. He nuzzles her neck and croons, 'Hey Ed Sheeran, where's your rendition of "Give Me Love"?'

Mum swats him with a tea towel. She winks, and says to me, 'Would you like to finish cooking dinner?'

Dad kisses her again – this time with tongue. It's beyond puke-worthy.

'God, kill me now,' I groan, sitting down and banging my head on the dining table.

This is how my parents are. They have no filter. They're randy, hormonal twenty-somethings hooking up at every opportunity. Everyone else's parents have long since reached the I-hate-you-I-can't-stand-to-look-at-you-what-the-hell-was-I-thinking-marrying-you stage, and meanwhile mine are groping each other in the kitchen. In the living room. The carport. The shower. Anywhere else that lends itself to upright sex. Once I caught them doing it on my weight bench. It's downright depressing when your parents are getting more action than you are.

Dad sits at the table, face flushed. He grabs the newspaper, rests it over his crotch and asks breathlessly, 'How was your day, son?'

'Yes,' Mum chimes. 'Anything exciting?'

'Oh, you know ...'

'No, we don't know,' Mum says. 'That's why we asked. It's called Being Interested. We're also capable of other amazing feats like Pretending to Give a Toss and Actually Giving a Damn.'

'Fine. If you really want to know, it was a total shitcake of relationship breakdowns, transport issues, peer-pressure Chupa Chup smoking, and navigating complex moral dilemmas for which I have no prior frame of reference. Okay?'

Dad blinks. 'Sounds intense.'

I roll my eyes. 'It was your basic boring school day, Dad. Nada on the report card.'

'Well, I'm relieved to hear it.' Mum switches off the burner and fans the pan. She moves it to the corkboard on the bench.

I can't believe she cooked. When she said she was thinking Mexican, I thought she was ordering in. We live on a two-week rotation of takeout menus, broken up by the odd frozen supermarket dinner. Mum says she didn't ace Accountancy to be chained to the kitchen sink. Dad's idea of cooking is anything that can be nuked. (Mum uses our oven for tax-file storage.)

'Why'd you leave the house in such a hurry?' Mum fluffs her long hair, then knots it into a bun. She wipes her hands on her sauce-stained T-shirt. 'What blows, Joe?'

I use the excellent excuse I prepared earlier. 'I maxed out on chocolate cake, was gunna spew, and I needed fresh air.'

'That's not like my growing boy. I thought your stomach was a bottomless pit.' She spoons taco mince into a tortilla, drizzles sauce, overloads it with lettuce, tomato and cheese, and places it in front of me.

I take a bite. It's drool-worthy good. When she cooks, it's not at all bad. Owing to the diverse culinary options on offer, I'd consider living here indefinitely if it weren't for the nightly Guantanamo Bay-style interrogations. And upright sex.

'What exactly were you doing at Ingle Farm?' Mum presses.

'Questions come, questions go,' I Chip-ism through a mouthful. 'Anyway. Can't I have secrets? Privacy? Can't I be an International Man of Mystery?'

'Evasiveness,' Dad observes. 'It can only mean one thing.' He gives me a friendly punch. 'You went and saw about a girl, eh, champ?'

I feel my eyebrows reach new levels.

'Is she nudge, nudge, wink, wink, say no more?'

'Are you channelling *Good Will Hunting* or John Cleese? I can't tell. Your references are all over the place.'

'I mean, is she a bit of alright?' Accompanying elbow jab and a giant wink to cement his point.

'Ooh! Yes! Tell us!' Mum says. 'Was it Cass?'

I sigh extra hard. Mum has wanted me to get it on with Cass since forever – even though I've told her six-point-eight billion times that we're just friends. *Were* friends. Platonic air-kiss-on-the-cheek, don't-perve-on-her-cleavage-even-though-it's-right-there-in-my-face friends. Mum says we've been in the throes of puppy love since our sandpit days, we just don't know it. I like to think I'd know it. Besides, if Cass felt that way she would've tried something by now. I'm sure if The Thing hadn't happened, things would be different.

I'm struck by a memory of us on my thirteenth birthday. Mum said I was permitted to invite one friend because I was grounded. Earlier that week she'd busted me playing frisbee with her Pink Floyd LPs and she said until I learned respect for other people's belongings my party was cancelled. In my defense: (A) LPs are a dated technology, (B) I *was* attempting to employ environmentally friendly pest management, scaring the cockatoos nesting noisily on the back brick fence, and (C) I enjoyed the irony of launching each LP at another brick in the wall. (Google Pink Floyd's biggest hit.) Anyway, Mum stuck to her guns and said one friend was my limit.

I chose Cass.

Cass, like me, was bummed our friends couldn't come, and said Mum was a gutter-trolling heinous bitch. When Mum served up birthday cake and she was momentarily distracted, Cass grabbed Mum's plate and blew her nose on it. I'd never felt such solidarity. Or revulsion. Mum was sick with a rhinovirus for two weeks. I didn't catch it and Cass said that was proof that what goes around comes around. She made me feel like she had my back – even when I'd done the wrong thing. That's what friends do, right?

But this time she didn't have my back. After The Thing, she was nowhere to be found. I still don't know how to process that.

'Cass and me: not happening.' To really seal the deal, I think about telling them she dumped me today, but I hope it will soon blow over and that next week we'll be back to sharing Spotify playlists, shouting each other canteen hot dogs with dodgy toppings, and plagiarising each other's assignments. (Cass takes the maths/science bullets. I take the arts.) The fact Cass will undoubtedly fail English without me gives me hope. This whole stupid debacle will be another pee-stain on my already impressive pee-stained record.

'This is the age you should be playing the field,' Dad starts.

I've heard this speech before. It ends with an awkward inroad into discussing contraceptive devices. I want to faceplant my taco.

'When I was your age, I was Casanova with a Capital C.'

'Oh Darren!' Mum laughs.

'I remember Hayley Hadley, God love her. Now that girl could do things with her tongue tornados only dream about.'

'Dad ...'

'Next was Jacinta Di Alberto. She could snog so hard her lips turned blue. Back of the disco, we did things to make your toes curl—'

'Dad!'

'And then came your mother—'

I stand up. 'Okay. Thanks for that. It's been a long day. I have homework to do.'

'But you haven't finished your dinner,' Mum sulks. 'I supermarketed! I trudged aisles, agonised over retail options, self-served, bagged, lugged it home.' She makes it sound like an epic cross-continent crusade Harrison Ford might've starred in. 'I stood by that hot stove and slaved away the hours.' She drops her bottom lip, ready for the grand finale. 'I invested every *single* shred of my love and care in that meal.'

'What do you want?'

One hand to her forehead, she grips her chest with the other. 'Such suspicion! Such distrust! Can't I spoil my family? Can't we talk to each other once in a while?'

I stare her out.

She bails. 'Printer's jammed. Your father made it worse. There's an Amazon rainforest stuck in there. Loggers, too. I saw booted feet poking out. And a hairy orange hand. I need help. Like this-will-probably-take-half-the-night-SOS-send-vodka-and-cigarettes kind of help.'

I grab my plate. 'Regular snacks equal sustenance, highly recommended for studying. I'll rescue you in an hour or so?'

She gives me a grateful smile. 'Thank you, darling boy. But please record this for prosperity: tonight I cooked. I'm officially off the hook for the next financial year.' She nudges Dad. 'You clean up, honey. I'm off to sneak in another eppy of *Mad Men*.'

In the sanctity (or sanity – take your pick) of my bedroom, I check my texts for the first time since arriving home from The Adventures of Taylor and Chip (which I *do* promise to revisit shortly). I check Facebook, Insta and Twitter. Snapchat, too. No Cass. No Lia, Jack or Riley. No *Sorry for behaving bovine.* No *I didn't really mean it.* No *I made a mistake.* No *Please Taylor, I screwed up on an epic scale. Please please please forgive me.* They haven't gone as far as blocking me, but I am universally ignored on all media platforms. (My shared pimple-popping video only got one 'like'.) I resort to checking Gmail and discover I have three hundred and ninety-four notifications from JB HiFi, to which I don't remember subscribing.

Feeling like a stalker, I go to Cass's Facebook profile and search for photos of us. Hundreds pop up. Years' worth. Parties, sporting events, school stuff. Some are as banal as us sitting together on the bus or in the cafeteria. Others are pivotal, like a birthday or graduation. She's been there my whole life – a lot longer than I've had a Facebook account. I stare at a photo of her wearing a princess crown, auburn hair cascading across her shoulders, freckled nose wrinkled with laughter. How do you go from talking every day, to nothing? This has to be about The Thing. What else is there?

I search Kelly Nixon's Facebook page. Her profile pic, Kermit kissing Miss Piggy, remains unchanged. It will never change. Not unless someone accesses her account. Kelly Nixon is dead. She died a year ago. She's perpetually sixteen years old, frozen in time.

There's a post on Kelly's wall from her older sister Mia, from two days ago. I must've missed it; it didn't come up in my feed. Mia's written: *I miss you so bloody much, Kel.* Simple. Truthful. Below is another post from a week earlier, from Kelly's friend, Maddison Roberts. Maddy's posted a shaggy cairn terrier dressed in a tutu meme with text: *Saw this, thought of you.* There are hundreds like it – people talking to Kelly, missing her, wishing her back, pining for her. If I scroll far enough, I'll find my post from a couple of weeks ago, too. I could've deleted it, but by the time I wanted to, the whole school had already seen it. And not only had everyone at school seen it, but anyone Kelly was connected to: her family, her Krispy Kreme workmates, her basketball team, her music friends, the handful of randoms she accepted to up her friends quota. It was too late. The damage had been done.

I shut my laptop. I text Cass: *Call me*. Then I stare at the wall.

After ten minutes, my phone buzzes and my heart leaps. It's not Cass. It's a photo from Chip: a bunch of lycra-clad arses.

And so, here I'll return to the earlier Adventures of Taylor and Chip:

Chip's last stop before delivering me home this evening can only be described as a combination of genuinely terrifying and weirdly stimulating. In a nutshell, we snuck into a yoga class. Not just any yoga class – one instructed by my maths teacher, Miss Hooper. Of course I didn't know it was *her* yoga class we were sneaking into. It's one of those bizarre enigmas, like pineapple on pizza, or the independent nature of Guy Sebastian's eyebrows – destined to be, despite overwhelming evidence that it probably shouldn't.

Turns out Miss Hooper moonlights under a yoga instructor alter ego, Miss Flexy. Of course, this pseudonym appealed no end to Chip when he scooped the advertisement ticket-flag from the supermarket pin-up board and decided that this was *our* ticket to finding local talent. (Why expend energy advertising when it can come to you?) Classes were open if you signed up for the twelve-week program. Chip said he wasn't that committed. He decided to sneak us in instead.

We loitered in the hallway at the community club for over twenty minutes, with Chip intermittently peering through the windowed-door, waiting until the class was in full swing and everyone was sufficiently sweaty not to notice two teenage boys entering at the back of the class. Don't ask me why I didn't bother to look through the window *before*.

Blindly trusting Chip is a fateful error never to be repeated.

We rolled out the rubber mats, which we'd borrowed (okay, *stolen*) from the nearby locker room and got comfortable. When I saw the instructor turn and reposition herself, I pretty much shat my pants.

*What?* Chip mouthed, legs stretched at ungainly angles on his pink rubber mat.

*My maths teacher!* I gesticulated wildly before burying my head between my thighs.

'Miss Flexy?' he whispered.

I nodded, head still buried.

Chip patted my back. 'Nice!'

To be honest, seeing Miss Hooper up there rocking it in tighter-than-tight black lycra explained a whole lot. Like how her derriére *does* look unbelievably toned in Target jeggings in comparison to most teachers. And how you always see her stuffing her face with vegan falafels. And how the male staff contingent are forever falling over themselves to buy her coffee and carry her teaching supplies. Also, there was the time I witnessed her shimmy through an open window to unlock a jammed classroom door, which she did without so much as breaking a sweat. The woman is limber.

'Taylor Kennedy?' she called out. 'Is that you back there?'

Cue the part where I ran from the room like a squealing pig, thirty-something pairs of eyes trained on me.

Chip caught up with me in the carpark. He fake-lit a Chupa Chup and smoked it like he'd just got laid. 'I think that was useful as far as reconnaissance missions go. No potential candidates, but it did prove inspirational.'

'She'll think I'm crushing on her!' I wheezed, doubled over.

'She's probably on the phone to the principal's office right now.'

'Relax. It's entirely probable you'd be there.' He poked my belly so I got the hint.

I *am* a little on the chubby side, granted, but he didn't have to point it out.

'I can't help being squidgy around the edges, Chip. It's genetics. I have the metabolism of a comatose tortoise.'

'Does Miss Flexy give you good grades?'

'No.'

'No harm done, then!' Chip unlocked the hearse and we got in. 'On with the plan, soldier! Where's another place we can find talent?'

'Haven't you considered something traditional?'

'Like?'

'Going to a nightclub or a bar.'

'Hmmm. Old school. I like it.' He drew on his Chupa Chup, forehead puckered. 'However, it's problematic.'

'Why?'

'Well, for one thing it's hard to segue from *Do you come here often?* to *Have you considered a career in adult entertainment?*'

'And you think you could have done that in a yoga class?'

He shrugged. 'I *had* prepared an excellent opening line.'

'Let's hear it.'

'No,' he pouted. 'I feel judged.' He wound down the window, blowing fake smoke. With a cursory glance at the back seat, he said, 'And that's enough out of you. You can shut up, too.'

I looked over my shoulder at the empty back seat.

'Yes,' Chip said. 'You.'

'Um ... Chip, who are you talking to?'

'Barry.'

I looked again at the back seat.

'Barry Henderson the Third. Former occupant. *Passenger,*' he corrected. 'We have this sparring thing going, Barry and me. I say stuff and Barry likes to take the piss.' He winked at the rear-vision mirror. 'Don't you, Barry?'

'Hang on a sec. Are you—?'

He nodded. 'Barry's not the only one. There are several visitors. They come and go.'

I gulped. The hairs on the back of my neck stood on end. 'Several?'

'I can't recall them all off the top of my head. The main ones are Barry, Jolene, Edgar, Lily and Richard. They make regular appearances, mostly to give me a hard time. The dead give you no peace, I swear.'

'You see dead people?'

He roared with laughter. 'I appreciate the *Sixth Sense* reference, Taylor, but no, I don't see dead people.'

'Then how—?'

'I hear them.'

'You can hear this Barry person right now?'

Chip laughed, though not at me. 'I told you he's like that.'

'What's Barry saying?'

'He says you're high-strung. I assure you that's the pot calling the kettle black. Barry also says I'm chicken-shit and I should place a business advert in the newspaper. That's the most foolproof plan according to Barry. Barry was an investment banker, you see, and he was used to getting things done. He lived a very comfortable existence before he met with an untimely death in a Cessna light plane disaster. He doesn't comprehend that advertising is an expensive exercise nowadays and a lot has changed since the seventies.' At this, he stopped to argue with Barry. 'No, you don't, Barry, and I'd be grateful if you stopped talking over the top of me. It's rude. I've told you that before.'

'Barry died in a plane crash?'

'Uh-huh.'

'And there was something left of him to put in the coffin?'

Chip shot me a stern look. 'Not *all* plane crashes end in fireballs, Taylor. Some planes limp down the runway and nosedive into a ditch. Either way the outcome is equally fatal.'

'What about the others? Lily and—'

A wave of his hand. 'You'll meet them later. I don't summon them. They show up. It's how things are. Barry's already left.'

'He has?'

'Don't take it personally. He's easily offended. We're still working through his issues.' He crushed his Chupa Chup stick into the Smokemart ash-catcher. 'I'd best get you home. Being your neighbour, I don't have anywhere to go if your parents send a lynch mob.'

He slotted Cannibal Corpse into the CD player and started the hearse.

We headed home with the radio screaming, my ears ringing, and me wondering what the hell I'd got myself into.

I'm still wondering now.

# CHAPTER FOUR

'We need to rethink our pornography business.' This is my opening line to Chip. Predictably, it goes down like head lice in a childcare centre.

'We need to *whaaaaat*?' he squawks.

We're sitting under my pergola, eating microwaved popcorn and guzzling milkshakes I whizzed up in Mum's ancient blender using ice-cream, choc syrup and bananas. They turned out soupy. I was going to top them with whipped cream until I found the can on Dad's bedside table at room temperature. No, not kidding.

Mum and Dad are out shopping. Dad's a garage roller-door installation consultant. He needs new pants for an industry dinner thingo. Mum texted me that if she let him go rogue at Myer the credit card would never recover. She followed that with a message saying she should supervise him in the change-room, coupled with laughing-crying emoji.

This is my life, I swear to God.

'I thought you were on board with my business venture?' Chip pouts, fidgeting with his red-and-white polka-dot cravat.

I have no idea why he's wearing one. It clashes with his Tupac T-shirt, also a questionable fashion choice.

'Why are you piking?' he asks.

'I foresee a lot of hurdles.'

'Who are you? Nostradamus's stable boy?'

The truth is, after arriving home from our reconnaissance mission *and* fixing Mum's printer (she was right, it took hours), I decided to do some online research. If I was going into business with Chip – and I was *still* debating if this would even happen – I needed to educate myself. I couldn't go along for the ride. I had to know stuff. Have an opinion. Take a position.

And boy, did I learn some positions.

Now I know what you're thinking: *You've never searched for porn?* Yeah right, and Donald Trump's hair is real. I mean, okay, I've stumbled across my parents' questionable browser history. (Honestly, Hansel left less breadcrumbs.) A girl in my Research Project class showed me some sexties she'd received from some chick who lives in Idaho. But it hadn't occurred to me to go searching for it. (I confirm I am a seventeen-year-old with a pulse.) I guess I've had better things to do. That, and my imagination and a tube sock serves me quite efficiently, thank you very much. Sad thing is, we don't even have Net-Nanny. Other families are all about parental-lock systems on their smart TVs and tech, but my parents don't bother. I guess they trust me. Or they're apathetic. Maybe they don't see the point in avoiding the inevitable?

I have access to whatever I want, and that meant last night's research mission left me in a combined state of shattered innocence, chronic sleep deprivation, and if I'm honest, total and utter exhaustion. I don't how Chip thinks he has any chance of getting in on the act.

'What are these hurdles you speak of?' Chip says.

I pick a place in the long list of No-Gos to start. 'I follow this one particular writer crowd online – you know, because I'm considering a writing career of sorts – and they're freakin' militant. I saw a Twitter thread that went on longer than Jimmy Barnes' career.'

Chip nods. 'It's sad to be an ageing rock star.'

'Don't forget Keith Richards.'

'Is he still alive? Shit! What a fine exhibit of taxidermy!'

I laugh. 'Anyway, in this thread, they were doing their trolley over Hugh Hefner's death, saying it was a good thing the old sleaze croaked it, because he was a pimple on the face of humanity. I watched some docos on his early court challenges and what he did to champion free speech and censorship, which the Twitter mob didn't mention. But this was eclipsed by satin pyjamas, a pipe and a smoking jacket, and some seriously dodgy workplace practices involving unprotected sex, deprivation of liberty and coercive control. Had we been born in the age of flares, grottos and disco fever, we might've stood a chance. But if we do this now, we'll be publicly roasted. We'll lose all credibility. Potential employers might find out about our online history and I'm not sure I'm a thousand percent down with the idea of my would-be boss noting my early foray into exploitation of the flesh.'

Chip takes this in. 'What are you suggesting?'

'You repackage.'

'Repackage?'

'Rebrand. We start a website: *Hotties of the Northern Burbs*.'

Chip rotates his hand, summoning more information.

'The beauty will be, it's not about the beauty. It'll be about what people are into. What they like to eat. What they like to read. Their political persuasions.'

Chip throws back his head and fake-snores.

'What music they listen to. What movies they like.'

He looks me squarely in the eye. 'You're forgetting the adage *sex sells*.'

'Yeah, but their photos will achieve that.'

His eyes spark. 'We'll curate them?'

'We'll ask them to submit attractive selfies. We'll post example pics with people showing skin.'

'I note the gender non-specificity of this discussion.'

'It won't just be chicks, Chip. We'll have a guy section too. Queer. Non-binary. I'm still thinking it through.'

His eyebrows go up.

'This is the age of inclusiveness, Chip. The world has moved on from *Mad Men*.'

'Mad-who?'

'My mother's bingeing it. It's this series set in the sixties depicting rampant sexism. What I mean is: we won't discriminate.'

Chip strokes his chin. 'Have you considered a career as an equal opportunity lawyer? I think you're showing some early flair.'

'Look, if we put up pics showing skin, it will undoubtedly induce similar submissions. We'll get them to do Permission to Publish forms.'

'Again with the lawyer stuff.' He picks popcorn from between his teeth. 'How are we paying?'

'I haven't figured that out,' I say.

'Top models cost a bomb. I've priced them before.'

'So you *did* do financial forecasting?'

'Spoken like the son of an accountant.'

'I thought you said you were a trust fund baby?'

'I still have to budget!' Chip leans back in his chair and sighs. 'Fine. We'll need to devote brain cells to income. Crowdfunding could be an option. I dunno. I'll get back to you on that.'

'So you're with me on the website idea?'

'I'd like to raise some concerns: chiefly, there's no nakedness or fornication involved.'

'You have to concede there are existing industry players who've already cornered the market, Chip.'

'Who?' He flexes non-existent biceps. Tupac couldn't look more flaccid if he tried.

'Outlaw motorcycle gangs, I suspect.'

'I thought that was tattoo studios?'

'That's not what my research would indicate,' I say. 'And I don't want to end up with my bodily fluids smeared on a deserted warehouse wall, or find myself buried under ten feet of concrete. Or dangling by my neck from an industrial water pipe. Or—'

He holds up a hand. 'I get it.'

'Are you disappointed?'

He mimes a flagging erection. 'It's only my lifelong dream.'

'The first rule in business is to know your limitations.'

'Are you sure?'

'Dunno. It sounds right.'

'It *could* work,' Chip says, considering my plan. 'We could venture into product endorsement deals.' He scoffs popcorn and talks through it, showering my feet in wet corny bits. 'I heard about some dude who makes a mint spruiking haircare products. We could go for body wax? Hair removal?'

'Is that a thing? I thought hairy armpits were back in?'

At this, Chip chokes. I think he's joke-choking, but then I realise he's waving madly, pointing at something on the other side of the yard.

I look at our garden shed. My heart skids to a halt. I shit you not, there's a guy there, both hands in the air like we might pull a gun.

'Don't freak,' he says, stepping forward.

He sports a buzz-cut, is clean shaven, maybe in his late twenties, with huge pecs bulging from a tight grey T-shirt. He's wearing matching grey track pants – which somehow, through my shock and confusion, I identify as a fashion fail. There's a black bracelet thingy around his ankle.

'Don't yell or anything,' he pleads.

Chip cradles the popcorn bowl to his chest. As defence barriers go, it's light on. 'Who the hell are you?'

'Jackson,' the intruder says. 'Jackson Rollock.'

Chip's mouth falls open and a piece of popcorn drops out. 'No way!' He looks at me. 'Taylor! It's the famous painter!'

Jackson sighs. 'Jackson *Pollock* is American. He's also worm feed. And my assertion is that his art was on the lazy arsehole side of things—'

I interrupt, 'What are you doing in my backyard, Jackson Pollock?'

'Rollock.'

'Whatever. Speak fast or I'm calling the cops.'

He puts a foot forward.

'Stay where you are!' I lunge for the garden hose and aim it at him. It has a mean spray. On full blast, it should keep him at bay for all of ten seconds. 'Talk!'

He takes a deep breath. 'Fine. I'm from the inside.'

Chip looks at the back door. 'Did your olds come home early, Taylor? Did they let this guy in?'

Jackson shakes his head. 'No. *Inside*. Yatala.'

Chip stares. 'The prison?'

On cue, sirens wail. Jackson curses, head swinging, looking for somewhere to hide – or to run. He plucks tin snips from Dad's toolbox just inside the shed, cuts off the ankle bracelet and flings it over the fence. I hear it splash into the neighbour's swimming pool.

'You have to help me,' he pleads.

I brandish the hose, ready to fire.

Chip stuffs in more popcorn (in a moment like this – *really*?) and says almost unintelligibly, 'We don't have to do shit, mate. There's this thing called a power balance and the scales ain't tipping in your favour.'

Jackson falls to his knees and throws his hands wide. 'My gran is dying. I want to see her. That's why I broke out. I love her more than anyone. I *have* to see her.'

There's truth in his eyes and desperation in his voice. I don't know a thing about him, but I can tell he's for real.

'Your gran?' Chip asks. 'Prove it. Tell me three things about her. Go!'

Jackson doesn't miss a beat. 'She's seventy-seven, her favourite food is pizza, and she can recite the national anthem backwards.'

Chip blinks. 'Backwards?'

'Well, she does get the odd word wrong. And once she sang "God Bless America". She's a few streets away in that nursing home over there.' He points beyond my backyard fence. 'Help me to see her? I promise, the authorities can do what they want with me after that.'

I lower the hose. 'You mean the nursing home next to the supermarket?'

He smiles. 'Yeah. It isn't far. And the screws wouldn't let me visit her. Bastards.'

'How long has your gran got?' asks Chip.

Jackson scratches his spiky head. 'Don't know exactly. My sister visited her a couple of days ago. She reckons Gran could bite the big one any time.'

Sirens wailing, it occurs to me there could be a string of murdered prison guards lying in this guy's wake. A nervous flutter eats my chest. 'How'd you break out?'

Jackson appears antsy. 'Look, mate. Choppers will be hovering any minute. The neighbourhood will be crawling with door-knocking stiffs. I'll fill you in on my Houdini moves later, alright? Can you help me or not?'

'Time *is* of the vanilla essence,' Chip says. He picks a corn kernel from his teeth, examines it and flicks it over his shoulder. 'The dude's gran is dying,' he says to me. 'What harm can it do?'

Kelly Nixon's Facebook page flashes before me – all the desperate people wanting to talk to her one last time, me included. And here's someone who has the chance to see a loved one before they die.

'You're for real?' I ask. 'You just want to see your gran?'

He grins like I've agreed. 'Your uncle said you'd be up for it.' He reads my blank face and his assured smile dissipates. 'You're Chip Carter, aren't you?' He looks me over. 'This is number twenty-four?'

'Twenty-six,' Chip says, thumbing his chest. '*I'm* Chip Carter.' He points at me. 'This is Taylor Kennedy. You know my Uncle Roger?'

Jackson nods, grinning. 'Top bloke. Best on the inside. Said you'd give me a hand.'

I look at Chip. 'Uncle Roger, as in Grand-Junction-Road-naked-as-shit-helped-prang-a-hearse-Roger?'

Jackson cracks up. 'You heard about that, huh? And all the poor guy was after was a decent burger, hey.'

Chip puts down the popcorn bowl and brushes his hands. 'The nursing home isn't far. We'd best drive so you're not seen.'

'We're doing this?' I ask Chip. But he's already headed for the door.

Jackson follows him. On the way out he says to me, 'Hotties of the Northern Burbs is an awesome idea. When my time's up, I'll subscribe for sure.'

# CHAPTER FIVE

After loaning Jackson my dad's jeans and a flannie (sidenote: Jackson dearly wanted to wear Dad's AC/DC *Jailbreak* T-shirt but I said it was best not to draw attention), we headed for the nursing home.

Pulling a hearse into a nursing home is probably something we should have given more thought to. Former investment banker Barry thinks so, chastising Chip over the decision.

'Yes *alriiiiiiiight* Barry.' Chip groans, switching off the ignition. 'I heard you the first time.'

From the back seat, Jackson asks, 'Who are you talking to?'

Chip doesn't explain. He taps the steering wheel. 'You need to chill, Barry. I know, I know. But trust me, unwanted attention is my thing. I can handle it.'

Jackson looks behind him through the small sliding windows into the hearse tray. 'Is someone back there?'

'Just you,' I tell him, getting out. 'And Barry.'

I can't believe we're doing this. My brain feels separated from my skull, floating above me, watching my body go along for the ride.

We've parked under a verandah next to an ambulance, its

doors open, a half-emerged green-sheeted gurney awaiting a customer. The engine is running but there's no one behind the wheel. It occurs to me the ambos could be here for Jackson's gran. What if we're too late? What if she's already dead? What was I thinking agreeing to this? Why didn't I tell Chip to go it alone? I should have said, *I'm out, I'm done, I'm cashing in my Chip/chips, see you later.* What the hell am I doing here?

A male orderly with a scary seventies haircut and handlebar mo meets us at the automated doors. He's not positioned there like a valet, he's chuffing a fag. He wears a pale blue uniform with the nursing home logo: a spray of yellow flowers and a rocking chair. I've seen staff at the nearby supermarket after work. They always look half dead, exhausted from a day of running around after old people. Given most old people move like sloths on tranquilisers, it's something I've never really understood.

The orderly raises his voice over the prison sirens. 'You guys are late. The other mob just left.'

I look at Chip. If he's good with unwanted attention, now's his moment to shine. Of course, he's silent as a cinema fart.

'The other hearse,' the orderly explains. 'They did the pick-up.' He puts out a hand and after an awkward moment, Jackson shakes it. The orderly gives him a confused once-over. 'You think this is the Prince of Wales welcoming ceremony, mate? I want your paperwork. There's been a mix-up.' He looks us up and down. 'Have you guys been out for a pub lunch or something? Your staff usually wear suits and ties.' He fingers Chip's polka-dot cravat. '*Masterchef* fan? My wife can't get enough of that show. Wish she could bloody cook like one.'

'We've clocked off,' Chip says, the cravat assault somehow

reviving him. 'We decided to call in on our mate's grandmother.' He pats Jackson's shoulder. 'Carpark's full. You don't mind if we leave the beast here a few minutes, do you?'

The orderly shrugs. 'Not like it looks out of place. Who's your gran?' he asks Jackson.

'Daisy Ames,' Jackson says.

A loud snort. 'That old broad! Hey, did you hear what she did last week? She craft-glued Kevin Peterson's toupee to his crotch. We thought the poor bugger was signalling to use the loo. Couldn't figure out why when he's been wearing adult diapers for the last five years.' He butts out his smoke. 'She's a firecracker that one. Follow me.'

We enter the glass doors and the next Ice Age; the air-conditioning blast is pre-freezing elderly inhabitants, ready for the mortuary. An old lady wearing a thick woollen cardigan and mittens hobbles past on a Zimmer frame. I swear I hear her false teeth chatter.

'Jacks—' I begin, but then I quickly change his name for security purposes. '*Ralph* heard that Daisy is gravely ill.'

Jackson mouths at me, *Ralph?*

I spread my hands.

He makes an *Oh* face.

The orderly grins. 'Hearse humour?' He reads my blank look. 'You said *gravely*.' Now he seems annoyed that his joke fell flat. 'I don't think she's sick. My last shift was Sunday. She was fine.' He leads us up a pink corridor lined with a wooden rail and a paisley green frieze. We pass door after open door. Dark rooms, flickering TVs, empty lunch trays, sagging elderly mouths catching flies. 'Daisy and her friend Mary were in the common room watching that pissant game-show host. Know

46

the one I mean? Bottle-blond hair and neon teeth. God I hate game shows.'

'I don't mind them,' Chip says defensively.

I glare at him, then at Jackson. If Daisy isn't sick, what's going on? This had better not be some elaborate ploy to do over a nursing home. Are there valuables here? Jewellery? Then it hits me. This is a medical facility. He's after drugs!

'Here we are,' the orderly says, pushing on a door with *Daisy Ames* listed in little black letters. He steps aside. 'I'll leave you to it.'

Chip salutes him. Jackson wastes no time hurrying into the sunlit room. 'Granny?'

A tuft of curly white hair sticks up above a puffy salmon-pink recliner. A wrinkled hand rests on the arm, clutching a remote. The wall-mounted TV blinks some dreary British soap opera with subtitles. There's a railed single bed with white sheets folded into precision nurse's corners and a knitted throw rug nesting red-rimmed reading glasses and a book. On closer inspection, the title surprises me: *The Making of Magic Mike, The Movie.*

'Is that you, Dixon?' comes Daisy's gravelly voice. It has a distinctive twang to it. 'Did you bring chocolate?'

'It's Jackson,' he says, crouching at her side and cupping her hand. 'Your other grandson.'

'Jackson?' Daisy sounds confused. Then angry. 'Jackson! You little blighter!'

'Come now, Granny. Don't be like that.'

'Don't you *Granny* me! You stole my last reefer!'

Chip does a double take. 'Did she just say—?'

Jackson tries to shush her, but she yanks her hand away.

'Where the fuck have you been, boy? You think it's funny being locked up in here? They took away my phone! I can't order pizza! The food here tastes like horseshit! They won't even let me have a ciggie! Get me out of here! I want to go home!'

Turns out Daisy has a not-so-daisy-like mouth on her.

'You can't go home, Granny,' Jackson says gently.

'Why not?' Daisy demands. 'Who's stopping me?'

Jackson ushers us to stand in front of her. 'Granny, I want you to meet my friends. This is Chip and this is Taylor.'

I see her properly now. She's shrunken, with sun-spotted skin and whiter-than-white thinning hair. Her haggard face bears a bright-red, just-applied lipstick slash. She's wearing a black velvet vest over a white shirt, elasticised blue jeans and pink tennis slip-ons. A faded forearm tattoo looks like it once was a fairy, but now it's more a withered wizard. She squints at us and croaks, 'Who'd you say you were?'

'I'm Chip,' he says half bowing. Or curtsying. I can't work out which. 'And this is Taylor.'

I give her a friendly wave.

'Get me my fucken glasses!' Daisy snaps. Jackson passes them to her. She puts them on. The thick lenses magnify her blue, bug-like eyes. She hones in on Chip and points at his cravat. 'What's that thing you're wearing?'

I look at Jackson. 'She doesn't seem like she's at death's door.'

He tugs his earlobe, brow furrowed. ''Spose not.'

Daisy snorts. 'Death's door? I've been knocking! The pricks won't let me in!'

An apologetic smile from Jackson. 'She can be a little feisty.'

'I hadn't noticed,' Chip says.

'Don't talk about me like I'm not in the room!' Daisy shrieks.

'You're as bad as these cockwombles who pretend to look after me!' She turns her attention to Chip. 'What have you got on you, boy? Any good stuff?'

Chip opens his mouth to respond but clams up just as fast.

'Don't play innocent,' Daisy adds. 'I might be old cheese, but I know how to party.'

'We should probably leave,' I say to Jackson. 'It won't be long before the cops are looking for you. You need to hand yourself in. It'll look better than getting caught.'

'Cops?' Daisy panics. She waves at Chip. 'Quick! Top drawer, behind the Bible! Don't dither, boy!'

After a confused moment, Chip opens the bedside drawer. He pulls out a Bible, reaches in again and comes up with a purple chocolate box. On Daisy's instruction, he opens it and removes a top layer tray of foiled treats. Underneath is a small plastic bag of white pills, a wad of cash and a hand-scrawled list.

Jackson sighs. 'Granny! You've been stealing from the med cart again? You almost killed Mr Bone last time! You can barely read the labels!'

'I *can* read the labels if I have my glasses on,' Daisy asserts. 'And how was I supposed to know Viagra makes his heart race?'

'You're dealing Viagra?' Chip interrupts.

'To someone called Mr Bone,' I note.

Daisy beams a gap-toothed smile. 'Big market.' She holds her hands at erect penis length. 'Huge.'

'I didn't even know old people do it!' Chip exclaims, like he's just discovered Mars for the human race. 'Did you?' he asks me.

'You haven't seen my parents.'

'What if they put a hip out?' Chip ponders, considering sexual logistics for octogenarians. 'What if someone walks in?'

'They join you,' Daisy says matter-of-factly.

I try to rein it in. 'Chip, we need to leave. We're not getting caught with him.' I point at Jackson. 'No offense, Ralph, but I think our job here is done. You've seen your gran. She's clearly got more fight left than Mike Tyson. It's time for us to go. Thank you very much and have a nice life.'

I grab Chip by the arm and go to steer him from the room, but Daisy screeches, 'You're not leaving here without me! I'll scream!' And she does just that.

Jackson lunges for the door and closes it. 'You two,' he barks at me and Chip, 'don't move. And you,' he says to Daisy, 'put a cork in it.' Daisy keeps yelling like someone dunked her feet in a urine-filled bedpan. 'I said shut it!' Jackson hisses. 'Let me think!'

Daisy pipes down.

'What's there to think about?' I say. 'We need to go. *You* need to hand yourself in.'

Jackson goes to answer, but Daisy pulls up her top, flashing a saggy white bra. Her wrinkled midriff is covered in blood-black yellowed bruises. I suck in my breath. It's a confronting sight. 'They're mean to me,' she pouts.

Jackson leans in for a closer look. 'What in the name of—?'

'Shower time,' Daisy explains.

Chip blinks. 'On the set of *American Psycho*?' He turns to Jackson. 'Mate, this is all kinds of messed up. I wouldn't let a dog stay under these conditions.'

'I slipped,' Daisy adds. 'They cut off the hot water. I turned it back on.'

Relief washes over Jackson's face. 'You mean this was an accident, Granny?'

'It's still their fault!' Daisy protests, dropping her top. 'They're idiots! Morons! Loopy-loons! You need to get me out of here. I've got money. I'll pay.'

Jackson shakes his head. 'Where will you go, Granny?'

'Mount Gambier,' Daisy says. 'To see Errol.'

Jackson rolls his eyes. 'You separated from your second husband years ago.'

'I have to see Errol!' Daisy maintains. 'I'm dying.'

'You're *ageing*, Granny. There's a difference.'

'No, I'm dying.' Daisy points to the chart at the end of her bed. 'Cancer. It's in my liver.'

Jackson picks up the paperwork and flips through it. After a minute, he says in a choked voice, 'This must've been what my sister was talking about.'

'I'll pay,' Daisy repeats. 'Name the price. Just take me to Mount Gambier.'

Jackson slips the chart back on the rack. Wiping the corners of his eyes, he says tightly, 'You haven't got any money, Granny. Your estate is run by a guardian.'

'I'm not completely stupid!' Daisy spouts. 'I didn't tell them about everything!' She waves a hand at Chip. 'You got a phone?'

Chip obliges, handing his over.

I glare at him. This has gone on long enough. We need to get out of here and we need to do it fast. I don't dispute it sucks major eggs that this poor woman has cancer, and I'd be lying if I said I don't feel for her, or Jackson, but how is any of this our problem? How is it *my* problem?

Daisy takes one confused look at the smartphone and hands it to Jackson. 'Ring this number.' She rattles off a list of codes at a rate that'd make Stephen Hawking spin in his grave. Jackson plugs them in. His eyes widen as he listens. He hangs up and hands the phone back to Chip.

'See?' Daisy says smugly.

'Did you rob a bank?' Jackson asks.

'No, that's your caper.' Daisy quips.

When she says it, it occurs to me I haven't asked what Jackson's crime is. *Did he rob a bank?* You need guns to do that. Is he violent? Should we be more worried?

Chip isn't shy to ask. 'How much moolah are we talking?'

Jackson smiles. 'Enough to have the four of us on a plane to Barbados and sipping mojitos in a five-star resort for the next twenty years.'

Chip looks at me. 'Is that so ...'

I don't have to be a mind reader. He wants the money for his business. 'Uh-uh,' I say, taking a backwards step. 'Forget it! No way!'

'She only wants to go to Mount Gambier.' Chip's words are loaded with insincerity. 'It's a short trip, Taylor. Five hours on the road, five hours back. We could do it in two days.'

Daisy nods enthusiastically. 'Yes, yes!'

'No fucking way,' I say.

Chip bats puppy-dog eyes. 'Come on, Taylor. Are you *really* going to deny this sweet old woman her dying wish? Where's your sense of obligation? Your compassion for the elderly?'

'No, Chip. No means no.'

'Come on,' he pleads. 'Fantasia hasn't made it through parliament yet.'

'*Euthanasia*,' I correct.

'*Fantasia* is a freeform musical composition,' Jackson offers. 'Quite delightful.'

Chip pulls a face at Jackson. 'Whatever.' He turns to me. 'Where's your—'

'My brain? We're already harbouring one escapee prisoner. You want to harbour two?'

'We can give them up when we get back.' He glances at Jackson. 'No offence.'

'None taken,' Jackson says coolly.

'And Daisy,' Chip says, 'won't mind providing us with a little incentive payment for our trouble. We can use it for our website.'

I was right. There it is.

'You mean hush money?' Daisy says.

Chip nods. 'Something like that.'

'Done deal,' Daisy agrees.

I throw my hands up. 'Fine! Do whatever! But count me out! My loose morals might have supported your whole harebrained pornographic ventures thing, but aiding and abetting criminals is another ball game. I don't need friends this badly. I'm quite happy friendless. I'm out.'

I go to leave. Jackson stops me. He digs a finger into my collarbone. 'You're doing it.'

I shake him off. 'No, I'm not.'

'It's one day. Two, max. Besides, I can't let you go, you might squeal.'

I look at Chip. 'Is he for real?' I turn back to Jackson. 'Are you kidnapping us?' Who is harbouring who?

'Abduction,' Jackson says. 'At least I think it is.' He scratches his head. 'I'm not sure. I know I googled the difference once.'

I fire at Chip, 'This is *your* problem, not mine! He's your uncle's friend! It's your car ... hearse! This is your mess!'

'And you're here with us, friendly neighbour.' Chip bends

down and cups Daisy's chin, pressing his cheek to hers. 'Besides, how can you resist this adorable face?'

Daisy flashes me a triumphant grin. 'Fucken' oath,' she says.

# CHAPTER SIX

'Hold the gurney still, would ya?' Chip barks at me.

'Do I look like an ambo to you?'

'Can't you lock the wheels or something?'

Jackson helps Daisy from her leather recliner and loads her onto the borrowed gurney (okay, *stolen*.) He covers her with a green sheet and wraps around three black straps, clipping and yanking them tight. Daisy's outline looks like a pork roast. I wonder if this is how bodies are sent into the cremation oven. All she needs is a sprig of rosemary.

'I can't breathe!' comes her muffled cry.

Jackson peels back the sheet and hisses, 'Shut it! You're supposed to be dead!' He throws the sheet over her head, shoves the bag of pills and wad of notes into his pocket, grabs her reading glasses and puts them on his head like sunnies. We rush the gurney through the corridor. 'Quit wriggling your toes!' he snaps.

Seventies-haircut-handlebar-mo meets us by the front door. 'Ah! Found one after all.'

Jackson glances at me. 'Um, yeah. Got the call ten minutes

ago. Typical,' he adds with a forced laugh. 'Always when you've clocked off, right?'

'Which one croaked?' The orderly goes to lift the sheet. 'Bagged and tagged?'

Heart in my throat, I jump in. 'How long have you been nurturing that?' I point at my top lip, then at his. 'I'd like one just like it. What's your secret?'

The orderly lets go of the sheet. He throws back his shoulders, stands tall, and smiles ear to ear. 'Beard oil,' he announces proudly. 'Amazing stuff. They've got some really nice fragrances too. Feel it. Go on. *Feel it!*'

I reluctantly reach out and pinch his moustache, running my fingertips along it. It's surprisingly smooth and on an aesthetic level, quite pleasing. As I let go, it snaps back into a tidy curl.

He double-winks at me. 'The missus loves the smell. Doesn't mind the odd tickle either. Facial hair is making a comeback. These days men are consistently emasculated. There's a war out there, a battle of the sexes, and facial hair is the final frontier. If there are women who protest social norms by not shaving their legs, then I refuse to shave my moustache.' He's super passionate about it – passionate enough not to notice a muffled sneeze from under the shuddering green sheet.

'We should get moving,' Chip says, pushing the gurney.

The orderly taps Daisy's sheet-outlined legs. 'Who'd you say this is? *Was.*'

'Kevin Peterson,' answers Chip.

After a WTF look at him, I remember he's talking about the man who had a toupee stuck to his crotch. I'm mildly impressed at his composure under pressure. He has a memory for names. Or hairy crotches.

The orderly twirls his mo. 'Huh. The old fella mustn't have eaten much in the last few days. His guts is usually the size of Everest.'

'Gas,' Chip says.

'Gas?'

Chip nods. 'The dead expel gas. It leaked out.'

*The dead bloat, don't they, Chip? They don't deflate like fucking balloons!*

On cue an enormous fart erupts from beneath the sheet. The orderly's prized moustache almost falls off his face.

'See?' Chip says.

Jackson gives a nervous laugh. He grabs Chip in a headlock, forcing him down so he hovers over Daisy's midriff. 'Ready for your second Dutch oven today, mate?'

The orderly's mouth hangs open. I thumb at them. 'Industry joke. It can be a depressing business. How else do you stay sane?'

The orderly collects himself and joins in on the gag. 'Yeah. I get it. Try working in God's Waiting Room. It's purgatory.' He waves us on. 'I won't hold you up. Have a good day. And remember,' he says, pointing to his mo, 'beard oil. You can't go wrong.'

Outside, the ambos have returned to their vehicle. A man and a woman stare at the back doors as if their missing gurney will magically reappear.

And now it has.

*Shit.*

'Hey!' The guy says. 'Isn't that ours?'

'No,' Chip lies.

'Yes it is,' the woman argues. She's dirty about it too. 'It has a sticker.' She points to a little white square on the rail. *Property of the SA Ambulance Service.* Grabbing a black box radio thing pinned to her shoulder, she side-mouths into it, 'Call off the search party. We found it. Over.'

Jackson gives me an accusing glare and biffs me across the top of my head. 'Charlie! You grabbed the wrong one!' He looks apologetically at the ambos. 'Sorry. This goober is on probation. It's the third time this week he's screwed up. Dunno what they teach kids these days, do you? Distracted by their iPhones. Nothing better to do than to watch YouTube. Wouldn't know a work ethic or clear instruction if it bit them in the arse.'

If Jackson thinks this will save us from further scrutiny, he's wrong. The male ambo smiles forgivingly. 'That's a bit rough, mate. He's only a kid.' He asks me, 'How long you been working, champ?'

'Um ... two weeks,' I stutter.

'And this is your chosen career path?' He pulls a business card from his shirt pocket. 'You might want to consider joining a union. I can get you started.'

'Here we go,' mutters his colleague. 'He's recruiting *again*.'

'Name's Bob,' he says, stuffing the card in my hand. 'Bob, like the legendary PM Bob Hawke. My family are unionists from way back. Do your parents vote Labor?' He doesn't wait for an answer. 'I'm guessing you'll be eligible to vote soon. We workers have to stick together. Shove it to the big guy.' He gives Jackson the evil eye. 'Workplace bullying is a serious matter.'

'Now listen here,' Jackson argues. 'If you're insinuating that I—'

But right at that moment, four cops rush past on foot, crackling two-way radios blaring from their hips. They enter the nursing home. Only now do I register the prison sirens still wailing in the background.

Proud unionist Bob is baffled. 'What's that all about?'

'Speaking of people who don't listen,' says his colleague, 'it was on the radio. There's been a breakout. A prisoner is on the run.'

Heart beating wildly, I feign shock and surprise – and I'm pretty sure I nail the awe factor. 'Wow! It's like that movie *Escape from Alcatraz*!'

Chip seizes the moment to open the hearse doors. The tray is empty – nothing but a set of silver rails and a tattered cardboard box of vintage LPs bearing yellow-dot price stickers. The lead singer of Guns N' Roses, Axl Rose, glares at us, probably pissed at being flogged for two-bucks-fifty. (Dad has that record. It's not bad.)

The ambos give us a once-over. The woman asks, 'You weren't going to take our gurney, were you?'

'Of course not!' Chip says like it's the most insulting thing he's ever heard. 'We'll just load her in and—'

'Him,' I correct.

'Him,' Chip says. 'And we'll be on our way.'

'What are you putting the body on?' The woman persists. 'Are you from one of those budget funeral places? Wow. I've heard of your practices but I've never actually seen it. Didn't Channel Seven do an exposé on you last year? I swear I've seen your face somewhere before.'

She looks squarely at Jackson. I realise his image must be all over the news. Did they see him on TV when they were inside the nursing home? *Shit shit shit*. We really need to get out of here.

She pats the body. 'Poor soul.' Extracting a silver cross necklace from beneath her uniform, she kisses it and whispers, 'Lord have mercy.'

Union Bob sighs. 'Don't be sanctimonious, Lorna.' He says to us, 'She's a lapsed Catholic, you know.'

'Am not!' Lorna cries.

'Are so! And what do you expect?' Union Bob huffs. 'We treat each other like crap when we're alive, what makes you think we'll be any better behaved towards the dead?'

At this, Kelly Nixon's Facebook page flashes through my mind – and the argument I posted that saw me ostracised by the entire student body.

'Not everyone is cashed up enough to pay for a Rolls Royce exit,' Bob continues. 'The corporate capitalist A-holes who control our wages make sure of that. That's why a workers' union—'

He's interrupted by an enormous fart from beneath the green sheet. This one could trigger a global tsunami. *What the hell are they feeding old people?* Both ambos look questioningly at the body, then at us. Chip and Jackson hurriedly unclip the straps, gather up Daisy's sheet-swaddled frame and slide her into the hearse.

Chip slams the doors shut behind her. 'We'd best make tracks,' he says. 'Nice doing business with you.'

I tap their gurney. 'Solid construction. Good ergonomic height. Wheels a bit dodgy-shopping-trolley. I'd get that seen to.' I head for the front passenger seat and jump in. The others follow. Chip fires the engine and we take off, a cloud of dust billowing behind us – or so I imagine.

Halfway down the road, adrenaline pumping, I select a strawberry Chupa Chup from the glovebox, peel the wrapper and plug it in my mouth. I unwrap a banana one for Chip.

He fake-smokes it with trembling fingers. 'Man, that was peak *Get off my gurney!* And you can shut your trap, Barry. I'm not in the mood.'

'Who *is* he talking to?' Jackson demands. He doesn't wait for an answer. He turns and slides the little glass window open, peering into the tray. 'Are you alright back there, Granny?'

I hear Daisy's squeaky reply, 'I think I sharted.'

# CHAPTER SEVEN

With Daisy and Jackson tucked safely next door at Chip's, I head home, heart hammering faster than a laboratory rat testing stimulants. I don't know what's happened. I'm spinning out of control. One minute my life is completely run-of-the-mill normal – school and friends, hanging with Cass, Lia and Riley, doing normal stuff – and the next I'm friendship-orphaned, adopted by a wannabe online pimp, hanging out with a prison escapee and a potty-mouthed elderly Viagra dealer, about to embark on a cross-country pilgrimage to see some old guy called Errol. If this is one of those dreams where you wake up and go, *Oh, thank fuck that's not my life*, and gladly get on with the day, then it's gone on long enough. I'm over it.

I find my parents seated at the dining table, wine glasses in front of them, a dusty bottle of red open and three quarters gone. There's a whiff of officialdom in the air. I promptly panic. They must know about Jackson. They must know about the nursing home. They've seen it on the news. How do I explain?

'There you are,' says Mum.

'We've been waiting,' says Dad, rapping his fingers on the table, Dr Evil-style. All he's missing is a cat to stroke and a spinny chair. He lifts his wineglass and takes a slow, deliberate sip, maintaining eye contact. If he's attempting to build tension, he's being obscenely successful. 'There's something we need to discuss.' He puts the glass down, reaches for the laptop in the middle of the table and drags it to him. I register the familiar Middleborough High peeling stickers. *My laptop*. Hang on, why do they have my laptop?

'We'll get straight down to it,' Mum says.

Maybe this isn't about the breakout after all. Do they know about Kelly Nixon's Facebook page? Has someone told them about what I did? Has Mum spoken to Cass?

'Our shopping trip was sadly unsuccessful,' Mum begins.

'There *was* that success we had in the Myer change-room,' Dad notes, blowing her an air kiss.

She smirks and fidgets with the hem of her skirt.

*Really?*

'I'd shut down my computer,' Mum continues, grinning stupidly at Dad, 'and we wanted to scout some online outlets, so we used yours.'

My head fires at speed. Did my password kick in? Did I leave Facebook open? What was the last thing I searched?

*Oh.*

*Holy.*

*Crap.*

Dad chooses his words carefully. 'You know, Taylor, I thought we'd crossed this bridge a while ago. I thought we'd covered the things there were to cover during The Talk.' He uses quotation fingers. 'But it would seem you're still curious. *Very* curious from what I've seen.' More quotation fingers.

'Dad, I can exp—'

'I'm not judging you for looking at pornography—'

'I—'

'Because it's a natural thing to be wondering about sex—'

'I'm not—'

'Especially at your age. Although when I was seventeen, unlike you, I'd already had lots of … experiences.'

*Way to rub it in, Dad.*

He goes on, 'But I'll also admit to spending a considerable amount of time looking quite closely at lingerie catalogues. Also nude diagrams in *National Geographic*. Plus there was a period where your grandmother, God rest her soul, got quite shirty about the state of my sheets.'

*Please, someone kill me now.*

'Also, I'd be lying if I told you that your mum and I didn't occasionally dabble in the odd bit of *inspiration*.' Again with the quotation fingers. 'When you've been married as long as we have, you need to keep it fresh.' Mum blushes and looks at the ceiling. I fantasise about earmuffs – a vast sea of earmuffs. 'But there are limits, Taylor. Healthy limits.'

'Not to mention something called good taste,' Mum butts in.

'And the sheer size and scope of your *investigations*,' quotation fingers, 'would suggest, at best you're insatiably curious, and at worst, obsessed or addicted. I want to make sure it's not the latter. Everything alright, mate?'

'It's a school project!' I gasp, like I'm the one taking a breath. But as the words leave my mouth, I can tell he doesn't believe me. 'For health class. Everyone is doing the decriminalisation of marijuana thing, which is soooooooooo predictable, and I wanted to be original. I chose Sexual Health.'

'I *did* see you'd looked at some legal sites,' Mum says, sitting forward, eager to buy into the idea. 'And I saw some stuff about domain names too.'

'Exactly. All part of the project.'

She turns to Dad. 'I think it's fabulous that our son is so open and forward-thinking. I knew there'd be a rational explanation.'

Dad isn't convinced. 'I'm concerned that when you get a partner, Taylor, that you'll think this,' he points at the laptop, 'is the real deal.'

'Their boobs aren't real,' Mum says.

Dad gapes at her. '*They're not?!*'

'Also: why do you think you always see those penis enlargement adverts?' Mum adds.

I laugh. Even when they're grilling me, they're funny.

'I want you to be a gentleman, Taylor,' Dad continues, pseudo-serious again. 'I want for you to be a respectful, caring boyfriend.'

This wounds me. 'You think I wouldn't be?'

'Of course you would be, honey.' Mum reaches for my hand and squeezes it. She gives Dad a pointed glare. 'I've seen how nice you are to Cass. Speaking of, why don't you ask her over for dinner?'

'Um ... she's ... um ... she's got a lot on.' I look at the floor, at the ceiling, anywhere but her face. 'If that's it, I have homework to do.'

'Don't take this the wrong way, son,' Dad says. 'We can be open with each other, right? I'm looking out for you. It's my job. Plus, anything you do that's bad reflects poorly on me. It's all about how *I* look.'

I smile. 'I get it.'

'Good,' he says, satisfied. 'Now we have something else to

share with you before you bunker down in Study Land. We're going on an impromptu trip. Well, not *we*. Us. Your mum and me. We'll be away for a few days, leaving on the red-eye special tomorrow morning.'

I think of Jackson and Daisy. Gone for a few days? Maybe I *am* going to deal with this situation without my parents being any the wiser?

'We're attending the Roller Door Extravaganza Conference in Queensland,' Dad says. 'Brenton Wakefield has a bad case of tonsillitis so they're sending me as company rep. Cool huh? I never get these perks.'

At this, Mum stifles a giggle.

Dad looks at her. 'What?'

'Nothing ...' She sips her wine. 'It's just ... *Extravaganza*? They're talking about garage roller doors for goodness sake.'

Dad appears hurt. 'You have something more appropriate to call it?'

Mum catches herself. 'Oh honey ... I'm sorry.'

Mum does this – drinks too much and makes fun of Dad's job. It's not like he planned to be a garage-door salesman. I'm not sure anyone leaves school thinking their life's dream is to safely contain people's prize belongings behind a durable Colorbond barrier. And who would've thought the roller-door trade was so reliable? Dad says he stays in business thanks to the crims. Security never goes out of style.

'That was careless,' Mum apologises. 'It's a wonderful opportunity, darling. I'm very proud of you.' She pats Dad's knee. 'We're going to have a rolling good time.'

Dad grins. 'Definitely. The only way is up. Or down. Mostly up.'

Mum turns to me. 'You're old enough to look after the house for a few days, Taylor.'

'Yes, but you'll need to be vigilant about locking up,' Dad warns. 'Remember, we've been burgled before. And there was a prison breakout this afternoon. Did you hear? A police officer door-knocked about an hour ago. Not sure if they've since found the guy?'

My heart hammers. The police *did* come looking. I bet that means they knocked on Chip's door too. Was that when we were at the nursing home? Would they be coming back? They need a warrant to search a home, don't they? I wish I'd paid more attention when I was bingeing *Line of Duty*.

'I've always worried it could happen,' says Mum, pouring herself more wine. 'Living next to a prison has its pros and cons.' She takes a swig and chortles, 'Cons. Geddit? Hey! Remember when we used to threaten you, Taylor, that if you didn't go to bed on time we'd dump you over the razor-wire fence and let the guard dogs eat you?'

Dad slaps his thigh, cracking up. 'You totally believed us.'

'I was six.' (But I was more like ten.) 'Now, if you're both finished reminiscing about your history of psychological abuse, I have homework to attend to.'

'Invite Cass over for dinner!' Mum calls as I slink away. 'Bill's Takeaway. We're ordering the Bill and Noelene special.'

'The what?' Dad asks. 'Oh, you mean that woman doing work experience? They've named a special after her?'

Mum nods. 'She created it herself. Combo pack: aged duck, pulled turkey and re-fried sausage.'

Dad snorts. 'Sold!' He stops me. 'Hey Taylor, you forgot your laptop.' He gets up and knights me with it, tapping each shoulder, then hands it over. 'Go forth, study hard, make your elders proud.' He leans in and whispers, 'I know we missed anal sex from The Talk, but if you want to discuss it, we can.'

I make a bolt for my room.

I know what you're thinking. Your parents don't seem so bad. They seem up-front and pretty nice. They have a sense of humour. They're good to each other and they obviously care about you. They seemingly endeavour to do all the things people passing as parents do. Why are you so reluctant to tell them about Cass? Or confide in them about the breakout? Hell, even tell them what happened with Kelly Nixon's Facebook page?

The answer is: they *are* good people. They could definitely cool it on the whole randy rootarama thing, but outside of that, they're harmless. Most kids I know hate their parents with a passion reserved for serial killers and crime overlords, but I've got to admit I kind of like mine. Mum is super-smart and business savvy. She keeps her clients happy, the show running at home, and she *always* has time to help me with my homework or drive me to an appointment. Dad's the same. There's nothing he wouldn't do for us. And they love each other. They genuinely do. That, or they're on the cusp of menopause/middle-age and their bodies are purging egg/sperm reserves, chucking it all out there for one last hurrah. Who am I to burden them? Isn't it noble to protect the people you love? There's not a lot they can do about the stuff I face, so why stress them with it? I like to think of it as a kindness.

I sit on my bed and cycle through my socials. Still no messages from Cass – *or* the others. We're now bordering on a communication blackout record.

I remember one time we argued. It was over toilet paper.

We were on school camp and the facilities were rudimentary to say the least. Cass needed a Number Two. There was no paper. She'd begged me to find some, but in the end, high up Shit Creek without a paddle, she used her underwear, discarded it and went commando. Half an hour later I remembered Mum had packed me emergency wet-wipes. Cass went troppo and accused me of holding out on her. (I wasn't, I just have a crap memory sometimes – kinda apt, really.) Later, when Cass calmed down, we weren't just fine with each other, we were better than fine. Riley likened it to make-up sex; people fight, release poison, and the balance is redressed. I don't know about that, but I took comfort in the idea there were no deal-breakers. That no matter what happened, we'd figure it out.

This time feels different, though. And it *has* to be about The Thing. I don't care if Cass says it isn't. Nothing else makes sense.

I open my laptop and search Kelly Nixon's Facebook page. There's a new post from her cousin, Angie. She's older than Kelly, maybe in her twenties, and in her profile pic there's a cherubic little girl balanced on her lap. She writes: *I could use a big squishy Kelly-hug right now. Life's so shit sometimes, cuz! I need you. You knew how to make me laugh. You were always so carefree. I loved that about you. I loved so many things. I wish you were here.*

I stare at Angie's words. I don't know the first thing about Angie, but I can't help but ask, would she say this to a living-breathing friend? Surely she knows by posting this that she's not just talking to Kelly, she's revealing her private struggles to *all* of Kelly's friends' list? How often did she turn to Kelly when she was alive? Did she? If she did, would she have called her or DM-ed her instead of writing something public?

*If I was no longer here, would Cass be posting nice stuff about me?*

I go the search function and search my name coupled with Kelly's. It comes up quickly – *my* post, the same post I've re-read countless times since I wrote it; the post that sparked major outrage. That thing I did.

*Taylor Kennedy commented on Kelly Nixon's wall:*
Fact: People lie. Even when they say they're not, they usually are. They're not telling you the full truth – only versions. They say shit they don't mean. They say stuff they think you want to hear. They say it to cover their backsides, because it sounds good, because it ticks a box and serves a purpose and keeps their noses clean. People are self-conscious conservative arseholes. They're ill-equipped to say I love you – especially to the people they love the most. They protect themselves. They think it will give them space to backtrack; if it goes wrong, if the other person doesn't love them back, they can say they never really cared. They're idiots. We know. Love is visible. Love is there – even when we think we're good at hiding it.

All these people commenting here are arseholes, Kelly. They didn't love you – not like they love themselves. If they did, they would've done something. Said something. Listened. They would've heard your silent screams. Paid attention. Made space in their busy lives. Tried harder. Now they want to alleviate their guilt by gushing about how fantastic you were. *Now* they want to tell you that they love you. Why didn't they tell you when you were here, when you needed it the most? Why didn't they pick up the phone? DM you? Post messages on your wall? Hunt you down.

**Where was the outpouring of love then?**

**Arseholes. All of them: arseholes.**

No matter how many times I look at it, it doesn't change. Brain snap. Uncensored fury. Out there. I fancied myself a truthsayer, but overwhelming public opinion would suggest not. In hindsight, it probably was a rookie fail to post such vitriolic garbage and not check on the comments for a whole day. I don't know what I was hoping for but it wasn't what greeted me – a sledging deluge, more f-bombs than a Jim Jefferies stand-up routine, and more than a handful of thinly veiled threats to rearrange my nether regions and tie them in a neat bow around my head. Cass added her two cents: *Thanks for the insight, Dickwad in Chief.* Straight to the point, of course. Still, I didn't take it to mean we were dead in the water. I didn't think it was a deal-breaker. I thought we'd tussle and then have metaphorical make-up sex; argue, get it off our chests, wisecrack our way through it and find our way back to each other. Optimism at its finest.

I log out, go to the *Advertiser* and pull up today's Death Notices. I've done it every day since my grandfather died six years ago, but in the last few days I haven't had time.

It's been a slow week – only thirty-nine names appear. That's light on. Across the state, across the country, hundreds of people die every day. All that's left of them is a few lines of text crammed into a tiny box. That, and maybe a graphic of a rose or a musical instrument, depending on what people were into. Sometimes there's a photo, but more often than not it's some boring professional headshot. The messages are always the same: heartfelt words of love and sympathy, and a desire that loved ones rest peacefully. (That's what they were like when

Kelly died.) Some notices refer to charities you can donate to, revealing the illness to which the person succumbed. The whole thing is depressing – and not because it's the death notices, but because there's nothing real about it. It's window dressing. These dead people are mannequins. This is how it felt when Grandpa died. It's like no one really knew him – not like I did – and this is what I want to change. I want to honour people's lives differently; breathe life into death and tell their stories in the same way we give eulogies at funerals. But do it online. Not everyone receives an obituary and that's not fair. I want to start a database of the dead – an accessible portal of stories that lasts for all eternity.

I scour the names and come across John Bates. *Died in tragic unforeseen circumstances*. I google his name. Up pops an article from a week ago.

> John Bates was crossing the road carrying groceries and a Keno ticket purchased from Fairview Heights Foodland when he was hit by an ambulance en route to an emergency. One witness recalls splattered bananas on the windscreen. An investigation is pending. Sadly Mr Bates will never collect his $345 Keno win.

And I thought *I* was having a bad day.

I shut the laptop and try to focus on my homework, a book review of *The Perks of Being a Wallflower* by Stephen Chbosky. But that would require reading said book and I don't really feel like it right now, *especially* seeing as I've read some Goodreads spoilers and it's a novel that explores pretty dark territory. Right now I'm calling my apathy *self care* and choosing not to go there. I consider searching the Teacher Notes and fudging it, but I can't be bothered with that either. A new level of laziness even for me.

My phone beeps. Once again my heart plummets when I see it's not from Cass. It's a message from Chip: *We leave at 9 am sharp*. I'm about to text back, when my screen does this weird blinking thing. The dreaded rotating circle appears, then it vibrates and dies. After plugging it in to charge and restarting it, it's obvious it's officially cactus.

Terrific. Is there anything else that can go wrong?

Here's a tip:

Don't ask that.

*Ever.*

# CHAPTER EIGHT

Chip leans over Fone Wizards' glass display cabinet and blows hot-breath rings. A misty filter appears, muting the collection of colourful phone covers. Chip rubs it off with his cravat, almost choking himself. (I really should get around to asking him why he's wearing one.) We decided to give his mate Cam a miss, not just because Tony's Phonies is a stupid business name instilling immediate customer doubt, but because I don't want to be recorded on shop-cam with an escaped criminal. Fone Wizards is security-camera free. Unless they have those small ones you stick in teddy bear noses to spy on babysitters, but I can't see any bears in store, nor people fitting the 'we're suspicious of our baby-sitter' profile. There's one of those gold cats with a waving arm, but that's it.

'You could've picked next week for this to happen,' Chip says, like I have a choice in my phone shitting itself. 'The plan was to leave at nine. We'll be late.'

'Late for what?'

'Road trips run to schedules, Taylor. You have a plan and you stick to it.'

It's the first time I've heard Chip sound anxious. Maybe

this whole harbouring fugitives thing isn't washing well with him either.

'Why does stuff like this *always* happen when you're headed off on holiday?' he says. I'm about to say this isn't a holiday, but he whines, 'It's in the playbook.'

Daisy and Jackson are waiting outside in the hearse. They slept at Chip's place. Overnight, Daisy got Chip to do an online banking transfer (nothing like leaving a paper trail), and this morning Chip raided the ATM and subsequently invested in a shit-tonne of groceries, enough to see us ride a sugar high all the way to Mount Gambier and back. Pringles, Tim Tams, three boxes of Cadbury Favourites, soft drink, travel tissues and Vaseline. When I asked what the Vaseline was for, he got flustered, mentioned a skin-friction issue, and wouldn't elaborate.

I touch my pocket to check there are no home-group absenteeism texts or last-minute reminders from Mum and Dad before they boarded their flight, when I realise my phone is with the repair lady behind the counter. *Uh Duh.* She's hunched over a tiny tool repair kit, my phone dismantled in front of her. With the focus of a brain surgeon, she twists a pin-sharp rod into the SIM tray, but she slips and drops it. It tinkles on the floor. She bends to get it, mutters, '*Shit* ...' then comes over to me and declares, 'I'll have to send it away.' There's something black stuck between her front teeth – a seed? I have a vision of her stuffing her face with multigrain toast at breakfast. 'It'll take a few weeks. I can give you a loan one.' She opens a drawer to share an impressive array of shabby secondhand phones. 'Twenty dollars a week,' she says.

Chip opens his overstuffed wallet and hands her a pineapple.

She takes it, shoves it in the till, then gives Chip his change. 'I broke your SIM.' She shrugs. 'It happens.'

Great. Now my phone *and* all my contacts are gone. I'm not even sure of my passwords. I wrote them in my school diary so I wouldn't have to remember. My diary is safely tucked in my locker. It's not like Chip's going to swing by my school to get it. Hang on – don't some apps have tracking devices? Maybe a social media blackout isn't a bad thing? Then I think of Cass – how is she going to contact me to apologise? Did she already try?

I remember an apology text Cass once sent me. It said: *Dangerfield is having a thirty percent off sale*, the subtext of which was: *Let's forget it and get into Afterpay debt together.* She isn't one for sentimentality – something I admire. But at the same time I also resented that text. Couldn't she bring herself to send a simple *I'm sorry* ? What was so hard about those words?

'I'll give you a new SIM.' The repair lady gets one from the dodgy phone drawer and writes my new number on scrap paper. She shoves a yellow contract at me. As I sign away my human rights to who-knows-what, she slips the SIM into a phone with a bright pink Pokemon cover. I really want to ask for a different cover, but I restrain my ego. 'There's no charger,' she says. 'Use a generic. Should be enough battery to get you through a few solid hours.' She starts it up and hands it to me. The seed that was stuck in her teeth is now stuck to the screen. *Ew.* I flick it off and it lands on her shirt. Hakuna Matata, seedling.

As we leave the shop, my new phone beeps. Chip shrugs as if to say it's not from him. *You think?*

Geoff, it's time for your annual prostate check. Please phone Anderson's Clinic to make an appointment.

Apparently I have Geoff's SIM.

Fabulous.

In the carpark, Chip nudges me and points to a woman locking her car. She's dressed head to toe in purple – purple shoes, purple jewellery, purple scarf, the works. Even her hair is purple. Her dog, a white shih tzu, has its tail and ears dyed purple. I'm almost certain PETA would have something to say about that. I'm surprised they're not standing behind her waving placards. Maybe I should phone it in?

'I'm going to miss Radelaide,' Chip laments, watching the purple lady. 'You won't see that kind of thing in the country.'

'Prince fan?' I suggest.

'Best keep our distance. She might eat us.' He's aghast at my blank face. 'You've never heard the Flying Purple People Eater song?'

'I no compute.'

'I saw it on YouTube. Search it.'

I try, but I can't. My loan phone may as well be a Morse code clicker, good for calls and text and that's about it.

'I'll play it for you later,' Chip promises. 'Something to look forward to.'

We return to the hearse. Daisy and Jackson are cozied up in the back seat, both of them wearing brand-new aviator sunnies. I know they're new because there's an elasticated price tag dangling from Daisy's.

'Where'd you get those?' I ask my distorted reflection.

Jackson points out the window. 'From that stand by the chemist.'

Chip slaps his forehead with an audible whack. 'You weren't supposed to get out of the car! There are security cameras everywhere!'

'I needed to wash my hands,' Jackson says.

Daisy says, 'He's a homophobe.'

'*Germaphobe*,' Jackson corrects.

'That too,' says Daisy.

'Granny! I may be a germaphobe, but I'm *not* homophobic!'

'That's not what you said when I told you I pashed Maisy Winterfeld behind the bowling green scoreboard.' She pushes her sunnies up the bridge of her nose. 'Hot diggety, that woman could kiss!'

Jackson explains, 'My distaste, if you recall, was about her fashion choices, *not* her sexuality. Who the hell wears Crocs and socks?'

Daisy replies, 'When you get to our age comfort takes precedence. She has bunions – not that I did a Fergie on her toes. Just saying.'

'What the hell is a Fergie?' I ask.

'Long and sordid tale involving royalty, foot fetishes and invasive paparazzi,' Jackson says. 'Best left buried with the three-point-six-bazillion other royal scandals.'

I'm still none the wiser.

And if I had a phone that worked, I'd Google it. *What the hell did the human race do before Google?*

Chip triple blinks. 'I think I need a Chupa Chup. Hit me up.'

I open the glovebox and recoil when I see what's in it. 'What the—?'

'Oh,' Chip says sheepishly. 'That.'

It's a handgun. A real-life actual handgun. 'You've got to be kidding me, Chip!'

'Chillax,' he sighs. 'It's a replica. I got it at Comic Con. At least I think I did. It *is* possible my cousin Gary knocked it up on his

3D printer. I dunno. I vaguely recall a chocolate box involved when I inherited it. Maybe he gifted me chocolates and hid it inside?'

Daisy extends her hand for a fist bump. 'Word.'

'And you thought this was the perfect opportunity to take it for a spin?' I ask.

Chip points at Jackson. 'No, he did. He saw it in my cosplay collection and thought it might come in handy.'

Jackson shrugs. 'It was that or the Viking sword.'

I select a lemon Chupa Chup (Chip's least favourite flavour), and slam the glovebox shut.

He starts the engine and pulls out of the carpark. 'We need petrol,' he says. 'Servo first, then we're out of here.'

I spend the next ten minutes regretting lemon. I've come to learn Chupa Chup wrapper-wrangling can be mega disagreeable. This one is titanium super-glued.

Daisy launches into a rendition of the 'Going to see Errol' song, which I note is largely reminiscent of the 'We're Going to Bonnie Doon' song from the movie *The Castle* except it goes: 'We're going to see Errol. We're going to see Errol. We're going to see Er-ro-rolllll!!!!!!!!!!!!!!! Errol, we'll see you soon.'

Even former investment banker Barry quickly gets jack of it. Apparently.

'It's okay, Barry,' Chip says. 'I've got this.' He turns to smile sweetly at Daisy. 'That's lovely, Daisy, but do you think you could save it until we get a bit closer?'

She crosses her arms. 'Got Spotify?' For someone who's been living in God's Waiting Room, her pop culture knowledge is impressive. 'Anything but that blonde Swifty girl. Or the redheaded guy with a guitar.' I assume she means Ed

Sheeran, but I'm reluctant to ask, lest an argument ensues.

'No problem, Barry.' Chip doffs a non-existent hat. 'My pleasure.'

'For the last time,' Jackson says, 'who the hell are you talking to?'

'Barry,' I tell him. 'Barry Henderson the Third, Investment Banker. Clocked off in a light plane crash, boarded this hearse and never left.'

Chip glares. 'I told you, Taylor, he doesn't *stay*, he comes and goes. And remember he's sensitive.' He glances at the rear-view mirror. 'Apologies Barry.'

Jackson gapes. 'Are you freakin' serious?'

'As a heart attack,' I say. 'Sorry, Barry. I'm aware that was an ableist comment.'

Chip laughs. 'Barry says you're an arsehole, Taylor, but he's starting to like you for it.'

Jackson is silent for a moment, contemplating this revelation he's sharing the back seat with a ghost-cum-former investment banker. 'My Aunty Rita is a clairvoyant,' he says. 'Reckons she once talked to Harold Holt, the Aussie PM who went for a swim and never came back.'

'Pfft,' Daisy spits. 'If you could talk to anyone who's dead, would you really pick some balding dickhead politician?' She makes an excellent point. 'I'd contact Steve Irwin.'

Chip pulls into a servo. There's an early-morning run on fuel. Every bowser is occupied. We park behind a white Toyota Camry and wait for a woman who's wearing furry brown slippers that look like she murdered Chewbacca and kept his feet as souvenirs.

'Why Steve Irwin?' I ask.

Daisy smirks. 'I have a thing for khaki shorts.'

'What? Wait! Really?' Chip gasps. 'No way!'

'What?' We ask in unison.

'Barry's met Steve!'

It takes me a short second to digest this. Considering Barry died in a seventies plane crash, I'm assuming the connection wasn't made here. Does that mean they have spiritual LinkedIn for former movers and shakers? Heavenly red carpet cocktail parties? Green Room meet-and-greets?

'Barry once wrestled a crocodile,' Chip explains earnestly. 'Apparently they got to talking.'

'Of course Barry wrestled a crocodile,' I say. 'Because bloody Barry did it all, on the thirteenth floor of an investment banking building.'

'Barry notes your disparaging tone, Taylor,' Chip says. 'He hopes you never have to face the jaws of death on a Kenyan holiday. Travel World never refunded him for the privilege of saving their tour guide.'

Chewie's feet shuffle over to the self-serve credit facility, swipe, then climb into the Toyota and take off. Chip moves us forward and pops the fuel cap. 'Anyone want anything?'

'Ciggies,' says Daisy. 'And one of those monster hits that improve you a bit.'

'I could smash a pie,' Jackson says.

'You?' Chip asks me.

But I'm distracted by a wispy, jittery girl standing by the servo sliding doors. She's wearing black: black T-shirt, black leather jacket, black miniskirt over black fish-net tights, black Doc Martens. Even her cropped hair is jet-black. She's the purple lady minus the purple dog and ... well, the purple. The only smidge of colour is her thick pink eyeshadow. She sucks a freshly lit cigarette and hugs herself, hopping from foot to foot. She looks around as if waiting for something or someone, then crushes her smoke in a planter pot and heads inside.

'Earth to Taylor?' Chip prompts. 'You want something?'

'Nah, I'm right.'

Chip fills up and goes in to pay. Daisy and Jackson resurrect the homophobia debate but thankfully they don't attempt to drag me into it. I glance at my mobile. There's another message for Geoff: **Herbert's Dry-cleaning: Job No 1294 is ready for pick up. NB: We couldn't remove the armpit stains.**

Chip returns carrying a bulging plastic bag. He gets in and passes it to Jackson. 'Dibs on the strawberry creams,' he says.

The smell of hot meat pie wafts through the car. My stomach rumbles. I regret not getting something now, but I do worry about the lifespan of the humble servo pie. Food provision isn't their chief priority, is it? The last one I ate was drier than a dog biscuit. It could've cracked the pavement. Plus I got the runs and you *don't* want the runs on a road trip. Public toilets are the worst.

'What's that?' Daisy asks, pointing at the windscreen.

I turn around. A black blur runs toward us. Seconds later, the back door is flung open and the girl I saw hopping from foot to foot is now hopping into our back seat. She wedges herself alongside Daisy, slams the door shut and hits the lock, activating the others to do the same.

'Drive!' she shouts at Chip. *'Drive!'*

An overweight security guard is hot on her heels. He lunges at the door, bulging belly bouncing. When he can't get the door open, he bashes on the window. Then he pushes buttons on a two-way radio and I hear his muffled voice say something about the police. A high-pitched alarm sounds – the staff must've hit the button.

'Shit!' Jackson cries, pummelling the back of Chip's headrest. 'Go! Get out of here! Go! Go! Go!'

My heart races. There's no time to think. 'Do it!' I yell at Chip. 'Do it! Go!'

He fires the engine and floors it into traffic, the hearse swinging sideways and narrowly missing a bus. He rights us and plants his foot, swerving around two more cars and then down a side street. It's some serious *Fast and the Furious* shit.

I swivel to look at her. Either she's suddenly nine months pregnant or she just inhaled a basketball. 'Keep driving!' she shouts at Chip, extracting a calico bag from under her top. Twisties and biscuits and bags of lollies stick out of it.

'Geez Louise ...' Jackson breathes, gaping at the bag. 'You nicked all of that?'

'Is she coming with us to see Errol?' Daisy asks.

Chip makes a fast right, hooking onto the main road, then through another red light and another, to a choir of honking horns. The girl pushes up her jacket sleeves. I spy a blue love-heart tattoo the size of a five-cent coin on her left wrist.

'Who are you?' Chip demands, crunching gears and making another hard right.

'Just drive!' She yanks a green gum-string from her teeth, twirls it round her finger and sucks it back in. 'And quit staring!' she says to me.

I struggle to speak. 'What makes you think we won't turn around and dump you back there?'

A knowing smile. 'Cos you guys are in the shit.'

'How do you know that?'

She points at Chip. 'This douchebag scoped the security cameras as he went in the store, kept his body turned away, stood on tippy toes by the police height sticker on the door frame and measured himself, ordered a pie at … what is it, 9.30 am? … perused *Woman's Day* commenting loudly on Princess Mary's possible boob job, selected a random Sudoku magazine without even opening it,' at this, Jackson checks the plastic bag – sure enough, there's one in there, 'and word-vomited to the attendant about what lovely weather we're enjoying, paid cash, made more word-vomit with the security guard about how uncomfortable starchy uniforms can be … Do you want me to go on?'

Jackson facepalms.

Chip shifts his weight and gives me a shrug. 'I was *trying* to be friendly,' he mumbles. 'And that's enough out of you, Barry.'

It crosses my mind to ask where Barry is sitting now that the backseat is now full, but given the present state of affairs, I don't linger there.

Mystery Girl shakes her head. 'What. An. Amateur.'

'Is she coming with us to see Errol?' Daisy asks again.

The girl turns and blows a giant bubble in Daisy's face.

Quick as lightning, Daisy smacks it flat. 'Are you fucking deaf, girly?' Daisy shrieks. 'Answer me!'

The girl blinks at her, picking green splat from her cheeks. 'Um … where's Errol?'

'Mount Gambier,' says Daisy.

'Sure. Okay. Mount Gambier it is then.'

'Good.' Daisy settles into her seat. 'Strap yourself in.' She hands over her aviator sunnies, price tag still dangling. 'Put them on. No one will know it's you.' She claps loudly. 'Where's the bloody Spotify? Jesus, Mary and Joseph! I'll be stone-cold dead before you find it!'

My phone beeps again. **Looking for the perfect getaway? Contact Travel Gurus for a free quote. To unsubscribe, click here.**

You're a right smartarse, Geoff. A right smartarse.

# CHAPTER NINE

As we exit Portrush Road and turn onto the freeway, our mystery passenger gives us a name. Whether or not it's her real name is irrelevant. It's something to work with.

'Chloe,' she says, cracking gum. 'What's yours?'

We introduce ourselves.

Once the Jackson Rollock-not-Pollock thing is established, Chloe's next question is, 'Are you related?'

I point at Jackson and Daisy. 'They are. We're acquaintances. But in a few days, we hopefully won't even be that.'

Chip frowns. 'I thought we were friends.'

Daisy dons her earphones, the thin auxiliary cable running to the dashboard sound system. Eyes closed, her head rocks from side to side.

Chloe cradles her bulging calico bag, hugging it tight.

'What did you score?' Jackson enquires.

'Food, toiletries, NoDoze, stuff like that.'

I'm struggling to process that our sum total of on-the-run passengers has now reached three. Thankfully there are no seats left. And I *still* haven't worked out where Barry is sitting.

'Did you really rob the servo?' I ask.

Chloe says flatly, 'No, I asked them nicely for the goods and they gladly handed them over. What do you think, genius?'

My fingers itch to open the glovebox. If she knew we were packing (well, packing cosplay plastic) she might not be so arrogant.

'You know, people usually do it on a smaller scale,' Jackson says. 'That's why it's called *petty theft*. It's a handful of stuff, not even a shopping basket. You've gone for full trolley minus the trolley.'

Chloe side-eyes him. 'And who are you? The CSI? What *do* you do for a living?'

Chip butts in, 'See? The eternal question!'

Jackson avoids her gaze. 'I'm kind of on the lookout right now.'

'Yeah,' I say. 'For the police.'

Chloe glances at me. 'Huh?'

'Nothing. So I'm trying to understand ... you nicked stuff from a service station *because*?'

She scoops gum from her cheek and sticks it to the windowsill. 'I needed supplies. It was that or Bill's Takeaway. And I like Bill. He does good chips.'

I'm not sure I heard her right. *Bill*? If she's a Bill's customer, that means she can't live far from us. God, if we get caught this is definitely going to look like we deliberately hooked up together.

'He has this annoying woman working for him,' Chloe says. 'She stuffed up my last two phone orders.'

Chip nods. 'Noelene. Happened to me too.'

Chloe's surprised. 'You go to Bill's?'

'Number One Customer right here,' Chip declares proudly.

'That doesn't explain *why* you robbed the servo,' I press. Keeping this conversation on track is harder than navigating the freeway. 'Why would you do something like that?'

Chloe peers at me over her aviators. 'I woke up this morning and went, *On today's bucket list I might try …* You know what? You grilling me is a bit rich.'

'How do you work that out?'

'You haven't told me *your* story.'

'You hitched a ride in our car! You don't get to ask the questions!'

'Questions come, questions go,' Chip says.

'This isn't a car.' Chloe turns to look into the back tray. 'Do you carry dead people?'

'Not often enough,' I say through clenched teeth.

'Barry,' Jackson reminds me. 'Don't forget Barry.'

'Oh yes. Barry.'

'Who's Barry?' Chloe asks.

'You'll meet him soon enough,' says Jackson.

'And the rest of them,' Chip adds. One hand on the steering wheel, he fidgets with his cravat, loosening it.

'Why are you wearing that thing?' Chloe asks.

Chip moans. 'What's wrong with it?'

'I *have* been meaning to ask you,' I confess.

He adjusts the small wedge of material. 'Pornographers wear them.'

'I thought they wore robes?' Jackson says.

'I can't wear a robe on the road,' Chip says. '*Obviously.*' He looks at me. 'Though that kind of fashion foresight could've saved Uncle Roger from the clink.'

Oh. Now I get it. Though I'm not sure why. It's not like I'm schooled in pornographer-accepted attire, but somehow a cravat makes sense.

Chloe's still playing catch-up. 'You wear a cravat because pornographers wear them?'

'I want to be one,' Chip says. 'Like Hugh Hefner.' But with a dispirited look my way he adds, 'However, apparently I need to sanitise that dream to conform to our progressive modernist society. I've recently been reassigned as Website Manager of Physically Appealing People Content.'

Chloe puts her aviators on her head, drawing her dark hair away from her face. Once you get past all the clumpy black mascara and the thick pink eyeshadow, she's really quite striking – in a kickarse, servo-robbing chick sort of way.

'Are you for shiz?' she asks. 'You really want to be a pornographer?'

'Yes I'm serious!' The hearse accelerates in line with Chip's indignation. He clocks the speedometer and slows down. 'Why's it so hard to believe? Look at your city street corners! Look at the adult bookshops! Who do you think runs them? Who do you think supplies the stock? Who *makes* the stock? It's an industry like any other. There are jobs to be had and money to be made. Just because your career counsellor never mentioned it, doesn't mean it's not an option.'

Chloe seems impressed. 'Guess I've never really thought about it.'

'You and almost everyone,' I say.

'I've watched it,' she admits with no hint of embarrassment, 'but I didn't think too much about where it came from.'

'Exactly,' Chip says. 'Like it's made by the magical porn fairies or something.'

'You've watched it?' I blurt. Then I realise how judgemental that sounds.

I'm not sure why I'm surprised. Maybe because my only real measuring stick of girls has been Cass and Lia. We'd talked about sex, definitely, but in a charades kind of way: hinting, joking, glossing over what went down at a party, never really discussing it in any outright detail. Maybe they talk differently when I'm not around? Or maybe they don't talk about it with me because I have no experience to speak of and nothing to share. I know the whole world thinks our generation is hung up on sex, but a lot of the time we've got better things to talk about.

'You don't think girls watch porn?' Chloe asks me. 'What kind of antiquated chauvinistic crap is that?'

'You're not supposed to watch it,' Jackson butts in. 'What are you? Fifteen?'

'Almost seventeen,' she says. 'How old are you?'

'Headed for thirty,' Jackson says.

Chloe retrieves her gum from the windowsill and recommences cement-mixer chewing action. My stomach churns at the thought of the dust mite and tiny dead skin cell particles she's potentially ruminating on.

'That's some majorly naïve shit if you think age has anything to do with getting hold of it,' she says. 'Most kids have seen it, or a version of it, by the time they start high school.'

'And you know this *how*?' I ask.

She blows a bubble, pops it, sucks it in and keeps chewing. 'Reported research. I had to do one of those Protect Yourself Online courses. Anyway, I've seen some A-grade productions. There was this one where a doctor and a nurse—'

'All that stuff,' I interrupt, trying again to steer the

conversation back to earlier. I point at the calico bag. 'Why'd you do it?'

She looks at me straight-faced. 'Drug debt. I smoked myself blind on crack and now I owe people.'

'They accept Twisties?'

'Sodium is very satisfying.'

'The truth please.'

She stares out the window. I'm sure I see her blink back tears. Her voice changes and becomes tight. 'I've never done drugs.' She puts on her sunnies. 'Not the big ones anyway.' She glances at Daisy, whose eyes are closed, head swaying, one hand riding an orchestra conductor invisible wave. 'Truth is I'm pissing off, making a fresh start. Apparently via Mount Gambier. And after I see some old guy called Errol.'

'Her ex,' Jackson says. 'Granny wants to see him before she ... she ...' But he can't finish the sentence. By way of explanation, he adds, 'Cancer.'

'Oh.' Chloe looks at Daisy, taking this in, absently running a thumb over her tattooed wrist. 'I'm sorry to hear that.'

'Won't someone be missing you?' I ask. 'If you go to Bill's, do you live near there?'

'*Did* live near there. *Live* is a loose description. I stayed at my aunt's place on and off.'

'And your parents?'

She removes her sunnies, scowling. 'Where are your parents, Taylor? How come there's no search party looking for you?'

At this, I wonder if Cass is looking for me.

There's nothing to be gained from lying, so I tell Chloe the truth. 'My folks are on a plane headed for the Roller Door Extravaganza conference in Queensland.'

Jackson snorts, 'Extravaganza!'

'Well yay you,' Chloe says bitterly. 'Not everyone has parents.'

I'm about to ask more when Chip cries, 'Shit!' and hits the brakes. We lurch forward, seatbelts tightening, pulling hard. Gripping the wheel, Chip wiggles a single finger, pointing ahead. 'Tell me that's not what I think it is.'

Police cars. Witches hats. 25 km signs. My blood is alive with a rush of prickly tingles. A breatho? On a weekday?

In the back seat, Jackson cranes his neck to see the side mirror. 'You'd be surprised how many gin-slinging parents they catch on the morning school run. Hang back, drop behind that truck, weave round its side, use it as a cover.'

Chip tries, but the truck, impatient with the slowing traffic, speeds up and hooks past, coughing a diesel cloud. 'Shit!' Chip panics as we close in. One lane is blocked, a policewoman with a reflector bar waving down traffic, directing it through orange cones. 'What do I do?'

'Don't avoid it,' says Jackson. 'That's a red flag. They chase you down side-streets. In fact, they probably have cars lying in wait.'

'There are no bloody side-streets!' Chip yells. 'It's a freakin' freeway!'

So this is how it ends: busted before we get started. We're the worst absconders in history. News outlets will have a field day. Headline: *Bumbling five foiled by breatho*. I guess that ends the suspense. We were bound to get caught, it's just a case of when.

Chip slows the hearse. We're in a chain of cars now, gradually being ushered into the turn-off. My stomach burns with terror and feels like it's going to fold in on itself, bypass my intestines and fall out my butt.

Daisy must register our sluggish momentum, because she opens her eyes and croaks, 'What's going on?'

My heart beats so fast it might break out of my chest. 'Breatho,' I tell her.

'What?' Daisy shouts.

Jackson yanks the earphones. 'Breatho!'

'Have you been drinking?' Daisy asks Chip, as if that's our chief concern.

Chip pales, beads of perspiration running down his cheeks. 'Oh god. Why didn't I think of that? You're right, Barry!'

Impeccable timing. Barry's back. (If he actually left.)

'What did Barry suggest?' I ask. 'Get a Tardis, go back in time and undo this stupid decision?'

I open the glovebox to grab a Chupa Chup to calm my nerves, when I see the gun and slam it shut again. *Shit!* What will happen when they search the car? I imagine all of us face down on the pavement, fingers interlocked behind our heads, a detective shouting interrogative abuse. I already know I'll be the first one to crack. The others will lynch me.

'Barry reminded me that they drug test you too,' Chip says, looking like he might throw up. 'They run those little scraper things across your tongue.'

'I *knew* you had some on you!' Daisy cries.

'When did you last ...?' I pretend smoke.

'My cousin Mikey gave me a cookie last week,' Chip says. 'But whether it had anything in it is a matter of dispute because I think he mixed up the bag of parsley. It happens in a pressurised kitchen environment. All that heat and steam and people yelling Gordon Ramsay style. I've used basil instead of rosemary before. It's easy to do. Herbs are not my strong suit.'

'They are mine,' says Daisy.

'Oh no, oh shit, oh fuck,' Chip sweats. 'I'm so screwed!'

'We're *all* screwed!' says Jackson.

But then, like some early Christmas miracle, the police officer waves us on. The breatho turn-off is full.

We drift past as if in a dream, everyone frozen in shock, except for Daisy who gives them a little wave.

Stunned silence. I don't think any of us can believe how close we came.

A couple of kilometres up the road, a relieved breath rushes out of me.

Daisy snaps at Chip, 'Hold out on me again, boy, and I swear I'll hand you in myself!' She puts the earphones back in and raps, 'My mutha's down with da bros, ya know. My mutha's down with da bros. My brutha's mutha blows, ya know. My mutha's down with da bros.'

# CHAPTER TEN

Geoff receives another message: **What time's Zumba?** I haven't as yet had the headspace to form a firm opinion of Geoff-my-anonymous-SIM-friend but somehow Zumba doesn't sit right with me. A follow-up message: **You can safely wear the pink leotard today, I'm wearing white.** Huh. Go figure. Maybe Geoff's a raging dance queen? Does he dress in full retro legwarmers? A cut-off Gymshark T-shirt? A terry-towel headband? Then: **Had my period last week.** A final message: **Shit, sorry, wrong number.**

I should learn to trust my gut.

The Zumba thing makes me think of my maths-cum-yoga teacher, Miss Hooper/Miss Flexy. Has she mentioned me to the principal's office? Has Principal Fitzpatrick called Cass for advice? *Taylor Kennedy is stalking teachers. What should I do?* Had the school sent an absenteeism text to Mum and Dad? They'd be en route right now, phones on aeroplane mode. I imagine them disembarking at Brisbane airport, switching on, notifications going apeshit. *Please explain Taylor's absence immediately!* Then I imagine them trying to ring my dead phone at Fone Wizards, only to receive message bank. Then trying Messenger.

Then emailing. Sending up smoke signals. Reporting me as a missing person. My face appearing on the six o'clock news. Me, on *60 Minutes*, my decomposing body found in a shallow, partially covered grave in a remote national park, discovered by international foodie tourists using pigs to sniff for truffles. And given I can think through all of these scenarios faster than a toddler cartwheeling on red cordial, I'm not sure why I didn't think through any of this before. Again it feels like I'm outside of my body looking down on myself. I wonder if this is how it feels to be dead. Maybe I should ask Barry.

'Taylor?'

'Huh?'

'I said we're coming into Tailem Bend.' Chip gestures at the green highway signage. 'You wanna stop for a leak?'

'Nah, I'm good.' I reposition myself, uncrossing my half-numb legs. Pins and needles burn my left foot. I give it a good shake. 'Keep going. I'll do a roadside job if I need to.' The sooner we get this over, the better.

Daisy tosses her earphones into the front seat. 'Speak for yourself, young man. Some of us aren't equipped with racehorse bladders. Or with built-in hoses.'

'I am,' Chloe says.

Daisy places a gentle hand on Chloe's thigh. 'Oh, I didn't realise, dear. Are you transitioning?'

Jackson chokes on his strawberry cream. 'Granny!'

'What?' Daisy says defensively. 'Jeez! Get with the times, boy!'

Chloe blinks. 'No. I meant I carry a She-Wee.'

'A She-what, dear?'

'A She-Wee. It's a portable funnel you use to pee standing up.'

Daisy's impressed. 'I suppose that beats incontinence pads. Do you have to check which way the wind's blowing? Cos I free-peed near a hand dryer once. It wasn't pretty.'

Chloe laughs. Something about the sound makes my chest do a surprising flip. 'Nothing worse than copping it in the face, is there? Or back-spraying an open car window.'

Daisy nods. 'Word.'

'I think we'll pull over,' Chip says.

He drives us to the rear of a busy roadhouse, where as many as fifteen trucks and semis are parked. Burly men with beer guts bulging from tight work-shirts lean against cabin doors, munching on hamburgers, washing them down with litre cartons of iced-coffee.

'Do you think you can restrain yourself from robbing *this* service station?' Chip asks.

'That depends,' Chloe says. 'Can you not draw attention to us by acting like a doofusburger?'

Chip puts out his hand. 'I fancy the full seafood pack with extra scallops. Your buy. Petrol's not cheap.'

Chloe sighs, digs a fifty from her pocket and hands it over. 'I want change,' she says.

'Of course,' he says. 'Good to see you have some manners. Also that you're paying your way. There's no such thing as a free ride. Unless of course you're Barry.' He pauses a moment. 'Oh sorry! Is that you, Lily? Hey, how's it going, hon? Long time, no sip a cocktail!' He cups his hand to his ear, listening. 'Sure, sure.' He nods a few times. 'Yep, no worries.' He turns to Chloe. 'Lily wishes to convey she would've appreciated She-Wees had they been around in her day.'

'Who's Lily?' Jackson asks.

'Lily Rendlesham,' Chip says, not missing a beat. 'Died in her early twenties under circumstances that will blow your tiny neurons.'

Chloe's neurons are blown. '*You talk to dead people?*' She looks at the rest of us. 'Hang on ... before when you were talking about that Barry person ... that was a ghost you were referring to?'

Chip nods. 'Lily was out celebrating her hen's night, being chauffeur-driven in a flash limousine, sipping champagne, mucking around with her bridesmaids, having the time of her life. That was until she made the fateful error of sticking her head through the sun-roof as they entered the dark underpass—'

'It knocked her block off?' Jackson guesses.

Chip shakes his head. 'She let out a sustained whoop of unbridled joy and that's when a dive-bombing pigeon flew full pelt into her open mouth. The pigeon's wind speed velocity coupled with the force of the vehicle moving at sixty clicks clean snapped her neck.'

I envisage a giant puff of feathers, twitchy bird feet, the woman choking and keeling over in front of her stunned bridal party.

I burst out laughing.

Chip glares at me. 'Barry warned Lily that you're an arsehole, Taylor.'

'I bet he did.'

'Lily was a nineties nightclub disco diva,' Chip continues. 'She says she tried to pee standing up, often in the Men's when the Women's was full, but she never quite mastered it. Mostly she just stained her satin high heels.'

'Lily sounds cool,' Chloe says admiringly (and to her credit, simply just shutting up and going with it.)

'She was,' Chip says. 'She loved nothing more than hitting the dance floor and busting a move to Chocolate Starfish.'

'Who?' Chloe says.

'Chocolate Starfish,' I explain. 'Nineties Aussie rock group. They had a big hit with a remake of Carly Simon's "You're So Vain".' I think about it. 'Lily just lost my respect.'

'You know that's the dopest name for a band *ever*, don't you?' Chloe argues. 'Think about what it means.'

I'd never given it any consideration. Now it hits me like the pigeon. 'Ew! Gross! Are you sure?'

'No. But it figures and plausibility is everything,' Chloe cracks up. 'Don't forget to wipe!'

We get out and head for the toilets. I tell myself that the stares from truckers have nothing to do with our criminal escapee status and everything to do with our unconventional mode of transportation. Honestly, we couldn't have picked a more attention-seeking ride if we tried. As we round the corner, I glance back to see one of the men with his nose pressed against the hearse window. I hope Lily busts a disco move, pirouettes and moons him.

After peeing (and not taking it for granted that I can do it standing up) I find Chloe perched on a fence rail by a garden bed littered with candy wrappers, discarded coffee cups and cans. A rubbish bin is only metres away. No wonder this planet is on its way to enviro hell in a handbasket.

Chloe puffs a cigarette. The others are inside ordering food. I take a seat.

'Chupa Chups are better for you,' I tell her. 'The resulting lung cancer isn't nearly as fateful.'

She inhales, exhales from the corner of her mouth and

shrugs. 'We all have our drug of choice.' She gives me a quizzical look. 'What's yours?'

For some reason, I'm totally honest with her. 'Writing.'

'Writing?'

'Yeah, it's this thing you do to spread ideas. You puke up your insides so they don't boil you alive. Ancient Egyptians were into it.'

She smirks. 'What do you write about?'

The stiffness in my bones loosens and I feel my body relaxing, a calmness washing over me. My prickly foot comes back to life. 'Things that piss me off, mostly.'

'Like?'

'Stuff.'

I have this overwhelming surge of gratitude she's even asked. Cass doesn't ask. She listens, sure, but she never asks. And she certainly doesn't make it obvious she's interested. More like she entertains it, tolerates it. I'm not one hundred percent sure, but I think it all stems from the time I wrote a primary school play and got my classmates to perform it at recess and Cass didn't get the part she badly wanted.

I skip my formative playwright years. 'I started off by venting in a journal about school and friends and bad haircuts and shitty canteen options and the economic inequities of structured seating at rock concerts.'

Chloe arches an eyebrow at the concert thing and nods like she gets it.

'Then I dabbled in fan fiction, but there were too many weirdos cramping my style, telling me I couldn't do this and I couldn't do that, critiquing what I'd produced, and I basically found it creatively stifling. So then I went through this serial essayist stage, writing epic arguments in comments sections on blogs and chatrooms.' I don't mention the Kelly Nixon Facebook debacle. 'After that I started writing eulogies and obituaries.'

'Death notices?'

'Fake ones.'

'Why?'

I don't say anything about my grandfather either – not because I'm embarrassed, but because I'll get choked up. 'It began as an English assignment. We had to do our epitaphs. Then we had to do someone in our class.'

'You killed a classmate?'

'Metaphorically speaking.'

She sucks the last of her cigarette and butts it out in a Coke can. 'If that was me, I wouldn't hesitate to wipe out Year Eleven.' She reaches in front of her, tracing the shape of a headstone. 'Here lies Year Eleven, dearly missed by the accounting staff who now have to figure out a way to finance the budget shortfall.'

'Private college?'

'Arts scholarship. You?'

'Public. Middleborough High.'

She pats my shoulder. 'Commiserations.'

'You've heard of the place?'

'I heard a rumour that the principal has a paid roll-call of student spies. True?'

I laugh. 'Something like that.'

She plucks a gum packet from her pocket, counts the number of pieces and puts it back. 'So these eulogies ... what would you say about me if I were dead?'

My stomach flips again and I feel kind of breathless. 'I don't know enough about you.' I want to know more, but I don't say that.

'What *do* you know?' A cheeky smile – it's a challenge.

'Okay. Let's see … You smoke. You chew gum. You dress like you're going to a funeral – which is somehow entirely appropriate, riding in a hearse. You must be good at art because you have a scholarship. Your relationship with your family is estranged. You've robbed a service station, so there's an element of kickarseness to you coupled with give-a-rats insanity. You enjoy the freedom of peeing standing up. You think Chocolate Starfish is a great band name, which I wouldn't make mention of if I was writing your eulogy lest I permanently scar your reputation.'

She's impressed. 'Wow. Observant. In a creepy, librarian-cataloguing sort of way.'

'I'd have to ask more questions.'

'But if I was dead, how would you?'

'I'd consult my resident psychic medium.'

She laughs. 'You know that's all in Chip's head, right?'

'*You think?*' Though a part of me is slightly unnerved by his conviction.

'Seriously,' she presses, 'how would you write my eulogy?'

'I'd ask people who knew you to tell me about you.'

'But that would be *their* version of me. How would you know if they got it right? I mean, it's kind of a big deal to write the last word on someone. You'd want to make sure it's correct.'

'I'd have no choice but to trust those left to speak.'

Her expression goes dark. She kicks the dirt, stands up and brushes off her black miniskirt with a few swift movements. 'Well. I can tell you that would be a mistake.' She heads for the hearse. She says over her shoulder, 'No one really knows me, Taylor. Not for real. No one's even got close. And the one person who did …'

'Chloe, that tattoo on your wrist—'

She stops, spins on her heel and stares me down. 'What about it?'

She touches it a lot. I was wondering if it had a special meaning. Now I've lost my nerve. I'm not sure where it came from to ask. 'Nothing. It's none of my business.'

'Damn right.'

Her angry reaction tells me it *does* mean something. 'Sorry, I didn't mean to—'

'You know what, Taylor? Let's forget we had this talk. And maybe forget what you think you know. The less we know about each other, the better. That way I can't die any time soon and you can't write about me.' Nose in the air, she walks on ahead.

Back at the hearse, Chip leans against the driver's-side door. He's scoffing unidentifiable fried food from a Styrofoam container. Jackson is scouring a newspaper spread on the car bonnet, flipping pages, presumably looking for any mention of himself. I must remember to ask if he's found any. And Daisy is – what *is* Daisy doing?

She's sitting on the hearse roof, legs folded, thumbs and forefingers pinched and rested on either knee, eyes closed, face turned to the sun.

Jackson glances at my confused face. 'Meditation,' he explains.

'How the hell did she get up there?'

'Not sure,' Chip mumbles. 'We think one of the truckers helped. That or there was a magic carpet involved.'

Jackson talks in a low voice so he doesn't distract her. 'It helps with her pain management. The prescribed meds only do half the job.'

Chip sucks a prawn tail dry and flings it across the carpark. 'It's this or weed. We don't have any on us.'

'Just make sure she doesn't swallow a bird,' I sigh, getting in the hearse.

Chloe climbs in behind me. She picks up her calico bag, checks the contents and puts it back by her feet.

'Do you feel bad?' I ask.

She studies me, confusion evident.

'For shoplifting from the servo, I mean.'

With some effort she levers her gum from the windowsill, molds it and sticks it in her mouth. 'Taylor?'

'Yeah?'

'You know before when you said something about the Ancient Egyptians?'

'Yeah?'

'Well this is how I think of it: In two thousand years from now, is anyone going to care what happened at some city servo? Is anyone going to care about the people who worked there? Are they going to care about what happened to me? Will there be proof I even existed?'

Morally she's up the Nile without a paddle. That said, I'd be high off my arse right now to debate morality considering the circumstances I find myself in.

'I did what I had to do, okay? If you knew what I was facing—' But she catches herself. After a long, deep breath she surprises me with, 'Okay. I admit it. I feel bad. Satisfied?'

I nod.

'But not bad enough to return the stuff,' she says.

'That'll come.'

She shrugs. 'I wouldn't hold your breath.'

Chip gets in, stinking of seafood. He adjusts the mirror and inspects his forehead, which has bloomed in line with his grease consumption. 'We must make haste, children.' He picks a pimple. 'I scheduled a twenty-minute stop. I suspect we've gone over that.'

Jackson gets in and puts on his seatbelt. He folds the newspaper and rests it in his lap. Massaging his temples, he stares at the paper with an expression I can't read.

Chip fires the engine. We gently roll forward and halt, waiting for a truck that's blocking the exit.

'Where's Daisy?' Chloe asks.

We look at the empty seat beside her.

Then at the roof.

Shit.

Jackson's halfway out the door. 'Don't worry. I'm on it.'

# CHAPTER ELEVEN

As we turn onto the road to Meningie, Jackson tells Chip to turn up the radio. It's 11 am, news bulletin time. After the usual swathe of boring political updates and the latest football star scandal (which notably involved a lion-tamer whip, sequinned hot pants and a stack of leaked selfies), there's a piece on the Yatala breakout.

A male newsreader dryly reports, 'Police are searching for an on-the-run prisoner today after a daring escape from Adelaide's major security prison. They maintain the public is in no immediate danger. Prison authorities advise that twenty-nine-year-old escapee, Jackson Pollock—'

'Oh for fuck's sake,' Jackson moans.

'—sorry, *Rollock*,' the newsreader continues, 'was a model prisoner nearing the end of his six-year sentence for armed robbery. Renowned criminal psychologist Dr Larissa Hardy spoke with us earlier today.'

The newsreader's voice cuts to plum-up-the-bum Larissa. 'We often find that when prisoners near the end of their sentence, panic sets in. Reintegration can be a daunting prospect. Some inmates deliberately reoffend to extend their sentence. This fear is known as *institutionalisation*. In Rollock's case, I believe six years was enough time for him to develop an unhealthy psychological attachment to his surroundings, possibly even a—'

Chip shuts off the radio.

I switch it back on. 'Hey, I was listening to that!'

Chip switches it off. 'It's exactly as she said: unhealthy.'

'Unhealthy?'

'Not even accurate,' Jackson sighs, sliding down in his seat.

'Which bit?' I turn to glare at him. 'The part about armed robbery? When were you going to fill us in on the reason you were locked up? Or your so-called Houdini moves?'

He looks out the window. 'I'm not sure now's the right time.'

'I'd say it's the perfect time. We have lots of time. Hours, in fact. You have a captive audience. Emphasis on the captive. Pretty sure your beloved Granny here is about as non-judgemental as they come.'

Daisy nods. 'No Judge Judy.'

Jackson throws his hands up. 'Fine! Which story do you want first? The break-out or the break-in?'

Chloe – mid-bubble – stops. Her bubble deflates. '*You're an escapee prisoner?*'

Jackson does jazz hands. 'Surprise!'

She looks at me. 'You're covering for a robber?'

The irony doesn't seem to resonate with her.

'It's a long story.' I glare at Jackson. 'Which he's about to tell.'

He sighs loudly. 'Alrighty then! I hope you're ready!'

Daisy tugs her seatbelt. 'Locked and loaded.'

'It was a cold day in June—'

'This sounds like the long version,' Chip notes.

'It was a cold day in June when I decided to duck into my local Baby Bunting store.'

'Come again?' I say.

'Baby Bunting. They sell baby stuff.'

'You have a baby?' Chip asks.

'No.'

'But you were in a baby store?' I say.

'Well if you shut up for a second and let me get to the *why* bit.'

'Okay, sorry.' Chip and I say in unison.

'I was stocking up on baby formula—' Jackson continues.

'You drink baby formula?' Chloe asks.

'Oh my god!' Jackson gasps. 'Are you going to let me get this out or not?'

'Sorry, sorry...'

'Which I was sending to Cambodia ...'

'Oh that is so shit!' Chloe interrupts again. 'You're one of those horrible people who makes a killing by buying formula and sending it offshore to China, aren't you?'

Jackson is clearly cranky now. 'Look. First of all: Get a map, sweetheart. Cambodia and China both begin with C, both have an Asian population, but that's where the similarities end. Secondly, for your information, I was sending the formula to a charity.'

'Oh.'

'Yeah. *Oh.*'

'Sorry.'

'Anyway,' Jackson says, twitching with annoyance, 'I was busy checking out the Baby Bunting shelves, considering my options, when this woman with a pram came in. Her baby was quiet, sleeping, covered by a blanket, the pram hood down. She went to the counter, which was unattended. There was only me and her, no other customers. I don't know where the shopkeeper was at that stage, probably in the storeroom.' His nostrils flare as he relays the next part. 'I went and stood behind her, politely queuing. She remained there, one hand rocking the pram, the other drumming the counter. She looked irritated. I assumed it was because she was in a hurry and neither of us were getting any service. I didn't think too hard about it. The truth was, she wasn't much to look at. There was nothing noteworthy about her. She looked like any other mother, dressed in track pants and a hoodie, barely functioning on two hours' sleep. What I didn't notice, and now realise I probably should have, was that she was wearing gloves. Admittedly it was cold, but most people take gloves off when they go inside. Anyway, the shopkeeper finally turned up, apologising about being tied up on the phone, and she was carrying a stack of magazines. In her hurry to get behind the counter, they slid from her arms and fell onto the floor. As she bent down behind the counter to get them, that's when the woman pulled back the pram's crochet blanket and drew a shotgun.'

'Her baby was sleeping next to a shotgun?' Chip gasps. He shakes his head. 'That's bad parenting right there.'

Throwing a perplexed glance at Chip, Jackson continues. 'I didn't think. I acted. I wrestled her for the gun. She was small-framed and easy to overpower and it all happened quickly. Before I knew it, the shopkeeper stood up screaming, hands in the air, the woman with the pram screaming too, both of them pointing at me, and right then, like some unholy citizen-of-the-year miracle, this off-duty police officer guy walks in, sees me with the gun and starts yelling at me to drop it and to get on the ground, which I do, and then next minute they're all sitting on top of me.'

'A classic case of mistaken identity,' Chip says.

'Thing is, I tried to tell them that the woman with the baby was the culprit, but the shopkeeper lady never saw her with the gun, and the mother was so good at covering her tracks, what with her innocent little baby and no fingerprints on the weapon, they didn't believe me, especially with my history.'

'Oh wait,' I say. 'You *already* had a rap sheet for armed robbery?'

'Three months earlier I was arrested for assault at an animal rights protest,' Jackson says stiffly. 'And the idiot I clopped deserved it. He'd painted his face with chicken blood and was chanting something about cavemen eating animals since the dawn of time. There was also the dick graffiti I painted on Parliament House, admittedly not my smartest move, *and* the time I was arrested for trespass in a costume hire store dressed as a Hell's Angels bikie, but that *was* a case of mistaken identity. There were no security cameras to record what really happened at Baby Bunting and they reckoned they had an open-and-shut case, so they pinned me for it. It's good for their statistics.'

'You expect us to believe that?' I ask.

Jackson looks wounded. 'I don't expect for you to believe shit, mate. Believe what you want. But it's the truth. And the truth will out.'

'*You're* out,' Chloe says.

'I'm innocent,' Jackson asserts.

'Okay,' I say. 'Tell us how you got out?'

'It was a cold day in June ...' Chip begins.

'Shut up. I didn't ask you.'

'I was smuggled out in a bread delivery van,' Jackson says.

'That was the short version,' Chip recaps.

'Surely it wasn't that easy?' I say. 'Everyone would be doing it.'

'As you near the end of your sentence, you get more and more privileges,' Jackson explains. 'I've been working in the kitchen for some time. There's this guy, Jonah, who delivers supplies each day. He lugs around heavy things, flour bags and boxes and stuff, and he likes a decent shoulder massage. Every time he comes in, I give him a massage and he slips me some ciggies or chocolate as payment.'

'You mean you were lovers,' Daisy says.

'Granny!' he baulks.

'I can't believe you have the audacity to give me stick about kissing Maisy Winterfeld,' Daisy says.

'I did *not*—'

Daisy puts up a hand. 'Tell it to Judge Judy.'

'Jonah and I *talk*,' Jackson says, shaking his head at Daisy. 'He's a good friend.'

'This guy really helped you to break out?' I ask.

'Yes,' Jackson nods. 'He understood how I felt about the possibility of never seeing Granny again, though right now I'm wondering why I went to all the effort. Jonah's grandmother died when he was eleven. It happened on the weekend he was supposed to see her, but he chose to go to soccer training instead. He's always regretted it.'

'So there's no string of murdered prison guards left behind you?' I say. 'No maiming or bloodshed?'

He cocks his head at me. 'You watch too many movies.'

'I think it's endearing,' Chloe says. 'But when the authorities catch up with you, they will extend your sentence. Like that psychologist woman said.'

Jackson agrees. 'When I made the decision to do it, I'd already accepted that. *Carpe diem*, right?'

'You never know,' Chloe says. 'When they hear about why you did it, they might go easy on you?'

Jackson gives a sarcastic laugh. 'Like they have in the past?'

Out of the blue, Chip asks, 'Hang on. Why were you at an animal rights protest? You said you punched a guy for eating meat. I bought you a meat pie this morning.'

I'm surprised by Chip's flash of intelligence. It *is* a flaw in Jackson's story.

Jackson shifts in his seat, the heat of shame filling his cheeks. 'I *was* a vegan. But you don't get a lot of options in prison and I found it a difficult lifestyle choice to maintain. I hate to admit it, but I redeveloped a taste for meat.'

'So you're passionate about animal rights?' Chloe asks. I wonder if it's a cause of hers.

'Definitely,' Jackson says, smiling. 'I can't stand to see animals hurt. They can't speak for themselves, can they? There are so many instances where we can treat them more humanely, more thoughtfully, more—'

It happens quickly. The wheels squeal and Chip brakes suddenly, the hearse zig-zagging over the road. I dig my nails into the seat, holding on for dear life. There's a horrible thud and something large and furry springs up from the bumper and hits the windscreen.

Chip pulls over. Blood drizzles down the glass like rain, a

dark puddle forming by the wipers. The furry thing comes to rest, slumped on the bonnet.

We stare at the massive beast – a glossy eye staring back at us.

I squeak, 'What was it you were saying about animals, Jackson?'

# CHAPTER TWELVE

All five of us stand by the roadside, surveying the dead deer resting on our windscreen. Trucks, caravans, Hertz hire cars zoom past, completely disinterested. That or they're too frightened to stop and assist, lest one of us turn out to be Ivan Milat's budding protégé.

'I think we broke its neck,' Chloe says.

Chip scratches his head. 'I thought kangaroos were the chief road hazard in Australia?'

I side-step to get a better view. 'Did it crack the windscreen?'

Chip investigates. 'Don't think so.'

'Cos you're not supposed to drive with a cracked windscreen,' I tell them. 'Dad says they can shatter at any time. A faulty roller door came down on this guy's car, and it started out this tiny chip in the glass, but it grew into a big mother fissure that—'

I stop talking and blink with disgusted awe at Chloe, who's prodding the beast, picking up its (presumably) still warm entrails, examining them before flinging them into the bushes. Jackson gags and runs around the back of the hearse to hurl.

'You need to help me to get it off,' Chloe says.

I look at the empty spaces either side of me.

'Yes, you.' She points at Chip too. 'And you. It's not like Daisy has the muscle to move it.'

Daisy lights a cigarette. 'I'm not touching that thing. It could have a ven-deer-real disease.' She cracks up at her joke.

Chip rolls up his sleeves, then he drags his cravat up and over his nose. I'm about to tell him that decomposition takes more than mere minutes, but he says, 'Righto. Let's do it. There's enough bottled water to wash up. We'll buy more when we get to Meningie.'

I'm not usually a subscriber to the whole alpha-male-versus-wild thing, *especially* since Australian author Tim Winton gave an impassioned speech on toxic masculinity, but I'm privately surprised and ashamed at my lack of stomach for such a predicament. I poke a hoof to make extra sure the thing is well and truly dead before grabbing its leg and yanking it, with all the heart of a kid picked last for Sports Day's tug-of-war.

'Put some effort into it,' Chloe huffs, tugging another leg. There are four legs (obviously – though it is possible one could encounter a three-legged deer, it would be uncommon) and thus there being four, there's enough to go around. Chip takes a third. With our combined effort, we manage to move it only several inches.

'What if I get behind the wheel and jerk it off?' Chip suggests.

'We don't have time for *that*,' Chloe says.

I snort-laugh.

'Never mind,' Chip mutters, red-faced.

We try again, this time really going for it. Who knew deer were so bloody heavy?

Chloe lets go, hands on hips. 'This thing weighs more than an elephant's dick.'

'Pretty soon we're going to have to call in the army,' I say. I look at Chip. 'Maybe we should consult Steve Irwin, seeing as we're one step removed.'

Jackson recovers, wiping his mouth. Frustrated by our lack of progress, he comes over to grab the fourth leg. We manage to drag the deer onto the ground. It lands with a thud and we stand there staring at it.

'Now what?' Chip asks.

'We leave.' I go to grab a water bottle and wash up.

'I feel bad,' Chip says. 'Shouldn't we say something? You know ... to send it off?'

'We should be respectful,' Chloe agrees. 'Give last rites. It's good karma.' She looks expectantly at me. 'You're the eulogy writer.'

I can't believe this.

'Fine,' I say.

I look at the brooding sky as if it will somehow provide inspiration. I draw a deep breath, close my eyes and collect my thoughts.

'We gather here today to celebrate the life of our dear (deer?) friend, Deery McDeer Face. We're sorry that your utopian existence freely roaming bushland, trampling native fauna and traumatising unsuspecting motorists has been tragically cut short. We can only hope that in deer heaven there are vast fields to run wild in and no hearses to speak of. We don't know what else to say except we're eternally sorry.'

I open my eyes.

Chip pats my back. 'Inspired.' He dusts off his hands and heads for the car.

Daisy leans over the carcass. She butts out her cigarette and plucks a weed flower and lays it on top. 'Too bad I don't eat venison.'

Back on the road, everyone is surprisingly sombre. Chip tries to clean the windscreen by squirting it and turning on the wipers, but stubborn streaks of blood remain.

No wonder when someone dies, the authorities get in and clean that shit up as fast as possible. No wonder we attempt to shield others from seeing it. It's confronting. How anyone works in an abattoir is beyond me. There must be a piece of their heart that's black and dead. How else do you spend your days firing stunguns and sticking knives into living, breathing things and walking away unaffected? I've stumbled across YouTube videos of men dressed in heavy rubber aprons and blood-spattered Wellington boots, separating baby calves from their mothers and shoving them into concreted rooms ready to end their short lives. The animals cry. The noises are bone-chilling. I could barely sleep after watching.

God, I'm hungry, I could *really* go a triple-beef burger with extra cheese.

'How long till we get to Meningie?' I ask.

'Twenty minutes,' says Chip.

'Then what?' I pull a tattered street directory from the behind the seat and flip through it. It's useless; it only has Adelaide's CBD. No wonder GPSs have been so successful. That, and you don't have to point them upside-down in the direction you're going – which I'm told is a girly trait, but I totally do it.

'Policeman's Point, Salt Creek, Kingston, then inland via Millicent to Mount Gambier,' Chip says. 'On the way back, there are a few other little towns scattered between. Coonalpyn is one. I hear there's some really impressive silo art. We should go see it.'

I'm about to remind him that this isn't a sightseeing trip when at the mention of Mount Gambier, Daisy starts singing the 'Going to See Errol' song. After three renditions, we tell her to put a sock in it.

'Wanna play I Spy?' she says.

Chloe's excited. 'Can I start?'

If Chloe doesn't have parents, she's probably never been on a family holiday. I feel a tug of sadness for her. I think of *my* parents and that tug pulls harder. Then I think of whipped cream and I quickly recover.

'I spy with my little eye,' Chloe begins, 'something that starts with P.'

I thumb at Chip. 'Pornographer.'

Chip grins like he's won an Oscar. 'Thank you. It's so nice to be acknowledged.'

Chloe shakes her head. 'Nope.'

Jackson points at Chloe. 'Pilferer. Plunderer.'

Chloe points back. 'Peckerhead. Penis-breath.'

Daisy cracks up. 'Ah! This reminds me of when my kids were young! Oh, the memories!'

'Police,' Jackson says.

'That's not funny,' I say.

'No ...' Jackson repeats with renewed urgency. 'Police!' He points ahead.

*Shit.*

Up ahead, a white cop car is parked on the side of the road. It's in the middle of nowhere. Why would a cop car be in the middle of nowhere? Surely this isn't some licence checkpoint thing? It's not a long weekend, is it? Have they put out an APB on us? (I'm not sure what that acronym means but I've heard it used on TV shows and whatever it is, it sounds threatening.)

'What do I do?' Chip says, reverting back to this morning's panic. 'Oh god ... oh no ... oh shit ...'

Every muscle in my body tenses. 'Keep driving,' I tell him. 'Whatever you do, don't go over the speed limit.'

As we draw closer, I hold my breath, frantically searching for signs of life – someone in the driver's seat, leaning against the car door, searching for something in the nearby shrubs. I can't see anything.

We drive past. In my side-view mirror I see something I can't unsee: a female police officer crouched by her front tyre, back to me, navy blue pants bunched around her ankles, black holster belt dangling, bare white bum, pissing in the wind.

Chloe states for the record, 'She needs a She-Wee.'

At Meningie, we stop near at the public toilets by Lake Albert. Thick reeds skirt twinkling water that stretches as far as the eye can see. Pelicans sail past, riding the wind, and land, perching on decaying timber pylons jutting out of the lake. They watch us watching them.

There are shops on the opposite side of the road: supermarkets, takeaways, a hairdresser and a real estate agent. The road is wide, cars diagonally parked. Townspeople come and go, paying little attention to us. It seems they're more than used to it being a tourist thoroughfare.

I don't need the toilet. I need food.

I go it alone, over to the Chickens-R-Us Takeaway and order a triple drumstick pack, chips and a Coke. A Noelene lookalike tells me to help myself to the drinks fridge while she prepares my order. I crack a can, guzzle a third, and look up at a tiny

TV fixed to the wall, subtitles on, a familiar face looking back at me.

I snort the Coke. It goes clean up my nose, stinging my sinuses. My eyes water. Behind the counter, the Noelene doppelganger glances my way with idle curiosity as she tongs hot chips into a paper bag and loads them with chicken salt.

'Acid,' I tell her, holding up my Coke and pinching the bridge of my nose. 'I'm told you can clean windows with this stuff. Toilet bowls. Dirty coins. Scrub ovens even.'

She screws up her nose and doesn't comment.

I look back at the screen and read the subtitles. *Missing seventy-seven year old grandmother, Daisy Ames, was last seen at an Adelaide retirement home in the company of three men masquerading as funeral directors.* The picture cuts to the orderly twirling his moustache. *They seemed like regular guys to me,* he says. *Daisy was a sweet old lady. She got up to mischief, for sure, but she wouldn't hurt a fly. I hope they haven't taken her for, you know... experimentation. Gerontophilia is a thing. Trust me, when you've worked in God's Waiting Room as long as I have, you've seen it all.*

The bulletin cuts to an advert for Barber's Beard Oil.

'Your order,' says the Noelene lookalike.

I take it and leave, ambling blindly across the road towards the lake, almost getting cleaned up by a honking tractor – in retrospect I'm not really sure how I missed it, given it was bright red, ten-foot high and doing about ten ks.

Back at the hearse, Chip is smoking a Chupa Chup. I've lost my appetite. The others are nowhere to be seen; they must be in the restrooms.

Before I can get a word in, Chip says, 'Hey Taylor. Guess what? I've just uploaded our first two candidates for *Hotties of the Northern Burbs*. We're up and away.' He swipes at his fancy iPhone. It reminds me to check *my* phone. There are three messages, all for Geoff. I decide to revisit them later. 'Where'd you get that case?' I ask, noting his glittery cover, feeling jacked all over again that I'm in Pokemon land. He could've thought to buy me one.

Chip points at a hardware store across the road. It wouldn't be my immediate go-to for technology needs, but then again we're not in Kansas anymore. 'I created us an Insta profile. Don't worry. I set it up under a pseudonym. I might as well work while I'm on the road.' He grins at me. 'You know, I feel like a legit certified businessman. There's something sexy about hotels, airports and layovers.'

Did I mention that Chip really is in a league of his own?

'Who'd you upload?' I point at two cosy-looking pelicans nestled in the reeds. 'I thought you were thinking of a different kind of bird.'

Chip smiles. 'Daisy and Chloe kindly agreed.'

I want to choke him. I want to ram my chicken drumstick down his throat. 'Are you freakin' nuts, Chip?' I point at the chicken shop. 'I just watched a news report on a missing Adelaide grandmother! *Our* missing Adelaide grandmother. You've uploaded evidence! I can't believe this! Don't you think anything through?'

'Settle, Petal.' Chip calmly shows me the account. 'I'm starting us off with a bang.'

There, staring back at me, are two sets of pure cleavage. And by that I mean: no headshot, arms, clavicles – all boob canyon, no nipple. One is pert and supple, the other wrinkly and sun-spotted.

'You said you wanted diversity,' Chip says, thoroughly pleased with himself. 'No age discrimination here.'

I hate to admit my own patheticness, but I can't help but linger on what is obviously Chloe's cleavage. (Daisy's I look at with a more scientific fascination as to the ravages of time.) But Chloe's takes my breath away. She's beautiful. I imagine falling in there and never coming back up for air. Then I curse myself for being a creepy perv. God. What is Chip turning me into?

He notes my longing face. 'Good huh?'

I swallow a mouthful of drool. 'At least they're unidentifiable. How'd you get them to do it?'

'I was telling them about our business plan. Daisy revealed she'd posed for *People* magazine back in the day and she'd love to relive that time in her life. Chloe said she's been taking private selfies to hone her life-drawing skills. She offered to do some artwork for our website. When we get around to setting it up, that is. Cool huh?'

For some reason, neither explanation surprises me. 'Hey. You have a phone with internet. Can you google the meaning of gerontophilia?'

Chip searches it up. I read over this shoulder. *Gerontophilia: sexual attraction to old people.*

'Ew,' Chip grimaces. He looks at me. 'You're not considering this for our website, are you? I mean, I'm all for innovation, but I think this might be a little out there. Even for us.'

I don't get to explain. Daisy and Chloe return, Daisy beaming triumphantly. She does a pirouette. 'I used the She-Wee! Who says you can't teach an old dog new tricks?'

Chloe reads my unease. 'I washed it between uses.'

I go to tell them about the news report, but Chip cuts me off.

'Save it for the road, Taylor.' He slips the phone into his pocket and looks around. 'Where's Jackson? He was here a minute ago.'

I share the hot chips. Everyone digs in.

Chip eats with his mouth open. 'Wow. These aren't bad. Almost as good as Bill's.'

We look across the road. Jackson is shaking hands with a skinny, scruffy guy dressed in a green flannelette shirt, ripped jeans and brown Blundstone boots. The guy hands him something in a plastic bag and Jackson stuffs it in his pocket. He salutes him goodbye and walks over to us.

'Got you sorted, Granny,' he says.

For the first time since we hooked up, I witness unbridled affection from Daisy. She falls into his arms, bestowing a loving hug and a loud smoochy kiss. 'That's my boy!'

I don't need to be Einstein to work it out what's in his pocket. Supply and demand works a treat, even in the country.

Daisy grabs my chicken drumstick, tears a mouthful of meat, passes it back and says, 'Keep some of this for later, for when I have the munchies.'

# CHAPTER THIRTEEN

A few kilometres out of Salt Creek, Chip gets a phone call. I'm about to suggest that maybe he shouldn't answer, when he says, 'Parental units. Excuse me while I take this. And keep it on the lowdown, would you? They think I'm still in Radelaide.'

He puts it on speaker and says in a super-posh voice, 'Chippolata Magna Carta speaking. How may I direct your call?'

'Ah! Connection!' comes a deep voice not at all unlike movie star Sean Connery. 'We've been trying to get hold of you for days, Chip. You agreed you'd pick up no matter what time we rang.'

'Sorry. What can I say? Man in demand.'

'So you got the job at the dog wash then?'

Chip adjusts his cravat. He seems short of breath. 'Turns out I shouldn't have answered *Yes* to animal dander allergies. Who knew?'

'Chip ...'

'Remember the time I petted a sheep at the zoo? My face blew up like an artichoke. Besides, I'm not really a fan of being bitten on the hand by the hand that feeds me.'

'We talked about this, Chip.'

'I'm working on it, Dad, I promise. I have an interview tomorrow.'

'And?'

'Can't say much. Might jinx it.'

An exasperated sigh. 'You sound like you're driving. Are you driving, Chip? We talked about this too. You know how I feel about your Uncle Roger's hearse. If you prang it, the insurance issues are more complicated than a Tom Cruise marriage contract.'

'I'm in a friend's car. You remember Taylor, don't you?'

There's an extended pause. 'Oh! You mean the dorky kid from next door?' Then laughter. 'Hey, is he the one whose aunt posted the bathtub pic? Those bubbles didn't cover everything.'

Chip chuckles.

'Oh cripes,' says Mr Carter. 'You don't have me on speaker, do you?'

'Nah, you're good,' Chip lies. 'I'll tell Taylor that you say hi and that you remember him fondly.'

'Good, good. Now listen, your mother wants to speak to you. I'll put her on. But remember,' he lowers his voice to almost a whisper, 'if she brings up the cruise ship stewardess again, don't buy into it, okay? We need to let it die a natural death. My back is killing me. I can't take any more nights on the couch.'

There's muffled fumbling, then Chip's mother's voice comes through, smooth like hot chocolate and somehow complementing the Conneryesque quality of his father. 'Chip? Is that you, honey? How are you, darling? Did you get the silk pyjamas? I mailed them ten days ago. They should've arrived by now.'

*Silk pyjamas?* I mouth at Chip.

He smiles and asks, 'They weren't perchance royal blue?'

'Oh good! So you received them?'

Chip mutes the call and hisses at me, 'I *knew* when I saw Mrs Harvey in her garden last week that those new threads weren't hers! She's been accosting Dave the delivery guy again, promising to pass on packages. Sticky-handed wench.' He unmutes. 'Thanks Mum, they're awesome! Comfy as.'

'Wonderful. Now tell me, darling. How are my petunias? Are you watering them?'

'I held a roadside stall, sold them by the bunch and made a killing.'

Mrs Carter laughs. 'Oh you tease! Just make sure you remember to fertilise them. Sorry honey, can you hang on a minute?' Her voice becomes shrill. 'Louis, don't use *those* teabags! For heaven's sake! I used them this morning for my facial! Fresh ones are by the kettle.' She comes back. 'I meant to say, sweetheart, I received a Neighbourhood Watch email alert. Something about a prison escapee. I hope you're locking up. I'd hate to be burgled. My mother's Barbara Cartland collector's box-set is worth a mint. Every book is signed by the woman herself. I couldn't stand to lose it.'

'Trust me, Mum,' Chip assures her. 'Grandma's Barbara collection is tucked safely under lock and key.'

'Oh, thank you sweetheart. It's such a relief to count on you. Holidaying is much more relaxing when you know things at home are being taken care of. Well, my dear, must fly! Your father booked another day cruise.' In a quieter voice she adds, 'He hasn't mentioned the stewardess, has he?'

'Not a word. Talk soon, Mum. Love you. Bye!' Chip hangs up.

'Silk pyjamas?' I say.

'Your father's a philanderer?' Chloe asks.

'Barbara Cartland?' Jackson says.

'Your elderly neighbour steals deliveries?' Daisy finishes. 'Ha! Genius!'

Chip is flustered. 'Look, I'll answer one at a time and in order of presentation.' He takes a deep breath. 'The silk pyjamas were a request – not that my mother knows *why* – she simply thinks I enjoy the feel of fine thread against my skin. If you must know, pornographers wear them. I'm getting into the spirit. Hey, it worked for Hugh.' He takes another deep breath. 'Yes, my father has an eye for the ladies, but no, he doesn't cheat, he's been fishing in the same fishing hole for over twenty years. The stewardess was a former chiropractor and she was adjusting his mid thoracic. *I believe him.* Barbara Cartland, I'll have you know, was a hugely accomplished bestselling author who wrote over seven hundred books during her lifetime, definitely nothing to be sneezed at, including some really steamy romance and seriously hot sex scenes. She also – notably – wore pyjamas and fluffy slippers to work. This, my friends, is my ultimate career goal. I'm not sure of any other professions where this occurs. Pornographers and authors are quite possibly it.'

'Sex workers,' Chloe suggests.

'They don't wear anything.' Jackson sounds like he knows.

'Peter Alexander quality control testers,' I say.

'Wake-up Jeff from the Wiggles,' Chloe giggles.

'Australian cricketers,' Jackson throws in.

'Fine. So there could be one or two others,' Chip admits. 'We all need something to aspire to.'

'And the deliveries?' Daisy asks.

'Ah yes. Mrs Harvey. Bless her. All I can say is the woman

knows how to sweet talk Dave's bike helmet off his head. I swear she snaffled the vintage Atari joystick I ordered last month. One day that woman is going to die and they'll enter her house and discover an Aladdin's Cave of suburban treasures – Tupperware orders, a forest full of home-shopping catalogues, probably Amelia Earhart's missing plane.' He stops talking and listens. 'No way! Wait. *Really?*'

'What?' I ask.

'Lily knows what happened to Amelia's plane.'

'You're kidding. And?'

'Can't say. It might jeopardise newspaper sales worldwide.'

We sail past Salt Creek. It's nothing more than a tiny roadside shop with toilets, a petrol pump, and a national park entry. We're now on the road to the seaside town of Kingston South East, where Larry the Lobster, a world-famous crustacean the size of an office building, resides. I've always wanted to see Ballina's Giant Prawn, so I'm quietly psyched for this (not that I'll say that out loud given this isn't supposed to be a sightseeing trip).

'We have about an hour until our next stop,' I say. 'We should probably talk about what I saw on the news.' I turn to Daisy. 'You've been advertised as missing.'

She crinkles her wrinkles. 'Which photo did they use?'

Like that's our main concern.

'I hope it wasn't the Studio Four one my granddaughter commissioned,' she says. 'You can see every hair on my double chins. And if you look really closely, I have a bat in the cave.'

I dry-swallow. 'You looked fine, Daisy. Maybe chubbier, but the camera *does* add ten pounds. Thing is, they're looking for you. It won't be long before they figure out Jackson is related to you, if they haven't already, and they probably have the hearse rego from servo security footage. I want to know what happens when they catch up with us. Because chances are they *will* catch up with us.'

'You're such a pessimist,' Chip says.

I survey the back seat. 'What are we going to say? We should get our story straight. We need to sing from the same songbook.'

Chloe clucks her tongue. 'You sound like you've done this before.'

'I told you, I tell stories. Stories have to make sense.'

'Not always.' Chloe nods at Jackson as if he's proof. 'But fine, in the spirit of playing along, Jackson kidnapped me. He forced me into this car, using me as a human shield, and I had no choice but to comply or be killed in nasty ways. I've seen *Silence of the Lambs*. I know about skin suits.'

'You're a little on the svelte side,' Jackson observes. 'He was after size sixteen.'

'Hey! Spoiler alert,' Chip says. 'I haven't seen it yet.'

Daisy shrugs. 'The police won't charge me. I'm old. I'll tell them this whole thing was my idea and I forced you into it.'

There's truth in that, but I can't see the authorities regarding Daisy as an influential criminal mastermind.

'That's the thing about dying,' Daisy adds. 'I can now live without a care in the world.'

At this, Chloe retreats, sinking in her seat, her smile fading. She stares out the window at the passing paddocks and shrub-dotted landscape, her thumb tracing her love-heart tattoo.

Chip brakes. 'I hope dying isn't what these idiots have in mind.' He flashes lights at the approaching minivan. It's on the wrong side of the road – *our side* – headed straight for us. My heartbeat quickens. Fortunately the driver comes to his senses, rights the vehicle, and flashes lights back as if to say *Thank you*. He passes us safely.

Chip wipes his brow. After he's collected himself, he says to me, 'See how so much of everything is up to chance, Taylor? What if this wasn't a straight patch of road? What if we'd been coming round a bend? We never would have seen him. He wouldn't have seen us.'

'So?'

'If you're on the road, you're taking a chance. That's the deal. But remember, you're also going somewhere.'

'To Mount Gambier,' I say, playing dumb. 'To see Errol.'

'You worry too much,' Chip says. 'You're bringing down the mood. Can't you think positively for a change?'

'That's rich coming from the guy who lost his shit over not one, but *two* cop cars.'

'At least my worries are circumstantial,' he says. 'What if we *don't* get caught? What if we make it to Mount Gambier, see Errol, and get back to Adelaide, mission accomplished? We'll have the money we need for our business, Daisy will have got her wish, and Jackson will have fulfilled his grandsonly duties before returning to prison and fulfilling his sentence.'

'Hey, go easy,' Jackson winces.

'Everyone wins.'

'You forgot me,' Chloe says quietly.

'And Chloe here,' Chip adds, 'will have successfully run away from whatever it is she's running away from.' He looks at her in the rear-vision mirror. 'What is that again?'

'None of your business.'

'Right. My bad. You don't owe us an explanation. You're just along for the ride. You know what? For all we know, *you* could be the chink in the chain. You could be the red herring. You could be the one who murders people and sews skin-suits. You could be the one who—'

'Killed her best friend,' Chloe finishes.

Chip's mouth hangs like he's dislocated his jaw.

'So I'd shut up if I were you.'

And Chip does exactly that.

# CHAPTER FOURTEEN

Cross off sighting a towering man-made crayfish from life's to-do list. *Tick!* Been there, done mega-seafood. Doing it in the company of a busload of tourists? Could have forgone that one. If I ever have to duck-dodge another selfie stick, it'll be too soon. I wonder about statistics – people who've lost eyeballs, been clopped over the head or copped fat lips by the wand of Narcissus. If God had wanted us to have Inspector Gadget arms He would have granted them. We are, however, an improvement on the T-Rex, so I guess that's a win.

I find Chloe sitting cross-legged in the tail of Larry the Lobster, an enormous scooped-out cocktail bowl dug into the ground. Throw in chopped lettuce, mayo, a lemon wedge and cracked pepper and she's good to be served.

I join her. She stretches out, and we lie side-by-side, looking at Larry's underbelly. In places, scaffolding pokes through, tangled with heavy industrial wiring, destroying the illusion.

I don't beat around the seafood basket. 'You say you killed your best friend.'

She stretches her arms, fingers twinkling. I do the same. Together, we comb the air. We brush fingers and part just as quickly – but not before a tiny volt of electricity courses through me.

'Is that why you stole from the servo?'

She glances my way. 'A tenuous connection.'

'Not really. One thing always leads to another.'

'There *were* steps between.'

'You mean the part where you hid the body?'

She turns and her eyes meet mine. 'I'm not joking, Taylor. I killed her.'

'Yeah, you seem the type who'd knife someone.'

Her lips curve.

'No, wait. Not a knife. A pickaxe. Hours of diligent video gaming have taught me that pickaxes can cave a skull with one blow. Impressive blood-spurting trajectory too. Not easy to clean up unless you're in a tiled space. I'm imagining you had one purpose-built for your serial killer's dungeon?'

She clutches her chest. 'You got me. It was Chloe. In the kitchen. With the pickaxe.'

'You suck at Cluedo.'

She rests her hands on her stomach, knitting her fingers. I wait for her to say something, but she doesn't. She sighs hard and stares into space. Well, into crayfish.

I try to bring her back. 'I can't imagine you kill-*killed* your best friend. Something happened. You blame yourself.'

She shoots me a look. 'Your powers of perception are unparalleled.'

'There were clues.'

'Like?'

'Like most people who commit murder generally end up handcuffed and behind bars. You're good at evading the law, I'll grant you that, but you're also young and inexperienced, so I suspect you're not that good – *yet*. Also, there's a growth period; a progression from petty crime to full-blown murder.'

She tilts her head. 'Uncannily intuitive.'

I shrug. 'I used to watch a lot of crime dramas. You haven't killed any small animals, have you?'

'I *was* farming gerbils for such a purpose.'

'We should probably curb this discussion. We don't want Jackson overhearing, given his former life as an animal activist.'

She looks around. 'Where are they?'

'There's a park down the road with a toilet block. I think they went there. That, or they suffered a surprise selfie-stick attack and were stuffed into a tour bus luggage compartment.'

She points to a crack in the crayfish shell. 'Can you see the internal structure? The rods and bolts?'

I twist my head to get a glimpse. 'Parts of it, yeah.'

'It's proof you shouldn't look too hard at something. It takes away the magic.' She turns her whole body toward me, tucking her hands under her head, her dark eyes searching mine. I feel her warm breath on my face and everything I'm made of grows hot. 'Mystery is what keeps us invested, Taylor. When you know everything there is to know about a person, there's nothing left to want. You get bored.'

'You're saying I should keep you a mystery?'

'Don't you find me more intriguing that way?'

I want to say I find her intriguing, mystery or no mystery, murder or no murder, but instead I ask, 'Do you think we ever really know everything there is to know about a person?'

She runs her finger over her wrist tattoo. 'People who've been married for twenty years *must*.'

'Didn't you just debunk your own theory? Why would they stay together?'

Her eyes flicker. 'How long have your parents been married?'

'Twenty years.'

'So you believe in love?'

'I believe in horniness.' I scratch my chin. 'Yeah, when I think about it, I probably do believe in love.'

She rolls away. 'Good for you.'

'It's not easy.'

She looks back.

'Romantic love, friendship love – neither are a picnic. I had some friends. One friend I really cared about. Her name was Cass.'

'Had? Past tense?'

I run a finger across my forehead. 'See this enormous neon sign? Dumped.'

'Romantic dumped or friend dumped?'

'Definitely the second one. She was just a friend! But my best friend. So.'

'What'd you do?'

'I like how you assume it's my fault.'

'Is it?'

I sigh. 'Don't know. Not sure.'

'You must've done *something*. What did she say?'

*I'm hard work.*

'I'm pretty sure it was owing to a difference of opinion,' I tell her, 'and it was all downhill from there.'

She pokes me, wanting more. 'Did you have an argument?'

*Yes. No. Sort of.* I feel myself tensing. Maybe talking about this isn't something I'm ready for. 'Not exactly. I did something. *Said something.* There was fallout.'

'Sounds like an argument to me.'

'There wasn't any fist-throwing or name-calling,' I tell her. 'More there was this lame discussion and things kind of petered out. Much like Barry's plane crash, come to think of it. I limped down the runway and nose-dived into a ditch.'

She nods like she gets it. 'And I'm guessing they haven't sent a rescue party?'

'Not yet.'

'You're holding out hope?'

I shrug. 'I'm not sure what I'm hoping for. Things to go back to normal, maybe?'

'I hate to tell you, Taylor, but she doesn't sound like a real friend to me.'

'Why?'

'Because *you* sound like you're the one who's sorry. Unless you killed someone like I did, friends forgive each other. Friends let shit go. *True friends stab you in the front*, said Oscar Wilde. You're the writer. You would've heard that.'

When she says it, a corner of my heart cracks open. I'm like the crayfish: I'm sure she can see my internal structure. It's a truth, but not one I'm sure I want to face. In fact, I've been actively avoiding it. It means that all those years were a lie.

I remember a time not so long ago when Cass rang me, pissed off with Lia. Straight after, Lia rang me pissed off with Cass. Normally I took Cass's side on pretty much everything, but this time I could see Lia's point of view. I rang Riley and got his opinion, and confident I knew where we all stood, I rang Cass and suggested maybe she should rethink it. I didn't criticise her, judge her, attack her. I didn't shame her for feeling the way she did. I simply suggested she might want to reconsider.

Wrong move.

Cass came out all guns blazing. She got off the phone with me and did the ring around, got Lia and Riley back on side, and next thing I knew, *I* was the villain for interfering and passing judgement. (Not long after that, I heard a saying coined by cowboys: *Never corner anything meaner than you.*) I thought I was being diplomatic; I thought Cass had involved me because she wanted help to calm the farm. But Cass didn't want help – she wanted validation. She wanted me to reinforce her choices and to bitch behind our friends' backs. Cass didn't want to be stabbed in the front, thank you very much Oscar Wilde. She was baying for blood and a public assassination, Julius Caesar Ides of March style – except she was Brutus and I was Julius, copping daggers for daring to love Rome more.

It was when I started to realise we came at things from very different angles; that what had floated once *now* sank our ship. We were butting tectonic plates spurring seismic shifts neither of us saw coming. I wonder if Cass saw it then too.

I shake off the thought and change the subject. 'You said you lived with your aunt. What happened to your parents?'

Chloe runs a hand through her dark locks, scooping them away from her face. I notice a tiny black love heart tattooed behind her ear – one that matches the one on her wrist – and I resist the urge to press my lips against it.

'They split when I was five,' she says. 'Dad lives interstate with his new family. We were his false-start family.'

'He has other kids?'

She nods. 'I have a brother and a sister. I know *of* them, but I don't know them.'

'And your mum?'

'Committed relationship with a bartender.'

'Oh.'

'Or maybe it's over?' she says. 'I haven't been home in a while.'

'She's not looking for you?'

She shakes her head. 'No search party. Guess that means I'm in the ditch with you.'

I spread my hands wide. 'Ta-da! It takes a level of skill to get here.'

Her body shakes with the giggles, but her eyes betray her – they glisten. And in that moment, I know what I'm feeling is something far stronger than I've ever felt before. Whatever it is that's blooming inside of me is growing roots, spreading out, creeping down my limbs.

My pocket vibrates. I dig out the phone. I forgot about the messages for Geoff – all four of which have something to do with a debt and legal action for a chiropractic bill at The Bone Joint. There's also a message from Chip – one far more threatening: *Houston, we have a problem. Engine won't start. Marooned. Repeat: Marooned.*

Chloe looks at me. 'What? Who is it?'

'I think we're up crayfish creek without a paddle.'

'Huh?'

'Car trouble. Errol might have to wait a bit longer to be reunited with the love of his life.'

She gets to her feet and offers me her hand. I take it. She pulls me up – *and* pulls me close. 'Stop talking about love,' she whispers, her breath warm on my neck. 'There's no such thing.'

She drops my hand and walks away like she didn't just drop a bomb on my heart.

# CHAPTER FIFTEEN

'Starter motor,' says a balding, middle-aged mechanic with grease under his nails and up his nose – I don't even want to think about how it got there. 'Have to send for the part.' Stubby fingers stab a keyboard possibly unearthed from the Neolithic period and trace across a screen. He leans in, squints, then rummages a drawer before donning a pair of reading glasses with diamante trim. He's a hillbilly Boy George. 'Naracoorte has one in stock. I'll rustle up a courier. Should have you back on the frog and toad by tomorrow, all things going to plan.'

'Tomorrow?' Chip stops fiddling with a spinny rack of pine-tree air fresheners and comes to lean against the wooden counter. Above us, on a cluttered shelf piled with trucking magazines, dog-eared paperwork and promo catalogues, a Coke-brand radio crackles the end of the midday news and The Rolling Stones sing, 'You can't always get what you want'. 'There's no way you can do it sooner?' he asks.

The mechanic scratches his sweaty neck. He has a blackhead patch requiring surgical excavation. Pimple-popping video addicts would go mad for him.

'Mate, in case you haven't noticed I'm busier than the

supermarkets baking Easter buns in January. Hate to tell ya, but you're out of luck. My idiot apprentice went to an eighteenth last night, got shitfaced and made the intelligent decision to take a long walk off a short balcony. Kid's in plaster up to his eyeballs. My other guy's got gastro so bad he's redecorating his house. There's two jobs booked ahead of yours. Best I can do, I'm afraid.'

'Crap,' Chip says. 'So we're stuck in Kingston for the night?'

'Arse end of the world, mate, but not the end of it.' The mechanic takes off his glasses, fishes for something behind him. He passes me a tattered tourist flyer with the carcass of a dead blowfly stuck to it. 'Good tucker at The Crown Inn,' he says. 'Damn fine schnitzels and salads. Caravan park can probably put you up for next to nix. Oh, and there's a footy club shindig on tonight. Fancy dress.'

The ancient flyer advertises The Football Club Annual Night of Nights, though admittedly it's the 2017 version.

'Free choice, come as you like. But here's some advice ...' He leans in close, lowers his voice. I'm not sure why when there's no one here but us. 'Don't dress as Franz Ferdinand a-la Rocky Horror. Local sheep-shearing gun, Bootstrap McGee, dresses as Franz every year and he gets super peeved if anyone else pulls on the fishnets.' He chuckles, wiping the corner of his eye. 'Get this. One year, on a dare, junior footy coach Adrian Hollingsworth gave it a crack. He landed in Soldier's Memorial ER hog-tied and sporting a fractured jaw. They found an applicator lipstick wedged You Know Where.' He stands straight and talks at normal volume. 'But I can't be certain of that last part because Josie Smith told me and she's renowned for embellishing her stories.'

'Fair enough,' I say. 'I forgot to pack my Sweet Transvestite outfit anyway.'

He eyes me. 'Where'd you boys say you're headed? Mount Gambier, isn't it? Got relatives there or something?'

'Yeah,' Chip says. He grabs my arm and drags me to the door. 'We'd better go call them and tell them about the delay. See you tomorrow.'

'Hang on!' the mechanic calls. 'Don't you want to know how much?' His keyboard receives another hammering. Dust clouds fly. 'That'll be three hundred and fifty-six fifty. Cash or Paywave? I'll need some details too. Contact number and all that.'

'Cash,' Chip says. 'We're good for it. We're not leaving here without the hearse, mate. We'll be back in the morning.' He ushers me through the door before we can be interrogated further.

Outside, the others are crowded around our bags piled on the footpath. Daisy sucks a cigarette. She blows smoke rings in Chip's face.

'You can get cancer from that,' Chip says.

'Oh you're hilarious,' Daisy retorts, giving him the finger. She dips her aviators at me. 'Don't tell me we're stranded?'

'Overnight.'

Jackson is holding a tourist brochure, presumably picked up from Larry the Lobster. 'It looks like a nice holiday spot, Granny. There's a lighthouse, a jetty, and it says here that the bakery does the meanest apple-turnover this side of Adelaide.'

'That puts it on the map,' Chloe says dryly.

'Is it a one-horse town or two?' Daisy enquires.

Jackson scrutinises the brochure. 'Two. The Crown Inn and The Royal Mail.'

Daisy butts out her smoke. 'I'm overdue for my midday spritzer. Lead the way.'

'That way,' Jackson says, pointing up the road toward a turn-off. 'I'm pretty sure the pub is up there.'

'Onward!' Daisy declares, marching up the footpath.

Jackson follows. I grab my bag and swing it over my shoulder. 'Shouldn't we make it a priority to book the caravan park?' I ask Chip. 'It sounds the cheapest place to stay. If we don't book, we might miss out.'

Chip picks up his backpack. 'Relax, Taylor. It's not school holidays. We'll be fine.' He oscillates from panic mode to chill-pill mode so fast it makes my head spin. 'You know, I'm totally down for this fancy dress thing they have on tonight. We should go.'

Chloe falls into step beside us. 'Fancy dress?'

Chip nods. 'At the footy club. I have an outfit in mind.'

'We shouldn't draw attention to ourselves,' I tell him. 'We should lie low for the night.'

He ignores me. 'Guess my outfit.'

'Hugh Hefner,' Chloe says.

Chip huffs and straightens his cravat. 'How'd you know?'

'Wild guess,' Chloe says. 'And if you think I'm dressing as a Playboy Bunny, think again. What are the rest of us supposed to go as?'

'Yeah?' I say. 'I can't imagine a town this size has a costume hire shop.'

'There'll be an op shop we can raid,' Chip says confidently.

'I still think it's a stupid idea.'

Chip stops and turns to pat my head. 'I say this with love, Taylor: Your over-anxiousness is starting to shit me. You're forgetting that if we rock up in costume, no one will know who we are. They don't know who we are *period*.'

He has a fair point, though there is a chance *some* people may have seen the news report about Daisy.

'And it's not like we have anything better to do,' he adds.

Decent point number two. *Dammit.*

'Our matriarch-biaaaaatch,' he thumbs at Daisy, 'is cashed up sweet. We can fully afford the night out.'

Chloe smacks his head. 'Hey! Call her your bitch again, gangster boy, and I'll kick your butt. She gets to decide who she spends money on, you got that?'

'Hush money,' Chip says, rubbing his head. 'She coughs up the bickies and we won't spill. That's the deal.' His phone pings. He extracts it from his jeans pocket and inspects it. 'Well whaddaya know.'

'What?' I ask.

'Submissions.'

'Huh?'

'For our website.'

'Oh.'

He rolls his eyes. 'We're still on the job, Taylor. Don't forget. Real businessmen combine business *and* pleasure.'

I wonder where the pleasure part is.

'I'll need to devote some brain cells to these over a schnitty. Preferably one with crayfish topping.' He gauges Chloe's approval and she reluctantly nods. He grins and stuffs the phone in his pocket. Next, he gives his groin a substantial adjustment, shaking a leg at four o'clock. Not satisfied, he rams a hand down his pants and *really* moves things around.

'Chip,' I hiss. 'What are you doing?'

'There's a gun in my pants.'

Chloe scoffs, 'Said every male *ever*.'

Chip pulls the glovebox gun from his crotch. Chloe reels back, gasping. I stare at him, frozen, not sure what I'm more upset about – the fact he's waving it around in broad daylight, or that I believed his crotch could actually be that well-endowed.

'What?' he asks. 'You think I'd leave it in the hearse?'

I snatch the gun, spin him round, unzip his backpack and stuff it inside. Chloe blinks at me, clearly terrified. 'It's isn't real,' I tell her, zipping the backpack. 'It's fake.' But the look in her eyes is one of disbelief. 'We're not that stupid. Or dangerous. It's plastic.'

Her voice is small and unsure. 'It's just ... you're hanging with an escaped prisoner, so ...'

'In case you haven't noticed, he's not the only one on the run.' I place a gentle hand on her shoulder. 'Trust me, okay? It's not real.'

I feel her shoulder dip, relaxing. She smiles. 'Okay. Well, it looked pretty real to me. I wouldn't let anyone see it.'

'Exactly,' I say, glaring at Chip. 'You want to scare the good townsfolk? Have the local law enforcement on our backs? Think first next time, okay?'

'Fair enough,' Chip says. He laughs at Chloe. 'Hey, you could've asked, *Is that a gun in your pants or are you happy to see me?*'

Chloe runs with it. 'Well, Mr Carter, you are packing a very powerful weapon.'

I hide my smirk. 'Lay off. He doesn't need any encouragement.'

Chloe winks and Chip pretends to shoot her with his finger. He blows the tip. 'Smokin'.'

After a mad tasty schnitzel at The Crown Inn Hotel – which notably involved a lengthy and pointless discussion with the waitress about why the local crayfish industry catches *crays*, but Larry the Lobster is a *lobster* – we're given directions to the op shop. We leave the pub and walk up the road. Daisy, under the influence of an unchecked quantity of wine spritzers, makes the walk longer by pinballing all over the footpath.

'Can't we push her in a shopping trolley?' Chloe says.

'One day you'll be old and vulnerable too,' Jackson scowls. 'I hope someone dumps *you* in a shopping cart like a bag of potatoes.'

'She doesn't look vulnerable,' Chloe says, head tipped sideways evaluating Daisy's rear-view stagger. 'Next I'll be holding back her hair while she pukes.'

'Be careful what you wish for,' I say.

Daisy, not hard of hearing, gives Chloe an over-the-shoulder salute. 'I'll have you know, young lady, I was strutting the town when you were but foam on your father's beer froth.'

Chip slaps his head. 'I really hate that euphemism. We were all spoof once, I get it, but it's not nice to be reminded.'

Chloe says, 'You men always focus on the male contribution. Don't forget we're the incubators.'

Chip shudders. 'Childbirth is soooooo *Aliens*.'

'We're drifting off topic,' I say. 'We should have some idea of what we're dressing as, so we don't spend too long at the shop.'

'You should go as Franz Ferdinand,' Chip says.

'Be serious.'

Exasperated, he moans, 'Why do we have to have a plan, Taylor?'

'That's rich coming from *road trips run to schedules and we need to stick to them*.'

Nose in the air, Chip says, 'Let's just see what they have in stock, okay?'

Piper, the teenage op shop attendant (Piper – *Volunteer* is on her nametag), tries and fails to conceal her annoyance we've disrupted her quiet reading time. Perched on a rickety wooden stool behind the counter, she huffily folds her page in half and turns it face-down, spine bent and cracking.

Chloe makes conversation with her while the rest of us check out the racks of musty secondhand gear.

She leans over a display counter, cracking gum. 'What are you reading?'

'*Doing It* by Melvin Burgess,' Piper replies.

She has straight blonde hair and an impressive mouthful of multi-coloured braces. A love bite marks her neck. There's another on her collarbone almost hidden by her Gang of Youths T-shirt. I wonder how her partner fared. Images of *The Walking Dead* run through my mind.

'I started reading it this morning. I'm already halfway through,' she says.

'I've read it,' Chloe tells her. 'What do you think so far?'

I don't know if Chloe's telling the truth or making conversation. The fact that she reads gives me a buzz.

'Pretty sick hey.' Piper nudges the book with a purple nail. 'My teacher wants us to read a pre-approved English Lit text for our project, but I'm taking the free choice option.'

'Year Eleven?'

'Twelve. They hide this book behind the librarian's desk. You have to request it.'

Chloe grumbles. 'They do it at my school too. What'd they say when you asked for it?'

Piper beams. 'Wanna see a re-enactment?' She tosses her head back, neck exposed, trailing a nail across her collarbone. Her voice is velvet. 'Miss, do you have that book? You know, the one about doing it. I want to know what it's like. You know, *doing it*. I haven't done it yet. It's important to be educated before you do it, don't you think?'

Chloe stifles laughter. She sticks a finger in her mouth, extracts her gum and twirls it round the tip of her finger. Something about her body language puts me on edge. She's not ...

*Is she flirting?*

'What'd the librarian say?' Chloe asks.

Piper shrugs. 'She got all shirty, but she had to suck it up because they have to give you the book if you ask for it and you're in the right year level. That's the policy. She checked it out and handed it over.'

'You're shameless then?'

'Abso-freakin-lutely.'

They smile at each other, not losing eye contact.

'What's your name?' Piper asks.

'Chloe.'

She points to her nametag. 'Call me Pipes. In town long?'

'Just tonight. We're going to that fancy-dress thing they have on.'

Piper looks at the rest of us. 'Cool. Well, the boss keeps all sorts of random crap just for that very reason. The op shops in Robe and Millicent throw us their costume-y stuff, too, at this time of year. So, you know, you might get lucky.' She looks at Chloe.

Daisy has a black-and-white maid's costume in hand and she's headed for the change-room. Chip has found a set of red satin pyjamas in the women's clothing section and he's now busy searching the shoe-rack. Jackson has found a black hat, blue shirt and black sunglasses. It's not a far stretch to assume he's dressing as a Blues Brother. I might've thought he'd choose something a little less close to home, but far be it from me to judge. There *was* of course the time he was mistaken as a Hell's Angels bikie in a costume hire store, so this is an improvement. Meanwhile, I haven't found a stitch. I'm too busy watching Piper and Chloe talk – in a totally non-stalkerish way, of course.

'I thought it'd be busy today,' Piper says, 'but it's dead. Everyone sticks to the same thing they wore last year. Or they swap. Or they rent something from Mount Gambier.'

'You're going?' Chloe asks.

'Hadn't planned to.' Piper fans her blonde hair across her shoulders. 'But now that you ask, I guess it could be fun.'

'So you'll go?'

Piper smiles. 'Sure. Why not.'

'Cool,' Chloe grins back.

Piper runs her tongue across her braces and winks.

I fumble a china bowl of men's cufflinks. They crash onto the floor. The bowl doesn't shatter, but rather bounces and rolls, and the cufflinks scatter. Chloe turns to look at me like she forgot I was in the room.

'Sorry,' I mumble, getting down on my knees to rescue them. I find a few from under a coat rack, my heart sinking into my stomach all the while.

I spot a set of varicose-veined legs nearby. I look up. Daisy, dressed in a full maid's uniform, is waving a pink feather duster. She adjusts her breasts so they sit as perkily as they did before (she must have some seriously gravity-defying structural support going on under there) and says, 'I'm not sure about this. I think I'll try biker chick instead.' She snatches a black vinyl jacket and ripped jeans from the rack and hobbles off to the change-rooms.

I look at Chloe. She's not looking back. Her fingers are on the counter, inching toward Piper's. She strokes her purple nail polish. 'Smooth,' she says.

A demure grin from Piper. 'Very.'

I know right then that I like her – *really like her* – and I'm disappointed she doesn't like me. She likes girls.

I bite my lip and turn away.

# CHAPTER SIXTEEN

After getting ready in a public shower block (and fretting about the prevalence of athlete's foot after Chip took it upon himself to relay a gruesome story about the time his mate caught it and almost had to have his leg amputated) we head for the footy club, dressed to impress.

We stand in a queue, shivering. Pterosaur-sized moths zoom around glowing yellow bulbs, the sky blacker than black. I've never seen insects so big they look like they could seagull-shit on your head.

'That'll be seven bucks fifty,' says the door attendant, holding out his hand. Inside the club, music thumps.

The carpark is full and most of the parking spots around the oval are taken. It's safe to assume the whole town is here. Kids run amok on the floodlit oval, shrieking, chasing each other and tearing up the freshly-cut grass, brandishing glow-stick swords and necklaces. Light-up shoes twinkle, whizzing by in a trippy psychedelic swirl. Unleashed dogs give chase, barking, snapping at their heels. Car headlights flash. Somewhere in the distance a firecracker goes off.

This really is Kingston's night of nights.

Chloe does a head count, rifles through Daisy's handbag and hands over a couple of twenties. I notice our door attendant bears an uncanny resemblance to former Australian cricket great, Merv Hughes. Maybe it's his fancy-dress outfit? I can't be sure.

He hands back a twenty. 'Seven fifty *total*, love. Family concession.' He gives Chloe her change.

Chloe looks at him as if he's speaking a foreign language. 'I've never paid for a family ticket before.'

Merv leans in and side-mouths, 'Well, I don't know if you *are* a family, love. But trust me, this lot will make a squillion on the bar tonight. I think we can afford it. Besides,' he says, winking at Daisy, 'I like her outfit.'

Daisy pats her bouffant blonde wig. 'Sandy from *Grease*. Not virgin Sandy. Badass Sandy.' She does a twirl in her shiny black spandex leggings and tugs her vinyl jacket straight. She spits a smoke butt, twisting a ballet flat on top. (The high heels were too high and thus remained at the op shop. Osteoporosis is a bitch, apparently.)

'You look good,' Merv says.

Daisy beams. 'Tell me about it, Stud.'

He turns his attention to my outfit. 'Are you a wizard or something?'

I pull my black sheet-cape together and switch my elasticated mask from the back of my head to the front. Chip hands me my staff. I beat it on the pavement. 'Death,' I say in a gruff voice. 'I've come for you.'

Merv is unimpressed, but he says kindly, 'We could've used you last week when Kingston played Edenhope in the semi-final. Would've liked to have given the kiss of death to those smug bastards.' He looks at Chip. 'No prizes for guessing your caper. No Playboy bunnies?' He looks behind him, hope fading. 'First time we've had Mr Hefner grace us. Don't know why no one's thought of it before.' His attention is momentarily diverted by a bloke in fishnets, holding up what I presume to be a pre-purchased ticket. He glides on past and Merv moans, 'Aw shit, looks like we're in for some trouble tonight.'

Chloe adjusts her army-camo tank top, jingling a wrist of black rubber armbands. Fake tattoos from the two-dollar shop line her arms and chest bone. She's Ruby Rose inspired. Not *actual* Ruby Rose. A tribute. A homage to hot-Australian-went-OS-and-made-it-big-as-TV-royalty.

'What kind of trouble?' she asks.

Merv shakes his head. 'That was Franz.'

'Franz Ferdinand?' Jackson says.

Jackson has embraced his inner Pollock-not-Rollock and gone full beatnik artist with beret, art smock, paintbrush and paint tray he found at the hardware store. He's even donned a fake moustache that the orderly from Daisy's retirement home would be envious of. He agreed with me that his initial Blues Brothers idea had been too close to home.

'The wrong Franz,' Merv explains.

'You mean that *wasn't* Bootstrap McGee?' Chip says. He really does have a memory for names.

Merv's impressed. 'You've heard of the local legend then?'

Chip shrugs. 'Surgically removed applicator lipsticks are hard to forget.'

'Well, if Bootstrap sees him that won't be the only thing shoved towards Christmas. Some people might as well paint a target on their heads, I swear.'

'Hey!' A woman at the back of the line calls out. 'Are you lot having a family reunion up there or what?'

'Hold ya horses, Meredith!' Merv yells back. 'Let's not forget ya made me wait in line for my bacon and egg sanga last week! And it was stone bloody cold by the time I got it. I've eaten roadkill that tasted better.' He waves us on. 'Go on. Have a good night, folks. Steer clear of the fish-nets.'

We head inside.

The place is packed. I spot at least five versions of Elvis within thirty seconds. I'm not sure if it's owing to a local fascination with The King, or coincidence. There's Fat Elvis holding a fake plastic hamburger, Skinny Elvis in sleek black pants and black shirt (thank you very much), Druggy Elvis with a bottle of pills swinging from his neck (not as he wore it, obviously), rhinestone-spattered White Jumpsuit Elvis with cape and aviator sunnies (Viva Las Vegas, baby!), and Marine Elvis – probably my favourite, at his purest – with Priscilla hanging off his arm, looking like a post-surgery dermatologist's dreamboat. I wonder if there's an Elvis convention on tonight. I hope they get on stage and bust out some karate moves. I'd like to see that.

'This wasn't a bad idea after all,' Chip says, cutting a path to the bar.

We dodge two of the fatter Elvises and then a white haze of Bo Peeps.

One of them bats her stuck-on eyelashes at Chip Hefner. 'Help! Help! We lost our sheep and don't know where to find them!'

The massive blue bow under her chin is a winged beast. She's busting from a tightly-strung corset. It's probable her sheep are lost in her cleavage.

She swings an empty Cruiser bottle in Chip's face. 'Quick! Get me to the baaaaaaaaaaar.' Her gaggle of Peeps dissolve into hysterics.

'Country humour,' Jackson Pollock says, raising his voice above the music. 'Wouldn't be surprised if tonight ends with a bit of cow tipping. Hey, get me a whisky sour, would you?'

'Do artists drink whisky?' I ask.

'This artist does.'

'I'll have a vodka,' says Chloe.

Daisy holds up two fingers. 'Make that another.'

Hugh Hefner gives me a friendly shoulder punch. 'What'll it be, Mr Death? Bloody Mary?'

'Coke,' I tell him.

'And?'

'Coke.'

He turns to the barman, a stubbly-faced guy dressed as Wonder Woman (more power to him) and orders me a Bundy and Coke.

'Chip, I said—'

'Oh grow a pair, Taylor!' He chucks a fifty on the bar. 'Ask yourself, What would Mr Death do?'

Wonder Woman makes our drinks and lines them up on the bar. Chip hands me a Bundy and Coke. 'Drink up, friend. Tomorrow is a new day of death and destruction.' He hands out the others' drinks and grabs his own – a pink cocktail garnished with a cherry and a red umbrella. 'What?' he says, when he sees me looking at it. 'Hugh would've drank it. Now if you'll excuse me, I have to go see a woman about her sheep.'

'You know, Hef didn't write the How-To Bible, Chip. He wouldn't be my chief reference.'

'I get it you're not a fan.' Chip shrugs. 'Each to their own.'

'Chloe?' says a voice behind me.

I turn around. *Piper*. Or rather Piper's alter-ego in a nineteenth-century costume with wide-brimmed ribboned hat. I'm not sure who she's meant to be, but it's not a look I expected she'd go for. Not that I know her, because I don't, but with all her talk about *doing it*, I thought she'd do something more along the lines of Daisy's *Grease*-inspired get-up.

Chloe kisses Piper's cheek like they didn't just meet hours earlier. 'You did it!'

'Did what?' I ask.

Piper does a one-eighty. 'I'm a suffragette,' she says proudly.

Daisy fist-bumps her. 'You've got my vote.'

'Thanks Livvy!' Piper beams.

'It's Sandy,' I correct her. 'Olivia Newton John was the actress. Sandy is the charact—'

'I know,' Piper snaps irritably. 'Though your mansplaining really helped. Who are you meant to be? Another cloaked male from the shadows making all the decisions that fuck up this planet?' She plants herself between Chloe and me and turns her back, her stiff grey dress like a Teflon sound barrier.

I turn away. Jackson, artist-extraordinaire, joins me and together we survey the crowd. We spot a giant foam lobster (sidenote: is it a crayfish or a lobster? – the jury is still out), a colourful clown (makes me shudder – I hate clowns) and a plastic-rifle-toting Ned Kelly (people keep trying to post drink coasters and serviettes through his helmet.) There's not a single person who hasn't got into the spirit.

Jackson guzzles his whisky sour and pulls a face. 'What say ye, Death? Is this living?'

'Not sure. When you were hunkered down on your thin government-supplied cot at night dreaming about freedom, is this what you'd hoped for?'

A baby elephant passes us by, vacuum cleaner hose trunk swinging, giant flappy ears sagging under their own weight. He's a clinically depressed Dumbo.

Jackson shrugs. 'I hoped there'd be Bo-Peeps and whisky sour.'

'What drugs were you on?'

'Speaking of ...' Jackson nudges me and points to the dance floor. 'Looks like Granny's have kicked in.'

Daisy is wrapped in the embrace of a young footballer a quarter of her age. I say 'footballer' because he's dressed *as* a footballer, with the number 28 on his Swans guernsey. It's not the local Kingston colours of red, white and black, so I wonder which regional football team he represents and why he hasn't as yet had his head beaten in. His muscled arms lift Daisy up and spin her round. She laughs like a debutante and flops into him.

'She smoked the weed?' I ask.

Jackson nods. 'Helps with her pain management.'

'Did she give you the money?' I ask.

'Nah, I traded some of her Viagra stash. It's good to see her enjoying herself. That's the Granny I know.' He smiles, pleased. 'When I was a kid, she let me sneak sips of her riesling. She bought chocolate and stuffed it in my hand when no one was looking. I feel like I'm repaying the favour. She's the only one who really loved me – unconditionally, that is. She made me feel strong, like I could take on the world. Everyone else made me feel like shit. Not her. You repay those debts, right? Someone helps you, you help them. You do it no question. And you do it before it's too late.'

I think of Kelly Nixon and my infamous Facebook post. I'd said something about not waiting to return love, thinking tomorrow would be there. I wonder if Jackson and I aren't more alike than we think. We stand up for something even if it costs us.

*Why didn't my friends stand up for me?*

I remember a political argument. We were talking about climate change. Cass argued the most ridiculous theory (no doubt garnered from some internet whack-job) about the blanching of the Great Barrier Reef. She said the coral wasn't dying owing to our planet slowly heating up, but rather because coral is like a hair colour; nothing can live forever, everything turns old and grey. (Yes, I shit you not.) Lia and Riley thought this plausible. I thought I'd been sucked into the Twilight Zone. I cited a bunch of scientific studies, quoted renowned experts, sent them a bunch of peer-reviewed journals, but no, apparently I was a panicky snowflake hippy-tree-huggin' greenie who needed a teaspoon of cement in my chamomile tea. Don't get me wrong. Friends can have political discourse. They can debate and be on opposing teams. But this felt different. This felt like the people I hung out with weren't on the same page as me at all. At times lately I've felt like *all* we had was history – they were what I knew, what I'd always known, but something inside me wanted to know something different, even if I wasn't ready to admit it.

Chip interrupts my reflective daze. 'Hey, check it out.' He pushes between me and Jackson and holds up his phone. Our Insta account has new photos – photos I assume Chip has executively curated, approved and posted. There are several headless shots of a couple presumably in their mid-forties dressed in their underwear, who, looking past their saggy-but-tanned skin and small paunches, are otherwise fit and attractive. No ageism here. However, when I look closer there's something strangely familiar about them. The woman in the photo has a bluebird tattoo on her left ribcage just under the line of her bra – a tattoo I've seen countless times on summer holidays by the pool. The photo has been taken in a darkened hotel room, but in the background I can see a can of whipped cream on the nightstand.

'Cool huh?' Chip says, shrinking the screen. 'They claim to be locals of our stomping ground.'

My mouth goes dry. I feel dizzy. 'What email address did they submit under?'

He thinks a moment. 'Something about going down on you?'

*Fuck*. My dad's unofficial roller-door account.

Chip's about to say something else and I'm about to throw up, when the people around us suddenly roll back and we're swept up in the tsunami. The crowd washes over us and before I know it a space has cleared, forming a circle around the dancefloor – an *empty* dancefloor except for two people: both dressed as Franz Ferdinand.

'Here we go!' someone shouts.

It's like they dinged a bell. Both men lunge for each other and a tangle of fish-nets crashes on the parquetry floor. The larger of the two, presumably Bootstrap McGee, quickly has his Franz nemesis in a crotch-headlock – and by that I mean he's sitting on the guy's neck about to lay a punch into his head. But there's an almighty groan as Bootstrap's

not-very-well-protected-behind-shiny-nylon-panties-nutsack
cops the mother of all crunches. Biting down like a rabid
dog, the pinned man's head is a lethal weapon. That's when
Bootstrap sticks his hand down his corset, yanks out a lipstick,
and shoves it into the biter's eye.

'I hope that wasn't the same one he used on the other guy,'
Chip says. 'He could get a nasty case of pink eye.'

The crowd cheers, drinks held high as if this is tonight's
scheduled entertainment. Franz rolls off Franz and the two
scuffle, satin material and fish-nets meshing in a semi-erotic
pose. I peer over the crowd and notice one guy cupping his
groin. At the same time, behind him, I see Daisy and the hunky
football player hand in hand, sneaking out the door.

No one looks to be making an effort to break up the fight. A
woman dressed as a sexy police officer back-steps through the
throng as if she might be confused for the real deal.

Fish-nets rip, corset strings fly, pearl necklaces unravel and
scatter across the floor. Blood seeps from somebody's nose.
It all takes place in a blurry haze *not* induced by my Bundy
and Coke.

And then, like the champion cricketer he is, Merv Hughes
rushes in. Franz and Franz are split. Merv grabs Franz-not-
Bootstrap by the scruff of the neck and steers him to the door.
It's fair. He is the troublemaker. He knew the rules. Don't mess
with I-owned-it-first Bootstrap McGee.

As I witness his public ejection from Kingston's night of
nights, I notice Piper and Chloe on the sidelines, clutching each
other, about to kiss. I tell myself it's one of those 'the world is
about to end, we'd better kiss now' kisses, but I know it's not.
And I'm jealous as all hell.

Jackson notices too. 'Right,' he says. He looks at me, regret in his eyes. 'Sorry mate.'

*How does he know? Am I that obvious?*

'Don't worry,' I say. 'I have choices. I choose Bundy.' I leave him and head for the bar, looping my arm through a Bo Peep along the way.

We clink staffs. 'Hey,' she says. 'Glad to find you in my paddock.'

'Just a warning,' I tell her. 'My tail's between my legs. Don't expect to find it.'

# CHAPTER SEVENTEEN

'And that, Mr Death, explains the mystery of Deery McDeerFace.'

Bo Peep sloshes the last of her vodka cranberry and slams the empty glass down on the table. Her blonde ringlets have fallen limp, pink lipstick smudged up her cheek. One of her fake eyelashes is unstuck and hanging from her eyelid.

She rubs her face. 'I neeeeeeeed another drink.'

This statement is one thousand percent up for debate.

The crowd has thinned. I have no idea what time it is. I don't know where the others are. My head roars like a convoy of garbage trucks leaving the depot. It feels so heavy it might tip me over.

A group of stragglers sway on the dance floor, dishevelled costume items on nearby chairs, shoes and handbags littering the floor. Druggy Elvis is lying face down under a table, stroking the carpet. Someone joins him. It's Wonder Woman from behind the bar. Together they scoop polyester fibres and bury their noses in them.

I slurp more Bundy. I miss my mouth and some of it dribbles on my cape. 'So you're telling me, Bo Peep,' I pause to emit the mother of all burps, 'that a local farmer had these deer on his property and they escaped and went feral in the woods?'

She hiccups. 'Feral in the *scrub*.'

'They're pests? We hit a pest?'

'Yep. You performed a public service.'

'Huh. Well, fuck me.'

'Thought you'd never ask.'

Before I know what's happening, she's straddling me like I'm a woolly ram about to be shorn. She grabs my hair, yanks my head back and squashes her lips to mine. Tongue, teeth, more tongue, more teeth. I taste cranberry, oily lipstick, and (possibly?) a chunk of tooth-saved pizza. I gag, pull back, and struggle for air before she suction-caps my mouth again.

This *isn't* how I envisaged my first kiss.

She yanks her fluffy skirt up around her waist and pushes down, grinding – or Beyoncé twerking – I can't decide which. It's immediately evident my tube sock is a better companion. My flag remains at half-mast. No mast, really. I thought alcohol was supposed to *improve* your chances of getting laid.

She grabs one of my hands and smacks it flat against her breast. Now, not only have I experienced my first kiss, but I've progressed to second base. I didn't anticipate things moving this fast; I thought there was a grace period. I lightly squeeze. It's not what I expected: a kind of sand-filled beanbag and I can't find the nipple. Am I supposed to? Perhaps I should accept my limitations and know there isn't anything I can do with incarcerated funbags. I could attempt to liberate them, but that's probably taking things too far in public. How far can we really go? Despite having consumed a bucketload of booze, I still have wits enough to know that I don't want to end up like Franz-the-Second, kicked out on my butt, the cops called to collect me.

She breathes fast. 'You're the best I've ever had.' She throws her head back like the women in the porn I watched. (Make that *researched*.) 'Oh god, you feel so good! You're so so so *sooooooo* good!' she squeals.

Now I *know* she's lying. I'm sitting on a chair doing little else other than being ridden like Phar Lap in the Melbourne Cup.

I look over her shoulder. Nobody's watching. We're in a dark corner and we have all our clothes on. People can't be arrested for simulated sex, can they?

She moans, riding, and I wonder where the finish line is. I don't have to wonder long. She gasps, 'Oh god, I'm going to ...' She stiffens, digs her nails into my shoulders, and with a final thrust and bounce of her hips, her whole body shudders.

She falls limp against me. 'You're amazing.'

'Thanks,' I squeak.

I'm not sure if I should tell her she's the best not-sex I've ever had. Maybe that's a backhanded compliment? To be honest, I feel a little shaken. Every coming-of-age story I've seen on the big screen or portrayed in books focuses on boys unloading too soon and girls getting no joy. Not this. Does this even qualify as a first time? Should I be concerned I didn't even leave the starter's block, let alone join her at the finish line?

'I've gotta get going,' she says, unsaddling herself and straightening her skirt. 'My boyfriend will be peeved if I don't get to his place soon.' She notes my stunned face. 'Oh, don't worry. We have an open relationship. At least, I told him we do after he got busy with Melanie Hogarth in the supermarket cool room.'

'Wait ...' I say, heart pounding. 'He's not here? His friends aren't here?' I look around in a frantic panic.

She smiles. 'Are you scared?'

'No. Yes. Maybe. How big is he?'

She giggles and bends down to kiss me. 'You're adorable. Thanks for the ride.' She leaves me there, staring at my Bundy and Coke.

Jackson appears, grabs a chair, swings it round, straddles it and takes a seat. This vision is too soon post not-coitus. A little bit of vomit comes up in my mouth.

'Hey, Mr Death. How's it hanging? What'd I miss?'

I stare straight ahead. 'My loss of innocence?'

He goes to high-five me. 'You got a peep at Bo Peep?'

'Is this how it feels after sex?'

'You had sex?'

'Is this how it feels?'

Jackson peels off his moustache and flicks it over his shoulder. 'What do you mean?'

'Is it ... anticlimactic?'

He scratches his head. 'Technically it can't be anticlimactic if you've climaxed.'

'On TV, people smoke afterwards.'

He nods. 'You want a cigarette?'

'A Chupa Chup maybe. Not strawberry. Too close to cranberry. Speaking of, where's Chip?'

'He's conducting *business*,' Jackson uses quotation fingers, 'in the Men's Room. I think he's been spreading the word about your website. I mean your Insta account. Whatever it is you're doing.'

'But they're supposed to be from the northern suburbs. That's false advertising.' Then I remember my parents. Then I drink more Bundy.

He shrugs. 'Do you have your postcode tattooed on your bum?'

An excellent but inconvenient point. 'Where's Chloe?' I say.

'You really want to know?'

'We should be keeping an eye on her, Jackson.'

'Why?'

'We're a team.' It slips out. I try to rephrase it. 'We should be working the buddy system.' *Fail. Again.*

'Is she looking out for you?'

I'm about to answer that loaded question when Chloe makes an appearance, minus her suffragette friend. 'You ready to get out of here?' she asks me sheepishly.

I'm kind of done with all things sheep-related.

'Where are we going?' Jackson asks. 'We didn't book anywhere to stay.'

'There are shelter sheds the other side of the footy oval,' Chloe says. 'We could crash there.' She grabs my hand and drags me from my seat. 'Taylor and I planned to take a walk on the beach first.'

'We did?' I don't recall this agreement. Bundy further impedes this memory from surfacing.

'You go on ahead,' Chloe says to Jackson. 'I know your granny has been taken care of.'

Jackson grimaces. 'Grandad was younger. Errol was too. She's always liked 'em that way.' He stands and straightens his beret. 'I'll go and rescue Chip. Or rescue his newfound friends. See you at the sheds.'

Chloe takes my hand and leads me through an obstacle course of tables, chairs, empty glasses, passed-out bodies, and one super depressed elephant. I wonder if we should stop to console him. Or summon David Attenborough.

'Where's Pipes? Did her drain get blocked?' It's not my finest joke. It's actually majorly pathetic. Drunk as I am, I have some comedic standards.

'She's gone back to her book. Reckons it's a better fit.'

'I didn't realise you were—'

'Bi? You didn't tell me you were into sheep-shagging.'

'You saw me?'

'I saw you getting cosy at the baaaaaaaar.'

I give an uncomfortable laugh. Hopefully that means she didn't see anything else. Wait. What was *she* doing all that time?

She stops to peel a sticky bit of paper from the heel of her shoe. 'Are you drunk?' she asks.

'Tanked, I think is the expression. You?'

'Smashed. Let's get out of here.'

We head into the cool night air, cross the empty carpark and make our way up the moonlit road. It's quiet, no one around. Either everyone has gone home or they're still at the club. I should be cold, but I don't feel it. There's a strange heat radiating throughout my body. I could attribute it to Bundy, but I think it's more because Chloe is still holding my hand.

She lets go.

I stagger behind her. In front of her. At her side. To the left. Off to the right. Over to a tree for a leak. Left. Right. Back at her side again.

'You're making me dizzy,' she says.

I do the Hokey-Pokey and I turn around.

'Your dance moves need work.'

I keep up, striding along, but I can't keep the green-eyed monster at bay. It leaves its cage without warning. 'Did you get with her?'

Chloe scowls. 'What business is it of yours?'

166

'Did you?'

She rolls her eyes. 'We kissed, okay?'

'And?'

'Nothing … exactly.' She stops in her tracks. A frustrated sweep of her hair and she adds, 'I'm not sure what happened. I'm not sure I got it right.'

It sounds as if things didn't go the way she expected, either.

'Tell me,' I say.

'Why?'

I don't admit it's because I like her and I want to know if I have half a chance. 'We're drunk. Now's the time to declare our deepest, darkest secrets.'

'You don't want to know my secrets.' She stalks off.

I chase her and grab her by her arm.

She shakes me off. 'What?'

I meet her steely gaze. 'You hardly know me,' I say. 'I barely know you. You're in my life for this trip and that's it. Like you said, in two thousand years from now, who's gunna care what you told me?'

She stands with her back to me, kicking at the gravel, drumming her fingers on her hips. 'Will you tell me yours?'

'My darkest secrets? Of course.'

She whips around, regarding me with suspicion. 'They can't be that bad if you can agree to talk about them so easily.'

I point to my head. 'Hello? *Drunk*. Drunkenness and oversharing go together. Also terrible dance moves.' I do the Hokey-Pokey again.

She smirks and looks at the sky. 'I'm not sure you can handle it.'

'Trust me. After tonight I can handle … Well, I can handle animal husbandry.'

We turn a corner and pass under a savagely bright streetlight, a million bugs buzzing overhead. A dog barks, gate rattling, making us both jump. We move quicker, vying for the forgiving cloak of darkness. I assume she knows where she's going so I blindly follow her. I'm tingling with anticipation. Maybe she'll not only tell me about Piper, but also her friend, the one who died.

'You only want to know about Piper because you think it will turn you on,' Chloe accuses. 'Boys are predictable.'

I feel a stirring in my pants. *Dammit.* Is this what attraction is? Love? 'That's not true,' I lie. 'You're upset. I want to help.' This *is* the truth.

She gives me a once-over. 'Fine. I'll tell you. But you have to walk alongside me and not look at me, okay?'

'Like a confessional?'

'Like a confessional.'

We walk and she says nothing. 'This isn't how confessionals work,' I say.

'Stop looking at me!' She keeps walking. Taking a deep breath, she says, 'Okay. Here goes. We went to those shelter sheds, the ones across the other side of the oval.'

'Uh-huh ...'

'We kissed. It was good. And then ...' She shakes her head, struggling to explain. 'Piper wanted to go further. I didn't. She was good about it, so we just sat and talked – about some pretty personal stuff. After a while I admitted something to her I've never told anyone.' She takes another big breath. 'I said I haven't ever ... you know ... got *there*.'

I'm not sure of what she means.

She blurts it out. 'I haven't ever successfully self-serviced.'

'Oh ...'

I get it now. Self-servicing is something I understand. Self-servicing, until now, has totally been my thing. I assume everyone does it, they just don't talk about it. I mean, it's not like you meet your friends at the bus stop at 8 am and when they ask you how your morning's been, you tell them you ate waffles, watched the news, argued with your parents, and jacked off twice in the shower before you left the house. You just shrug and say, *Yeah, it was fine.* I remember someone once saying that masturbation is like practise for the big game. I liked that. It made me feel less ashamed.

'Piper showed me how.'

I gulp. 'Showed you?'

'We didn't touch each other, only ourselves. We did it together until it happened.'

I don't know what to say. It seems like nothing in relation to sex is what I thought it would be and I feel a sudden surge of anger. What was Chip thinking, wanting to be part of the porn industry? Why do they flood the net with that shit? Isn't this the real stuff? The awkward, shitty, sticky, heartbreaking reality of it?

She looks at me, face crinkled. 'I shouldn't have told you.'

'No, no. It's okay.'

'Really?'

'Yeah. It's fine. I get it. More than you know.'

She blushes. 'I didn't know it could feel that good. I didn't know I could make *myself* feel that good.'

'So what happened after? Did you argue?'

'Piper wanted to do more and I wasn't into it. I didn't think girls pressured girls. I thought it – that *being with girls* – was a safe space.'

'I think people pressure people, period.'

She smiles. Then she gathers herself and says, 'Okay, now it's your turn. I told you mine. Tell me yours.'

Perhaps it's the amount of Bundy I've consumed, or it's the intimacy of the moment, but I say without hesitation, 'I've never kissed anyone before tonight.'

She stares. 'Never?'

'Never done anything.'

'Until tonight?'

'Until Bo Peep.'

'Oh.' She sounds disappointed. 'What happened?'

I feel my cheeks flood. 'The usual casual hook-up, I think. She attempted to rip my lips from my face and rode me like I was Phar Lap.'

'Phar Lap?'

'Famous horse. Stuffed and in a glass box in the Melbourne Museum, I believe.'

'So you didn't—?'

'No. Clothing, as it turns out, is a highly effective barrier. Better than a condom.'

'And you didn't—?'

'Get aroused? You mean, did it happen for me like it happened for you?'

She nods.

'Major anticlimax.'

'Riiiiiiight.'

I smile. 'I'm starting to think that's what everyone says after sex. *Riiiiight.*'

'Um, would we call it sex?'

'Would you call *yours* sex?'

She bites her lip. 'I'd call it a sexual act.'

'Do you think I'm a loser virgin?' I hold my breath.

She takes my hand. 'It's not a bad thing, Taylor. I'm one too.'

I can't believe it. 'You are?'

She nods. With a lopsided grin she says, 'Come on. Let's go to the beach, lie on the sand.'

'Sort of Mondo Rock lyrics, except it was the boy saying it, not the girl.'

She laughs. 'I actually know that song. My aunt plays it. "Come Said The Boy".'

'It's an Aussie anthem.' I'm quoting Dad here.

She squeezes my hand. 'You're okay, Taylor. You know that?'

I thread my fingers through hers. 'You're not thinking we should remedy the situation, are you? Cos that's kind of gross on the same night. I'd feel like a bit of a tart.' But a small part of me is hopeful.

'Relax,' she laughs. 'I'm not a fan of crotch sand.'

'Yeah. No. Me either.'

She reads my disappointment. 'Oh, that's right. You didn't get to—'

'I had an invitation, didn't make it to the party.'

'There'll be other parties, Taylor.'

'I hope so.'

Hand in hand, we head for the beach, my drunken heart beating with hope.

# CHAPTER EIGHTEEN

We lie on a bed of damp sand, the dark starlit sky our ceiling. A gentle sea breeze strokes my skin. Salty air fills my nostrils and I taste rum on my tongue. Rum seems fitting for a shipwrecked pirate marooned on an island with a sassy wench. Maybe I should get dreadlocks. Wear black eyeliner. Grow my nails long. Adopt a parrot.

The rhythmic swish and slap of the ocean is our background music. I roll nearer and sneak a peek at Chloe's silhouette, filled with wonder that I, Taylor-inexperienced-except-a-nursery-rhyme-lap-dance-Kennedy, am in the dead of night *and* in a clichéd romantic setting, alone with a girl. A real-life girl. And a beautiful one.

I roll onto my back. 'Doubt thou the stars are fire—'

'You're not quoting me Shakespeare, are you?'

*She knows Shakespeare?* There's that stirring in my pants again.

'That's cheeseburger with extra cheese, Taylor.'

'My bad. I didn't know you're lactose intolerant.'

She snorts.

After a moment's consideration, I say, 'If thou can't recite

Shakespeare to thy lady, what would impress? I have an awesome repertoire of fart jokes.'

'What kind?'

'*What kind?*'

She stifles a giggle. 'Do you know girls can fanny fart?'

This is a topic I've not previously discussed – *with anyone*.

I readily embrace it. 'Actually, I *had* heard that. Not an actual fanny fart, of course, as I imagine one has to be within close proximity *and* have it declared an official fanny fart, lest it be confused with the common bum fart. But I have heard of fanny farts and I must say it's good to have their existence confirmed. I'd started to wonder if they were one of those *tree falling in the woods* scenarios – if you don't witness it, does it really happen?'

She dons a schoolmistress persona. 'There are two types known to womankind. First, where air has been pumped inside – use your imagination – and the other kind. The kind which requires a primary source.'

I'm genuinely invested now. 'Do educate me.'

'First you have to be seated. This is a must. Picture me in class, unable to get the teacher's attention and be excused for the bathroom. By now I've already bravely bum-swallowed a succession of farts.'

'Ah. Bum swallowing.' I nod emphatically. 'Those farts you can't freely emit so you hold them in. They internally dissipate, providing momentary relief, but it's an empty promise. They go off, gather strength, redistribute, and return as a suppressed shit-storm with twice the vengeance.'

She laughs. 'So eventually you have to let one go, right? If you're lucky, a silent one. But with a seated barrier, anatomically it has nowhere to go. It must follow the female escape route trajectory.'

'Of course ...'

'When it finally bursts, it flaps the ... erm ... *flaps*. Sometimes with an audible *pop!*'

'Incredible.'

'Yep.'

'Well that certainly leaves dick farts for dead.'

She blinks. 'You can *dick* fart?'

'No, not that I'm aware of. Not enough sheeting. Further stymied if you've been circumvented.'

'Circumcised.'

'That's what I meant. When you think about it, the humble dick really is a useless conduit.'

'Meanwhile vaginas can stretch around a baby's head and snap back to size,' she says. 'Tell me why history deemed us the fairer sex? The shit women's bodies can do is impressive. Think milk, for example.'

'I'd rather not.'

'Cos boobs are playthings?'

'"Milkshake" was a popular song for many reasons.'

She slaps my arm. 'Milkshake?'

'You know. That old song about bringing all the boys to the yard.' I wiggle my torso at her. She makes a face.

'I like milkshakes,' I say. 'Vanilla is my favourite.'

'You were probably breastfed.'

It's not something I've thought to ask. Also, a mental image of Chip's recent Insta acquisition reminds me that I'm pretty sure I don't want to know.

'I wasn't,' Chloe says. 'Guess that's why I have no connection.

I didn't bond. My mother had postnatal depression and my grandmother took care of me for my first couple of years.'

'Do you want to tell me about that?'

'About my family? What's to tell? They're terrible people. I'm the runt of the litter left to die in the woods. It's a wonder they didn't eat me.'

'It's widely speculated by zoologists that parents who eat their young do it for the nutritional value,' I volunteer.

'Guess I don't even have that.'

'I'd eat you. You look tasty to me.'

She punches my shoulder. I notice she's touching me a lot. 'You don't give up, do you?' she says.

'Thanks to Bundy? No.'

'Bundy is urban slang for a boy's boner he's trying to hide.'

I roll onto my front, propping myself on my elbows.

She laughs again. The sound is magical. It lights up every cell in my body. I imagine myself on a CT scan, glowing like the nightlights of the fishing harbour. I want to stay in this moment – her smiling at me, relaxed and comfortable, and me watching her. I'd watch her for millennia.

She stares at the sky. It seems like minutes go by before she says, 'I wonder which star she is?' She glances at my confused face and adds, 'My best friend. It's what I tell myself. Better her up there than in the ground.'

I wait, but she doesn't say anything else. I reassure her, 'Chloe. We're drunk, remember? After what you told me earlier, plus schooling me on the intricacies of fanny farts, I'm not sure there's anything left that will shock me. Well, except if you told me you were into collecting belly button fluff. But apart from that.'

'What's wrong with that?'

I shudder. 'It's unhygienic. And mega weird. There's an Australian librarian called Graham Baker who harvests his own fluff and keeps it in a jar. He's in the *Guinness Book of Records*. True story.'

'I *knew* librarians were dodgy.'

'He plans to knit a jumper. Actually, I'm not sure if that part is accurate, but if it is, it's the ultimate recycling operation. Kudos to him. Saving the planet one hairball at a time. I'm thinking of doing a similar thing but with ear wax. I could make candles.'

'Entrepreneurial.'

'Or bikini wax. I'm keeping my options open.'

She shakes her head, amused.

'So are you going to tell me about your friend or not?'

Without losing eye contact she says, 'I killed her.'

'Yes, we agreed on that. With the pickaxe.'

'Can you be serious?' She bites her nails and searches my face like she's trying to see through me; see deep within, right down to my core. *Can she trust me?* 'You promise you'll never tell anyone, Taylor? If you meet someone in the future, someone who knows me or who knew my best friend, you'll never say anything?'

'I swear. In two thousand years from now, no one will know.'

She grasps my hand and squeezes it. 'Okay.' She inhales deeply. 'I slept over at her house the night before she did it. You know what I told you about Piper?'

'Yeah?'

'Well, the night I slept over, my friend confessed she'd been in love with me for two years.'

I don't know what to say. 'Shit. That's ... *Wow*.'

'I had to say I didn't feel that way about her.'

'Oh … that's tough. For both of you.'

'She started crying. She accused me of not being honest. She said I led her on. We had this massive argument where we blamed each other, then she blamed herself, then I blamed myself, and then everything we said to each other from there just caused more and more hurt until she said she never should've told me; that in doing so she'd lost me for good. But she hadn't. She hadn't lost me at all.'

She's crying hard now. I squeeze her hand and wrap my other hand around it. She sobs and gasps like she's been holding this inside her for a lifetime. It rushes out, a burst dam, no way of stemming it or stopping the flow. 'I tried to tell her we could still be friends. I could've got past it, Taylor. *We* could've got past it. We could've stayed friends, couldn't we?'

I draw her into my arms and hold her. I don't know the answer to that. Can you be *just friends* with someone you're in love with?

What I do know is that this isn't Chloe's fault. It's a shitty situation with no winners. And it's not her friend's fault either. The heart wants what it wants – that much I'm coming to learn. I'd said things on Kelly Nixon's Facebook page; things about not waiting until tomorrow to say you love someone, things about telling the truth, about gutless people who only share their true feelings after someone is dead. But here was a story of someone who'd taken a chance when they were alive – a girl who'd told her friend the truth of her heart.

Why is it I think these things are simple? Love – *and sex* – is more complicated than I ever imagined. I'd judged people in Kelly's life, saying things online with complete conviction, with no idea how complex it could potentially be. How could I think it wasn't? No wonder people hated me for it.

I stroke her hair and whisper, 'You weren't to know how badly she'd take it.'

'What if I'd gone along with it for a little while and *then* let her down?' Chloe suggests. 'Maybe she could've handled that? Maybe it wouldn't have felt as bad for her?' She sobs into my chest. 'I miss her, Taylor! I'm so angry! Couldn't I have loved her like she wanted me to?'

'You can't force yourself to feel what you don't feel, Chloe. You were honest. You didn't lie. Someone you love deserves the truth. You gave her *your* truth.'

'And she gave me hers. What did I do with it? I fucked it up.' She shudders, breaking down again. 'I don't know how to go on without her. Kelly was everything to me.'

*Bang!*

Someone straight-up shot me. My mind rushes back to the moment in the car where Chloe said she visits Bill's Takeaway. She lives locally. I don't have to ask her friend's last name.

Fuck. Fuck, fuck, fuckety fuck.

I, Taylor Kennedy, had been one of those people making public judgements about something I know nothing about – about a girl I'm now falling for.

'Stay?' Chloe whispers, snuggling into me.

I let her bury her head in my chest. 'I'm not going anywhere,' I say.

Until she makes the connection that I'm an absolute out-of-this-world arsehole and she kicks me from here to next Tuesday.

# CHAPTER NINETEEN

I wake with seaweed stuck to my face. Seawater slapping my feet. Sandflies biting my legs. I'm being environmentally assaulted.

The roar of the ocean is no match for the roaring in my head. It feels like I slammed my skull into a brick wall fifty times in a row.

Chloe is sleeping on her side, her head resting on prayer hands. I have a sudden vision of that black-and-white movie *Here to Eternity*, passionate lovers locked in a steamy embrace on the beach, oblivious to the surf rolling over them. I want to wake her with a kiss, but that would mean waking her to the fact that the boy next to her is the *same* boy who vented online about her best friend. (You didn't sing about *that*, Mondo Rock.)

Chloe knows my full name. How can she not have made the connection? My Facebook profile *is* my name. The only logical explanation (outside of alcoholic impairment) is that she doesn't have an account. A teenager not on social media? Now there's a revolutionary act.

She stirs, rubbing her eyes, shielding them from the sun. 'Hey you.' She smiles. 'What time is it?'

In my pocket, Geoff's phone is dead. I hold out a finger and squint at the sky. 'Judging by the sun's positioning, I'm guessing it's eight am?'

She sits up. 'Are you a boy scout now?'

'Nah. Boy scouts are good. I'm a bad boy. I'm Mr Death.' But by mentioning death I've stuck my foot in it. I've reminded her about last night's conversation. *Shit*.

'It's okay,' she says, reading my discomfort. 'I don't want this to be one of those *regret the night before* things. I'm not ashamed of what I told you.'

Maybe she doesn't have any regrets, but I do.

'You should be ashamed,' I tell her. 'Fanny farts are a taboo subject.'

I grin with the full knowledge I'm a right prick. Everything I say from now on makes me a liar. I'm keeping a piece of the puzzle from her. Omitting crucial information is as good as being a liar, isn't it? I'd like to say I'm protecting Chloe, but I know who I'm really protecting.

Chloe senses something's wrong. 'What is it?'

'Nothing. We should get going.' I get up and make my way up the beach. 'We'll go to the mechanic's. The others are probably waiting there.'

We trudge through the sand, up to the road. She picks seaweed from her hair, then from mine. She reaches out to clasp my hand, smiling at me. I look down at our interlocked fingers and feel that wonder again; that amazement I'm hanging out with a girl – one who's clearly into me. Then I see the love heart on her wrist and wonder if it has something to do with Kelly?

She sees me looking and untwines herself. 'I got this,' she says, pointing to the tattoo, 'to remind me to be kind to myself.'

She lifts her hair and points to the one behind her ear. 'And this one is to guard against evil whispers.'

'Do they work?'

She taps her chest. 'I wish I could put a tattoo on what's in here.'

It's a beautiful idea – one that makes *my* heart swell so big I want to turn and kiss her and never let her go.

'I think it's why we let others in,' she says. 'So they'll write on it for us.'

My thumping heart skips faster. 'I can do *very* impressive things with a Sharpie.'

'You can draw?'

'I wouldn't call it drawing. Scribble is a better description. You're looking at the toilet-rating pioneer of Middleborough High.'

A peal of laughter. 'I heard about that! The Full Dump on the Full Dump. That was you?'

I nod. 'Who knew restaurant-like lavatory reviews would catch on? My only failing is I didn't patent the five-turd rating. Or start the Insta account.'

'Someone at my school copied you, but they used tampon icons instead.'

'Well that's sticking it up them.'

We crack up. She whacks my arm. I whack hers. She shoves me. I shove her. She throws an arm over my shoulder and we keep walking.

And despite my guilt I feel so bloody happy. I wonder if there's a chance I can get away with what I've done; if she'll never find out what I wrote. We can move on, fall madly in love, get married, apply for a joint loan, buy a slice of land in an overpriced housing estate, pop out two-point-five kids, gain an average of twenty kilos, binge-watch Netflix every night, complain about our shitty desk jobs, and turn old and grey while living happily ever after in nauseating domestic bliss.

But lies are like cancer – they eat at your core. I'm already a gutted cadaver on a chopping block waiting for the axe to finish the job. She just doesn't know it.

Hey. No one said I have to come clean immediately. I can put off the truth a little longer. Just as long as I eventually *do* fess up. That's the main thing, right? Emphasis on the *eventually*.

Shit. Who am I kidding?

We find the others waiting outside the mechanic's. The hearse is parked in a bay, ready to go. The backpack with the gun is resting on the back seat. Full points to Chip for looking after them. He manages to get some things right.

Daisy has swapped her aviator sunnies for a red-and-white footy scarf. It's wrapped around her head like she's about to go Sahara desert-hopping. I'm going to ask, but she volunteers, 'I can't afford to be seen.' *Now* she says that. 'I snuck out before dawn. He proposed last night and I said yes.' She glances at Jackson's shocked expression. 'What? You would've too if you'd seen his abs.'

Chip asks me, 'Do you think *this* qualifies as gerontophilia?'

'Not if she's the instigator.'

Jackson opens the car door for her. 'Get in, Granny.'

Chip gives me and Chloe the once-over. Recognition flashes like he knows we spent the night together. I can tell he's about to make some smartarse remark, but something stops him. Instead he says, 'I met with the police.'

It's a good thing Daisy's already in the car because the rest of us suffer a collective coronary.

'*What?*' we all say.

'That chick in the sergeant's outfit.' It takes a moment for the penny to drop. He's talking about the girl from the fancy-dress party – the one I saw during the fight. My muscles relax so fast I almost fart. 'Seriously arresting,' he adds.

'You're such a tool,' Jackson grumbles, getting into the hearse. 'Let's get out of here.'

We get in and resume our positions: me in the front seat, the others in the back. Chip fires up the engine. The hearse purrs. For a death-mobile, it sounds pretty healthy. Points to the mechanic. I wonder if he offloaded the grease from his nose. Maybe it's his secret to automotive success.

Chip pulls onto the main road. I find my phone and plug it into the car charger. After a few bars, notifications appear. Geoff Messages. I spy something about spaghetti, which admittedly piques my interest, but I resist the urge to further investigate. I don't have the patience or the inclination right now.

As we turn onto the highway, Daisy sticks her earphones in and begins humming to the music. About a kilometre past the green Millicent road sign, Chip says to no one in particular, 'How do you know that?'

I've come to recognise these red flags – a visitation is upon us.

'Sure,' he adds. 'I see.'

'Lily?' I ask.

Emphatic headshake.

'Barry?'

'Nope.'

'Who?'

'Edgar.'

'Have we met Edgar?'

Chip holds up a finger. He listens intently, then says, 'Look. We've talked about this before, Edgar. I agree Lily and Barry are big personalities and it's hard to get a word in, but that doesn't mean you can't own your place.' He nods a few more times. 'Sure, sure. Well now that you have the floor, say what it is you want to say.' He listens again. 'Okay, I see. Gotcha.'

Chloe entertains him. 'What is it?'

Chip says, 'Edgar reckons Errol isn't worth it.'

'Sorry?'

'Edgar says he knows Errol. He says the trip to Mount Gambier is a mistake.'

'And you needed Edgar to tell you that?' I look at Jackson. 'Do you know what he's talking about?'

Jackson rolls his eyes. 'No.'

Chip listens again. 'The Es,' he says.

'The what?'

'Edgar. Errol. Ernie. Eugene. Ewan. The Es. It's a celestial categorisation thing. A cluster. They take note of each other.'

'But Errol's not dead.' I look at Daisy. Her eyes are closed, lost in the music. I turn back to Chip. 'Fine. Tell us about Edgar. No doubt you're going to anyway.'

'Ah, Edgar's tale is a *very* unfortunate one,' Chip says, his voice filled with sympathy. 'Ice-cream is supposed to invoke happy memories. Colourful candy sprinkles. Choc topping. Sticky sweet fingers. Long summer days. Stripy beach umbrellas—'

'Why do I feel a Cold Day In June story coming on?'

'It was a hot day in February, actually,' Chip says crisply, 'when Edgar unwittingly drove his ice-cream van into the wrong territory.'

Chloe snorts. 'Where was he? The Bronx?'

'Semaphore foreshore, Adelaide,' Chip says. 'Edgar was unaware that the area had already been spoken for. In hindsight, he admits the telltale *Greensleeves* melody should've been a giveaway, but he wasn't really wholly present at the office that day owing to what had happened that morning.'

'What *had* happened?' Chloe asks.

'His wife had packed her bags and left him.' He says the next bit with abject horror. 'For their pool cleaning guy!'

I swear I hear a digital *Dop-Dom!*

'Ouch.' Chloe winces.

'Ouch indeed,' Chip says. 'Anyway, to his credit, Edgar was getting on with business, doing a roaring trade selling Bubble O'Bills, Golden Gaytimes and milkshakes by the bucketload, unaware that the other vendor, Peter Streets, didn't take too kindly to the competition. Peter got—'

'Wait a sec,' I interrupt. 'Peter Streets?'

Chip laughs. 'Yes, Edgar and I have already conferred over this bizarre little nugget.'

Jackson doesn't follow. 'Huh?'

'Aptronym,' I say. 'When a person's name strangely matches their occupation. Also referred to as nominative determinism.'

'Like Usain Bolt being a runner?' Jackson asks.

'Or William Wordsworth being a writer?' Chloe suggests.

'Yes,' I say. 'Margaret Court, controversial Australian tennis star, is another who springs to mind.'

Chip is annoyed. 'You're hijacking my story, Taylor.'

'Oh. Sorry. Beg your pardon. Do go on.'

'So Peter Streets marched up to Edgar's van and told him to get the hell out of there or he'd do things with a Cornetto that Edgar would live to regret.'

'Cornettos *are* pointy,' Jackson says.

'Edgar, having already had a crap start to the day, didn't take kindly to being told what to do. He decided to stand his ground. He threw the first punch, metaphorically speaking, by scooping the contents of a Dixie cup and lobbing it into Peter's eye.'

'I like Dixie cups,' Jackson notes. 'They're so cute and bite-sized.'

'Anyway,' Chip says. 'It was a mistake. Peter marched off, jumped in his van – which *did* have a massive fibreglass Cornetto on top – and he drove up and rear-ended Edgar. Edgar had recently let his insurance lapse so he decided to cut his losses and bail before he was publicly butt-fucked by a giant Cornetto. But Peter Streets wasn't done. Peter, enraged *and* riding a potent sugar high – he was renowned for eating his own stock – gave chase.'

'Streets took to the streets,' I say.

'Yes. And he rammed Edgar again. That's when the refrigerated ice-chest in the back of the van dislodged, toppled over and chlorofluorocarbon vapours began leaking through the cabin.'

'CFCs,' Chloe contributes. 'The stuff that caused the hole in the ozone layer.'

'Indeed,' Chip says. 'Under a growing CFC cloud, Edgar became dizzy and disoriented. He drove a surprising distance before passing out at the wheel. The van careered into a Macca's Drive-Thru. Maccas had only recently started serving thirty cent soft-serve, potentially putting Edgar out of business anyway, so it was a cruel irony.'

'Maccas took out the competition,' Jackson tsk-tsks. 'So unlike them.'

'Actually, it was by Edgar's own hand. Or by his ice-cream,

rather. The collision roused him and he pulled himself up from the driver's seat and staggered through the van, opening the doors to life-giving oxygen, but as he did, he slipped on melted ice-cream and milkshake-milk and tumbled headfirst into the concrete, cracking his skull.'

'So there *is* a point to crying over spilt milk,' I say.

'CFCs put holes in people's *heads* too,' Chloe says.

'Take what you want from Edgar's demise,' Chip says. 'Not every story has a moral.'

I rebuff in a cutesy voice, 'No, cos it's all about the *journey*.'

'I think it's a cautionary tale about the dangers of transporting deadly chemicals,' Jackson offers.

'Well,' I say. 'That sucks fat Magnums for Edgar. But coming back to Errol. What's the deal?'

'Ah! Edgar says that Errol isn't worth the hassle.'

'But *why*?'

'He didn't elaborate.'

'You mean we just went through an epic ice-cream saga turf war and now you're telling me Edgar isn't going to explain?!'

Chip listens for a moment. 'Edgar says if that if you can't take him at his word, he's disinclined to further engage.'

'What?'

Jackson translates, 'He's middle-fingering you.'

'I thought you couldn't see them?' I say to Chip.

'I can't,' Chip says calmly. 'Edgar's response *is* the middle finger. He's giving you his digitus medius.'

'His what?'

'Digitus medius,' Chip says. 'The anatomical term for the middle finger.'

'Well screw you with your digitus medius, Edgar!' I say loudly.

'You're dead. I'm alive. How do you like dem ice-creams?'

'Urgh! So insensitive!' Chip cries. 'I'm not listening to you anymore, Taylor. You're being unreasonable. It's the time-out corner for you, my friend.'

He starts singing a weird song about a Flying Purple People Eater. He does it at the top of his lungs. He'd promised me I'd get to hear it and now I am. He sings the 'one-eyed' bit really pronounced and looks over at me, glaring.

'Keep your eyes on the road!' I yell.

Daisy removes her earphones. 'What's all the ruckus about? And why are you singing that insipid out-of-the-ark song?'

Chip stops singing. 'There was one-eyedness going on.'

'Speak the Queen's English!' Daisy barks.

'Taylor is being a douchebag,' Chip says.

I get a banana-flavoured Chupa Chup from the glovebox, peel it at record speed and shove it in Chip's cakehole. 'Apparently your Errol isn't worth the trip,' I tell Daisy.

'Says who?'

'Says Edgar.'

'Who the fuck is Edgar?' she bleats.

'Former ice-cream peddler and jilted lover,' Chloe explains. 'He reckons we shouldn't be making this trip.'

Daisy looks at us all in turn like we're completely mad. 'Errol *is* worth the trip. Trust me. He deserves to see me again.' She traces the withered wizard tattoo on her arm. 'Did I tell you how I got this?'

'No,' I say. 'But if you start by telling me it was a cold day in June or a hot day in February, I'm going to leap from this moving vehicle.'

'Stop being so dramatic,' Chip says.

'Actually,' Daisy says, 'it was a dark and stormy night ...'

'Oh, for the love of—!'

'It was a dark and stormy night in early December,' Daisy says. 'Errol had just finished making love to me for the fourth time.'

'Granny!' Jackson freaks.

She hands him the earphones. 'Be my guest.'

He shoves them in his ears and turns away.

'As I said, Errol had just finished—'

'We get the picture, Daisy,' Chloe says. 'Continue.'

'We were laying there having a smoke—'

'I knew it!' I blurt. 'Oh. Sorry. Go on ...'

'—when Errol said we should do something crazy. Something spontaneous. Something YOLO.'

Chloe blinks. 'You know what YOLO means?'

'Errol said we should go see Chris Hemsworth and get a tattoo.'

'Chris—?' Chloe starts.

'Not *the* Chris Hemsworth,' Daisy says. 'Another one. He worked out the back of a butcher's shop. Errol said he owed him. By that stage I'd taken three pharmaceutical Quaaludes so I was up for anything.'

Chloe looks questioningly at her.

'Muscle relaxants,' Chip explains. 'Banned from the market after widespread recreational abuse. Hugh Hefner probably did, like, three billion of them.'

'Led Zeppelin were big at the time,' Daisy says. 'I wanted some trippy Tolkien fairies floating in an airship. Errol said that was doable. We braved the wind and the rain and took a cab to Meat Treats. Chris was in his usual spot out back putting the finishing touches on an awe-inspiring carpet python curled across a woman's abdomen. When he was done, the chick left, and we joined him for a few tokes on the magical flute. I told him what I wanted and he was good to go. I lay back and got my first tattoo. It wasn't even painful. It was a pleasant experience. When Chris finished, he handed me a mirror. I sat up, looked at my left hip and couldn't believe my eyes.'

'Hang on,' I say. 'I thought you were talking about your arm?'

'This,' she says, pointing at the wizard, 'came later. This was the replacement one.'

'The replacement?'

'Yes. Chris was hard of hearing from all the meat band-sawing next door,' Daisy says. 'Instead of fairy airship, he thought I'd said *hairy bear shit*.' She shrugs. 'Hey, maybe I did. Maybe it was the 'Ludes talking.' She twists herself sideways and pulls down her elasticated jeans to reveal a faded, wrinkly Winnie the Pooh crouched down, taking a dump. Eeyore stands by, covering his mouth in shock.

I almost wet myself. Chip snorts then gasps so hard he inhales his banana Chupa Chup. I thump his back to dislodge it as we zigzag across the road. Chloe's laughing so much, she's wheezing.

Jackson pulls the earphones out. 'Are you done now, Granny?'

When we pull ourselves together, I turn to see Daisy reaching for Chloe's arm. She rubs her thumb across Chloe's love-heart tattoo.

'Every tattoo has a story.' Her thumb moves slowly, working its way across Chloe's wrist. 'Some of us wear our hearts on our sleeves, others keep theirs under wraps. Don't let it fool you. Both bleed exactly the same.' She runs her hand up and down

Chloe's arm, gently stroking it. 'Hurt is by design, my dear. It's to remind us we're alive. If you're not hurting, you haven't been living.' She lets go and leans back into her seat. 'When I was younger, we were expected to be tough, to keep stuff private, to keep a stiff upper lip. It's why I did enough drugs in the sixties to kill a herd of pygmy hippos. But the days of shame are gone and I'm glad to say I lived long enough to see them.' She pats Chloe's leg. 'Remember, dear, talking to someone you trust is as good a drug as any.'

Chloe looks at her, tears shining. Then she looks at me, a smile curling her lips. Her face says it all. *You're my confidant, Taylor. You're someone I trust.*

I smile back, but inside I feel like an even bigger prick than I did before.

# CHAPTER TWENTY

With nothing but bare paddocks, the odd stray sheep and hundreds of kilometres of barbed-wire fence rolling by, I brave Geoff's text messages – all of which are from a disgruntled partner. Jilted lovers must be the order of the day. (You're in good company, Edgar.) It's probably more common than I think. A global epidemic. I know *I'm* not a jilted lover per se, but I *am* a jilted friend. And when it comes to Chloe, it's definitely on the cards.

**You're** [sic] **dick is like limp spaghetti.** That explains the spaghetti I saw earlier. Also, people who don't know the difference between *you're* and *your*? I'm with you on this one, Geoff. You can do better. **You couldn't find your hose if your ass was on fire.** American spelling of *arse*. What do donkeys and mules have to do with it? I'm further offended. **In what relm** [sic] **is buying homebrand chocolate over Lindt Lindor Selection Box acceptable?** Maybe he should've gifted you a dictionary, sweetheart. **I'd rather have root anal.** I think that's *root canal* – talk about typo of the century. **Why don't you answer me?** Cos you get more flies with honey, Honey? **Call me. We can talk this out.** Ending on a conciliatory note.

Too little, too late, I might've thought, but who am I to judge? Perhaps Geoff finds this behaviour endearing. For all I know, he might enjoy an illiterate text-bashing.

I get the impression these messages are fresh data. Not sure what's going on here, but it's obvious Geoff has only recently retired his SIM. Could he be dead? A dire leap I know, and for Geoff's sake I hope not, but it *is* a possibility I can't rule out. Maybe I should check with Edgar? But Geoff being a G, a couple of celestial letter categories over, they might not know each other.

The interesting thing is, now that I'm Geoff's unofficial personal assistant, I get more correspondence than I ever did. It's uplifting. Like likes on a post – you get a little buzz. But my Kelly Nixon Facebook post made me feel the reverse: I suffered a manic meltdown, cowering under my sheets with cortisol stress hormones shitting all over my dopamine. For some of us, social media only produces anxiety. I can't even count the number of times I've agonised over a post, drafted it, overthought it, redrafted, perfected it and ultimately deleted it. (Why I didn't do that with Kelly's, I'll never know.) I wonder as to the worldwide energy spent on this exercise, all the problems that could be solved if we redirected our brainpower. We could've tackled global warming, cured cancer, found Bigfoot. Explained the parliamentary enigma that is Barnaby Joyce. Changed the date. Converted to genderless toilet blocks.

As I empty Geoff's text cache, I wonder if Cass has contacted me. I *did* send Cass a message right before my phone shit itself. Has she responded? My phone could be lighting up in Fone Wizards' drawer right now, pinging a string of apologies – if it had a SIM, which it doesn't. On one level I have to admit it's good *not* to know. That way I can invest the expertly cultivated self-deception I've come to rely upon. I wonder if Mum or Dad have tried? Whipped cream, half-naked headless photos suggest not. The roller-door extravaganza conference must be a raging success. Dad's dopamine levels are clearly off the charts. He's probably parked his car more than once.

*Ew! Scratch that unholy thought! Focus!*

I just need to survive this trip. After that, life can go back to normal. Once we reach Millicent, we have roughly half an hour's drive to Mount Gambier. When we arrive, we can visit Errol and Daisy can say her goodbyes. We can turn around and go home, mission accomplished. Theoretically we can do all that today and we can *still* make it back to Adelaide by tonight. The end of the tunnel is in sight.

*Chloe.*

All she'd wanted was a ride to Mount Gambier. She hadn't said where she was going after that. By this afternoon she'll be out of my life for good. Were the police after her? Had someone declared her missing? Had they identified her on the service station security footage? Put out an APB? (I still don't know what that means.) It doesn't make sense for her to go back to Adelaide. She's probably a wanted woman. *My* wanted woman. Why hadn't I thought of that until now?

And what about Jackson? What will happen to him? If he hands himself in to the authorities like he promised, how will he be punished? He seems a really decent guy. (For the most part, anyway.) Seeing him penalised – for doing nothing more than loving his grandmother and trying to respect her dying wish – doesn't seem fair.

Part of me has become complacent. We've got this far. We

haven't suffered any genuinely close calls other than a roadside breatho and a bare-bottomed police officer. I'm comfortable with my surrounds. *Dependent*. It's possible I've developed what they used to call Stockholm Syndrome: an unhealthy attachment to my captor. Make that *captors*. Actually, I still haven't figured out what's going on. Strange how quickly we adapt and form emotional attachments. How we make fast friends or fall in love.

*Chloe*. I'm not ready to say goodbye.

'We must be getting submissions,' Chip says, rousing me from my thoughts.

'Huh?'

He taps his pocket. 'Good vibrations. I'd take a peek, but those *Don't text and drive* ads scare the bejesus out of me. Have you seen the one where the tree branch goes through the woman's windscreen and into her groin?' He shudders. 'I get it that they have to shock us, but skewered bodies and chunky brain matter? Why'd they have to go *there*?'

It *is* an unsettling image. It spawns an idea. 'Hey Chip. Have you noticed something about Barry, Lily and Edgar?'

'What?'

'They all died in road accidents.'

He gives me a Robert De Niro lippy head-nod. 'I hadn't before made that connection.'

'Technically Barry's was a runway,' I say, 'but whatever.'

'Both are asphalt surfaces,' Chip agrees.

'Maybe that's why they haunt a hearse? Intended purpose aside, it *is* a vehicle.'

Chip ponders this. 'I dunno. Would you put yourself in a triggering situation?'

'What about the others?'

'Huh?'

'You mentioned others. Joelene and Richard, wasn't it? You said they were main ones who visit. How'd they die? Bus? Motorbike? Spare me the extended version and skip straight to the gory end.'

Behind us, Jackson launches into a boppy rendition of Dolly Parton's 'Joelene'. He sings it loud, slapping his thighs.

'Don't do that!' Chip freaks. He bashes the driver's door with a fisted hand, punctuating his panic.

His reaction is so intense, I jump, hitting the roof – if you're tall and in a confined car space, that's totally achievable.

Chip slams his foot on the brake. At 100 km an hour, it's a bad move. We snake over the road, barely missing a honking Landcruiser, then a red Holden Commodore covered in bright yellow *Close the Mines* stickers (the fact that I can read what they say shows that in a moment of life-threatening peril, things *really do* go into slow-mo), and we narrowly dodge an oncoming forestry truck lugging logs.

I dig my nails into the seat, my life flashing before me – mostly the embarrassing bits.

Jackson stops singing. 'What'd I do?'

Chip releases the brake and accelerates, righting the hearse.

We coast along in silence for at least half a minute before Chloe lurches forward and belts Chip's headrest. 'What the hell, Chip?'

'Yeah, what the hell?' Daisy echoes. 'I might be on my way out, but I don't want to go that quick!'

Chip takes a breath. He enunciates each word carefully.

'Just don't. Whatever you do. Sing that song. *Again*.' It's an apocalyptic warning.

He drives on, clutching the steering wheel, shoulders tense, expression grave. Eventually he adds, 'You're messing with powers you know nothing about.'

'Jackson was celebrating a country music great,' I say. 'You make it sound like a deliberate attack.'

'Joelene won't see it that way,' Chip warns.

'Dare I ask why?'

'No! It's a sensitive topic!' Chip snaps. 'That's the end of it.'

We travel on in silence. I half expect him to come out with more, but he doesn't. Finally I venture, 'You didn't tell me how they died.'

Chip sighs. 'Richard passed away in a bank hold-up.'

'Oh.'

'But he was in an armoured vehicle at the time. Points to you, Taylor. Your theory stands.'

'And Joelene?'

From pressed lips, he mumbles something I can't make out.

'I can't hear you.'

Clearer this time. 'Clown car.'

'Say what?'

'You know those ones where your feet run along the ground? Some have pedals.'

'I'm not even going to ask.'

'Wise choice,' says Chip.

'So what you're saying is: they did in fact all die in motorised accidents of one kind or another.'

'Indeed.'

'Why doesn't Heathfield Smart hang around then?' I ask.

'Who?'

'The one in the accident with Uncle Roger. He slingshotted out the back.'

'He was already dead, Taylor. He can't die twice.'

'Oh.'

'Why do you keep trying to find holes in my story?' Chip asks, evidently hurt. 'I don't do that to you. I don't question everything *you* say.'

'You have to admit there's an epic suspension of disbelief going on here, Chip.'

'Why? What's so hard to believe?' The innocence in his voice is almost convincing. 'You think I'd lie about something so serious? People's former lives are at stake.'

'Sorry, but I've never met anyone who talks to the dead. I'm on a learning curve.'

'You're a sceptic,' Chip says. 'I get it. But don't knock it. People make a big living from it. Think Tyler Henry, psychic medium. I'm pretty sure I read somewhere that he drives a Lamborghini. And he has at least seventy mansions and fifty Rolexes.'

'That's just evidence of a lot of gullible people.'

Daisy speaks up rather matter-of-factly, 'When I die, I want to be donated to medical science.'

I turn to look at her.

She shrugs. 'You were talking about dead people. I'll soon be dead. That's what I want to happen to me.'

With the knowledge she has incurable cancer and her deadly outcome is a forgone conclusion, I feel a little queasy. It's been my dream to write people's obituaries and eulogies, to tell their stories and respect their lives, but I never expected to meet someone who was on their way out; someone who, if they wanted to, could tell me their story before they passed. For me, until now, death happened *after* the fact. Now I find myself sitting in the front seat, quite literally.

'You know what they do to you?' Chloe asks Daisy. 'I read about it in my aunt's *National Geographic*.'

Daisy clasps her wrinkled hands and smiles serenely. 'Of course I know. First they strip me naked and pickle me in formaldehyde. For several months I float around in a massive bathtub, turning yellow. Once I'm good and cooked, they dry me out and use a bandsaw to carve me into quarters. Then they slice me into thin sections like Bega cheese.'

Chip shudders. 'Gruesome.'

'It's not that big of a deal,' Daisy says, coughing a little.

'I wouldn't want them looking at my—' Chloe points to between her legs.

'They won't be the first!' Daisy laughs. 'Actually, they *will* be the last.'

Chip gags. 'I wouldn't want them chopping *mine* up.'

'They'd need a microscope for that,' Jackson quips. 'And tweezers. Probably detailed directions on where to find it.'

I stifle a laugh. Chip glares at me.

'I have cancer, so that's that,' Daisy says. 'By figuring out what went wrong with me, they might be able to save someone else.'

It's an altruistic act for sure, but not one everyone is comfortable with.

Jackson's face is a mixture of dread and dismay. 'I don't know, Granny. I partied with some med students once. Throw in a beer keg, things get crazy.'

'It's not like I'm going to know about it,' Daisy reasons. 'And I love a good party.'

'Our resident spooks might beg to differ,' I say.

Daisy is resolute. 'When you've stared death in the face as often as I have, there's nothing left to fear.'

'You mean the cancer?' Chloe asks gently.

'No, I mean Jasper Harnett.'

'Who?' Jackson says.

'In the nursing home,' Daisy says. 'He died in front of me. Faceplanted my rice pudding.'

'Heart attack?' I ask. 'Choking?'

'Diabetes. I saved him my desserts. Plus I snuck him Fruchocs and jelly babies from the vending machine.'

Jackson's confused. 'You *knew* he was diabetic?'

'He asked me to,' Daisy says.

'You killed him?' Jackson squeaks.

'Indirectly,' Daisy says.

'Wow,' Chip says, looking at her in the rear-view mirror. 'That's smokin' gun sort of shit.'

'He wasn't my first,' Daisy admits.

Jackson coughs. 'What?'

'Others asked me for help, too.' Daisy strokes her chin. 'Let me see ... There was Geraldine Lucas. She had a weak heart. *Texas Chainsaw Massacre* didn't require a lot of forward planning – it was already in the DVD cabinet. I'm not even sure I can take full credit. There was Lulu Chowchin. She asked me for a little push. On a daytrip to Anstey Hill, I undid the latch on her wheelchair, and boy, did she fly! There was William McMurtrie. Viagra took care of him.'

'So your drug dealing *did* kill someone?' Jackson asks.

'We could have the drug debate all the way to Darwin and back!' Daisy huffs. 'I'm just a tiny link in a broken chain, my dear boy. I'm not what drives the market.'

'You've given this a lot of thought,' I say.

Daisy shrugs. 'I'm soon to meet my maker. I need to make my peace. Hence, take me to Errol.'

Chip slows the hearse as we enter an 80 km zone. We're coming into Millicent, a spread-out rural township dotted with houses, car dealerships and agricultural suppliers. 'Anyone want to stop?' he asks.

'I do,' Daisy says. 'A woman's bladder waits for no man.' She looks at Chloe. 'Can I borrow the She-Wee? It's freeing. I feel twenty again.'

Chloe grins. 'Absolutely.'

Daisy takes Chloe's hand. 'I'm glad I met you, dear. Every person we meet is a gift. We learn something from them. You, my girl, have educated me.'

Blushing, Chloe says, 'I don't know about that.'

Daisy pats her arm. 'Nonsense. I think you're full of all sorts of gems we've yet to discover. I have a feeling. When you're old like me, you've learned to trust your gut. My gut tells me you've a grand, important life ahead of you that'll make a lot of people very happy.' She strokes Chloe's hair away from her forehead and gently cups her chin, looking right into her eyes. 'We all need to be told we're worth something. You, my dear, have enormous value.'

Chloe's voice, when it comes, is a disbelieving whisper, 'No one's ever said anything like that to me.'

Daisy kisses her cheek. 'That's what old folks are for. We've given up censoring the truth. Well ... *mostly*.'

# CHAPTER TWENTY-ONE

After a brief toilet stop in Millicent, we're on the road to Mount Gambier. In half an hour we'll get to meet the famous Errol. Half an hour and Chloe will say her goodbyes and be on her way. I tried to corner her at the restrooms before we got back in the car, but I was headed off at the pass by Chip, who wanted to share his recent batch of Insta submissions.

Honestly? I didn't expect *Hotties of the Northern Burbs* to take off the way it has. I thought one had to work at these things. Invest blood, sweat and tears. Hang over a keyboard in the dead of night trawling for desperate Twitter followers. I thought you actually had to give a shit.

'You know what?' Chip had said, closing his screen. 'For the first time in my young adult life, I feel like I'm in charge of my destiny. My dreams could really come true.'

I can't help but admire him. He hasn't deviated from his original goal. Not once. Achieving anything takes staying power, commitment and self-belief. A handful of supporters just as deluded as you. Porn isn't exactly a hard sell, granted, but even so, part of me is impressed by Chip's unshakeable faith and vision. If Daisy thinks the people you meet teach you something, then Chip has taught me that passion is everything. You make your own opportunities. You don't let dissenting voices sway you. Also: small business is a lifelong opportunity to fudge tax deductions. I must tell Mum.

As the highway twists and turns, and a dense pine-tree forest closes in around us, I feel like this road is leading me into a new world. I can sense it coming, like when you know you're just pages from the end of a book. New horizons, new adventures. And as much as I don't want to believe my chapter with Cass is over, I'm starting to realise it is.

Cass drew people in by mucking around and playing pranks, and she *never* took anything seriously. Hanging out with her had meant a whole lot of fun. Until recently I'd thought her care-factor attitude was an admirable trait, if not an aspirational one, *especially* because it feels like I overthink everything. But one day it's like I woke up with my blinkers off and I started seeing stuff. The snarky things she said behind people's backs. The times she snidely dissed things that were important to me, like my writing. How she basically relied on everyone else to do her homework. How her jokes *always* had a barb, a sting in the tail.

Unlike me, Cass doesn't doubt herself. She possesses that which mankind strives for: rock solid self-belief. (She is, for all intents and purposes, a middle-aged cis white dude in a teenage girl's body.) And all this time I've been reinforcing that – like one of those hired suits standing behind a politician, nodding in agreement. I'm a nodder. I give good head. (I'd best not tell Chip that.) And I'd been totally bank right up till the moment I dared to go out on my own with the Facebook post about Kelly. For that head-shaker, I was dumped on my arse.

But we have history. So much history. Isn't that a reason to try and make it work?

And that's *all* I keep coming back to: history.

School thrusts us together. It's the pool of friendship options we have to choose from. If you don't play district sport or have some other reason to mix with kids from outside, the schoolyard is your lucky dip. All these years, that's where I've been at: conforming, twisting, squishing myself so I'm not a Lone Ranger wandering the wilderness at lunchtime. I can't imagine I've been the only one doing that? How many of my classmates act like someone they're not? How many sell out for something that fits but isn't quite right? How many become smaller versions of themselves, and how many become larger than? I remember Mum once spoke gleefully about a girl who'd been Queen Bee at her school. Mum said she ran into her years after high school and she was anything but. At school she'd ruled, in life she failed. Mum admitted she took smug satisfaction in discovering her former bully's demise.

Despite being bullied, Mum went on to be happy in her adult life – *and* successful.

Why is it that we think *right now* is how it'll always be? The world isn't stagnant, change is constant. How it is that we lure ourselves into a place where we think we've got things 'as they should be' and we'll stay right there and be comfortable? How is it that we think we're in control? We're in control of absolutely nothing. Control is an illusion.

I've been trying my hardest to control my environment and limit the damage and keep myself safe. I thought I'd found a jungle pack to run with, but instead I've been a chameleon blending in so I don't get eaten. In the game of nature versus nurture, my true nature surfaced when I wrote that post; when my hand felt forced, nature took over – a deep, primal defence mechanism akin to protecting the herd and furthering the species. Pecking orders be damned.

Chip glances my way and notes my reflective expression. He slows us down, joining a convoy of cars caught behind a camper trailer. 'What's up, Tay-Tay?'

'Nothing. Thinking.'

'You think too much.'

'What can I say? Me and anxiety: best mates.'

'Best mates *beat* anxiety,' Chip says.

I've got to say I like it. I want it printed on a T-shirt. Possibly a billboard.

'Oh, that's right,' he adds, 'you lost your so-called best mate. Best mate, my butt. Bye-bye Cass. Sod off. Adios. Arrivederchi. Suck a fat—'

'It's okay,' I tell him. 'I'm working through it.'

'Good, because she's not worth stressing over.' He looks in the rear-vision mirror. 'Hey Daisy. We're almost at Mount Gambier. What's the address? Is it a nursing home we're looking for?'

'I'll take you there,' Daisy assures him. 'When I see those streets it'll come back to me.' She suddenly coughs really hard. She fishes for a tissue to cover her mouth.

'You okay?' Chloe asks, rubbing her back.

Daisy nods, hacking loudly. She pulls the tissue away from her lips. I spy a clot of glistening red blood. Chloe sees it too. She flinches and hugs herself. I wonder if it makes her rethink her own habits.

Daisy sees me looking. 'Lung cancer,' she croaks. 'The cancer in my liver is secondary.'

'Oh.' I want to ask her why she still smokes, but I know that's an accusatory question at best.

Daisy wipes her bloody mouth. 'I've smoked my whole life. Why stop now? And don't sit there judging me, boy.'

'I'm not—'

'Yes you are. I see it in your eyes. You know nothing of my life. You haven't walked in my shoes.' She balls up the tissue and stuffs it in her pocket. 'I don't expect sympathy, but remember, my generation didn't receive the same warnings yours has. I was good and hooked by the time all that rolled around.' She looks at Chip. 'And if you think lollipops are any better, you're dreaming. Sugar is deadly too.'

Chip spouts the same line he gave me. 'I have an addictive personality.'

'Maybe,' Daisy says, 'but immediate gratification has more to do with it. *Delayed* gratification is key. I've never mastered it. I'm a *right here, right now* kind of girl.'

'We've noticed,' I say. But I like her take. It's refreshingly honest.

'In porn world,' Chip says, 'delayed gratification is the goal.'

'And so we come full circle as to the relationship between sex and smoking,' I say.

Jackson gets my reference. 'Riiiiiight.'

Chip adds, 'If you blow straight away, where's the fun in that?'

'Like storytelling,' I say. 'You have to hold things back. Build towards a climax.'

Chloe kicks my seat. 'Or *anticlimax*.'

'Hey, I had an invitation,' I say.

'An invitation to what?' Chip wants to know.

'I speak not a peep,' I say, and zip my lips.

Jackson and Chloe crack up.

'Hey,' Chip whines. 'Excluding me is *not* cool.'

'You're not alone,' Daisy says. 'I have no idea what they're talking about.' She points at something. 'See that church on the hill? Up there, make a right, then a left, then a right again.'

We head towards the church. We're on the outskirts of Mount Gambier now, surrounded by quiet tree-lined streets, seventies cream-brick houses and picket fences. Swings and play equipment clutter front yards, and rambling garden beds and old cars abound. On the other side of town, there's an ancient inactive volcano filled with fresh water called the Blue Lake. I hope we get to see it. Again though, I have to remind myself this isn't a sightseeing trip. We're on a mission: a mission to see Errol.

You know when you look forward to something and you build it up in your mind to be bigger than it is? Like Christmas presents – they never really meet your expectations. Well, I half expect for Errol to greet us like some unearthly enigmatic figure dressed in kingly robes. He'll stride down a red carpet with an orchestra playing and birds tweeting, and court jesters skipping and plucking mandolins.

But that won't happen. Errol will probably be an anticlimax too.

Life, it seems, is all about climaxes of one kind or another.

'Turn right here,' Daisy says. As we sail past the church, she gives the grey granite building her digitus medius. 'Up yours, Father Smythe,' she wheezes.

Chloe looks back at the church. 'What did Father Smythe do?'

'Gave me ten lashes for taking the Lord's name in vain.' Daisy holds out her palms as if Chloe can see the cane marks.

'I was seven years old. He did it in front of the entire Sunday School. I didn't even understand what *Jesus Bloody Christ* meant. When they handed out the body of the Father, I simply repeated what *my* father said when my mother served up dinner. Anyway, it doesn't matter now. The old bugger got his just desserts.'

'Your father?' I say.

She shakes her head. 'Father Smythe. They burned him at the stake.'

'They did that back then?' I imagine an elderly priest dragged outside and tied to a cross, bonfire flames licking his feet, villagers dressed in plaid shirts and straw hats raising pitchforks, chanting, *Burn in hell! Burn in hell!*

'No,' Daisy says. 'But it would've been a fitting biblical ending. He'd been siphoning donations from the collection plate into his private Mercedes Benz fund. Contrary to Janis Joplin's wistful musings, the Lord doesn't bestow costly automotive gifts.' She points. 'Turn right here.'

'Chip!' Chloe suddenly shouts. 'Look out!'

He hits the brakes. We swerve left, wheels squealing. Chip narrowly misses a parked car before swinging back, slowing down and pulling up on the wrong side of the road. 'Shit ...' he breathes, his head hung over the steering wheel. 'Not again.'

'I'll do it,' Chloe sighs, getting out of the car.

Jackson's bewildered eyes follow her. 'Do what?'

I have no idea either.

'Didn't you feel the bump?' Chip asks, his face pale. 'We hit it. We definitely hit it.'

'Hit what?'

But Chloe is getting back in the car, a pocket-sized brown dog cradled in her arms. At least I think it's a dog. It could be a rat. Or an elongated guinea pig. *That's what we hit?* No wonder I didn't feel it. If I'd stepped on it, I wouldn't have felt it. It's a princess-pea scenario.

Oh, I spoke too soon about peas. It's lifting its leg.

Chloe reads from the tiny, engraved brass tag dangling from its collar. 'Chikki,' she says, holding it up and looking it over.

It's yapping loudly. To describe it as barking would be an insult to canines. I guess noise is a good sign?

'Chikki the chihuahua,' Chloe croons. 'I don't think anything's cut or broken.'

'Are you *sure*?' Chip presses, wiping his clammy forehead.

'Look at the size of thing,' Jackson reasons. 'It has a five-metre clearance.'

'I swear I felt a thump,' Chip says.

Chloe stares at him. 'That was the other one.'

Chip swallows hard. *'What?'*

She shrugs. 'I couldn't scrape it off the road so I left it there.'

Chip hyperventilates. I whack him between the shoulder blades, but he shoves my hand away.

'I'm joking!' Chloe laughs. 'Jeepers Chip. Calm down. Get a sense of humour already.'

I shake my head. 'A bridge too far, Chloe.'

Jackson counts on his fingers. 'They say things come in threes. We've hit a deer. Now a dog-rodent. What's next?'

This doesn't help to improve Chip's breathing. I unwrap a choc-vanilla Chupa Chup and plug it in his mouth. Then I turn to scowl at Jackson. 'Not helpful either.'

'We need to take it to a vet,' Chloe says. 'Have someone check her over.'

'But we're going to see Errol!' Daisy protests, throwing her hands in the air.

'What if we *did* hit Chikki?' Chloe says. 'What if she has internal bleeding? She could be suffering. Look around you. Do you see anyone? There's no one in sight and nothing on her name tag to say where she lives.'

Chip sucks his lolly pacifier with gusto, more annoyed now than anything. 'Just leave her on the footpath. Someone will find her.'

'And risk her being hit by someone else?' Jackson says.

A giant eye roll from Chip. 'Oh right, I forgot your animal activist thing.'

'It's called being a decent human being,' Chloe jumps in.

'What if the vet asks us for details?' Chip says. 'What if they lodge an accident report?'

He has a point. We've got this far. We don't want to draw unwanted attention. We don't want to be foiled at the last minute by pet detectives. Not least because there's something pathetic about that. Border Force or the Australian Federal Police? I could live with that. Pet detectives? No sir, not happening.

'Chikki is small,' I reason. 'We could take her to the vet clinic, stick her in the postal chute and do a runner.'

Chloe blinks. 'You want to post a dog?'

'I'll let you lick the stamps.' I laugh at her horrified face. 'Hey! I'm joking! Jeepers. Get a sense of humour already.'

Chip high-fives me.

'Thanks,' I say, taking full credit.

Chikki is yapping like crazy. The high-pitched noise could rupture eardrums within a five-kilometre radius.

'What are we going to do?' Chloe yells above the din.

'Does anyone have a better plan?' I ask. 'How do we leave her at the vet without being noticed?'

'We could build a giant wooden horse,' Jackson offers.

'Nope,' I say. 'I'm all Trojan-ed out this week. Next?'

Chloe smirks, 'Oh yeah. She rode you like ... which horse was it again?'

'Not relevant. Next?'

'We could catapult her over the back fence,' Chip suggests. 'Buy a drone and do an air drop?'

'I could stash her in a hotdog bun and pose as an Uber Eats delivery guy?' Jackson acts it out. *'Well, would you look at that! How did that get there?'*

'We could bake her into a loaf of bread with a nail file for escape,' Daisy says, getting in on the act.

Chloe gags. 'You lot are a bunch of sickos. This little dog could be injured. Come on. We need to do the right thing.'

'Take it to the church,' Daisy says. 'The one back there.'

'And *pray* for it to get better?' Chip says.

'There'll be someone on duty,' Daisy explains. 'They won't ask questions. We'll be strangers doing a good Christian deed.'

Jackson doesn't like it. 'You want to drive a hearse into a church yard? We all know how the nursing home fared.'

I turn to Chip. 'Daisy's right. It's the best plan.' I look at Daisy. 'Are you sure going there isn't going to upset you?'

She gives a casual wave. 'I took a whiz in his communion wine and watched him drink it. Among other things.'

I dry-swallow. I want to know what those other things were,

but given her Confessions of a Nursing Home Serial Killer, I'm afraid to ask.

Daisy adds, 'And those yellow-crusted sprinkles on his apple muffin?' She shoves a finger up her nose and twists it. 'Home-grown.'

'Snot funny,' Jackson says.

But he's laughing. And so are we.

# CHAPTER TWENTY-TWO

Chip drives through spiked wrought-iron church gates and steers us up a gravel driveway. He parks near the side door. Ahead of us is a clapped-out red Holden Astra bearing a *U-Turn to God* bumper sticker. As Daisy suspected, someone is on duty.

In a voice reminiscent of James Bond, Chip gives directions. 'Make the handover quick, people.'

I'm not sure if he's trying to sound dramatic or if he's being serious.

'If the deal goes sour, bite down on your cyanide pill.'

Yeah, okay, so he's being dramatic.

'Do we *all* get out or just Chloe?' I ask.

'We all do,' Jackson says firmly. 'Safety in numbers.'

We climb out. Daisy appears hesitant at first, but then she juts out her chin with a resigned *I can do this* face. Jackson puts a supportive arm around her waist and helps her from her seat. Chloe cradles Chikki. The little dog yaps like she has no off-switch. She's a built-in doorbell. We're barely out of the car when the church attendant comes running outside to see what all the fuss is about.

'Oh! Hello there ...' Her voice wavers, startled by our strange posse.

Chip *is* wearing his cravat, which admittedly tends to throw anyone.

She's short and dumpy, probably in her sixties, with saggy jowls and an impressive collection of grey hairs sprouting from her chin. She looks harried, damp hair stuck to her forehead, and she's wearing a floral dress and sneakers. Over the top is a barbecue apron that says: *The best threesome I've had is the holy trinity.*

Chip gives her the thumbs-up. 'Word.'

The woman decides this is a compliment. 'Thank you! It's new. My son gave it to me. He's never been pious. I think he's finally coming around.'

Jackson covers his mouth, stifling a laugh, and walks away.

'Goodness gracious,' the woman says, 'today's been crazy! Non-stop! You're the sixteenth delivery. *Volunteer*, they said. *It'll be fun,* they said. What I wouldn't give for the Lord to grant me an extra pair of hands.' She looks skyward as if He's listening. 'And a Jayco caravan.'

'We won't keep you,' Chloe says, beaming. She juggles Chikki, who's yapping loudly, trying to climb her shirt. 'We were in the neighbourhood and—'

'Where are the donations?' The woman looks at the hearse, which she doesn't seem to register *is* a hearse, and asks, 'Are they in the boot?'

'We don't have any—' Daisy goes to say.

The woman cuts her off. 'Sorry. I'm on a tight schedule. After I finish up here I have to go to Probus Club, turn on the urn and defrost the prawns. Seafood cocktail night. These things don't happen by themselves.'

Chloe juggles Chikki. 'Well we—'

The woman holds up a finger. 'Ooh! I left the sauce on the

stove. I forgot to turn it down.' She spins on her heel and scurries inside. 'Back in a jiff!'

We stand there looking at each other. 'Do we bite the cyanide pill *now*?' I ask Chip.

Before he can answer, an aggressive male voice shouts, 'Oi! Shut that mongrel mutt up!'

I scour the garden but I can't see anyone.

'Oi! Over 'ere!' He's hanging over the fence from the adjoining property. Bald, in his mid-fifties, with a massive beer gut and what looks to be a broken nose (there's surgical tape plastered across his face), he also sports a black eye. He belts a hand against the wooden slat fence, bellowing, 'Shut it up or I will! Don't ya test me! I'll stick a lump of lead between its eyeballs!'

'Now *he's* a charmer,' Daisy says, a twinkle in her eye.

Chloe says politely, 'We apologise for the inconvenience, sir. We won't be long.'

'Ah! Ya bloody do-gooders!' the man yells, waving a hand about. 'Yers all the same! Yers think yers doin' the world a favour, but yers not!'

The church attendant returns. 'Sorry,' she says breathlessly. 'Making tomato sauce is a *very* delicate business. Anna Phillipou has won the church fate cooking trophy four years running and this year I refuse to be beaten! Now, where are the boxes?'

Chikki yaps, and the man yells, 'Oi! You lot deaf or sumphin? I said, shut that mutt up!'

The church attendant hollers back, 'Twenty metres, Slicker! Don't you forget the court order!' She turns to us. 'See the birdbath?' She points to a gaudy concrete monstrosity in Slicker's front yard. 'That's his limit. He's not supposed to come any closer.'

'Shove a Bible up your oversized skirt, Betty!' Slicker yells. 'Yers been driving me mad all day! Cars coming and going, bells tolling, organ playing the same tune on repeat! I got rights too ya know!'

'I told you, Slicker,' Betty says, hands planted on her hips, 'that's the new boy. He's only twelve. He has to learn the song.'

'Well do it somewhere else! Me ears are bleedin'!'

Betty rolls her eyes. She says to us, 'Would you believe this barney started over fruit trees? Slicker Wilcock's apricots overhang our fence. Mary Cuthbert picked a batch to serve at Sunday School morning tea and all hell broke loose. Since then we've been the victim of intimidation tactics galore. Egg throwing, rotten tomatoes, wet toilet-paper bombs, you name it. It's not good for my condition. I have a dicky heart.'

'Yer spouting lies again, Betty?' Slicker shouts. 'You lot love your fictional tripe, don't ya?'

'Take a walk, Slicker!' Betty yells. 'Twenty steps backwards!'

'Get dem idiots to shut that mutt up!' Slicker blusters. 'I've reached the end of me rope!'

Chloe looks at Betty. 'Actually, we've come about the dog.'

But Betty is distracted by a battered white Toyota ute pulling up by the kerb. The door opens and the man himself gets out. And by that I mean Jesus.

Yes, I shit you not – Jesus drives a Toyota.

He's wearing brown leather sandals and a flowing white tunic tied with a waist rope. His shoulder-length brown hair bounces like a Herbal Essences advert, and there's a crown of thorns wedged on top. He goes round the back of the ute, drops the tailgate and reaches in to grab something. Moments later, he's striding up to us, a baby lamb trotting by his side.

He tugs the lead. 'Where do you want it, Betty?'

The lamb bleats, Chikki yaps, and Betty stares at Jesus with utter confusion (long enough for me to think the Lord really *has* returned) and says, 'Russell, didn't you get the email?'

'What email?'

'Nativity play practice was cancelled. Michelle Harris lodged an equal opportunity claim. She wants to be one of the three kings. It's held up the entire production.' She looks him over. 'And we spoke about your outfit, remember? You play older Jesus, not crucifixion Jesus. Lose the thorns.'

Russell-Jesus points at Chikki. 'Are you auditioning dogs? Cos I'm pretty sure there wasn't a dog at the birth of Christ.'

'No,' Betty says, 'these people are here with donations for the fate.'

'Well actually—' Daisy starts to say.

'That's it!' Slicker bellows, belting the fence. 'You lot've crossed a line! If you reckon I'm putting up with these shenanigans, you've got another think coming! If the law won't defend my rights, I will!'

'Oh calm down!' Russell-Jesus yells. 'Get off your high-horse and come over to the light side. We don't bite!'

'Hell will freeze over before I buy your mumbo-jumbo claptrap!' Slicker fires back.

Russell-Jesus turns to Betty. 'He's looking unstable again, Betts. Reckon you'd better call the boys in blue. You know what happened last time.'

At the mention of the police, Jackson side-steps towards the hearse. Chip snatches Chikki from Chloe and sandwiches himself between Russell-Jesus and Betty.

'Look,' he says. 'We brought this dog here because—'

But Betty's apron has caught Russell-Jesus's attention. He places a hand on Chip's shoulder and steers him to one side. 'What the devil are you wearing, Betty?'

She smooths the apron and gives a little twirl. 'Darren gave it to me. Isn't it sweet?'

Russell-Jesus goes to say something, but his tunic starts buzzing. His ringtone, Smashmouth's 'I'm a Believer', plays as he pats himself down trying to find it.

Chikki yaps, the lamb bleats, Smashmouth *dert-dert-derts*, and now Slicker has *really* lost his marbles. He's shouting a string of stuff I can't make out – apart from frequent profanities, religious slurs, and something about apricot jam being the true fruit of the gods.

'We hit this dog with our car,' Chip yells at Betty over the noise. 'We're passing through town and we're in a bit of a hurry, so we were hoping you can take her for us.' He thrusts Chikki at her.

She takes a step back. 'You want to leave the dog *here*?'

'That's it! I've had it!' Slicker yells.

He steps down from the fence, turns and marches across his garden and into the house.

Russell-Jesus answers his phone. 'Hey Gabrielle. Yeah, look, I'm gunna have to call you back. I've got a bit of a situation here.' He hangs up and dials someone else – presumably the police.

Shit. This isn't good. We need to get out of here. *Now.*

Slicker's fly-screen door clangs as he exits his house and huffs across his garden carrying – *Holy crap! Is that what I think it is?*

He climbs his fence-ladder, raises the giant slingshot and takes aim. 'I gave you fair warning! Now you can suffer the consequences!'

He lets the strap go. *Ping!* Something pellet-like flies past my nose and hits the stone-walled church, ricocheting into the garden bed.

We all stare at him, frozen in shock. Then Daisy squawks, 'Jesus, Mary and Joseph! What the hell are you doing, man?'

They say animals can smell fear. The lamb bleats louder, skipping in frantic circles. Chikki goes apeshit in Chip's arms. Slicker rummages his pocket for more ammunition and reloads, drawing back on the elasticated sling. Russell-Jesus fumbles his phone. Somehow through the chaos, I hear him speaking to the police. Betty runs for cover, cowering behind the church billboard, *Love thy neighbour – Matthew 22.*

Slicker lets fly. If he's aiming at Chikki, he's a lousy shot. The second pellet skims Russell-Jesus's head, dislodging his crown of thorns, sending it tumbling across the yard.

'It's okay,' Russell-Jesus calls to Slicker, phone pressed to his ear, 'I forgive you! I don't need it anyway!'

'We have to go,' I say to Chip, thumbing at Russell-Jesus. 'He's on the phone to the ...' I mouth, *cops.*

'Huh?' Chip says.

Oh for the love of —! *Cops!* I mouth again.

'Yes, thank you officer,' Russell-Jesus says, hanging up. He shouts at Slicker, 'The cavalry is on its way! Get off the fence now if you know what's good for you!'

This only enrages Slicker more. He reloads, taking aim at Chikki. 'Fire in the hole!' he roars, letting the elastic snap.

Chip turns his body to shield Chikki, but the next thing I know, Chikki is running past my feet and out the gate in a bid for freedom, and Chip has both hands on his backside, screaming, *'Faaaaaaaaaaaaaaaaaarrrrrrrrrrrrkkkkkkkkkkkkk!!!!!!!!!!!! He got me! I've been shot! I've been shot!'* He runs around clutching his arse like it's on fire.

Jackson chases him, aiming for Chip's pocket. He gets lucky and plucks out the hearse keys. Dangling them at us, he says, 'Let's go! Now!' He heads for the driver's-side door.

Chloe helps Daisy, supporting her to walk as quickly as possible. I go to Chip, toss one of his arms over my shoulder and haul him up the driveway. *Whoosh* – a pellet flies past my head, making a metallic *ping* when it hits the hearse number plate. Men shout, women scream, and Chip cries like he's mortally wounded. Religious war zones be damned, this *Black Hawk Down* shit is not for me.

Jackson gets into the driver's seat and fires up the engine. Daisy sits next to him. Chloe climbs into the back and helps me to lift our injured man to safety. Chip sprawls face down with his head in Chloe's lap. I wedge myself in under his legs and slam the door behind me. 'Go!' I yell at Jackson. 'Go!'

Jackson plants his foot. We fly backwards, the gravel driveway ripping up in a cloud of dust. Another pellet hits the bonnet as I watch Slicker, Russell-Jesus and Betty fade into the distance. Iron gates whizz past as we reverse onto the road, and I wait for the under-wheel thump of a Chikki Chihuahua. Then I recall the size of her and decide that this time if we hit her, I don't want to know about it.

Jackson manoeuvres into first gear and floors it. Somewhere in the corner of my mind, I hear sirens blaring.

'Lordy!' Daisy hoots, rummaging the glovebox. She fumbles a Chupa Chup wrapper, sets one free and fake-smokes it. 'That was peak *Get off my driveway!*'

# CHAPTER TWENTY-THREE

Halfway up the road, I decide to check out Chip's buttocks. (That's something I never thought I'd say.)

'Hold still,' I tell him, dragging down his jeans, jocks in tow. 'Let's see how bad it is.'

'It stings! Oh God, it stings!' He buries his head in Chloe's lap, crying, clutching her thighs in agony.

'Ow!' she shrieks, trying to pry his fingers loose. 'Chip! Cut it out!'

I yank his jeans. As his blinding-white arse crack comes into view, so does an angry red patch on his right butt cheek. There's no bleeding, no open wound, just a lump the size of a twenty-cent coin that's slowly turning purple.

'How bad is it?' Chip gasps.

'Looks critical. I think you're going to develop gangrene and lose a leg.'

'*What?*'

I extract his mobile from his back pocket, find the camera function and snap a pic. This is one we definitely won't be uploading to *Hotties of the Northern Burbs*.

I pass the phone to Chloe. 'Show him.'

He lifts his head to look. 'Oh my God!'

'Calm down, Chip. I've had bigger pimples.' I pull up his pants and smack his left (unharmed) butt cheek. 'You copped it square in the middle. The ample amount of padding you have seems to have cushioned the impact.'

Jackson laughs. 'I think that's what you call a million-dollar wound, Chip. Congratulations!'

'It kills!' Chip whimpers, head still buried in Chloe's lap. 'It hurts so bad!'

Chloe grabs a fistful of hair and pulls him away from her crotch. 'If you think it gives you licence to stay *there*, you've got another think coming!'

With an awkward flailing of arms and legs, Chip tries to sit himself up. He eases himself onto the middle seat, wincing. 'I hope you lot are happy. I hope the dog was worth it. Why is it always *me* who has to take one for the team? Why do *I* have to be the fall guy?'

'I hate to break up the pity-party,' Jackson says, 'but where are we going?'

'To see Errol,' Daisy reminds him, fake-smoking her Chupa Chup.

'Where exactly is that?'

Daisy looks around, orienting herself. 'If you take a left up here, then the next right, you'll be back on course. It's not far.'

When she says it, despite all the mayhem and distraction, I suddenly realise that when we get there Chloe will leave us. She'll get out of the car, walk away and I'll never see her again. My chest instantly aches.

'What's the plan, Daisy?' I ask. 'Are you talking to Errol while we wait outside?'

It occurs to me I haven't thought to ask Daisy about logistics. All this time we've been *going to see Errol*, but I haven't known exactly what that entails. Now I feel stupid for not asking. Is he boiling the kettle and offering us tea and scones? Is she declaring her undying love for him and spending the afternoon cuddling on an outdoor swing while they say their final goodbyes? Is she working out practicalities, like what to do with her possessions, her wealth, her last will and testament?

'You're welcome to come in with me,' Daisy shrugs. 'I don't expect it will take long.'

Something about this sounds odd. We've driven all this way for a short meeting? Then again, she is dying. I suppose any time is valuable time when you don't know when you'll take your last breath.

'I'd like to meet him,' Chloe says, glancing at me. 'I've put up with a lot to get here. Why not?'

I want to ask her what happens after that, but I bite my tongue, grateful to be in her orbit just that little bit longer. It probably doesn't make sense that she would leave us in the middle of some random suburban back street. We'd drop her in the city centre near a café or a bus station. Somewhere resembling a link to the outside world.

'Turn here,' Daisy says. 'This street. Slow down.' She sits forward, peering out the window, looking for a house number. 'There,' she says, pointing to a battered green weatherboard home positioned in the middle of a large block. 'That's the one. Right there. Number twenty-four.'

'You're sure?' Jackson says.

'Uh huh.' Daisy winds down her window and flicks her Chupa Chup stick into the gutter. 'I'll never forget *this* place.'

The way she says it sounds ominous – like it's somewhere she'd rather forget.

We pull into the driveway. It's not really a driveway, but parallel tyre-tread marks ploughed into the grass. It doesn't look like anyone has mowed it in months. You'd need a hatchet to cross the front yard from one side to the other. The front porch is littered with scattered home-shopping catalogues, and a straggly tabby cat perches on the edge of a concrete pot.

As Jackson opens his door, the cat leaps off and sprints around the side of the house. 'Now what, Granny? Do you want me to ring the bell?'

'No,' Daisy says. She points at the rusted gate. 'Back yard.'

I know a lot of home-owners direct visitors to side doors or around the back, but something about unhitching a locked gate and letting ourselves in makes me uneasy. We're not friends here, we're strangers. Well, Daisy might not be, but the rest of us are.

As if reading my mind, Chloe volunteers, 'My cousin lives in Nairne in the Adelaide Hills. It's a country town. Everyone goes around the back.'

Daisy opens her door and gets out. 'You coming?'

We look at each other. Chip agrees. 'The more standing I do, the better.'

We get out. Jackson goes to the gate, stands on his tippy toes and slings an arm over the top, fiddling with the latch. It's eerily still. No blaring TV from inside the house, no voices. There's the faint sound of a baby crying far away, but that's it.

The windows are closed, curtains drawn. If I didn't know better, I'd think that no one lived here. Then again, Errol is old and possibly incapacitated, so it makes sense his home has fallen into disrepair. Perhaps he has back problems and he can't push a lawnmower? Maybe he has a carer and doesn't even get out of bed.

Jackson unlatches the gate and pushes it open. I half expect a barking guard dog to bound out, but nothing does.

We follow Daisy into the sprawling back yard. As I walk in, the wind bursts through the gates, as if breathing relief at our presence. A nervous niggle eats my chest, but I'm not sure why.

Unlike the overgrown front lawn, this lawn, if you can call it that, is a dustbowl. Greyed tree stumps dot the corrugated fence line, along with the skeletal remains of a hedge. A dilapidated garden shed has its door propped open by a half wine barrel. Dirty glass window slats hang by their hinges and the roof sags. An enormous Hills Hoist stands smack in the middle of the yard, an uneven, weed-ridden pathway leading to it.

Daisy takes in the view. I wait for her to turn and climb the concrete steps to the back door, but instead she hobbles over to the Hills Hoist and places a hand on it as if it's some kind of touchstone. She looks around, then at the ground, like she dropped a coin or a wedding ring in the dirt. 'I know I put it here somewhere ...' she mumbles.

'Granny?' Jackson says.

'Shush!' Daisy hisses, scouring the ground. 'I'm thinking. I'm trying to remember where I put him.'

'Where you put what?' Jackson asks.

She didn't say a *what*, she said *him*.

'You mean a house key?' Jackson goes to her and rests his hands on her shoulders. 'We can knock on the door, Granny.'

Daisy shrugs him off. 'There's no one in there. The house has been empty for years.' She looks at the ground again, tapping her chin. 'I know he's buried here somewhere.'

Jackson clears his throat. 'Beg yours?'

'Under the clothesline,' Daisy says. 'I left him here.'

Chloe and I look at each other. I'm sure the shock on her face mirrors mine. Tentatively, she asks, 'Are you talking about a pet?'

'No,' Daisy says curtly. 'Errol.' She hobbles over to the garden shed and pokes her head inside.

Chip smacks the side of his skull like he's trying to rattle his brain into place. 'The pain in my bum must be making me delirious. Did she just say what I think she said?'

Daisy returns, dragging a rusted shovel. She passes it to me. The weight of it sinks my hand as if it's a bowling ball. 'Dig where I tell you to.'

I stare at her, not moving.

'Do it,' Daisy says.

We're all gawking at her. Lined up in a row, we must look like sideshow clowns: mouths open, eyes wide, heads swinging one way, then the other.

Daisy blinks. 'Oh for heaven's sake! If I'd told you he was dead you wouldn't have come.'

Oh. My. God.

What. The. Actual. Fuck.

We've been duped by an elderly criminal mastermind.

Chip states the obvious. '*Errol's dead?!*'

Daisy goes to the Hills Hoist, turns her back on us and counts steps like a pirate searching for buried treasure. 'One, two, three, four …'

Jackson's mouth stays open. Chloe puts her hand under his chin and closes it. It's obvious he had no idea. He's been taken for a ride like the rest of us – quite literally.

'Did you kill him?' Chip stutters.

Given Daisy's earlier confessions, this isn't an unreasonable question. She lived at this house at one stage in her life. Surely she didn't butcher poor Errol and use him as lawn fertiliser?

Daisy takes one more step and stops abruptly, approximately three metres from the Hills Hoist. She points to the ground. 'Here. Bring the shovel.'

'Why is Errol buried in the back yard?' Chip squawks, hands flapping about his face. I figured with his whole I-talk-to-dead-people routine that something like this would be plausible. Seems not. He's fully freaking out.

Daisy gestures at her feet. 'Dig. We haven't got all day.'

The thought of jamming the shovel into the soil and hitting bone makes me queasy. Vomit rises in my throat. I have a vision of myself as if I'm floating above my body. I look down: Oh, there I am in a random country back yard, holding a shovel, about to dig up a body.

*What is happening?*

'Hurry up!' Daisy barks. She breaks into a coughing fit and searches her pockets for a tissue. After hacking up a lung, she wheezes, 'I'll be stone cold dead by the time you find him!'

'And if we *do* find him, what then?' Jackson stammers, overcoming his muteness. 'Why are you bothering to move him? If you're worried about the cops, it's a bit late for that, don't you think? What are they going to do? Arrest you for murder? You'll be dead before it goes to trial. Possibly before they get to you the station!'

Daisy gapes at him with wounded disbelief. 'Murder? Is that what you think of me? I didn't murder Errol!'

There's a moment of confused silence. Then Jackson throws his hands in the air and cries, 'Who the hell did then?'

'Errol wasn't murdered,' Daisy says. 'He was bitten by a brown snake.'

Jackson's eyebrows almost leapfrog his buzz cut. '*A brown snake?*'

Daisy nods. 'He trod on it, right here. A long bugger of a thing, too. King Brown. Good two metres. I told Errol not to wear loose shorts and thongs. Do you think he listened to me? Serves him right he was bitten on the balls.'

'Errol died of a snake bite to the nutsack?' I can't believe it. I literally *can't* believe it.

'Yes,' Daisy confirms. 'First time in years a mouth had gone anywhere near it, too.'

I point at the ground. 'And you left him here to rot?'

'I let the grass grow over him,' Daisy says sarcastically. 'What do you think, dumbarse? He was cremated.'

'Oh.' I suddenly realise what we're digging for. 'You mean he's in an urn?'

Daisy smiles. 'A Nestlé coffee tin if memory serves.'

There's silence again while we take this in. Then Chloe asks, 'Okay. So once we've dug him up, what then?'

'We enjoy a hot cuppa?' Chip suggests.

I glare at him.

'We make things right,' Daisy says. She shuffles over to the porch steps, takes a seat on the bottom one and lights a smoke. 'We take him to see his brother Harold.'

'Harold?' we say in unison.

'Yes, Harold.'

And she starts singing the Going to Errol song, except now it goes:

*'We're going to see Harold. We're going to see Harold. We're going to see Har-ro-rold!!!!!!!!!!!!!! Harold, we'll see you soon.'*

# CHAPTER TWENTY-FOUR

As I unearth the rusted coffee tin from Errol's yard, I recall Edgar's warning, *He's not worth the trip.* The hairs on my neck stand on end. If Errol's been dead the entire time, maybe Edgar *does* know what he was talking about. Which means Chip knows what he's talking about – a genuinely terrifying thought.

'Ah! Hello Errol,' Daisy says, taking the tin from me. It hasn't fared well in the soil. What was probably once shiny silver is now tarnished brown. The lid looks welded shut. Daisy strokes it. 'It's been a long time, dear husband. I promised I'd come back for you. Today's the day.' She holds the tin at arm's length like a beacon. 'You know, I think there might be a God after all.'

Jackson hops around nervously, his eyes surveying the fence line. 'We should get out of here. We've been here too long. What if the neighbours see us?'

'Yes,' Daisy agrees, tucking the tin under her arm. 'We should. We're going to see Harold, but first I need to stop by the supermarket.'

Jackson's flummoxed. 'The supermarket?'

'Of course! I can't go to Harold's without taking afternoon tea!' She says it like it's some kind of unwritten rule he should know. Tin cradled under her arm, she wobbles on ahead of us. 'Come on you lot. Day's a wastin'.'

'I take it you never had much to do with Errol?' I say to Jackson as we follow her to the car. 'What about Harold?'

He shakes his head. 'Errol was her second husband. Mum didn't like him so I never had much to do with him or his family. When we saw Granny, it was usually without him. She told us she'd left him, *not* that he'd died. I vaguely remember Harold coming to Christmas lunch one year. I think the only reason I remember is because he was out on probation and his parole officer came to lunch, too.'

'Prison runs in the family,' Chip says, half-limping alongside us.

Jackson is bruised by this. 'I'm not related to Harold. Not by blood. I'm nothing like him. I'm pretty sure he was in the clink for strangling a kid.'

Chloe shivers. 'We're going to see a guy who did that?'

I notice she says *we're*. Knowing what I now know about Harold, my instinct is to dissuade her from joining us. We should offer to drop her in the city centre instead. But my selfishness quickly overrides that thought and I keep my mouth shut. (Yes, I really am a prick.) I haven't had a chance to tell her how I feel. I haven't decided if I'll tell her about Kelly.

'If Harold is an unsavoury character,' I say, 'why would Daisy want to see him?'

'Beats me,' Jackson says. 'But it must be good if we've come all this way.'

'You're not mad at her for lying to you?'

'What do you suggest? Hold it against her? Never speak to her again?'

He's right. Daisy *is* dying. Maybe soon. Never speaking again will happen soon enough.

I get in the front seat, consumed by thoughts of forgiveness. We're born to die, yet we all act like tomorrow is a given – that we'll have the next day and the next to mend our ways. We hold grudges. Stay angry. *Why?* Like the church sign said, *Love thy neighbour.* Holy crap. Maybe *I* should be Russell-Jesus? The dude was onto something.

I think of Chloe's argument: *In two thousand years from now is anyone going to care?* Jesus had the forgiveness thing figured out, and yet here we are two thousand years later, and not everyone has got the message – which goes to show the human race really *are* slow learners.

'Take me to Woolies,' Daisy tells Jackson as he starts the engine. 'They make the best flans.'

'Flans?'

She licks her lips. 'Crispy crust. Harold never could resist a pie.'

We're about to pull out of the driveway when Chip says, 'Stop, Jackson. I should drive. I have a licence. If we're pulled over, at least we have some prospect of getting away with it.'

He's right.

'Trade places,' I tell Jackson. Chip and Jackson get out and swap seats. Chip eases himself into the driver's side so delicately you'd think he'd just undergone a bad colonoscopy. 'You're playing on that,' I say. 'Sympathy vote?'

'Bruises can turn into hematomas,' Chip replies snottily. 'Clots can break off, travel through your bloodstream, reach your heart, block an artery and kill you.'

'You're telling me you're going to die of butt-cheek bruising?'

'It's a thing,' he says. 'There are heaps of people who've died from butt-cheek bruising, we just don't hear about it. It doesn't pull the heart-strings like other conditions.'

'You should start a foundation,' I suggest. 'Tax deductible donations supporting bums and arseholes.'

Chloe laughs. 'There's already one of those. It's called The Liberal Party.'

I crack up. So does Jackson. Chip, unimpressed by our jokes at his expense, huffs, 'One day you'll take one in the butt, Taylor, then you'll know what I'm going through.'

'Guys ...' Jackson says. 'Can we get going?'

'Sorry,' Chip says, reversing the hearse onto the road. 'Woolies was it?'

'Yes,' Daisy says. 'Does anyone have a Rewards card? The points can get us cheaper petrol for the drive home.'

Jackson smirks. 'I don't think a flan is going to clock you many points, Granny.'

'I know,' Daisy retorts, 'but the wine I buy from the BWS after I see Harold will.'


At Woolies, I grab a handbasket and follow Daisy. She makes a beeline through the fruit and veg section to the bakery at the back. The others are waiting in the car. Shopping centres have cameras, so the least number of us recorded on screen, the better. Besides, if we let Chip anywhere near the chocolate and magazine rack, we'll be here for hours.

The store is busy, but none of the customers or staff seem interested in us. They're too busy filling trolleys or stocking shelves. I'm just a kid buying flan for the brother of a dead guy I dug up. The usual.

'Do you know that if you position bananas in your basket *just so*, it signals you're up for some hanky-panky?' Daisy shares this as we pass by the banana display.

I'm eternally surprised by her contemporary knowledge. 'I think that's an urban myth, Daisy. Not everyone with bananas in their basket is looking for a bit. They probably enjoy eating them. Or they need the potassium.'

Daisy shakes her head. 'You really do suck the joy out of everything, don't you?' She shuffles over to the baked goods, where she selects a plain pressed-biscuit flan with no filling.

'That's what you're taking to Harold's?'

'No, I need other ingredients.'

'Daisy, in case you haven't noticed we're travelling in a hearse, not a campervan meals-on-wheels. Where do you plan to whip up a cake?'

'You don't know much about cooking, do you? Does Mummy do it all?'

'Mum's an accountant. She doesn't cook. Well, *sometimes*. Rarely.'

'Good for her,' Daisy says. 'I hate it.'

This confuses me even more. 'Then what are we doing?'

But she doesn't explain. 'Where's the custard? Plus I need a can of tropical fruit mix. That ought to do it.'

I take her to the refrigerated section where she takes her time inspecting the various labels. 'So many options,' she mutters, 'and yet the nursing staff fed us that same lumpy muck, day in, day out. Thank the Lord I'm not spending my last days cooped up in that dump. I'll go back there over my dead body!'

'Daisy, you *have* to go back. Where else will you go?'

'Barbados. Jackson says I have enough money.' She must be

recalling what Jackson had said when he checked her account before we left. 'He said we can sip cocktails. That sounds lovely. I've never been to Barbados. Where is it again?'

'I think he was being facetious, Daisy. Barbados is an island in the Caribbean.'

'Is it the one where those nice young men and women strut up and down the beach wearing thongs?'

'You mean g-strings. And that happens on most beaches, Daisy. You don't have to trek to Barbados.'

'Well, with scenery like that, who wouldn't want to go there?' She chooses a custard carton and drops it in the basket. 'Fruit?'

I take her to the canned fruit aisle.

She surveys the shelf. 'Harold likes the one with Maraschino cherries.'

'You remember what he likes?'

'I remember lots of things about Harold.' She selects a tin and hands it to me. Then she does an about-turn and goes to the kitchen gadgetry rack, where she grabs a sturdy-looking tablespoon and dumps that in the basket, too. She dusts her hands. 'Job done. Let's skedaddle.'

At the self-serve check-out, there's a lanky kid with reddish bum-fluff on his chin. I've seen kiwifruit with better hair coverage. He points to a free station. I put the basket on the side-table, grab a plastic bag, scan it and set it up in the bagging area. I'm about to start swiping when Daisy hip-and-shoulders me out the way.

'I love these machines!' She scans the custard, puts it in the bag, grabs the fruit tin and waits as a neighbouring customer scans an item, and bags the tin in tune with *that* beep. It's like watching synchronised swimming, except it's synchronised stealing. She does the same thing with the tablespoon. I wait for the red light to flash. It doesn't; the weight scale must be switched off.

'Daisy! You want to get us busted?' I look over my shoulder at Bum-fluff Junior, who's helping another customer. 'Scan them!'

Cupped hand to her ear, Daisy says, 'What did you say, dear? My hearing is terrible! Not to mention my Alzheimer's! Can't remember what I did two seconds ago.' She grins.

I reach around her, grab the flan and scan it.

'You're no fun,' she pouts. Clicking her fingers, she calls out, 'Oi! Boy! I need a packet of Marlborough Lights, toot sweet.' When Bum Fluff's back is turned, she grabs a handful of Cherry Ripes from the confectionery display and stuffs them in the bag too.

I point heavenward. 'I thought this mission was about making things right with whoever sits in the big chair upstairs. They're going to see you coming and lock the gate.'

She shrugs. 'Suits me. If Father Smythe is the kind of person they let in, I'd rather not get an invitation.'

Outside, Daisy stops by a homeless man who's sitting on the concrete footpath, leaning against the wall. She drops the Cherry Ripes into his lap and tells him to have a good day.

We pull up three doors down from Harold's place – a nondescript brown-brick unit in a block of eight ground-level flats. Daisy needs a moment to construct her afternoon tea, so Chip gets out and opens the hearse back doors to give her a preparation platform. He gets back in while we wait.

'So,' I say to Jackson, 'she sees Harold and then we're out of here?'

He nods.

'Then what?' I glance at Chloe, but she won't meet my eyes. 'What happens next?'

'We go home,' Chip says.

'Daisy doesn't think she's going home. She thinks she's going to Barbados.'

'Barbados?' Jackson says. Then it clicks. 'Oh. Yeah, no. That's not happening.'

'What about you?'

'What about me?' Jackson says. 'I get back and hand myself in.'

'What do you think they'll do to you?'

'Dunno,' he says. 'Probably nothing good.'

I feel bad for him. All he's doing is helping out his dying Granny. He hasn't done anything *really* wrong. Well, apart from abducting her from a nursing home and forcing me, an innocent teenager, to trek halfway across South Australia. But we'll overlook that for a minute.

'I've done what I intended to do,' Jackson adds. 'I can live with myself now.'

'You don't think this Harold guy will call the police?' Chloe asks.

'I doubt he even knows Daisy's been in a nursing home,' Jackson says. 'And he wouldn't know anything about me. And even if he did, if he saw us on the telly, a man with his background is unlikely to call the police. No, I think he'll just take it for what it is: an unexpected visit.'

I look up. Daisy is tapping on my window. The flan, on its silver cardboard base, is balanced on her hand. She's filled it with custard and fruit. It looks creamy good. If that came to my

237

door, I'd be happy. Maybe it *is* a nice thing to do for someone you haven't seen in a long time?

She thumbs at us to get out. Chip winds down the window. 'You want us to come with you?'

'Of course,' Daisy says. 'I need someone to take the photo.'

We look at each other, unsure of what this means.

'I've given up trying to get an explanation from her,' Jackson says, climbing out.

We follow Daisy to Harold's door. A wind chime tinkles on someone's verandah. A budgie in a hanging cage chirps, *who's a pretty boy* as we walk by. I think I see a curtain flutter like someone's watching, but I tell myself it's the breeze.

Harold's security door is broken, the bottom half of the flyscreen ripped like someone kicked it in. An overflowing ashtray rests in a near-dead pot plant. Several crushed beer cans litter the porch. There's a strong stink not unlike a urinal. I wonder if he throws open the door each morning and 'waters' his plants.

A weathered doormat reads, *Nice Underwear*. Chloe takes a step back. Jackson presses the buzzer. An electronic AFL club song plays, I can't place which one, and shuffling noises emanate from behind the door before it swings open and a tall, reed-thin elderly man greets us dressed in nothing but blue striped boxer shorts.

'Yeah?' He grunts, scratching his armpit. His wrinkled chest is covered in faded black tattoos. A colostomy bag hangs from a stoma on his lower abdomen, flat and empty like it's just been changed. His face resembles a squashed avocado, all ridged bumps and mushy bits. 'If you're selling, I'm not buyin',' he says.

'Harold!' Daisy steps forward, flan in hand. 'Why, would you

look at you! I almost didn't recognise you. You look … look …'
She holds out the flan. 'Like you need a good feed!'

He stops scratching and his jaw goes slack. *'Daisy?'*

'Surprise! I brought afternoon tea.'

He looks at the rest of us now with interest. 'Is this some kind of trick?'

Daisy pushes her way past him and into his flat. 'Let me get the kettle,' she says.

He looks at her, then at us, confused.

Jackson puts out a hand. 'Jackson Rollock, Daisy's grandson. Pleased to meet you.'

Harold limply shakes it. 'Er … the painter, right?'

Jackson goes with it. 'Yeah, I just finished a new piece, *Convergence*. All that paint-flinging sure takes it out of you. I needed a holiday, so I thought I'd chaperone the old girl. She's been pretty keen to see you.' He gestures to me, Chip and Chloe. 'Friends of mine. Road trip buddies. Wouldn't mind a cuppa if you've got one?'

Harold looks us up and down but he doesn't really seem to take us in. He's more concerned with Daisy, who can be heard rattling around in the kitchen. 'Come in, come in!' she calls.

Defeated, Harold stands aside. 'You heard the woman.'

I enter his flat. The first thing that hits me is the stink, like cat piss. Just inside the door there are three kitty litter trays and they don't look as if they've been emptied in ages. I gag and cover my face with my T-shirt. A brown-and-white cat scoots past my feet and shoots out the door, into the garden.

The room is dark, blinds down. As my eyes adjust I see there's stuff piled *everywhere*: books, cardboard boxes, newspapers, shopping bags, pots and pans and crockery, laundry baskets filled with scrunched-up sheets and clothes, a broken guitar, and six or seven baseball bats stacked in a teepee by the wall. It's like an op shop.

'Sit!' Daisy calls. 'I'll bring you a coffee.'

Harold parks himself in a recliner chair and flicks up the leg rest. The four of us take a seat opposite him on the three-seater leather couch, arms wedged by our sides. Daisy comes and clears the coffee table of DVD cases and remote controls by literally sweeping them onto the floor. She puts empty coffee mugs in their place. Then she gets the flan. She carves a big slice for Harold, plops it on a plate and passes it to him with a spoon. He accepts, somewhat bewildered. He looks at it, then at her, then at us, then at her again.

'I'm dying,' Daisy announces. 'It's time to let bygones be bygones, Harold.' She points to the pie. 'This is my peace offering.'

Harold stares at her. He looks at Jackson as if waiting for a second opinion.

'It's true,' Jackson confirms.

Harold doesn't seem to know what to say. He coughs a few times, clears his throat and says gruffly, 'I'm sorry to hear that, Daisy.' He digs a chunk of custard flan. Spoon hovering by his mouth, he asks, 'And you wanted to see me?'

'It's cancer,' she says, like he asked. She waves a hand, prompting him to eat. 'Go on. I remember how much you love pie. I made it fresh this afternoon.'

He takes a mouthful, chews, swallows, and grins. There's a piece of cherry stuck to his top teeth. 'You haven't lost your touch, Daisy. This is good. I remember you used to make a mean tiramisu.'

She watches him eat, smiling.

He points at his colostomy bag. 'Bowel cancer. Six years ago. Two rounds of chemo. Dodged a bullet but ended up with this shit of a thing.'

Chip laughs. 'Ha! Good one!'

Harold looks at him, mystified by his own unintentional joke.

'You understand what it's like then,' Daisy says. 'The cancer is in my liver.'

'How long have you got?' Harold takes another mouthful. He's really smashing it now. The old bloke can't have eaten a decent meal in ages.

'Don't know,' Daisy says. 'Not long.'

Sick of waiting to be offered a slice, Chip reaches forward to grab the knife and help himself, but Daisy slaps his hand away. 'It's not for you,' she says. 'I want Harold to have it. He can keep the leftovers and eat it later.'

Chip looks peeved, but Harold looks chuffed. 'That's real good of you, Daisy. I don't get much tucker on the pension. I get sick of eatin' baked beans.'

'My pleasure,' Daisy says. 'It's my way of making things right between us.'

Harold shifts in his seat, uncomfortable. 'You know that stuff's in the past, Daisy. Water under the bridge. I haven't thought about it in years.'

'I don't doubt it,' Daisy says stiffly. 'But I got to thinking I should try to resolve it. All these years, it's been like an unfinished sentence in desperate need of a full-stop.'

Harold nods. 'You gotta make your peace before you croak. Been there myself.'

When he says this, I think about what Daisy said earlier –

about making *her* peace. Where's Errol? We made all that effort to dig up the tin because she said she wanted to make things right with Harold. Wasn't she going to hand him his brother's ashes? Did she forget?

I'm about to offer to go and get the tin, when Harold finishes his last mouthful. Daisy immediately cuts him another slice. She takes his plate, loads it up, and hands it back, saying, 'Chip, would you do the honours?' She makes clicky flingers like she's using a camera.

'Oh. Right.' Chip un-wedges himself from the couch and jumps to his feet. He gets out his mobile and waits for her instruction. Daisy perches herself on the arm of Harold's recliner chair. Harold holds up his plate and Daisy points at it. The two of them grin side-by-side like Cheshire cats.

Chip snaps the photo. *Click!*

As I hear the sound, it hits me – what's in the pie.

Errol.

Errol is in the pie.

Harold is eating his brother.

'Well, we'd best get going,' Daisy says, getting to her feet. 'It's been a good visit. Short and sweet is always best, don't you think?'

'But we haven't had a coffee?' Chip says.

It's true. Daisy forgot to pour it.

Harold seems disappointed. 'Oh. Right then. I was just thinking it was nice to have company for a change.' He goes to get out of his chair.

'Don't get up,' Daisy says, pushing him gently back down. 'We'll see ourselves out. We have a long drive ahead of us so we'd best hurry along. Remember! Enjoy that pie. Don't scoff it all at once.'

Harold nods. 'I really appreciate the gesture, Daisy. I've got to say, I didn't expect it from you. It's nice to know there are still surprises to be had. You've done the right thing.'

'Absolutely,' she agrees.

'Take care of yourself.' Harold watches us leave.

'I always do,' Daisy says.

Outside by the hearse, Daisy asks Chloe for the She-Wee. Chloe obliges, handing it over. Daisy then asks Chip to open the back doors of the hearse. He does.

Errol's tin sits, quite appropriately, in a dead man's domain. Daisy takes it, jimmies the lid open with the spoon, puts it down on the roadside and drops her pants. She positions the She Wee and takes aim.

And there, in the middle of a quiet country street, Daisy pees all over what's left of Errol. 'First you were pie,' she says. 'Now you're cuppa soup.'

# CHAPTER TWENTY-FIVE

Following Errol's second coming *and* second demise, we drifted into the city centre. Chip followed the tourist signs to one of Mount Gambier's premier attractions, the Cave Garden – an enormous natural sinkhole smack in the middle of town. Once a water source for the community, it's since been turned into an impressive public park. I know because it says it on the sign. There's a sepia-toned photo of a group of people clad in early European get-up, picnicking under umbrellas. I wonder how they trusted the sinkhole wouldn't further open up and swallow them. Right now, after what we just did, I half expect it to.

It's late in the day and there's hardly anyone around. We sit at one of the wooden tables under a canopy of creeper vine, scoffing over-salted chips, dim sims, corndogs and battered fish. With every bite, Chip complains our fare is nowhere near as good as Bill's Takeaway. His assessment is right, but I don't care. I'm starving. The food is filling the sinkhole in my gut.

The no-smoking sign doesn't deter Daisy. She lights a cigarette as I ask her to recount her beef with Errol.

She gives me a crooked smile. 'Long or short version?'

Drawing back on her smoke, she exhales and talks through the haze. 'My first husband, Brian, was abusive.' She points her cigarette's fiery eye at Jackson. '*Your* grandfather. And I wasn't hanging round to be his punching bag, so I got out while the getting was good.'

Jackson nods as if this is something he already knows.

She takes a drag. 'Then I met Errol. He seemed different. He was cheeky and spirited and *very* good in bed.'

At this, Jackson winces.

'What I didn't know when I fell for Errol was that he and his brother, Harold, were inseparable – a two-for-one package – and between them Harold *always* wore the pants. What he said, Errol did, no question.' She nods at the cave opening. 'One of Harold's bright ideas was to attempt to find the bottom of this cave. The rescue effort took days. When they were brought to the surface, they were arrested for being a public nuisance. Another time they tried to copy Mount Gambier's favourite son, Adam Lindsay Gordon, by stealing a horse to jump the Blue Lake fence.'

'Adam-*who*?' Chip says, dipping a dim sim in tomato sauce and virtually inhaling it. He's avoiding the fish. He says it looks like lab-manufactured cat food.

Daisy waves her hand. 'Writer. Poet. Famous story around these parts. They were arrested for that too. Harold was always getting Errol into trouble.'

Chloe asks the obvious question. 'Why'd you marry him?'

'Because the serious stuff came later,' Daisy says. 'In the beginning it was mostly pranks. It started with the tin kettling and my patience wore thin from there.'

'The what?' I shove a piece of butterfish in my gob. It's

actually quite tasty. I think about telling Chip he's dipped out, but eating wins and I keep stuffing my face.

'Tin kettling,' Daisy says. 'It's an old country tradition that happens after a wedding. Friends of the happy couple wait a week or so to surprise the newlyweds. They gather on a nearby street corner, sneak up to your house and scare the crap out of you by bashing pots and pans and throwing them onto your roof. Unbeknownst to me, Errol gave Harold a house key. Harold decided to take the tin kettling to the next level by sneaking everyone *inside* our house to surprise us. Thing is, Errol wasn't home from work yet and I'd decided to surprise *him* by lathering my naked body in icing sugar and lying on our kitchen table – a welcome home present. All our friends and family burst in, banging pots and pans, and I publicly shat myself in a cloud of icing dust.'

Chloe cracks up. 'For real?'

Daisy smirks and nods.

'So that was the icing on the cake?' Chip asks.

'No.'

'*No?*'

She exhales a plume of smoke. 'A week later, Errol and Harold had a few too many, put on my underwear over the top of their workwear and went to the council meeting to protest changes to pub licensing hours. Hilda Burton was mayor. She'd held a grudge against me since high school, and—'

Jackson cuts her off. 'Granny, we get the picture. Errol and Harold were tools of the A-class variety. And you've got an elephant's memory for those who wronged you. But don't you think the Errol Pie was taking things too far?'

'I'm not finished!' Daisy says.

The sting in her tone makes me think something more significant is coming.

'The idiotic stunts continued,' she says, 'until one day I gave Errol an ultimatum. I told him it was me or his brother. Harold didn't take too kindly to that. First he killed my cat, Angie, by hanging her from our gum tree.'

Chloe drops her food and covers her mouth in shock. 'Oh my God ...'

'And when that didn't achieve what he'd hoped for,' Daisy says, 'he came around when Errol was at work and he beat me. I was carrying your aunt or uncle at the time.' She clutches her stomach when she says this and gives Jackson a sad look. 'I almost bled to death.'

I feel ill. 'Errol *let* that happen?'

Daisy flicks ash. 'A weak man is no better than a violent one. Errol was in denial that his brother would do such a thing. He told me I'd asked for it by attempting to lay down the law. After my first husband, I couldn't believe it was happening again. For a while there all the fight went out of me.'

Jackson rests a gentle hand on her arm. 'You've been angry all this time?'

Daisy surveys our faces. 'I know that forgiveness is said to be freeing, but they also say revenge is sweet. For years I blamed myself. *Me.* I thought it must have been something I did. I thought maybe I deserved it. When Errol died unexpectedly, I saw an opening and I broke free and left that life behind. But it's haunted me. Now I'll soon be dead and I have to live with myself.'

The last thing she says is confusing, yet somehow it makes perfect sense.

Chloe puts an arm around her. 'I would've peed on him too, Daisy.'

Daisy grins. 'Can I see the photo?' Chip obliges, showing her his phone. Daisy looks at it, smiling. But her smile fades. 'I'd like to say watching Harold eat Errol was the most satisfying moment of my life, but it wasn't.'

Chip cringes. 'Don't tell me there's someone else you want to put in a pie?'

Daisy shakes her head. She looks at Jackson. 'Sharing this trip with my grandson has meant the world to me.'

Jackson's eyes brim. He takes her in his arms and holds her tight. And despite everything I know, despite the criminal nature of our entire trip, watching them gives me a sense of peace that we've done the right thing – even if we do end up getting caught.

Daisy rubs Jackson's spiky head. 'This trip would be even better if you gave me another hit of my magic pain relief.'

Jackson laughs. 'Soon, Granny. Soon.'

Chip licks his fingers and takes the leftovers to a nearby rubbish bin. 'It's getting late. We should hit the road. Does anyone mind if we make a quick detour to the Blue Lake? I've never seen it. Should only take twenty minutes.'

Chloe shrugs. 'Why not?'

I look at her, surprised. She's not leaving us?

As if reading my mind, she says, 'I haven't seen it either. I wouldn't mind a lift. You can drop me back in town on your way out.'

We go to the hearse and get in. My stomach is winding itself into knots. This is it. This will be my goodbye to Chloe. How fitting – a pair of lovelorn virgins visiting an ancient volcano.

(Note to self: *I'm* the lovelorn one.) Is this the part where, in an effort to appease the gods, I'm thrown in? I half expected this trip might get some kind of climactic ending, but not the volcanic kind. Volcanos are said to be a gateway to hell. I should've paid more attention in English when we read Dante's *Inferno*. Did Dante make it out? I can't remember. I remember the nine circles of torment that await me, and to be honest, I'm pretty sure I've covered most of them. Limbo and Lust: been there, done that with Chloe. Gluttony: I just stuffed my face like a crazy person, plus there was the Bundy binge. Greed and Wrath: pocketing Daisy's money for this road trip of 'Errol-Harold Flan Revenge' covers that. Heresy and Violence: that would aptly describe our church visit. Fraud and Treachery: once again, Chloe and my lying arse for omitting the truth.

I have to tell her about Kelly. *I have to.* Yes, I'll be throwing myself into the proverbial volcano, but it's an extinct one, one filled with water, so I'll drown instead. Water beats fire. I can swim. I won my junior Nippers championship two years running. I have a medal to prove it.

Okay, that's the plan: throw myself in, swim like mad. Doesn't sound so bad.

Chloe reads my unease. 'You don't look so good, Taylor.'

'I *told* you that fish was dodgy!' Chip says, smoking a post-dinner Chupa Chup. He turns right, climbing the hill towards the tourist lookout, a small brick rotunda overlooking the lake. 'If you think we're cutting our trip home short because you're shitting through the eye of a needle, you can guess again. When we packed Daisy's gear at the nursing home, we packed adult diapers. I'm ready for you, friend.'

I'm not sure if it's my terror of confronting Chloe or if it's the fish, but either way she's right – I definitely don't feel good. In fact I feel *really* queasy.

'Wind down the window,' Jackson says. 'When I was a kid and I got bad motion sickness, that's what Mum said to do. Let the wind blow on your face. Fresh air fixes everything.'

I wind down the window and rest my chin on the ledge. The snaking, winding road isn't helping things. I feel dizzy. I close my eyes and try to concentrate on the steady breeze washing over my face.

'Be careful,' Chip warns. 'Don't forget how Lily died. Remember Pigeongate?'

Something wet hits my cheek. I draw my head back in and turn to look at the others. Jackson covers his mouth, snorting. Daisy and Chloe laugh too.

'I thought seagulls pooped on you when you were eating fish and chips,' Chloe says. 'Not afterwards.' She grabs a bunch of tissues from behind the seat and passes them to me. 'Here. And use this to clean it off,' she says, passing me a yellow tub.

It's the massive jar of Vaseline Chip bought from the supermarket before we left Adelaide. I lift the lid. A fair portion of it is gone. Oh God.

'Chip, *please* tell me you didn't do what I think you did?' I say.

Chip glances at it. 'Whoops. Didn't think anyone would see that.'

'What the hell, Chip!' I flip the sun visor and squint at the mirror. 'How could you have used that much Vaseline in only a couple of days?'

'Remember the police officer?' Chip says.

'Which one?' Jackson asks. 'There have been a few on this trip.'

'The fancy-dress one in Kingston.'

Oh. Right. Her. 'Yeah?' I say.

'Well I thought the handcuffs she had were fake,' Chip says. 'Turns out they were the real McCoy. It's a good thing I had the Vaseline in the backpack.'

'I don't want to ask,' Chloe says, 'but also I really do. What did she handcuff you to?'

Chip grins. 'The goalpost.'

'Is that a euphemism?'

'Not *to* it. *Around* it,' he says. 'Thank god she didn't do a runner and leave me there. I'd like to say her overly conscientious rescue efforts were because she cared about me, but I think it's because she'd borrowed the hardware from her dad. She needed them back.'

I scoop some Vaseline to clean my face.

'But the Vaseline came in handy *before* that too,' Chip adds.

I throw my used tissue at him.

He laughs. 'What kind of savage do you think I am, Taylor? I don't dip my wick! I dip my fingers exactly like you just did.'

'It's what you do with those fingers *afterwards*,' I say.

'Are you accusing me of double-dipping?'

'Do you? Cos I know what I do at a barbecue versus what I do when I'm at home alone, and the two are very different.'

Chip's horrified. 'You're one of those people who licks peanut butter from the knife and shoves it back in the jar, aren't you? Do you know that the residual saliva transfers from the knife to the food and starts breaking it down? By the time you serve yourself that next slice of toast, it's already partially digested.'

I swallow hard, more disturbed by this concept than I care to admit.

'I have to question your hygiene practices, Taylor,' he says. 'No wonder you feel sick. Did you wash your hands before you ate?'

'*Did you?*'

'I don't need to,' Chip says confidently. 'I'm blessed with a strong constitution. Also, I once ate a cockroach and nothing happened.'

My stomach churns and gurgles. 'Are you *trying* to make me throw up?'

'Come to think of it, it could've been a cricket,' Chip ponders. 'We were watching this hippy gastrointestinal foodie show on SBS and—'

'You mean *gastronomic*,' Chloe corrects.

Chip argues, 'No. I don't think so. *Gastroenteritis* maybe?'

'No, the word is definitely *gastronomic*,' Chloe asserts. 'Say it with me: gas-tro-nom-ic.'

'Gas-tro-nom-ic,' Chip repeats.

'Oh my god!' I squeak. 'Can you both stop saying *gastro*?!'

'And anyway,' Chip goes on, 'the science people said you should eat bugs because they're an excellent source of protein. Me and my mates had had a few brewskies and we were feeling brave, so we moved the couch, caught some on the run and chowed down. I gotta say the flavour was unexpected. They tasted nutty. And their legs still wiggled after a few bites. Actually, now I stop to consider it, I was also drunk the first time I tried oysters. Now *they* have the texture of straight-up snot sliding down your throat—'

I lean out the window and hurl. Vomit sprays up the side of the hearse, hitting Chloe's window. 'Urgh!' she cries, shrinking away from it.

'Better out than in,' Chip says. 'You could've waited and done it in the bushes. We're here now.'

He pulls into the carpark and stops the hearse. If I wasn't feeling like I'd just had my insides vacuumed out, rearranged and shoved back in, I'd leap out of the car, go round, drag him out by his cravat, strangle him with it and throw him in the lake.

I grab my water bottle and get out of the hearse. I slurp, swish and spit a few times. Then I wipe my face with my T-shirt. I'm covered in back-spray, so I empty the water bottle all over me, scrub, and wring out my shirt. Now I look like a drowned rat. It's probably the perfect outfit to wear to admit my arseholerey to the girl I like. If she punches me and gives me a blood lip, that will undoubtedly complete my look. My next fashion runway show: *Loser Inspired Collection, Blue Lake Period*.

'I'd forgotten how spectacular it is,' Daisy says, looking across the road at the lake.

Grateful for the distraction, I follow her line of sight and gaze with wonder at the massive ancient crater. The intense blue hue of the water is almost otherworldly. It's mind-bending to think this once was a raging inferno spewing lava and ash, but now it's calm and peaceful; a tourist attraction with flourishing wildlife. Proof that, over time, some things can change for the better.

There are two viewing choices: visitors can either climb the concrete stairs to the small rotunda lookout, or take the tunnel under the road to a viewing platform.

Chip is already halfway up the stairs. Jackson follows him, patiently helping Daisy to climb too.

Chloe rests a hand on my shoulder. 'You okay?'

I nod. I *do* feel better. Better out than in, as Chip says.

Her hand slides down my arm and she threads her fingers through mine. 'Come to the other side with me?'

We walk down the stairs and through a short concrete tunnel that shudders with the vibrations of cars overhead. We emerge into the setting sun. She walks across the parquetry platform and leans against the wooden railing, looking out at the flat blue water – no waves, no current, complete stillness.

'What do you think?' I ask, standing by her side. 'Hard to believe it was once ugly rivers of stinking sulphur.'

Her brow furrows. 'I don't know about *ugly*. Depends on your interpretation of beauty.'

*You're my interpretation of beauty.*

'It would've been spectacular,' she says.

'You're right,' I say, reimagining it. 'It would've been.'

'If I'm honest,' she says, holding the rail and rocking back on her feet, 'I'm actually secretly nervous. There's this irrational voice inside my head telling me it's going to blow.'

'Not irrational,' I say. 'More like representative of my luck. In twenty-eight thousand years nothing happens, and then the moment I stand near it? *BOOM!* You should get out of here while you can.'

She laughs. 'We'd end up like those Pompeii plaster casts.'

I nod. 'I've always thought the ones with their legs in a sitting position were on the loo when it hit.' I mime an unsuspecting Roman on the crapper. 'Caesar's ghost! What's that rumble? What's that smell? Jeez, think I'm gunna have to tell Claudia to go easy on the spelt bread. It's doing my guts no favours.'

She joins my routine, fanning her nose. 'It was the goat stew you ate, Romulus. You had three helpings. You're such a swine!'

'Too much pomegranate wine,' I agree. 'Oh! Actually, now I remember! It was that slice of Errol pie!'

She clutches her stomach, laughing. 'Stop it!' When she catches her breath, she says, 'Oh my god. Do you think Harold is feeling sick by now?'

'Possibly. I personally don't mind a little Ash Brie or Charcoal Chicken from time to time, but human ashes are something else. Especially ... *preserved* ones. Whatever's happening, I'm glad we're not there to witness it.'

'It's been a crazy ride, huh?'

'Sure has.'

She stops talking and gazes out at the water again. After at least a minute's silence, she says, 'I can't believe it's over.' She turns to look at me with something like guilt in her eyes.

I swallow. 'This is it, huh?'

She nods. 'This is it.'

'What happens now?'

'Um ... you guys give me a lift back to town, and I take it from there, I guess.'

'Where's there?'

She shrugs. 'I have time. I'll figure something out.' She sinks her hand into her pocket and pulls out a folded piece of paper no bigger than a fifty-cent coin. She passes it to me. 'I made you something. It's not much. Just something I did when we were in Meningie. You were in the takeaway shop and I had nothing to do, so I sat at one of the picnic tables and doodled. This is what came out.'

I unfold it. It's a blue pen sketch drawn on the back of a takeaway menu. When I see it in full my heart skips. It's a typewriter nestled in grass at the base of a headstone. Above it are the words to the poem 'Remember' by Christina Rossetti – the same poem I wrote in my childhood diary, the one that was stolen when our house was broken into.

I didn't tell her about the poem, did I? How could she know?

Her voice is gentle. 'Your hands are shaking, Taylor.'

The paper flaps. I try unsuccessfully to still it.

'You don't like it?' She sounds crushed.

'Don't … like …' I stutter. 'No! That's not it at all. I love it. It's amazing. It's … um … wow. You're, like, *really* talented.'

'You think?'

'Yeah. I can see how you got a scholarship. This is … it's so … I don't know what to say.'

She laughs. 'I think you've said all I need to hear.'

'How did you know?'

Her brow knits. 'Know what?'

'The poem. It's my favourite. I can recite it by heart.'

Her face is a picture of surprise. 'It was printed on the little service cards at Kelly's funeral. That's the first time I'd seen it. I thought it was beautiful, so I memorised it.'

I can't quite believe it. 'I like what it says about forgetting,' I tell her. 'The greatest sacrifice you can make is to set someone you love free.'

'Yeah,' she says, 'but I don't know how you can forget someone you love.'

Maybe it's wishful thinking, but it's like her eyes are saying so much more.

'I think it's about permission to move on,' I say. 'The person is letting you go.'

She nods.

I take a chance. 'If Kelly could speak, do you think that's what she'd say? *Let go. Move on.*'

She gulps and turns her back.

I hold her drawing out to her. 'You have real talent, Chloe. Are you really going to chuck it in?'

She looks back at me, eyes dark. 'I deserve to lose something.'

'But this is your future, Chloe. You have a life to live.'

She scoffs. 'Don't remind me.'

'How long are you going to punish yourself?'

'As long as it takes.'

'It won't bring her back.'

She hugs herself and stares at the lake. 'Maybe *you* can let go of things—'

'Chloe, I've been meaning to tell you something.'

Tears fall. She sniffs and wipes them away. 'We don't need to do this, Taylor.'

'Do what?'

'*This.* Say how we feel.' A frustrated sweep of her hair, she adds, 'Look, I admit it, okay? I care about you. Another time and place, maybe we could've—'

'That's not what I meant.'

Her cheeks flood red. 'It's not?'

I suck a deep breath. Here goes. I'm about to spew my guts up for the second time today. 'Did anyone tell you about a post about Kelly?'

She looks at me intently. I can tell she doesn't follow.

'On Facebook,' I say.

She shakes her head. 'I can't see her Facebook. She changed her settings right before she—' She looks over my shoulder, into the distance.

'So you *are* on Facebook?'

She drags her foot along the ground. 'Yeah. But Kelly blocked me right after we argued. I know her settings allowed for people to post on her timeline without her permission. Her mum told me that people still write her notes and stuff. They talk to her like she's still alive.' She looks at me hard. 'Why are you asking?'

'I was friends with her.'

She reels back.

'Online,' I add. 'Not in real life. I can't remember if I ever actually spoke to her.'

Her face contorts with shock. Then anger. Her whole body stiffens. I knew the storm would come and I thought I was ready for it, but I don't know if you can ever really be ready for a moment like this.

She explodes, *'And you only thought to tell me this now?'*

'You were upset the other night. I didn't think it was the right time.'

'You knew who I was talking about? When I made you promise not to say anything, you knew then?'

'I only realised when you said her name.'

She throws her hands up. 'We've had a full day together since then, Taylor! Why didn't you say anything?'

'I haven't had a chance. I was waiting for a private moment. You've got to admit it's cramped in the car. Do you think I'm going to blurt it out in front of the others?'

She seems to take this on board, but just as quickly she seethes, 'What about at the beach? We were alone then!'

She's right. We were.

She paces in circles, her head in her hands. 'Oh my god ...'

'Thing is, Chloe. Me knowing Kelly isn't the whole story.'

She looks up.

'I'm the one who wrote the post – the one everyone was talking about.'

She stares at me, mouth open, eyes wide. It's like I can see the pieces of her brain clattering into place, the puzzle coming together, forming a picture. 'Wait a minute,' she whispers. 'I remember now. My friend Jessica told me that some random … some guy from Kelly's school said something. She said he made awful judgmental comments about people's grief. You're telling me that was you?'

I nod.

She blinks slowly. 'Holy fuck.'

I reach for her. 'Chloe …'

She backs away, shaking, eyes clouded. 'Don't touch me!' She yells. 'Don't come anywhere near me!'

'Chloe, I—'

It hits her. 'Oh my god! Is that *why* you had the falling-out with your friends? That's the thing you did?! You said there wasn't a fight, they were angry at you for saying something.'

'They didn't understand what I was trying to say—'

She shakes a finger at me. 'Save it, Taylor! Don't say *anything*. I don't care about a single word that comes out of your mouth. You got that? I don't want to know.'

My stomach plummets. She's not going to give me a chance to explain. 'But you don't even know what I wrote,' I say quietly.

She's crying hard now. 'I don't need to know! Whatever you said, Taylor, you were judging Kelly! You were judging me! *I* killed her. Me! I told you that. It's my fault!'

'You didn't kill her, Chloe.'

'Shut up!' she screams. 'I can't believe I told you things. I can't believe I had feelings for you!'

The moment the words leave her mouth, her face falls like she didn't mean to say that part – it slipped out.

She marches up to me, puts both arms out and shoves me hard. 'You're such a prick!'

*Tell me something I don't know.*

'Don't come near me again, Taylor. Got it? Don't follow me. Don't try to contact me. Leave me alone.'

She spins on one heel and runs back through the tunnel. I chase her, pleading pathetically for her to listen, but she runs up the stairs, goes to the hearse, grabs her bag and strides off down the hill, yelling, 'Fuck off, Taylor! Go to hell!'

I stand on the footpath watching her leave, my heart dissolving with every step she takes.

When she's nothing but a dot in the distance, I turn back and look at the volcano. I don't know why I'm surprised with the way that went. Maybe I'd kidded myself into hoping for something better.

Serve me up a slice of Errol pie, folks – I got my just desserts.

# CHAPTER TWENTY-SIX

'Chloe is Cersei Lannister,' Chip declares between heavy puffs of his Chupa Chup. One hand on the steering wheel, he flicks thin air into the Smokemart ashtray and points his stick at me. '*Game of Thrones*. You know it, I know it.'

'How do you work that out? And PS, keep your eyes on the road!'

After visiting the lake and throwing myself into the proverbial volcano, I'd explained to the others that Chloe had decided to take off; she wasn't into emotional goodbyes, and a quick exit was a good exit. Chip didn't take too kindly to that. He thought her rude. Daisy looked disappointed, but she sighed and said, 'I guess it's too late now.' I wanted to tell them the truth, but as usual I didn't know where to start.

We're headed into town to get petrol. The tank is almost empty. Daisy is low on cigarettes and Chip's Chupa Chup supply is bankrupt. Jackson is craving another meat pie. It's a lesson in how addiction drives the consumer market, I tell you.

Chip indicates to turn left. 'I'm trying to alleviate your worries, Taylor. Drawing on literature's evil female characters will help you dissociate. *Game of Thrones* is an excellent starting point.'

'I thought Chloe was more Arya Stark.'

'Arya isn't evil,' Chip argues. 'Arya is kickass, but she isn't evil.'

'Exactly.'

He shakes his head. 'You're putting Chloe on a pedestal. You need to stop. Chloe was Cersei. Didn't you notice? She had that resting bitch face thing going on.'

'That's her face. She can't help her face.'

'Her face is a warning light blinking, *Stay the hell away*.'

Daisy pipes up, 'Why do you boys knock strong women?'

Chip shifts in his seat, not knowing how to respond.

'Chloe had nerve,' Daisy says. 'She had spark and backbone, and sure, she might not have always made the best decisions, but she's got a lifetime ahead of her to work on that. I, for one, liked her.'

'I liked her too, Daisy.' And saying it out loud only makes my heart ache more.

'*Trouble* is what you like,' Chip says, flipping the visor to block the sun's last rays. 'Besides, you knew her for what, a couple of days? A sparrow's fart. I've had longer relationships with Kleenex.'

'*All* your relationships have been with Kleenex,' I say. 'You could be sponsored by Kleenex.'

Behind me, Jackson cracks up. 'Don't forget the petroleum industry.'

'Yes!' I say. 'The Great Barrier Reef is under threat because of you, Chip. They're drilling for oil in an attempt to feed your insatiable appetite for lubricant. Don't you feel guilty? Sea creatures are suffocating. Coral is soon to become a daggy name associated with CWA ladies. The eighth wonder of the world will disappear because you're fixated on friction reduction.'

'Ooh, keep talking,' Chip interrupts. 'You're turning me on.'

'I believe you could fall for Chloe that fast,' Jackson says to me. 'I once fell in love pretty much instantly.'

Daisy pats his leg. 'Ooh. Do tell.'

Jackson hugs himself, his expression serene. 'Her name was Brindabella Rogers and she was nine years old. It happened at a Hungry Jacks indoor playground. She came down the slide with her skirt around her ears. That was it, my heart was sold.'

Chip coughs. 'I'm not sure where to begin with unpacking that image.'

Jackson rolls his eyes. 'I was nine years old *too*, dipshit. She was perfection. We spent an hour swinging from the monkey bars. We completed the colouring competition together. She let me share her onion rings—'

'Oh! That *is* love,' Chip agrees.

'—and she had soft brown hair, bright blue eyes, a smattering of tiny freckles across her cute button nose. And ooh! She wore those socks, the short white ones rolled down with little lacy bits around the edges.'

'Again,' Chip says, 'you're painting a concerning picture.'

'When her parents said it was time to go, she crash-tackled me on the rubber mat and stole a kiss behind the king's quarters. She whispered I was her prince and that one day I would climb a tall tower and find her. I've never stopped wondering if it could come true.'

'It's probably a good thing you never found each other,' Chip says. 'Bedding a princess comes with its pitfalls.'

'Speaking from experience?' I ask.

Chip side eyes me. 'The sexual practices of the monarchy have been closely monitored throughout history.'

I wave my hands. 'Look who's been watching the History Channel.'

'In the 1400s and 1500s,' Chip says, nose upturned, 'it was not unusual for attendants to stand by and watch the monarchy in the act of lovemaking. Personally, I'd find that kind of pressure a major buzzkill.'

'Says he who wants to make inroads into the porn industry, where people stand around filming other people doing it.'

'If pornography is to be my business,' Chip says, 'I'll make it my business to know all I can. That includes the historical aspects. Do you know that in order to prove kings and queens consummated their wedding night, their sheets were displayed to the court as proof of the act? That's where the phrase, *to air one's dirty laundry*, comes from.'

I shudder at the thought. 'Well, it's a good thing they don't display *your* sheets, Chip. Yours are probably so stiff they'd have to distribute them as crackers.'

Jackson snorts. 'Would you like some dip with that?'

'No thank you,' I laugh. 'I'm trying to mend the error of my double-dipping ways.'

'Make fun if you want,' Chip says, chin jutted. 'But I *know* things. I'm educated. Archaeologists have discovered some surprising artefacts of a pleasurable nature among the Aztec ruins.'

'Fertility statuettes, I think you mean.'

'Some, yes. Others, no,' Chip debates. 'It's speculated that some objects had a more hands-on purpose.'

'I wonder how scientists drew *that* conclusion?' Jackson cackles. 'Do they test drive the hardware? Also: where do I sign up for the research study?'

'Your knowledge base *is* impressive,' I grant him. 'I'm not disputing that. However, your interpretation and application of said knowledge could do with some work.'

'You're sounding perkier,' Chip observes, conveniently ignoring my constructive criticism. He pulls us into the service station and drives up to the bowser. 'It's a good thing because we can't have you sulking all the way back to Adelaide. If you accept the reality that you and Chloe were never meant to be Sonny and Cher, you'll be at peace.'

'Who?'

'Big-haired sixties music icons,' Daisy says. 'Cher was also famous for straddling a rocket, wanting to turn back time, and for wearing a strappy garment constructed by a seatbelt manufacturer. Not a good example, Chip. Their relationship was reportedly abusive,' she finishes.

'Fair enough,' Chip says. 'Let me think of another one ...'

'Lady Gaga and Bradley Cooper,' Jackson says eagerly. 'Did you see their Oscar performance? It was the bomb.'

'You need to cut me some slack,' I say. 'This is my second loss in as many days.'

Chip bats his eyelids. 'You still have me.' He crushes his Chupa Chup stick in the ashtray. 'Look, I agree your scoresheet is looking rather shabby. We can always fudge the data.' Someone behind us toots their horn. 'Yeah, yeah, keep your cravat on.' Chip presses the petrol cap button and gets out.

As he plugs in the nozzle and starts pumping petrol, Jackson asks me, 'Do you really think he's going to make it as a movie director?'

Daisy coughs into her tissue. 'That's a polite way of framing it.'

I pass her a water bottle. 'He's committed. You have to give him that.'

Jackson's shoulders sag. 'I should be grateful for the connection, I guess. When I get out of prison, the way the system works with declaring prior convictions, it might be the only decent paying job open to me.'

Daisy wipes her mouth and hands me back the bottle. She waves a finger, pointing at someone outside. 'Don't I know him? That guy, the one filling up over there. See?'

She's right – we all do. Bald head, big beer belly, threatening stance – it's the church neighbour from hell, Slicker Wilcock. And he's looking right at us.

'Shit,' Jackson mutters. 'This isn't good.'

The police obviously didn't arrest him or he wouldn't be here. 'Stay calm,' I say. 'Maybe he won't want any more trouble.'

It's an optimistic thought. Slicker moves in our direction. My window is open a fraction, petrol fumes wafting in, and amidst the noise of car radios, growling motors, and customers shouting *hellos* and *goodbyes*, I hear him yell at Chip something that sounds like, 'It *is* you, you little punk!'

Chip hangs up the petrol nozzle. He's not fast enough. Slicker is in his face. Cornered, Chip has no choice but to confront him. 'Sir, I think you have me confused with someone else.'

'Yeah?' Slicker says menacingly. 'Who would that be?'

Chip straightens his cravat. 'Your ignorance can be forgiven. It's an easy mistake to make. Allow me to introduce myself. Chippolata Magna Carta, highly respected film industry professional. You've probably seen me on the red carpet.' He flashes a winning smile. 'I'm usually photographed hanging out with celebrities so that's probably why you can't place me. I'm not an actor. I'm a producer-director.'

Slicker's angry expression slips like he's unsure of himself. He peers at the window, looking right at Daisy and Jackson. Then he straightens up and puffs out his chest. 'That your cast?'

'Key grips,' Chip says confidently.

Jackson whispers to me, 'What's a key grip?'

'Dunno,' I whisper back. 'But you always see them listed on the credits.'

'And my best boy,' Chip says, pointing at me.

Jackson pats my back. 'Aw, that's so nice!'

I shout-whisper, 'It's another film industry term, you dick.'

'What the hell are you talking about?' Slicker rumbles, his massive frame dwarfing Chip.

Chip places a hand on Slicker's chest. 'Sir, please take a step back. This is a limousine, a *very* expensive vehicle. I must maintain its pristine condition. Appearance, in my industry, is everything.'

Slicker looks at Chip like he's a Fruit Loop shy of a cereal box. 'It's a bloody hearse!'

Chip gasps. 'Sir, that's insulting! This vehicle is leased by the production company. The Actor's Guild have very strict guidelines when it comes to endorsing a particular standard of transportation and it's my obligation to adhere to them.'

Slicker sticks a stubby finger into Chip's chest. 'Mate, if you don't cut the bullshit, I'm gunna stuff you in the back, drive you to a cemetery and bury you six feet under.'

In my peripheral vision I notice a young, pimple-faced service station attendant standing on the sidelines, watching. 'Can I be of assistance?' He squeaks. I don't know if his voice sounds like that because he's nervous or because his testicles have yet to make the journey south.

Slicker looks at him as if he's a pesky fly. 'Not your problem, Zachary. Go back to your desk.'

Zachary's jittery, rabbit-like eyes flit from Chip to Slicker. 'You sure?'

'Sure I'm sure,' Slicker insists. 'By the way, did your mum get the apricot jam?'

Zachary gives him two thumbs up. 'Top shelf, Mr Wilcock.'

'Good to hear,' he sneers. 'Now run along. I've got things here covered.'

Zachary backs away and heads inside. Slicker turns his attention to Chip. 'Listen here you little shi—'

The door behind me opens. In the side-mirror, I see Daisy clad in aviator sunnies, a football scarf wrapped around her face, toting the plastic gun. She must've got it from the backpack. She digs it between Slicker's shoulderblades and thunders, 'Leave the kid alone!' Her whole body shakes. It doesn't seem like fear – more like adrenaline. 'I'm done with men like you!'

Slicker puts both hands in the air. 'Who *are* you people?'

'People with nothing to lose,' Daisy barks. 'Now, I suggest you go back to your jam jars – unless you want some in-built air-conditioning?'

Slicker nods like a frightened schoolboy. He takes a few steps forward before turning to see Daisy brandishing the gun. She lifts it, rotates it to the left, cocks her head like a gangland gangster and croaks, *'Chick chick boom!'*

Slicker 'sure-I'm-sure' surely shits his pants. He runs for his car, jumps in and takes off. Zachary comes running out, waving him down, yelling he forgot to pay for the fuel. He looks at Daisy who, in lieu of a holster belt, is shoving the gun down the front of her jeans. She gets back into the hearse.

Chip runs around to the driver's side and jumps in. This time there's no screaming, *Go, go, go!* We know the drill. Chip floors it from the servo.

Daisy unwraps her scarf, tosses the sunnies aside and holds her hand up at me for a high-five.

I slap it.

'Bitches be damned,' she says. 'That felt good.'

# CHAPTER TWENTY-SEVEN

'It's official,' Chip announces. 'I'm detoxing.'

He lifts a shaky hand from the steering wheel to wipe his glistening brow. Thin lines of perspiration run past his temples. He dry-swallows and licks his lips. He's out of Chupa Chups, and withdrawal is a cruel taskmaster. He says he's *edgy and on the brink*. Also: *more prone to risk-taking behaviour.* (Not sure what the last forty-eight hours qualifies as?) He has *all the classic signs of substance abuse: aches and pains, weight gain, anxiety.* (I could've said the weight gain was owing to excess sugar consumption, but I didn't argue.) His *relationships and employment opportunities are now at risk* (again, possibly a foregone conclusion) and he feels *isolated and alone.*

'Be my cheer squad,' Chip pleads. 'I need for you to tell me that this is a good thing. This is an opportunity to kick the habit once and for all. Gotta turn this frown upside down.'

He flicks the indicator, gives way to a hurtling double-semi packed with cattle, and turns onto the highway. We're headed to Adelaide via Coonalpyn, the small rural township with the silo art. Chip badly wants to see it. The sky is dark now, a full moon on the rise, but the towering concrete mural is apparently floodlit. I have to admit I wouldn't mind seeing it too. I only wish Chloe was here to share it.

She's well and truly behind us now. The realisation is setting in that I'll never see her again. I'm headed back to my pathetic reality: dumped outcast, friendless virgin, perpetual online idiot. The past two days briefly made it seem like everything has changed, but really nothing has.

'If Slicker hadn't have shown up at the servo I could've got my fix,' Chip complains. 'It's the universe's way of making me give up. A sign. A higher power is telling me I'm destined for greater things.'

'I know you're used to reading into stuff, Chip,' I say. 'But a higher power? Come on. That's stretching the truth even by your standards. Every servo across Australia stocks Chupa Chups. The universe is working *against* you giving up, not for it.'

*Click-click.* The sweet smell of burning tobacco wafts through the car.

Daisy waves her hand, passing me a cigarette. 'For God's sake shut him up,' she croaks.

I hand it to Chip. He looks at it like it's a foreign object. 'You *real* smoke it,' I tell him.

He cautiously brings the filter to his lips, draws back and promptly explodes into a violent coughing fit. He winds down the window and throws it out.

Jackson whacks his headrest. 'Hey! Don't do that! You'll start a grass fire.'

Chip clears his throat. He looks at Daisy in the mirror, blinking with amazement. 'How the hell do you do that every day?'

'Dunno,' she says, 'but the commitment has really paid off.'

Jackson asks, 'You've never smoke-smoked before, Chip? I

don't get it. I thought the Chupa Chup thing was a replacement for the real thing?'

'You thought wrong,' Chip says. He looks longingly at his empty hand, where a Chupa Chup would usually be. 'I was recruited at an early age.'

'Oh?' I laugh. 'What? The schoolyard bully cornered you in the sandpit and said, *Whatup Dawg. You up for harder thrills than mud pies?*'

Chip shakes his head. 'First, I was breastfed. Then my dad dipped my pacifier in honey. For a while I wore a mouth plate. I was susceptible to colds, so I sucked a lot of lozenges. I was prescribed gum to stop me from chewing on my tongue. It was a slippery slope into the spiralling black depths of Chupa Chup addiction, but in hindsight, entirely foreseeable I'd end up here.' He wipes away crocodile tears. 'Gosh, I didn't realise how good it would feel to talk about it. You guys are the best. I love you.'

'I think you have what's known as an oral fixation,' I tell him.

'He *did* say he wants to direct porn,' Jackson says.

'Not that kind,' I say. '*Oral fixation.* Psychotherapist Sigmund Freud famously identified it as a problem during the weaning process. A baby is supposed to grow and become independent, but some infants find it traumatic and require consolation. Freud postulates that's why some adults have problems with over-eating, drinking, smoking or nail-biting. They never really detached from the proverbial tit.'

Jackson chuckles. 'Who'd want to, is my question.'

Chip considers this. 'I *am* fond of boobs.'

'That's not what I meant—'

'Besides,' Chip says, 'what *is* the normal usage of one's mouth if it isn't for food-stuffing, nail-biting, drinking and smoking?

All very pleasurable acts. Once again, Taylor, you're sucking the joy from life.'

'How is nail-biting pleasurable?'

'Cavemen didn't have scissors,' Chip says.

I'm about to ask what the fuck that means, when Daisy interrupts, 'Freud was a strange little man.' She waves her hand dismissively. 'Try Gestaltian. Or Jung. That shit'll give you something to ponder.'

Jackson appears confounded.

Daisy pokes him. 'What? You don't read?'

A light shower of rain begins to fall. Chip turns on the wipers. 'Addiction is anything you do too much that becomes harmful.' He glances at me. 'Like obsessing over girls.'

'You're psychoanalysing *me* now? Oh right. And porn *isn't* obsessing over girls?'

'Procreation is fundamental to the future of the human race,' Chip defends. 'Porn is a public service. Inciting lust is vital to the survival of the planet.'

'The planet is overpopulated, Chip. Besides, you're telling me humans can't replicate without porn? How does the animal kingdom survive? I'll have to watch wildlife documentaries more closely. I must've missed the bit where the lion dials up laptop inspo before accosting a lioness in the field.'

'Funny you should mention it,' Chip says. 'Did you know that the orchid plant mimics the wasp's sexual organs so it can be pollinated? If that's not some natural pornographic magic, I don't know what is.'

Daisy coughs heavily. Jackson rubs her back. 'You okay, Granny?'

She catches her breath. 'Yeah, I'm all right. I think the last couple of days have caught up with me. I'm suddenly feeling every one of my seventy-seven years.'

'It's probably these guys,' Jackson says, motioning at me and Chip. 'Listening to them is exhausting. Maybe you should try to get some sleep?'

Daisy rests her head on Jackson's shoulder and closes her eyes. Within minutes, she's snoring lightly.

'Yeah, no, you're wrong,' Chip says to no one in particular. 'I can see how you got there, but nope, you're totally incorrect.'

'Who are you—?' Then it hits me. Another car spook is upon us.

'Wrong, wrong, wrong,' Chip says.

I sigh. 'Who is it this time?'

'Richard. He's weighing in on the oral fixation thing.'

'Remind me who Richard is?'

'Died in the bank hold-up.'

'Right. In the armoured vehicle?'

Chip nods. Then he shakes his head. 'Not in it, *underneath* it.'

'I don't follow.'

'Me neither,' says Jackson.

Chip rolls his eyes. 'It was a solo operation – no driver. Richard stole the armoured van *first* because he thought it would be a less conspicuous means of escape and if the cops followed him, they'd have zero luck shooting at the windows. Instead of parking it, he wrapped one of those stretchy, springy ropes around the steering wheel, put it in gear and left it running on full lock, doing unpiloted donuts of the carpark. When he ran out of the bank and jumped in, the van would already be moving and he could unhook the rope and take off.'

I don't get it. 'So how did he—?'

'End up underneath it? As he ran towards the van, the bank alarms sounded. He made the fatal error of turning back to see if anyone was following him. In the split second he looked away, the van ran over him, crushing his legs. The dude was lying there, a sitting duck. It circled back and flattened his head.'

'Crime never pays,' says Jackson.

'Richard was pulling a Robin Hood,' Chip explains. 'Stealing from the rich to give to the poor.'

'His cause being?' I ask.

'Underfunded chicken-poo sculptures.'

I don't have any words.

'Say what?' Jackson manages.

'He knows it's not the most attractive concept,' Chip says, 'but who's to judge what's art and what isn't? Countless academics have debated this very idea. Theses have been written, journals published. In comparison to sports, the arts is always fighting for financial support.'

Jackson snorts. 'Explain the need for chicken-shit sculptures to the general public, I dare you.'

Chip huffs. 'The public are uptight and unimaginative.'

'A sweeping assessment,' I say.

'But a true one.'

'Wouldn't it stink?' Jackson asks.

'Beauty is in the eye of the beholder,' Chip says.

'No ... I mean literally stink. *Smell*.'

'Oh. Well, yes,' Chip admits, 'but Richard says that's crucial to activating the brain's sensory lobe and connecting with the idea that an organic material is at play.'

I attempt to clarify. 'So basically you're saying you can justify anything with some fancy explanations and call it art?'

Chip snaps, 'We could debate this, Taylor, but it's already been done. I think there's relief to be found in accepting that not everything has or needs boundaries. Some things exist in the margins and by their very existence they can be exactly as they are. It's like before when we talked about stories, remember? There doesn't have to be a moral to every story. It is what it is.'

Jackson ponders, 'What do you think the moral to Richard's story is?'

'Don't stick a leg out?' I suggest. 'Don't lose your head? The road to hell is paved with good intentions, crushed skulls and splattered brains?'

Chip relays, 'Richard says the moral is: *Don't look back*. And PS, *our* intentions on this trip have been nothing *but* good. Do you see us on the road to hell?'

'A matter of perception,' I say. 'We're not back in Adelaide yet.'

'But we're on the home strait, Taylor. It doesn't have to go wrong. There's no pending doom. In fact, it's looking exceptionally positive.'

'You've lured yourself into a false sense of security,' I tell him.

'Catastrophic thinking will do you no favours.'

'Says he who's on a Chupa Chup downward spiral.'

'Says *I* who's conquering my demons and remaking myself.' Chip twirls a finger in the air. 'Spin it around, Taylor. Spin. It. Round. Pessimist, optimist. You have a choice. Is the glass half full or empty?'

'Irrelevant if the liquid is putrid.'

'You lack faith.'

'I've seen too much go wrong.'

'You're not seeing the stuff that's gone right.'

When he says it, something inside me heaves and shifts – the creature of burden, the shame of my mistakes. The Thing is stirred. Poked in its safe little cave, it grumbles. *Is it really as simple as the way I look at things?*

'If you're on the road, Taylor, you're going somewhere,' Chip says, repeating his earlier assertion. 'That's brave. Bravery doesn't necessarily look like someone in a superhero costume. Bravery is having faith in yourself; feeling the fear and doing it anyway.'

'I've been a passenger,' I say.

Chip nods.

'Cass said I'm hard work.'

'Cass wasn't up to the task.' He pats my shoulder. 'Cass isn't the authority on your life, my friend. *You* are.'

His words hit me like the cattle-loaded semi doing a hundred k: He's right. I *am* the authority.

'Start acting like it,' Chip says.

# CHAPTER TWENTY-EIGHT

Out of the darkness, the enormous concrete silos come into view – a series of giant black-and-white illustrations of primary-school children painted on an epic scale. Humans are capable of a great many feats and mind-bending creations, and this certainly qualifies as that; to construct something of this size and magnitude and to get it right is truly art. It's incredible.

'Beats chicken-shit sculptures,' Jackson says.

We turn into the carpark and pull up alongside it. There's no one else here. We have the place to ourselves. It's dark, so probably not the best time for viewing it in all its glory.

'Granny?' Jackson gently shakes her shoulder. 'Wake up. You have to see this.' Daisy stirs and lifts her head. 'What do you think?'

I grin. 'Feeling inspired, Jackson Pollock?'

He smirks. 'Actually, I am. Can we take a closer look?'

Chip nods. 'Sure.'

He leaves the headlights on. We get out and walk up to the silos, dodging puddles from the recent downpour. There's that fresh after-rain smell in the air. Crickets chirp in the nearby paddocks and moths swarm, circling the floodlights. We stand near it, then backtrack, trying to work out the best vantage point to appreciate it in its entirety.

The children are portrayed with their heads tilted, looking down at their feet. One of them wears glasses. His hand is on his forehead, either wiping his brow or sheltering his eyes from the sun – I can't tell which. The girl on the end silo has her back to the viewer, her messy hair in a bunched ponytail, her arm up, drawing on the wall above her head. The shading is incredible – the folds of her school shirt, the crinkles in the material. I'm convinced if I touched it, I'd feel the texture.

Jackson reads from an information plaque. 'It says it was created by Brisbane artist Guido van Helten. The children represent the future of the township.'

'We are the world,' I say.

Daisy lights a smoke. 'Huh?'

'That famous song by Michael Jackson and Lionel Richie for Live Aid. It says the children are the future.'

Chip nods. 'Art informing art.' He interlocks his fingers at the back of his head and rocks on his feet. 'I'm not saying that *was* Guido's inspiration, but that's the beauty of it. Concepts planted in our psyche through music and other media unconsciously inform what we create.'

We stare at him.

He looks at us. 'What?'

'Nothing,' I say. 'It's just … for a moment you sounded—'

'Intelligent,' Jackson finishes.

Chip unlocks his hands and pats his pocket. 'Ooh! That's surely the buzz of another submission.' He gets out his phone, swipes a few times and confirms. 'Oh yeah, baby. Now that's what I'm talking about.'

I'd almost forgotten about *Hotties of the Northern Burbs*. Or maybe I'm deliberately trying to forget.

I'm almost afraid to ask, after my parent's contribution. 'What have you got?'

'Yoga poses. Word's obviously reached Ms Flexy!'

I swallow hard. *'Miss Hooper?'*

He reads my panic. 'Relax. She has no idea who we are.'

I can't help my curiosity. 'Can I see?'

He clutches his phone protectively against his chest. 'I don't think that's appropriate. Feels like a breach of the student-teacher relationship to me. I'll keep this one quarantined until you graduate.' He wanders off, swiping and stabbing at his phone.

Jackson announces he needs to take a leak. He marches into the nearby trees for some privacy.

Daisy chuffs her smoke. She waves her free hand at the silo art. 'A shame your girl isn't here to see this.'

I don't bother arguing with her reference to Chloe as *my girl*. 'Yeah,' I say. 'She would've liked it.'

'I saw her drawing something when we were at Meningie,' Daisy tells me. 'She's very talented.'

She must've seen Chloe making the picture for me. I instinctively touch my back pocket where it's folded up, safe. When I get home I plan to pin it to my wall above my bed.

'Need an ear?' Daisy offers.

I shrug. 'There's not a lot to tell.'

She exhales a plume of smoke and waves at the silos. 'See these? They're packed with grain. Millions of tiny seeds. I'm willing to bet each one of them that there's stuff you need to get off your chest.' She puts out the palm of her hand. 'Sometimes all it takes is one grain to tip us over, Taylor. Go on, give me one. Let me hold it for you.'

I run my hands through my hair, a strange nervousness eating at me. 'I dunno ...'

She keeps her hand extended. 'We can hold a few, but after that we need to share the load.'

I give a defeated sigh. 'You're sure?'

She winks. 'I'll take it to my grave.'

I laugh at her dark humour. But it also makes me sad. 'I did something, Daisy. Something bad.'

'Go on ...'

'I wrote something. *Public*. On Facebook. I said stuff I shouldn't have about people.'

Daisy flicks ash and takes a drag. 'You gave unsolicited advice?'

'More like an unwelcome opinion.'

'About?'

'About a girl called Kelly who killed herself.'

Daisy comes close and strokes my arm. 'That's very sad. Was she a good friend?'

'That's the weird thing, Daisy. She wasn't. I didn't even know her. I knew *of* her. We were friends online. That's all.'

Daisy nods. 'I don't really understand this Facebook thing, but I'm guessing it's like when I was a kid and we had pen-pals. Friends you wrote to, but you hadn't actually met them in real life.'

'It's like that with some, not everyone.'

She sucks the last of her smoke and butts it out. 'When I wrote to my pen-pal, I told her all my secrets. I wrote the most intimate things; things I couldn't say out loud. Strange, huh?

Anonymity is powerful. Like how Catholics enter confessionals to talk to a priest.'

I think of Chloe walking up the road after the disco. *Like a confessional.*

'Do you know why the girl took her life?' Daisy asks.

'No. And no one is ever going to know. She's not here to tell her story.'

'Did she leave a note?'

I shake my head. 'Nothing. Well, not that I'm aware of.'

We watch as Jackson stumbles out of the bushes, zipping up his jeans. He heads for the hearse, opens the back door and leans inside, searching for something.

Daisy regards me more seriously. 'This opinion you gave. Why was it bad?'

I rub my palms on my jeans. 'After she died, people were writing this stuff on her timeline – stuff about loving her and missing her. It made me furious because I never saw any of them doing it when she was alive. Kelly would often post things – *sad things* – and no one would comment. Before she died, she did it with increasing frequency. It was like no one noticed. Where were they then? Why weren't they talking to her then? She was reaching out. She was trying to say she was hurting.'

'Did *you* say something?'

The words get stuck in my throat.

'Taylor?'

Tears come. I feel them, hot and stinging.

Daisy's voice is gentle. 'That's why you feel so bad, isn't it?'

I nod and wipe my cheeks with my shirt sleeve. 'I pressed *like* on a few things. I didn't comment. I should've. I can't stop thinking I could've done something ... *said* something. I feel like a dick for caring so much. I wasn't even her real-life friend.'

Daisy rubs my back. 'So you vented by blaming other people?'

I sigh, 'Yeah.'

Daisy keeps rubbing my back, her hand moving in a circular motion. 'Dear boy, it's wonderful how thoughtful you are, truly. But take it from an old biddy who's been around the traps a few times. In this life we don't have emotional space for everyone. I know that sounds harsh, but hear me out. This Facebook thing: equate it to my childhood pen-pal. Imagine if I'd had hundreds of them. Hundreds of letters choking my mailbox. Imagine the time it would take to respond to each of those letters. You couldn't possibly. It's too much for one person.' She points to the silos. 'When it's full, it's full. You can't cram more in there without tipping some out. It's the same with people. We have space for some, but not for all. The love and responsibility *has* to be shared. There were people close to this Kelly girl who should've been there for her.'

'But they *weren't* there for her, Daisy,' I choke. 'That's why others needed to step in.'

'Maybe they did? Maybe they tried. You don't know what went on, Taylor. You weren't there. Whatever you saw online was only one part of the picture.'

I think of Chloe. I'd told her she'd done all she could. I told her she shouldn't shoulder the blame. Why can't I apply that to me?

'Depression makes people think hopeless things,' Daisy says, 'and challenging those thoughts isn't always enough. Professional care is required. I know because I've been there.'

I think about what I know about Daisy, about what she's had to endure. It doesn't surprise me.

'When you come out of it, you wonder what the hell you were thinking. But at the time it's frighteningly real,' she says.

I nod. 'I think Kelly had been struggling for a while.'

Daisy clucks her tongue. 'What about you?'

'Me?'

She stares at me.

The penny drops. *She thinks I'm depressed?* I'm about to argue, but then I wonder. *Am I?*

'My generation thought it was shameful to discuss what hurt,' Daisy says. 'Being strong was prized. I think that changed when people began to realise that the weight of silence only compounds the problem. So we started speaking up. But speaking up doesn't necessarily mean you'll be heard. We're still failing each other in that respect and I think that's what you're grappling with. If we're told it's okay to talk, and we do talk, and nothing happens, then what?'

She's right. I *am* having a hard time wrapping my head around the *then what?* What Kelly did can't be the *then what*, can it?

'The biggest thing to know is that if you don't talk, you're worse off. You *have* to talk. No two ways about it. Talk until someone listens.'

I smile. 'I wish everyone was like you, Daisy. Maybe this world wouldn't be so messed up.'

'It's not *all* messed up,' Daisy says. 'Only parts of it. Or more so, some people. There'll always be rotten apples, Taylor. You can't eradicate them, so you just have to bin them and move on.'

'Or put them in pies?'

She gives me a wicked smile. 'Ram it down their sorry throats and hope they choke on it.'

A drop of rain hits my face. Then another. 'We should probably make a move.'

She reaches up and ruffles my hair. 'You're a good kid. You'll be okay.'

When she says it, everything inside of me feels suddenly calm. It's reassurance I desperately needed to hear.

We turn and head for the hearse, but we're blinded by the glaring white lights of a truck pulling into the parking bay. The roar of the engine is all-consuming. I shield my eyes, trying to see as the passenger-side door opens and someone climbs out. A girl's voice yells, 'Cheers for the ride!'

My body is swamped with prickles. *Chloe.*

The truck pulls out, onto the highway, and there she stands, duffle bag slung over her shoulder. 'Taylor?'

Before I can say anything, Chip yells, 'Oh hey everyone! Look who's back! Cersei Lannister!'

Chloe waves at him.

'My favourite character,' he says. 'Your chariot awaits. Get in.'

# CHAPTER TWENTY-NINE

Chloe's sitting in the back seat.

She's *back* in the back seat.

*Why* is she back? I thought she wanted to see the back of me? Technically she *is* – seeing the back of my head – but she's come back to me, to *us*. I don't get it. My stomach won't stop doing backflips.

Chip drives, not saying a word. I don't speak and nor does Jackson. Daisy is the one who finally breaks the silence.

'Good to see you, dear! Now, tell me about the trucker you hitched a ride with. I want *all* the details. Don't leave anything out. Make things up if you have to. Particularly the part where he showed you his debut calendar appearance in *Naked Truckers*.'

Chloe laughs. 'The trucker was a *she*, Daisy. Her name was Wendy. She's on the return leg, headed home to see her husband and three kids.'

Daisy pouts. 'Well that's a white bread story.'

Chloe doesn't get it. 'Huh?'

'No seedy bits,' says Daisy.

Chloe laughs. 'Hey, what's with the Cersei thing, Chip? Why'd you call me that?'

'Private joke,' he says.

'You have jokes about me?' She sounds wounded.

'When the cat's not around, the mice go to town,' Chip responds. 'And besides, it's a long trip. We need to talk about something. Speaking of, are you going to tell us why you've magically returned from the land of the sleeping volcano or do we have to play twenty questions?'

Chloe shrugs. 'I missed the road.'

Chip snorts. 'The road to forgiveness.'

I whack his arm.

He feigns innocence. 'What?'

He turns the radio dial, channel surfing, searching for a familiar beat. He finds an old-school classic hits station, listens briefly to the wailing misery I recognise as Sinead O'Connor (sidenote: as if the Irish didn't have enough to be sad about), then finds a country music channel where the presenter is mid-sentence saying, 'Here's an oldie but a goodie.'

Chip taps a hand on his thigh. When Dolly Parton blasts the opening lines to 'Joelene', he promptly has Meltdown Number Two.

'Turn it off!' he cries. 'Turn it off!' He fumbles for the button, but he can't seem to get there. I don't bother to help. Watching him freak out is fun.

Until he nearly runs the hearse off the road. Then it isn't fun anymore.

I switch it off. 'Chip, are you *trying* to add to your dead passenger count?'

'Too late,' Chip says, fingers trembling – mostly his pointer and digitus medius, which he wiggles at me, signalling for a Chupa Chup. He's forgotten we're out. I open the glovebox, find a ballpoint pen and pass it to him. He sucks the end, drawing on blue ink. 'She's here,' he stutters nervously. 'She's with us.'

'Joelene?'

He nods. 'God, please make her stop.'

'Stop what?'

'Screaming. It's deafening.'

'I can't hear anything.'

'Well der!' Chip says. 'Of course you can't. But I can. She's so angry.'

'In a poltergeist way?' Jackson asks.

'Exactly,' Chip says. 'Any minute, my head is going to spin around.'

I stifle a laugh. 'She's done that to you before?'

'Not yet,' he says, dragging on his pen and puffing. 'But I've watched a lot of horror movies and I'm across all the potential scenarios. None of them are good. Shit ... we don't have any piano wire on board, do we?' He holds his finger to his neck and makes *Eee-aww* scraping sounds.

I clear my throat. 'Chip, I think it's time you told us *why* Joelene is so upset. I know you said it's the mother of all sensitive topics, but I think you need to share. Talking helps things to lose their power. This crazy behaviour isn't acceptable at one hundred kilometres an hour. It's not acceptable, *period*.'

He emits a heavy sigh. 'Okay. Fine. Maybe you're right. Do you remember what I said about how she died?'

'You mentioned something about a clown car. My brain kind of short-circuited thereafter.'

'It was a sunny day in mid-November—'

'Here we go again,' Jackson mutters.

'— when Joelene decided to take her clown car for a test

drive. She was soon to appear in the community Christmas pageant and she wanted to be sure she could pedal fast enough – especially with giant clown shoes on. Anyway, after a successful test drive around her local streets, she returned home, pedalling up the driveway. Her husband, Billy, was pottering in the garage, humming along to 'Joelene' on the radio. As Joelene pedalled across the threshold, Billy turned to give her a welcoming wave. That's when the horror began. The automatic roller-door came crashing down, crushing her inside her clown car. Clown cars aren't subject to the same rigorous cabin-testing factory safety standards that most other cars must adhere to. They're basically death traps on wheels. They don't even have airbags.'

'Because they have balloons?' Jackson interjects.

Chip glares at him and keeps talking. 'Anyway, Billy lunged for the wall control and hit the emergency button in the vain hope it would paralyse the door motor. But pressing the button made it worse. The thing went haywire. Up, down, up, down, up, down, pummelling Joelene, leaving only her clown feet unharmed. And all the while, 'Joelene' played on the radio.'

'Ouch,' Daisy says.

'Indeed,' Chip says. 'Imagine if *your* theme song played as you died? Shocking. Just shocking.'

'Hang on a sec,' I say, icy chills coursing through me. 'Are you talking about Joelene McCaskill?'

Chip clutches the wheel. '*You can hear her?*'

'No. My dad's a roller-door consultant. I remember the incident. It was *his* company's roller door and it's plagued his business ever since. The insurance claim is still going through court.' I stop talking to stare at him. 'Holy shit! You're for real!'

'I'm for—?' He hits the brakes, turning us onto the roadside, ripping through the gravel, bringing us to a skidding halt. *'I'm for real?'* he repeats.

Chloe wallops his headrest. 'Again, Chip?'

But he's not paying attention. He's unclipping his seatbelt, yelling, 'That's it! I'm done!' He gets out and slams the door. We watch as he strides ahead of us, ditching his pen-cigarette into the bushes, before turning and crouching to sit cross-legged in the gravel under the glare of the headlights.

Jackson rolls his eyes. 'What the hell is he doing?'

'Staging a protest,' Daisy answers matter-of-factly. 'It's how we got things done in the sixties. We'd lie down in front of buses. Army tanks, even. It was epic.'

I throw back my head. 'He's offended.'

Chloe says, 'Of course he's offended. He thought you believed him. If you didn't want to kiss his arse when it was injured, you're going to have to kiss it now. We're clearly not going anywhere until you do.'

'Me?' I shriek. 'What about you lot? None of you believed him either!'

'Fine,' Jackson says, opening his door. 'In the interest of getting us home this century, we'd *all* best get out and go kiss his arse.'

We pile out one by one. Jackson leads the pack, marching up to Chip, flanked by the rest of us like we're some kind of intervention party. Chip sits with his arms crossed, steadfastly unmoving. Jaw set, chin cocked, he turns his head and looks away.

'We seek an audience with our master,' Jackson begins.

As opening lines go, it's a bit dramatic, but whatever.

'We realise the error of our ways. We wish to offer an apology.'

Chip re-crosses his arms, huffs, and refuses to look at him.

Daisy goes first. 'Chip, I'll admit that all this time I thought you were a moron. Please forgive me. It's an easy mistake to make.' Her apology could admittedly do with some refinement, but decidedly done, Daisy turns and walks back to the hearse, calling over her shoulder, 'I'm going to take a quick lie-down in the back. I need to stretch out for a minute. My osteoporosis is killing me.'

Next: Chloe. 'Chip, you've got to admit your I-talk-to-dead-people routine is pretty far-fetched. I mean, when you said Lily half-swallowed a pigeon, I had my doubts. But it turns out to be entirely possible. I googled it. She's not even the first person it's happened to.'

I want to know when Chloe's had an opportunity to google, but I don't ask. I also want to know the search terms she used. And if there were photos.

Chip glances her way.

She adds, 'Some people have really big mouths – like, physically big. The lead singer of a band called Aerosmith, for example. Big enough to fit a bird. Plus there was this rock star, Ozzy Osborne, who reportedly bit the head off two doves. I'm not sure if it's a vicious rumour, and I really didn't have enough time to trawl through all the articles, but there's enough evidence to indicate it could happen. I'm sorry for doubting you.'

Chip meets her eyes and slowly nods a thank you. 'Sounds like you made an effort.'

Chloe smiles, chuffed. She looks at Jackson.

He steps forward. 'Look, Chip, I didn't say I don't believe you.

I just never said I *did*. And like I said before, my Aunty Rita is a clairvoyant, and I believe *her*, so it stands to reason I'd believe you. Right?'

Chip raises his eyebrows.

'Okay!' Jackson sighs. 'I straight-up believe you! There! I said it. No ifs, buts, maybes. Are you happy?'

Chip nods. 'Forgiven.'

Jackson steps back.

I step forward. 'Which leaves me.'

Chip pulls an extra huffy face and turns away.

'You know I'm a sceptic, Chip. You called me one yourself. You can't blame me for needing hard evidence. I just needed enough to tip the scales of belief. And now you've done that.'

He jumps to his feet. With his nose an inch from mine, he growls, 'I *gave* you evidence, Taylor! What do you think the death stories were? Did you think I made them up? Did you think I'd joke about ice-cream trucks and giant Cornettos? You can't even make that shit up!'

'Peter Streets was pretty left of field, I'll give you that.'

'I also told you that Edgar had talked to Errol.'

I nod.

'And was Errol dead?'

'Yes.'

'Well?'

'I'm sorry,' I mumble. 'You were right, I was wrong.'

He puts a hand to his ear. 'I didn't quite catch that.'

'I said I'm sorry!'

He grins and slaps my back. 'That's better, Taylor! Admitting one's failings is the first step to moving forward.'

'If we don't get going, we won't be moving anywhere.'

'Settle Petal,' he says, leading me to the car. 'As usual, your anxiousness is shitting me.'

The four of us are poised by the hearse, ready to get in, when Jackson clicks his fingers. 'I forgot. Give me a minute.'

As he goes round to wake Daisy, I spot something that makes my blood freeze – flashing red and blue lights. They come hurtling out of the darkness and they don't keep going up the highway – they stop, pulling up right in front of us.

My pulse reverberates in my ears. Red tail-lights glow. An interior light comes on. A crackling two-way radio beeps. Red, blue, red, blue, red, blue.

None of us have anywhere to go. We're in the dark, by the roadside, in the middle of nowhere.

'Shit,' Chip whispers.

'Double shit,' Jackson echoes.

'Shit, shit, shit,' Chloe panics.

My phone goes off in my pocket. I pull it out. A Geoff Message: **Re: your ad on Gumtree. Is the parachute still available?**

# CHAPTER THIRTY

'Well, folks,' the cop says, climbing out of his car. 'What seems to be the problem?'

He's in his late fifties, in good shape, with a full head of black hair. *Dyed* hair. It's straight and slicked with gel, resembling a helmet – or a repurposed taxidermied American black bear. It's so shiny and thick, I want to stroke it. He adjusts his holster belt, taps his gun pouch as if to indicate he's packing, and flicks on a small flashlight. With the glaring headlights and rhythmic blue and red, his torch is a bit lost – until he shines it directly in our faces.

'Car trouble?' He shines first at Jackson, then at me, then at Chip and Chloe, then at the hearse. 'My, my. It's an unusual vehicle you have here. Is it a ... *is this a hearse?*'

Chip parts his legs and puffs out his chest in an authoritative pose. *Oh God. Here we go.*

'We're from the Sunnyside-Up Funeral Company,' he says. 'Good evening to you, sir. We're taking a ... how shall I say it politely? A *relief* stop. A woman's bladder waits for no man.' He points an accusing finger at Chloe. 'I'm willing to bet your wife has the same issue?'

'Husband,' the cop corrects. 'But yeah, Virgil *does* have a small bladder.' His hand rests on his holster belt, his expression unsure.

That's when I remember our plastic gun. *Shit.* What if he searches us? He'll find the gun. Maybe even Daisy's weed. We are *so* going down. What was it Chip was saying about us making it back to Adelaide without a problem? I bet he's silently choking on those words now!

The cop gestures at the hearse. 'Mind if I take a look?'

'Be my guest,' Chip says cheerfully.

I glare at him. Shouldn't he be attempting to distract the cop? Fob him off? Reassure him all is well and we can happily get going?

'Name's Henry Minogue,' the cop says, pointing to his badge. He walks around to the back of the hearse. 'No relation to Kylie. Though I have been to several of her concerts, and Virgil is doing one of those online ancestry registry things to work out if there's a connection. I think he wants something to discuss at dinner parties.'

He opens the hearse back doors and shines the torch inside. I wait for his scream when Daisy sits up and says hello, but it doesn't come. He walks back over to us, rubbing his chin.

'It's been a while since I've seen something like this. I'll have to consult my list of traffic violations and see what code it falls under. You *do* know that transporting bodies in this manner is not okay, right? The body has to be restrained. In the event of an accident, it can become a lethal weapon. It could catapult into the cabin and wipe one of you out.'

*He thinks Daisy is dead?* Credit to her. A small wave of hope rises in my chest. Maybe we *are* going to get away with this?

'Someone stole our gurney,' Chip explains. 'We haven't had time to report the incident. We're on a tight turnaround and we have to get the body back to Adelaide in time for the funeral. We thought we'd worry about the paperwork later. This woman's family is our priority and we don't want for them to suffer more than they already have. Stuff-ups like this only compound the trauma and make everything worse.'

Officer Minogue considers him. I think Chip has blown our cover, but the cop says in a sympathetic tone, 'Gosh. There aren't many businesses left with the customer's best interest at heart.'

'True,' Chip agrees.

'You know, I was recently the victim of the worst online transaction in retail history. They make you jump through hoops to obtain a refund.'

Chip enquires, 'May I ask the item in question?'

'Satin pyjamas. I ordered medium and they delivered extra large. And in the wrong colour. I mean, frog green makes me want to gag.'

'No kidding ...' Chip breathes. He glances at me with an expression somewhere between unbridled relief and incredulous awe. 'Same thing happened to me.'

Officer Minogue looks at him. 'It did?'

'Yeah,' Chip says. 'I mean, I didn't get the wrong size or colour. I didn't get my pyjamas at all. But I'm pretty sure it was the old lady in my street. She has a habit of accepting packages on behalf of her neighbours.'

Officer Minogue chuckles. 'Annoying stuff, hey?' He looks again at the hearse. 'So you're telling me you're willing to risk your company's good name in order to care for this woman's family?'

'Yes,' Chip says. 'There are some instances where you have to concede there's no way out other than to do what's morally right, even if it's not legally right.'

Officer Minogue reaches into his back pocket and pulls out a yellow pad and a pen. 'Look, don't tell anyone I did this, but I'm going to write you up for a standard traffic violation. Your tail-light is dicky, in case you haven't noticed, and you need to get it seen to. I'll make it about that and let you off with a warning. Got your licence handy?'

Chip fishes out his wallet, finds his licence and hands it over. 'That's mighty kind of you.'

'Yeah well,' Officer Minogue says. 'Virgil has been chewing my ear about good karma. He says if you put some kindness into the world, it'll come back at you tenfold. I'm not sure, but I'm willing to give it a try for the old softie.' He writes up the ticket, tears it off his pad and hands it back, together with Chip's licence. 'Besides, we're in the dark in the middle of nowhere with a dead body. Hats off to you for even doing this job. It's not everyone's cup of tea, but someone has to do it.'

Chip nods. 'True.'

'Right then,' Officer Minogue says, returning to his car. Window down, he gives us a wave as he turns onto the highway, tyres churning the gravel.

Chip stares after him. 'Did that really happen?'

Chloe starts singing the chorus to Kylie Minogue's 'I Should Be So Lucky'.

Jackson rushes around to the back of the hearse. 'Granny! That was awesome! Talk about an Emmy award-winning performance.' There's a long pause. 'Granny? Hey, Granny!'

Then he's staggering back and collapsing onto his knees, head in his hands. A guttural noise cuts through the dark.

I don't have to ask.

Daisy is dead.

# CHAPTER THIRTY-ONE

'Can't you talk to her?' Jackson pleads with Chip. 'Contact her. Do your thing. Ask her if she's okay.'

'I told you,' Chip says, flicking high beam to low as a car passes us by. 'It doesn't work like that. She has to come to me. And given her parting words to me, do you think that's likely?'

Daisy *did* call him a moron.

Jackson thumps his fist on the door ledge. Choking back tears, he cries, 'Shit, Granny. Why'd you have to go so quick? Why? Why, why, why?'

I feel his pain. My guts is in knots and I'm swallowing tears. I can't believe Daisy is not playing dead this time – she's *actually* dead. Here one minute, gone the next.

Chloe, who's crying too, reaches for Jackson's hand and tries to console him. 'You got a chance to be with her. You got your wish and she got hers. And you boys,' she says to me and Chip, 'did the right thing. Daisy was happy and relaxed. I think it happened the way it was meant to. Without unfinished business. She was ready.' She pauses a moment, then says, 'Hey … we should say something. You know, out of respect.'

I think of our earlier deer encounter. Surely she doesn't want me to—?

'The poem,' Chloe suggests. 'You know the one, Taylor.'

She means 'Remember' by Christina Rossetti – the one read at Kelly's funeral; the one she wrote the words to, coupled with her drawing. The one I'd written in my diary all those years ago.

'Okay...' I agree, a lump in my throat. 'That's a nice idea. Let's do it.'

'What are you talking about?' Jackson asks.

'It's just a poem,' Chloe reassures him. 'Something nice to say. You ready, Taylor?'

'Ready.'

We recite the poem together:

> Remember me when I am gone away
> Gone far away into the silent land
> When you can no more hold me by the hand
> Nor I half turn to go yet turning stay
> Remember me when no more day by day
> You tell me of our future that you planned
> Only remember me; you understand
> it will be late to counsel then or pray
> Yet if you should forget me for a while
> And afterwards remember, do not grieve:
> For if the darkness and corruption leave
> a vestige of thoughts I once had,
> Better by far you should forget and smile
> Than that you should remember and be sad.

'Wow,' Chip says when we finish. 'That's actually really nice. How do you both know the words?'

I'm about to answer, but Chloe simply says, 'Long story.'

Jackson shivers. 'I know that poem too.'

I'm surprised. 'You do?'

'And that's *also* a long story.'

'Tell us,' I encourage, not least because it's something to distract him, to keep him talking. I also really want to know how he knows it. I didn't think the poem was that widely known.

'Okay,' Jackson agrees. 'But keep in mind I was young and stupid, yeah?'

'Sure. Of course.'

'I was down on my luck,' he begins, 'and I was hanging out with some real dickheads. I wasn't part of what they did, but if I'm honest, I *was* a beneficiary of it. We were house sharing, right? None of us had a job. We bummed around week to week, living off social security and favours. Anyway, for a while there, a few of the guys were doing B&Es.'

'Is that a drug?' Chloe asks.

'Nah,' Jackson says. 'Shorthand for *break and enter* – my mates were robbing houses. When they brought home the loot, we'd sit there sucking back beers, plucking through the spoils, rummaging through people's stuff. Handbags, hatboxes ... sometimes the guys would take a whole bedroom drawer with jewellery and all sorts of crap in it. Anyway, this one time they brought home a briefcase.'

Something grips my chest. *Holy shit.*

'It took ages to open the bastard. It was leather and it had a lock. I think they ended up cutting into it. Anyway, after all that effort, there was nothing important. Just some kid's diary. The guys were passing it round, laughing at the shit that was written in it, and when they handed it to me and it was my turn to read something out loud, I randomly flipped to a page and found that poem. I remember it because it was written next to a photo of some old dude and it felt really sad and personal, and I felt shabby all of a sudden – dirty for even touching it – so I handed it back, glad to be rid of it.'

My voice is tight. I can barely believe it. It's another one of those weird sliding-doors moments. 'What happened to the diary?'

Jackson shrugs. 'How should I know? Anything that couldn't be pawned or traded, the guys either torched or dumped.'

My blood boils. I think about telling him it was *my* diary, but what good would that do? He's just lost his grandmother and he's already in pain. He wasn't even the one who broke into my house. Like he said, he was just the recipient of the spoils.

It's a cruel joke, an evil twist of the universe. Somewhere up there, the great puppeteer is having a lend of me.

No one says anything for a while. We coast along the dark highway, not talking, all of us lost in our thoughts. With the radio switched off, we hear the rumble of the road and the occasional growl of a diesel engine passing us by. Almost half an hour goes by before Jackson breaks the silence. 'What do you think the point is?'

'Sorry?' Chip says.

'Life,' Jackson says. 'Do you think there's a point?'

'Just a small philosophical question,' I say. 'No biggie.'

'I'm serious,' Jackson insists.

'There is no meaning,' Chip says confidently. 'It is what it is. Existence. Survival. Keeping sustained. Sleeping, waking, eating, drinking, shitting – on repeat twenty-four-seven. Same play, different backdrops, characters, but at the core an endless rotation of bodily functions keeping us breathing.'

Chloe sniffs and wipes her cheek. 'I think it's about love, laughter and friendship. The best bits. Even when you think it isn't.' Her take on it surprises me, and I feel her kick the back of my seat. She's trying to tell me something.

My phone vibrates. Another Geoff Message: **This is the sixth and last time we're contacting you. To collect your grand prize please be at Grayson's Convenience Store on Hampstead Rd at 11.00am tomorrow.**

'Hey Chip, isn't Grayson's near Bill's Takeaway?'

He nods. 'Yeah. It's across the road. The one with a spinning planet on the roof. Come to think of it, I've never really known what that's about.'

'It's a hangover from when it used to be a travel shop,' Chloe explains. 'They never took it down.'

'Oh right,' Chip says. 'I forgot you go to Bill's.' He looks at me. 'Why's that?'

'Nothing,' I say. 'Just a message.'

'From Grayson's? To you?'

'To Geoff.'

'Who's Geoff?'

'Geoff, my phone-SIM nemesis.'

'Huh?'

'Long story.'

'I'm all—' He pinches his ear and wiggles it. 'We have plenty of time.'

'Fine. It was a cool autumn morning a couple of days ago ...'

# CHAPTER THIRTY-TWO

When we arrive in Adelaide, it's close to midnight. The agreement is: Chip will drop us home and then Jackson will drive to the nursing home with Daisy's body. He'll surrender his liberty and confess to stealing the hearse.

In Chip's driveway, we say our goodbyes.

'Thank you,' Jackson says to all of us. 'For everything. I promise I won't breathe a word. I did it all on my own – that's my story and I'm sticking to it. And if they come asking, remember: I forced you into it.'

Chloe gives him a hug. 'Can we visit you?'

He shrugs. 'Not like I don't have the time. Hell, I might even take up painting. They've got a mean arts and crafts program I've never taken advantage of. Maybe it's time I live up to my name?'

'We can trade pictures,' Chloe suggests. 'I'll share mine if you share yours?'

Jackson smiles. 'Deal.' He looks at me and Chip. 'Thanks for everything, boys. Didn't think I'd say this, but I'm gunna miss our conversations.'

'We might visit too,' I say. 'If you're up for more?'

He looks chuffed. 'Sure. And hey, keep me posted on *Hotties of the Northern Burbs.*' He pats Chip's shoulder. 'I did a phone transfer of some of Granny's funds to your account. Not enough for a trip to Barbados, but enough to keep you in the lifestyle to which you've become accustomed – enough to buy loads of Vaseline.'

Chip shakes his hand. 'Cheers mate. That's very cool of you.'

Jackson looks at me. 'On ya, Taylor. You're the best Best Boy I've ever met.'

I side eye Chip. 'I suppose there are worse job descriptions.'

'And if Granny could say thank you, you know she would.'

I swallow a lump. I glance at the hearse where she lies. 'We'll be sure to pay our respects. And I'd like to write her obituary, if you're okay with that?'

'I'd like that.' He gets in and starts the engine. Window down, he calls, 'Time to serve me up a slice of Errol pie!' We watch him drive off into the night.

Chip turns to me and pats my back. 'Well, that's it, friendly neighbour. I'm wrecked. Think I'll hit the sack. Maybe unwind with some Barbara Cartland.'

'Are you coming tomorrow?'

'To Grayson's Convenience Store? Yep, I'll be there. Meet you at Bill's Takeaway first?'

'That's the plan, Stan.'

'Done.' Chip salutes me and Chloe. 'Adios! Arrivederci.' Quoting the ever-timeless Bob Dylan: 'I'm *blowin' in the wind.*' He lifts his leg and drops a farting goodbye.

'I'm glad he saved *that* until we got out of the car,' I say to Chloe as we walk over to my place.

'Me too.' She fidgets with her T-shirt, pulling it straight. 'Are you sure your parents won't mind me staying over?'

'Nah. They're cool. Advance apologies, though. They can be a bit handsy.'

'Handsy?'

'With each other. They're always bumpin' and grindin' and lovin' it up. I'm going to need a lot of therapy when I'm older.'

She laughs. 'They sound like fun.'

'Debatable. Oh, and hey, a head's up: if Dad offers you a Vienna coffee with whipped cream, don't accept.'

She gives me a bemused grin. 'I'll keep that in mind.'

With my hand on the doorknob, I say, 'Ready?'

'Ready.'

We find Mum and Dad seated at the kitchen table, sharing a bottle of red wine. At this time of night, I'd hoped they'd already gone to bed, but of course that isn't my luck.

'Ah! Right where I left you!' I say.

Mum opens her mouth to speak, but closes it when she sees Chloe standing behind me. She looks at Dad. Dad looks at her. If they were any more surprised, they'd be that painting, *The Scream*.

Dad gets up to hug me. 'Taylor! We'd expected you'd be here when we got back. We were really beginning to worry.' He stands me at arm's length, firm hands on my shoulders. 'I've sprouted grey hair! Look at me! Look. At. Me!' (Sidenote: he already *had* grey hair.) 'Not cool, buddy!'

'Beginning to worry is an understatement,' Mum says, shoving him aside. She gives me one of her panicked mother-bear hugs. 'Shitting bricks is more en pointe. Don't do that to us!' She biffs my skull. 'What the hell?! If I wasn't so relieved, I'd kill you! What happened to your phone? I messaged you a bunch of times. You freaked me out when you didn't answer. I rang Mrs Harvey and she said she'd seen you once or twice.'

Thank goodness for elderly neighbours – I don't know who Mrs Harvey saw, but it wasn't me.

'Oh! That reminds me,' Mum adds. 'Apparently she has a package for our neighbour, Chip. I must remember to tell him.'

Chip's satin pyjamas? 'Yeah, I said hello to Mrs Harvey,' I lie. 'And my phone is in for repair at Fone Wizards. I have a loan one. I tried to text you but it obviously didn't work.'

'*Do ya think?*' Mum says. 'We didn't reply, did we?'

'No, but you were at the conference so I didn't think much of it,' I say.

Dad looks at Mum. 'Well that explains that. I guess we should let him off the hook? Or maybe we should invoke … The List?'

I groan. 'Not The List!'

Mum composes herself, eyes lit with sudden glee. 'Ah! Yes! I've not had a decent foot rub in ages. And the bathtub drain is full of hair. After that, you can tackle the lost sock drawer and do an underpants inventory. Your father's jocks are so see-through it's like a thinly veiled fruit bowl down there.'

My mind flashes back to their Insta submission. *Ew!*

I know when I've been defeated. 'Fine. I'll do The List.' I glance at Chloe. 'I had some stuff to take care of.' I take Chloe's hand and steer her forward. 'This is my friend, Chloe.'

'Hi there, friend of our son,' Mum says, putting out her hand.

Chloe shakes it. She gives Dad a shy little wave. 'Hi.'

'Hi,' he says. 'I once knew a girl called Chloe—'

I cut him off. 'How was the conference?'

'Oh you know roller-door conferences,' Dad says, loosening up. 'They have their ups and downs.' He takes his seat, slapping his thigh.

'But we rolled with it,' Mum says, parking herself on his lap.

They clink glasses, laugh, and share a kiss. A *long* kiss. There are dental hygienists less thorough. Chloe watches them, her eyes wide.

I try to break up the pash party. 'Guys, Chloe's going to sleep over, if that's okay? On the couch.'

Dad looks pleased. Too pleased. 'Your parents don't mind, do they Chloe?'

'Nah, they're good.'

'We have to be somewhere early tomorrow morning,' I tell them. 'I have to collect a prize from Grayson's Convenience Store. Not my prize. On behalf of a mate. He's out of town right now.'

'Okay, son. That's better communication. I appreciate it.' Dad stretches and yawns. 'Well! This old bloke has been burning the candle at both ends. I'm ready to hit the sack.' He pats Mum's knee. 'Coming, sweetheart? Fancy a nightcap? I can make us a Vienna coffee with a shot of Irish Whisky?'

Mum gives him the thumbs-up. She says to us, 'Night, kids.' She points at me. 'You don't come home on time this time, I'll publicly shame you on KidSpot by requesting advice to help combat your OTT baked beans obsession.'

'But I don't—?' Then I get it. 'Okay. Yep. Fine.'

Dad goes to the fridge, grabs the whipped cream and they head off to the bedroom.

Chloe looks questioningly at me. 'Didn't he say—?'

'Don't ask.'

I go to the linen cupboard, grab some blankets and a pillow, and set her up in the living room. I unfurl the fold-out sofa, quickly make up the bed, and switch on the corner lamp, turning the dimmer down. Everything glows a dull yellow.

'Thanks for this,' she says, watching me fuss about. 'I suppose we get to actually talk now, huh?'

I take a seat and pat the mattress. She sits next me. We keep our voices low. 'I didn't expect to ever see you again,' I say.

She looks at me, her gaze steady. 'After you told me what you told me, I walked back to town. It gave me time to think. I went and sat in a cafe and contacted a friend. I asked if I could log into Facebook under her account. I went to Kelly's page and I searched up your post.'

I bite my lip. 'And?'

'I liked what you said.'

I stare at her.

She nods. 'You didn't hold back. You really let fly. I admire you for it.'

I don't understand. 'Everyone hates me for that post, Chloe. *Everyone.*'

'I think you said some stuff people needed to hear – me included. You said stuff no one wants to acknowledge, but deep down they know. And that's when it occurred to me.'

'What?'

'Everyone wants a scapegoat. I've wanted someone to blame, Taylor – I just chose myself. Let's face it. *All* of us are looking for answers about what happened to Kelly. None of us are going to find any. I can't go back and I can't undo what's done, so maybe it's time I accept that. I think hanging out with Daisy made me rethink a lot of stuff.'

I nod, feeling that tug in my chest – the loss of Daisy.

'She was in my life for a couple of days,' Chloe says, 'but she made a big impact. I don't want to spend my life looking back,

Taylor. I don't want to be angry. I can't do it anymore.' Her eyes fill with tears.

I reach for her hand. She lets me take it. It feels natural – like this isn't something new, but something we've always done. She feels like someone I've known a long time, not a few days.

She looks me over. 'You know what, Taylor? All things aside, I like how pathetic you are. You're equally pathetic as me. That takes real talent.' She gives me a cheeky grin.

'You're not pathet—'

She puts a finger to my lips. 'I *am* pathetic. I'm fundamentally fucked up for a thousand different reasons. But none of them matter right now. Not when I have you.'

I gulp. 'You *have* me?'

She looks at her shoes. 'If you want me?'

I lean in and kiss her. My first real kiss. It feels amazing – and not just because my lips aren't being hoovered into next Tuesday.

Coming up for air, she says, 'You know that party you missed?'

'Yeah?'

'There might be another invitation coming your way.' She adds with a shy smile, 'I don't know when, but I have a feeling it might be soon.'

I feel breathless. My stomach does star jumps. 'I'll need a new costume. I've been there, done Mr Death, and to tell you the truth, I'm kind of over him. I'm more into living. Also: fanny farts. In fact, I'm not sure I can accept your invitation without first sharing this intimate get-to-know-you experience.'

She pulls a face like she's trying hard to let one rip. 'Yeah, nope, I've got nothing. Chip must've stolen my thunder from down under.'

'Well, regrettably, until such time as I bear witness to this mythical phenomena, the party invitation will have to stay on hold.'

We kiss again. 'You're funny,' she says.

I point to my head. 'Middleborough's lavatory-rating pioneer. I'm not above toilet humour. Besides, who doesn't love a good fart joke?'

She pats my thigh. 'Love is like a fart, you know.'

'It is?'

'If you have to force it, it's probably shit.'

I laugh. 'I won't force it then.'

She kisses me again. 'You're a true gentleman, Taylor Kennedy.'

'I have my moments.'

# CHAPTER THIRTY-THREE

'I'm putting *Hotties of the Northern Burbs* on hold,' Chip declares. He stuffs his face with hot chips, tips back his head like a flip-top rubbish bin and squirts in the sauce. As serving suggestions go, it's disgusting and yet highly practical.

Chip, Chloe and I are seated in a window booth at Bill's Takeaway, looking at Grayson's Convenience Store across the road. Noelene has served us a platter of deep-fried delights, redeemed in the healthiness stakes by strategically positioned parsley sprigs. No longer on work experience, she has a real job now. Bill has taken her on for good. He says her turkey breast and refried sausage dish was a stroke of genius and you're obligated to reward ingenuity. I have to admit she's growing on me.

'What do you mean you're putting Hotties on hold?' I say, as I munch on a seafood cake with two prawn tails and a squid arm (leg?) sticking out of it. 'I thought we had a following?'

'I'm thinking I might try the clairvoyant thing,' Chip says through a mushy chip mouthful. 'Porn is my passion, of course, but perhaps it's not my true talent. Also, I should probably wait until I've *you know...*' He leans in and whispers, 'Done it.'

'Come again?' I say.

He laughs. 'Ha! Good one.'

I can't believe it. *Chip's a virgin?!*

'I need to keep my options open,' he says. 'Explore. I can always come back to it.'

Chloe slaps the table. 'Who will provide this essential public service now?'

Chip shrugs. 'There's an opening if you're interested.'

Chloe winks at me. 'Now *there's* a party invitation.'

I look at my loan phone. My old one still isn't ready for collection. 'We'd best make a move. Time to collect Geoff's prize.'

I'd checked my socials and emails on my laptop first thing this morning. No messages. (Actually, there was one: an email from Miss Flexy/Hooper relaying that her yoga classes are not free and I owe her $38.50 and if I don't pay up she'll crush my head between her muscular thighs. I'm not sure whether to be terrified or excited by this. Also, I got an A-minus on my maths test.) There are a few posts from Cass and Co., but no attempts to contact me, and the surprising thing is that when I looked at it, I found myself not really caring. An apology from them would mean I'd have to work out how *I* feel; if *I* want to forgive, and right now I don't know if I want to. In some ways they've given me an out – one I wouldn't have actively taken. We've grown apart. Maybe they'd known that and I hadn't. History can't be the only reason people stay together. There has to be something more – something that looks to the future.

My head-nodding days are over. I've survived hanging out with people who don't mind if I argue or hold a differing opinion. In fact, they seem to respect me more because of it.

We pack up the leftovers and bin them. 'You've got no idea what it is that Geoff's won?' Chip asks, as we head out the door and across the road to Grayson's Convenience Store.

'Not a clue.'

'I hope it's worth the effort,' he says.

As we enter Grayson's, a doorbell clangs. The place is dead. It's a small shop with a lot of stock crammed into it and there's not much space to move. We navigate our way to the counter, dodging display stands and precariously stacked soft drink cans. As we approach, I think I'm going to have to ring another bell for assistance, but then this guy pops up from behind the desk – he must've been tying his shoelaces or something. He's tall and lanky, and he has an impressive moustache. The dude from the nursing home would be green with envy. I resist an urge to reach across and touch it. *And* to ask if he uses beard oil.

'Pop-up service!' Chip jokes. It falls flat – which is a shame for a joke about pop-ups.

'Can I help you?' says the guy.

I get out my phone, find the text message and show him. 'I'm Geoff. I've come to collect my prize.'

The guy jumps up and down on the spot. He's mega excited. 'Finally! I was beginning to think you weren't going to show!' He comes out from behind the counter to shake my hand. 'I'm Grayson. Pleased to meet you.' He looks me over. 'Huh. For some reason I thought you'd be older. Don't know why I thought that.'

I gesture at Chloe and Chip. 'These are my friends.' When I say it, I realise how good it feels. They *are* my friends.

Grayson dips a non-existent cap at them. 'Nice to meet you.'

He turns to me. 'Okay, if you're ready, follow me! I've got it all set up.'

He steers us down a confectionery aisle to the back of the store. There's a bunch of cardboard boxes stacked as high as me. He reaches up for a Polaroid camera that's sitting on the top box and loops the strap around his neck. 'Stand here.' He guides me into position next to the cardboard tower. The area is cramped, so Chip and Chloe stand just off to my left, about half a metre away.

Grayson backtracks himself into position. He lifts the camera. 'Now put a hand on the top box, if you wouldn't mind.'

I do as he tells me. I wonder when he's going to do the big reveal. I'm dying to know what it is I've won – or rather, Geoff has won.

He lifts the camera, looks through the lens and moans, 'Uh duh! I forgot to give you the other prop!' He reaches over to the nearby confectionery stand, grabs something and passes it to me.

I look down at my hand as the camera starts flashing.

'Congratulations Geoff,' he says cheerfully. 'You've won a lifetime supply of Chupa Chups!'

That photo now hangs on Grayson's wall: me, standing next to boxes upon boxes of Chupa Chups, looking like a stunned mullet. Chip in the frame just off to my side, pulling the mother of all WTF faces. Chloe, doubled over, cracking her sides.

Here's what I know about life:

It has a sense of humour. It can suck sometimes, but it's also sweet.

Getting the wrapper off takes work. The good bit is under there – *somewhere*.

It has all flavours, all colours, and it's addictive. When your supply runs low, you've got to ride it out. You *will* be restocked.

It's best shared with friends. *Real friends*. The kind that don't suck. The kind who love you for you. The kind who have your back no matter what.

THE END

# FACEBOOK POST

***Taylor Kennedy commented on Kelly Nixon's wall:***
You'll recall my prior post. By way of apology, I write the following with the assistance of Kelly's best friend, Chloe Hart, and Kelly's parents. Recorded with love and truth.

***OBITUARY – Kelly Nixon***
Kelly Nixon was born in Adelaide to Mark and Connie Nixon, a sister to Mia. A restless baby, Kelly screamed the house down. She slept only if her milk was spiked with Phenergan. Unfortunately this practice was frowned upon, so mostly she screamed.

From an early age Kelly loved music and dancing. She wasn't good at either. At age five it was evident she was tone deaf. She sounded like a cat caught in a cheese grater. Her room was egg-cartoned to ward off noise complaints from the neighbours. Equally, Kelly's dance moves were some of the worst ever witnessed. She once attempted a scissor kick that left Mia with a permanent scar under her right eye. (The video evidence has been confiscated.)

Kelly enjoyed weird food combinations. Watermelon smeared with chutney, Scotch Fingers dipped in fish paste, Tabasco sauce in coffee. She thought deconstructed cheeseburgers were delicious, but gagged if they were presented intact. She always threw away the pickle.

Kelly loved Aussie teen fiction author Erin Gough. She underlined quotes from *Amelia Westlake*, faced-out books on shop shelves, wrote five-star ratings on Goodreads. She sent countless letters to Warner Bros, begging they make Erin's books into movies. When Erin was on literary shortlists, Kelly anonymously sent the judging committee Haighs Chocolates. She ditched the jar of pickles she'd had on standby if some other author won. (See pickles above.)

Kelly had a small mole behind her right ear she toyed with when nervous. It bled regularly and she had to tape it. She had an obsession with black nail polish and there were at least fifty brands stuffed in her dresser. When pressed, she admitted she liked the smell and sniffed them in order of preference.

Kelly cried easily. An advert with a Labrador pup frolicking in a field of wildflowers had her reaching for the tissue box. She was banned from the Hallmark Card display at the newsagent after her mascara-streaked tears warped the paper. Strangely, she laughed when the octopus gets killed in *My Octopus Teacher*. No one laughs when the octopus gets killed.

Kelly had a phobia of zebra crossings. She'd only step on the white lines and if she overstepped, she had to start again. (Getting to school in the morning took a while.) Kelly also had an aversion to door handles after an aunt told her they carry millions of bacteria. She opened them with her sleeve yanked over her hand. On Fridays she wore hot pink socks and no one knew why. She never explained.

Kelly was no angel. She shoplifted pregnancy tests and sold them at a profit to a Catholic girls' school. She spat on a teacher's seat after he made a racist slur (*the authors of this document think that totally understandable.) She wrote *Outlander* spoilers in TV chatrooms under a pseudonym 'Stone Maiden' and took twisted joy when people complained. When she was mad at her mum, she dunked her toothbrush in the toilet bowl.

Kelly's first job was in a hardware store. Within a week she was indecently assaulted by an elderly male customer who made lewd comments and grabbed her left breast. Staff detained him but the security footage was inconclusive and it ended up her word against his. Her manager demanded she stay quiet and forget about it. Thereafter, Kelly carried secateurs in her back pocket and almost neutered a guy who asked where the hoes were located. She soon left and landed a job at Krispy Kreme, gained five kilos, and developed an allergy to Cochineal food dye. She was shocked to discover it's made from dried insects. (She then sent a complimentary tray to her former manager.)

Kelly had a smile that lit up a room. Her giggles were contagious and her whole body shook when she laughed. She had a huge heart, but it meant she was sensitive and easily wounded. She acted tough, put on a show. The only person she claimed to tell the truth was her best friend, Chloe.

Kelly loved her best friend.

Her best friend loved her.

That love will live on.

That love is infinite.

Kelly would rather help someone else than help herself. She tried to talk about what hurt, but the words got stuck and she moved on to something else. She said everyone was a work in progress, no one was a finished portrait, yet she claimed the paint brush was done with her—the strokes had been made.

Kelly was a good soul. Like all of us, she just wanted to be happy. And loved. She was a bright star. We know she's shining down on us. We will never forget her.

# ACKNOWLEDGEMENTS

This novel was written thanks to me.

I should thank some other people though.

Daryl and Dillon: you come first. Not sure why, I probably need to rectify that. Thanks anyway. Love you loads. Thanks also to my extended fambam. I'll keep ya. Thousands wouldn't.

My Agent with The Mostest, Jane Novak: any author-agent relationship should incorporate a healthy amount of sucky-up mutual lovefesting. *slurp kiss slurp* You are all kinds of awesome. Mwah!

Jo Case, Michael Bollen, Poppy Nwosu, and the team at Wakefield Press: Getting into bed with you has been fun. Thanks for putting out. Hey, I was a sure thing but you made me feel coveted and desirable. I'm glad we still respect each other in the morning. (Jo Case: you're the best I've ever had.)

To whom this abomination of a novel is dedicated, Vikki Wakefield, my dearest bestest darling bud (*who dedicated one of her own books to biscuits): I love your Literary Hornbag cotton socks. The time I've spent with you—and I wouldn't have it any other way. Daisy is our nursing home go-to and I can't wait to ask you fifty times a day if you've seen my dentures, or about the hot nurse on nightshift. *waves to Russ*

To my other bestest darling bud, Andrea Altamura: your name has appeared in the back of every book. Your subscription is up. I accept wine, koala walks, and ... well, mostly wine. You make me look smart. This is a miraculous feat. You should be knighted or canonized or made into a bronze statue or immortalised as carved watermelon fruit art.

To Rebecca Burton and Adam Cece: You read this dumpster MS and laughed. Hey, I'm funny. Thanks for investing your time. Clearly my powers of persuasion work a treat. I'm grateful you're so gullible. Also: I kinda like you, like, a whole bunch, so there's that.

To Erin Gough: If I could bottle your voice I'd snort it for breakfast. Hurry up and move to Adelaide so I can harass you more readily. The current situation is untenable. Also: Lit crush, heart rush. *fans face*

To Robert Newton: One day we'll launch onto stage in front of a crowd of unsuspecting CBCA conference goers – you'll slide down a pole, I'll strut with a guitar, we'll duet, it will be epic call-the-fire-department stuff. Oh wait. PS. You can leave your hat on.

To Becky Lucas: Keep those GIFs coming. (Mandy Foot and Katrina Germein said to say that.) And sign me up for some more stuff. Charge double. Okay? Maybe shoot for a box of Haighs on top? Let's not get ahead of ourselves.

To Tania Ingram, Kristin Weidenbach, Kylie Covark, Hayley Lawrence, Briony Muhovics, Bec Hayes, and Kristina Schultz: Thanks for accepting me for who I am, broken bits and all. I have dirt on you, you have dirt on me. Methinks we're good till we drop.

To my readers: Points for being you. You're fabulous. I know so. It's evident owing to your choice of author.

To SCBWI, eKIDS, LoveOzYA, and the literary artfart community: This is what happens when you don't lock the gate. I love all of ya. With gumdrops on top. I'm this shy of sticking my tongue in your ear.

To the Chief Poobahs of Festive Festivals, podcasters, bloggers, teachers, librarians, reviewers, booksellers: I do what I do *not* because of you (like I said in the back of my last book) but because you probably did something very naughty in a past life and now you have to deal with me. Sorry. I'll do my best to make it up to you. Sending LOVE.

To the Pearl Clutchers: You inspired this novel. Thanks! Also: ___ ___ _____ (fill in the blanks)

To Hollywood: Yeah, I'm sure we can work something out. Always up for another notch in my literary bedhead. I'm not fussy. Seth Rogan? Sure! Byron Bay? Why not! Magda will play Daisy? That's a dream come true. Sign here? Done. My details? I'm opening a Swiss bank account as we speak. Hang ten, I'll flick em through.

Finally, and most importantly, to Jed Hitchens: Skate high, sweet angel. I loved you. So did my son. Till we meet again.

Wakefield Press is an independent publishing and
distribution company based in Adelaide, South Australia.
We love good stories and publish beautiful books.
To see our full range of books, please visit our website at
www.wakefieldpress.com.au
where all titles are available for purchase.
To keep up with our latest releases, news and events,
subscribe to our monthly newsletter.


Find us!


Facebook: www.facebook.com/wakefield.press
Twitter: www.twitter.com/wakefieldpress
Instagram: www.instagram.com/wakefieldpress

www.ingramcontent.com/pod-product-compliance
Lightning Source LLC
Chambersburg PA
CBHW060421030726
47495CB00003B/675